Praise for *Golden Hill* from the United Kingdom

Winner of the Costa First Novel Award
Named Novel of the Year by the *Sunday Times*

"Addictively readable."
　　　　　　　—Mark Haddon, author of *The Curious Incident*
　　　　　　　of the Dog in the Night-Time

"Francis Spufford has long been one of my favourite writers of non-fiction; he is now becoming a favourite writer of fiction as well. *Golden Hill* is a meticulously crafted and brilliantly written novel that is both an affectionate homage to the eighteenth-century novel and a taut and thoughtful tale."
　　　　　　　—Iain Pears, author of
　　　　　　　An Instance of the Fingerpost

"I loved this book so much. *Golden Hill* wears its research with incredible insouciance and grace; a rollicking picaresque, it is threaded through with darkness but has a heart of gold."
　　　　　　　—Jo Baker, author of *Longbourn*
　　　　　　　and *The Undertow*

"A narrative taut with twists and turns keeps you gripped until its tour-de-force conclusion. . . . Colonial New York is conjured up with tremendously informed verve and brilliancies of metaphor and phrasing gleam everywhere. Ranging from euphoric comedy to moments of bleak nightmare, it's a marvelous debut."
　　　　　　　—*Sunday Times*, Novel of the Year

"Every bit as superb as everyone says. As a reader, I was in a delighted swoon at the verve and prose; as a writer, I had a fit of infuriated envy that anyone could be so outrageously good."

—Sarah Perry, *The Guardian*, Best Books of 2016

"Nothing short of a masterpiece; eighteenth-century New York came alive for me and I say this as someone who doesn't usually care for historical novels."

—Penelope Lively, *The Guardian*, Best Books of 2016

"Set in the turbulent days before the American Revolution, this book is many things: a thriller, a meditation on the form of the novel, an examination of the beginnings of American politics. And it's a ripping good read."

—*New Statesman*, Books of the Year

"Utterly captivating . . . Pitch perfect from the opening sentence."

—*Saturday Review*, BBC Radio 4

"*Golden Hill* is a novel of gloriously capacious humanity, thick-woven with life in all its oddness and familiarity, a novel of such joy it leaves you beaming, and such seriousness that it asks to be read again and again. . . . This novel is verifiable gold."

—*The Sunday Telegraph*

"The intoxicating effect of *Golden Hill* is much more than an experiment in form. [Spufford] has created a complete world, employing his archivist skills to the great advantage of his novel. . . . This is a book born of patience, of knowledge accrued and distilled over decades, a style honed by practice. There are single scenes here more illuminating, more lovingly wrought, than entire books."

—*Financial Times*

"Like a newly discovered novel by Henry Fielding with extra material by Martin Scorsese. Why it works so well is largely down to Spufford's superb re-creation of New York. . . . His writing crackles with energy and glee, and when Smith's secret is finally revealed it is hugely satisfying on every level. For its payoff alone *Golden Hill* deserves a big shiny star."

—*The Times*

"Splendidly entertaining and ingenious . . . Throughout *Golden Hill*, Spufford creates vivid, painterly scenes of street and salon life, yet one never feels as though a historical detail has been inserted just because he knew about it. Here is deep research worn refreshingly lightly. . . . A first-class period entertainment."

—*The Guardian*

"Paying tribute to writers such as Fielding, Francis Spufford's creation exudes a zesty, pin-sharp contemporaneity. . . . Colonial New York takes palpable shape in his dazzlingly visual, pacy and cleverly plotted novel."

—*Daily Mail*

"*Golden Hill* shows a level of showmanship and skill which seems more like a crowning achievement than a debut. [Spufford] brings his people and situations to life with glancing ease. . . . They all live and breathe with conviction. . . . His descriptive powers are amazing. . . . Spufford's extraordinary visual imagination and brilliant pacing seems to owe more to the movies than anything else."

—*Evening Standard*

Also by Francis Spufford

Red Plenty

Unapologetic

Backroom Boys

The Child That Books Built

I May Be Some Time

Golden Hill

A Novel of Old New York

Francis Spufford

Scribner

New York London Toronto Sydney New Delhi

F
SPU

Scribner
An Imprint of Simon & Schuster, Inc.
1230 Avenue of the Americas
New York, NY 10020

Originally published in Great Britain in 2016 by Faber & Faber Limited
Published by arrangement with Faber & Faber Limited

First Scribner hardcover edition June 2017

For information about special discounts for bulk purchases,
please contact Simon & Schuster Special Sales at 1-866-506-1949
or business@simonandschuster.com.

The Simon & Schuster Speakers Bureau can bring authors to your live event.
For more information or to book an event, contact the Simon & Schuster Speakers Bureau
at 1-866-248-3049 or visit our website at www.simonspeakers.com.

Manufactured in the United States of America

1   3   5   7   9   10   8   6   4   2

Library of Congress Cataloging-in-Publication Data is available.

ISBN 978-1-5011-6387-6
ISBN 978-1-5011-6389-0 (ebook)

For Stella

"He advised me to correct the rebellious principles I had imbibed among the English, who, for their insolence to their kings, were notorious all over the world."
—Tobias Smollett, *The Adventures of Roderick Random* (1748)

1

All Hallows

November 1st

20 Geo. II

1746

I

The brig *Henrietta* having made Sandy Hook a little before the dinner hour—and having passed the Narrows about three o'clock—and then crawling to and fro, in a series of tacks infinitesimal enough to rival the calculus, across the grey sheet of the harbour of New-York—until it seemed to Mr. Smith, dancing from foot to foot upon deck, that the small mound of the city waiting there would hover ahead in the November gloom in perpetuity, never growing closer, to the smirk of Greek Zeno—and the day being advanced to dusk by the time *Henrietta* at last lay anchored off Tietjes Slip, with the veritable gables of the city's veritable houses divided from him only by one hundred foot of water—and the dusk moreover being as cold and damp and dim as November can afford, as if all the world were a quarto of grey paper dampened by drizzle until in danger of crumbling imminently to pap:—all this being true, the master of the brig pressed upon him the virtue of sleeping this one further night aboard, and pursuing his shore business in the morning. (He meaning by the offer to signal his esteem, having found Mr. Smith a pleasant companion during the slow weeks of the crossing.) But Smith would not have it. Smith, bowing and smiling, desired nothing but to be rowed to the dock. Smith, indeed, when once he had his shoes flat on the cobbles, took off at such speed despite the gambolling of his land-legs that he far out-paced the sailor dispatched to carry his trunk—and must double back for it, and seizing it hoist it instanter on his own shoulder—and gallop on, skidding over fish-guts and turnip leaves and cats' entrails, and the other effluvium of the port—asking for direction here, asking again there—so that he appeared most nearly as a type of smiling whirlwind when he shouldered open the door—just as it was about to be bolted for the evening—of the counting-house of the firm of Lovell & Company, on Golden Hill Street, and laid down his burden while the prentices were lighting the lamps, and the clock on the wall showed one minute to five, and demanded, very civilly, speech that moment with Mr. Lovell himself.

"I'm Lovell," said the merchant, rising from his place by the fire. His qualities in brief, to meet the needs of a first encounter: fifty years old; a spare body but a pouched and lumpish face, as if Nature had set to work upon the clay with knuckles; shrewd and anxious eyes; brown small-clothes; a bob-wig yellowed by tobacco smoke. "Help ye?"

"Good day," said Mr. Smith, "for I am certain it *is* a good day, never mind the rain and the wind. And the darkness. You'll forgive the dizziness of the traveller, sir. I have the honour to present a bill drawn upon you by your London correspondents, Messrs. Banyard and Hythe. And request the favour of its swift acceptance."

"Could it not have waited for the morrow?" said Lovell. "Our hours for public business are over. Come back and replenish your purse at nine o'clock. Though for any amount over ten pound sterling I'll ask you to wait out the week, cash money being scarce."

"Ah," said Mr. Smith. "It *is* for a greater amount. A far greater. And I am come to you now, hot-foot from the cold sea, salt still on me, dirty as a dog fresh from a duck-pond, not for payment, but to do you the courtesy of long notice."

And he handed across a portfolio, which being opened revealed a paper cover clearly sealed in black wax with a B and an H. Lovell cracked it, his eyebrows already half-raised. He read, and they rose further.

"Lord love us," he said. "This is a bill for a thousand pound."

"Yes, sir," said Mr. Smith. "A thousand pounds sterling; or as it says there, one thousand seven hundred and thirty-eight pounds, fifteen shillings and fourpence, New-York money. May I sit down?"

Lovell ignored him. "Jem," he said, "fetch a lantern closer."

The clerk brought one of the fresh-lit candles in its chimney, and Lovell held the page up close to the hot glass; so close that Smith made a start as if to snatch it away, which Lovell reproved with an out-thrust arm; but he did not scorch the paper, only tilted it where the flame shone through and showed in paler lines the watermark of a mermaid.

"Paper's right," said the clerk.

"The hand too," said Lovell. "Benjamin Banyard's own, I'd say."

"Yes," said Mr. Smith, "though his name was Barnaby Banyard when he sat in his office in Mincing Lane and wrote the bill for me. Come, now, gentlemen; do you think I found this on a street-corner?"

Lovell surveyed him, clothes and hands and visage and speech, such as he had heard of it, and found nothing there that closed the question.

"You might ha' done," he said, "for all I know. For I don't know you. What is this thing? And who are you?"

"What it seems to be. What I seem to be. A paper worth a thousand pounds; and a traveller who owns it."

"Or a paper fit to wipe my arse, and a lying rogue. Ye'll have to do

3

better than that. I've done business with Banyard's for twenty year, and settled with 'em for twenty year with bills on Kingston from my sugar traffic. Never this; never paper sent all on a sudden this side the water, asking money paid for the whole season's account, almost, without a word, or a warning, or a by-your-leave. I'll ask again: who are you? What's your business?"

"Well: in general, Mr. Lovell, buying and selling. Going up and down in the world. Seeing what may turn to advantage; for which my thousand pounds may be requisite. But more specifically, Mr. Lovell: the kind I choose not to share. The confidential kind."

"You impudent pup, flirting your mangled scripture at me! Speak plain, or your precious paper goes in the fire."

"You won't do that," said Smith.

"Oh, won't I? You jumped enough a moment gone when I had it nigh the lamp. Speak, or it burns."

"And your good name with it. Mr. Lovell, this is the plain kernel of the matter: I asked at the Exchange for London merchants in good standing, joined to solid traders here, and your name rose up with Banyard's, as an honourable pair, and they wrote the bill."

"They never did before."

"They have done now. And assured me you were good for it. Which I was glad to hear, for I paid cash down."

"Cash down," repeated Lovell, flatly. He read out: " 'At sixty days' sight, pay this our second bill to Mr. Richard Smith, for value received . . .' You say you paid in coin, then?"

"I did."

"Of your own, or of another's? As agent, or principal? To settle a score or to write a new one? To lay out in investments, or to piss away on furbelows and sateen weskits?"

"Just in coin, sir. Which spoke for itself, eloquently."

"You not finding it convenient, no doubt, to move so great a weight of gold across the ocean."

"Exactly."

"Or else hoping to find a booby on the other side as'd turn paper to gold for the asking."

"I never heard that New-Yorkers were so easy to impose on," said Mr. Smith.

"So we aren't, sir," said Lovell, "so we aren't." He drummed his fingers. "Especially when one won't take the straight way to clear off the suspicion we may be gulled. —You'll excuse my manner. I speak as I find, usually; but I don't know how I find you, I don't know how to take you, and you study to keep me uncertain, which I don't see as a kindness, or as especial candid, I must say, in a strip of a boy who comes demanding payment of an awk'ard-sized fortune, on no surety."

"On all the ordinary surety of a right bill," protested Smith.

"There you go," Lovell said. "Smiling again. Commerce is trust, sir. Commerce is need and need together, sir. Commerce is putting a hand in answer into a hand out-stretched; but when I call you a rogue, you don't flare up, as is the natural answer at the mere accusation, and call me a rogue for doubting."

"No," returned Smith cheerfully. "For you're right, of course. You don't know me; and suspicion must be your wisest course, when I may be equally a gilded sprig of the *bon ton*, or a flash cully working the inkhorn lay."

Lovell blinked. Smith's voice had darkened to a rookery croak, and there was no telling if he was putting on or taking off a mask.

"There's the lovely power of being a stranger," Smith went on, as pleasant as before. "I may as well have been born again when I stepped ashore. You've a new man before you, new-made. I've no history here, and no character: and what I am is all in what I will be. But the bill, sir, is a true one. How may I set your mind at rest?"

"You've the oddest notion in the world of reassurance, if you're in earnest," said Lovell, staring. "You could tell me why I've had no

5

letter, to cushion this surprise. I'd have expected an explanation, a warning."

"Perhaps I out-paced it."

"Perhaps. But I believe I'll keep my counsel till I see more than *perhaps*."

"Of course," said Mr. Smith. "Nothing more natural, when I may be a rascal."

"Again, you make mighty free with that possibility," Lovell said.

"I only name the difficulty you're under. Would you trust me more if we pretended some other thing were at issue?"

"I might," said Lovell. "I might well. An honest man would surely labour to keep off the taint of such a thing. You seem to be inviting it, Mr. *Smith*. Yet I can't be so casual, can I? My name's my credit. Do you know what will happen if I accept your bill, for your secret business, your closed-mouth business, your smiling business, your *confidential* business? And you discount it with some good neighbour of mine, to lay your hands on the money as fast as may be, as I've no doubt you mean to? Then there'll be sixty-day paper with my name upon't, going round and round the island, playing the devil with my credit just at the turn of the season, in no kind of confidence at all. All will know it; all will know I'm to be dunned for a thousand pound, and wonder should they try to mulct me first."

"But I won't discount it."

"What?"

"I won't discount it. I can wait. There is no hurry. I have no pressing need for funds; sixty days' sight, it says, and sixty days will suit me perfectly. Keep the bill; keep it under your eye; save it from wandering."

"If I accept it, you mean."

"Yes. If you accept it."

"And if I don't?"

"Well, if you protest it, I shall make this the shortest landing in the colonies that ever was heard of. I shall walk back along the quay, and when the *Henrietta* is loaded, I shall ship home, and lodge my claim for damages with Banyard's."

"I don't protest it," said Lovell, slowly. "Neither yet do I accept it. It says here, *our second bill*, and I've not seen hide or hair of first nor third. What ships d'ye say they're bound on?"

"*Sansom's Venture* and *Antelope*," said Mr. Smith.

"Well," said Lovell, "here's what we'll do. We'll wait and we'll see; and if the others of the set turn up, why then I'll say I accepted the bill today, and you shall have your sixty days, and if you're lucky you may be paid by quarter-day; and if they don't appear, why then you're the rascal you tease at being, and I'll have you before the justices for personation. What do you say?"

"It's irregular," said Mr. Smith, "but something should be allowed for teasing. Very well: done."

"Done," echoed Lovell. "Jem, note and date the document, will you? And add a memorandum of this agreement; and make another note that we're to write to Banyard's on our own account, by the first vessel, asking explanations. And then let's have it in the strong-box, to show in evidence, as I suspect, for the assizes. Now, sir, I believe I'll bid you—" Lovell checked himself, for Smith was feeling through the pockets of his coat. "Was there something else?" he asked heavily.

"Yes," said Smith, bringing forth a purse. "I'm told I should break my guineas to smaller change. Could you furnish me the value of these in pieces convenient for the city?"

Lovell looked at the four golden heads of the King glittering in Smith's palm.

"Are they brass?" said one of the prentices, grinning.

"No, they're not brass," said Lovell. "Use your eyes, and not your mouth. Why ever—?" he said to Smith. "Never mind. Never mind.

Yes, I believe we can oblige you. Jem, get out the pennyweights, and check these."

"Full weight," the clerk reported.

"Thought so," said Lovell. "I am learning your humours, Mr. Smith. Well, now, let's see. We don't get much London gold, the flow being, as you might say, all the other way; it's moidores, and half-joes, mostly, when the yellow lady shows her face. So I believe I could offer you a hundred and eighty per centum on face, in New-York money. Which, for four guineas, would come to—"

"One hundred and fifty one shillings, twopence-halfpenny."

"You're a calculator, are you? A sharp reckoner. Now I'm afraid you can have only a little of it in coin; the reason being, as I said when first we began, that little coin is current at the present." Lovell opened a box with a key from his fob chain and dredged up silver—worn silver, silver knocked and clatter'd in the battles of circulation—which he built into a little stack in front of Smith. "A Mexica dollar, which we pass at eight-and-fourpence. A piece of four, half that. A couple of Portugee cruzeiros, three shillings New-York. A quarter-guilder. Two kreutzers, Lemberg. One kreutzer, Danish. Five sous. And a Moresco piece we can't read, but it weighs at fourteen pennyweight, sterling, so we'll call it two-and-six, New-York. Twenty-one and fourpence, total. Leaving a hundred and twenty-nine, tenpence-halfpenny to find in paper."

Lovell accordingly began to count out a pile of creased and folded slips next to the silver, some printed black and some printed red and some brown, like the despoiled pages of a prayerbook, only of varying shapes and sizes; some limp and torn; some leathery with grease; some marked only with dirty letterpress and others bearing coats-of-arms, whales spouting, shooting stars, feathers, leaves, savages; all of which he laid down with the rapidity of a card-dealer, licking his fingers for the better passage of it all.

"Wait a minute," said Mr. Smith. "What's this?"

"You don't know our money, sir?" said the clerk. "They didn't tell you we use notes, specie being so scarce, this side?"

"No," said Smith.

The pile grew.

"Fourpence Connecticut, eightpence Rhode Island," murmured Lovell. "Two shilling Rhode Island, eighteenpence Jersey, one shilling Jersey, eighteenpence Philadelphia, one shilling Maryland . . ." He had reached the bottom of the box. "Excuse me, Mr. Smith; for the rest we're going to have to step upstairs to my bureau. We don't commonly have the call for so much at once. Jem, you can commence to close up; Isaiah, stop gawping, start sweeping. If you'd like to follow me, then. —Bring your winnings, by all means; we wouldn't want you to lose count."

"I see you mean to tease me back," said Mr. Smith, now possessed of a double handful of rustling, doubtful currency.

"One turn deserves another," said Lovell. "This way."

He led him through a door in the panelling, and Smith found himself in what was plainly the hall-way of the merchant's private residence, for it ran perpendicular to another street-door, whence fell the faint remaining light of the day; and where the counting office had smelled of ink, smoke, charcoal and the sweat of men, this had the different savour of waxed wood, food, rosewater and tea-leaves, with a suggestion of (what is common to both sexes) the necessary-house. At the end of the hall a stair spiralled steeply up in the dark. At each turn it passed a window but, the outlook being to the east, little came in through the glass but roofs and spars in black outline, upon the ground of a slice of heaven but one degree brighter. Stray gleams of polish showed the placing of the banisters and newel posts; picture frames set faint rumours of gold around rectangles of darkness or curious glitters too shadowed to make out, as if Lovell had somehow collected, and drowned, a stairwell's-worth of distant constellations. This being Lovell's home, it might be expected that the merchant would put off the weight of business, and resume the legerity of domestic life, yet on the first step he paused for a moment, and Smith saw the level of his shoulders fall, as if they had taken on them some effort, perhaps the effortful thought of the thousand pounds, and Smith anticipated a slow, perhaps a wheezing, ascent. But instead, that moment past, Lovell set off up the narrow house at the pace of a climbing monkey, swarming aloft in the boughs of a familiar tree, and it was Smith, his hands too full to balance with, who followed the dark stair warily—and when Lovell crossed a landing and rushed on, he paused, arrested at a door-way.

The long room it opened on did have western windows, a pair of them letting in the day's last glow of light, rather the silver of rain than of the metal, streaked with a faint crimson admitting to the distant existence of the sun; brilliant light to Mr. Smith, and it burnished with borrowed brilliance the faces of the three young women in the room, plain-dressed among the plain furniture. One, fair-headed, was standing at the window with her hand to her mouth; one, darker, was sitting and reading something; and one, an African servant in a white kerchief, was holding a taper to a fresh white candle. When they saw him at the door, they all turned and looked at him. He looked back.

What a difference a frame makes! To Mr. Smith, gazing inward, the uprights of the painted door seemed to set out the three of them like some tableau representing the New World itself, of which his acquaintance to this point totalled forty-seven minutes, and which therefore he could not yet feel to be entirely solid, entirely *terra firma* as ordinarily founded on its bed of earth; but only to constitute a kind of scene, backed by drops and flats, where you must step forth at your cue to act your part, ready or not, ignorant as yet of the temper of the audience; ignorant of the temper of the other players, which will so much determine the drama you compose together, turn by turn, speech by speech, line by line. —The blonde one was extremely pretty, with a wide mouth of candid pink. The dark one not much less so, though she seemed just to have left off scowling, and her brows met in a knot. The African was turning eyes black as liquorice on him, in a gaze of perfect blankness. —What was more, what seemed to him a rarity fitting them to model the Three Graces, none of the three was in the slightest marked by the pox. He would learn that this exemption was, in the colony, almost too common to deserve notice, but it had for the moment the force of an original astonishment. Thus Smith, on the one side, gazing in. To the three gazing outward, however, into the dark of the stairwell, where a face had bloomed, and two pale hands clutching paper, he had only appeared in the ordinary aperture of an ordinary day. For them the blue-grey pediment of Connecticut pine faced the everyday world, as it always did, and they were their everyday selves, well launched (it seemed to them) into the middle of their histories, with loves, sorrows, resentments, hopes, all far advanced and long settled already into three familiar fortunes. He was the one unshackled, as yet unconfined; the one from whom diversion, or news, or any other of the new worlds a stranger may contain, were to be expected. And perhaps desired. For if your fortune at present is not such as pleases you, there is a prospect of mercy, as much as of doom, in the thought that Fortuna is fickle. The goddess's renown is all in her changeableness, and strangers are her acknowledged messengers. They bear with them a glimmering of new chances. When this stranger came forward to the threshold, he could be seen to be a youth of about four-and-twenty dressed in plain green, wearing his own hair in short rust-brown curls, smiling in a fashion that crinkled the freckles across his nose, and staring shamelessly.

"Hello," he said.

The dark one yawned deliberately. "Zephyra, shut the door," she said.

"Don't do that," said Smith.

"Why not? This is a parlour, sir, not a peep show. The place of business is downstairs. A very little glimpse must suffice you—in proportion to your manners."

"But my curiosity is great."

"How sad for you. Very well. Zephyra, count to three, and *then* shut the door. —What? Not enough?"

"Never," Smith said. The fair girl dimpled. The African turned back to the candle with a slow shake of the head.

"Gallantry," observed the dark girl, with the air of someone naming a common insect. "Dull."

"My sister thinks everything is dull," broke in the yellow-haired girl. "Everything but a wounding tongue. Or she makes it so. But some of us aren't so sour. *Some* of us don't take compliments amiss a-purpose. You are a client of Father's, sir? Won't you step in?" A blush had appeared in her cheeks, as she made this speech of defiance. It was apparent that she was very young; maybe only sixteen or seventeen.

"You are kind," said Smith, remaining where he was. "Yet truly, it was not gallantry speaking, I swear, but gluttony. Six weeks I have been at sea, and every wave looking just like the one before, in wet procession. By now my eyes, being starved so long, have as many stomachs as a horse."

The dark sister snorted. "As many—? That is the most grotesque similitude I ever heard."

"And yet it served its purpose."

"None I can perceive."

"To make you smile."

"But I am not smiling."

"I would warrant you did for a moment."

"No; you and your eyes' horses' stomachs are all mistaken. Though I doubt that will stop them vomiting words."

"Now who is grotesque?"

"Your bad habits are catching. You have infected us."

"May I come in, then, and do it more conveniently?"

"We can hear you quite well from where you are."

"Tabitha!" protested the other, and was ignored.

"So, you'd stare as boldly at anything, would you? Any object would do?"

"Sorry: I have it on authority that gallantry is dull."

"Have you come from London, sir?" the fair girl tried again.

"Yes, I have," he said.

"I wonder, do you—do you—have you—perhaps—"

"What my sister Flora wants to say," said dark Tabitha, slipping into a mocking falsetto, "is: 'Do-you-do-you, could-you-could-you, might-you-might-you, possibly have in your baggage any novels?' For she consumes them like laudanum, and has read all that New-York can afford, so must beg new supplies from every traveller."

"Hush!" cried Flora, the spots back in her cheeks.

"I do have a book or two in my trunk," said Smith, "and I would be happy to look them out for you. You don't approve?" he asked Tabitha.

"I am not a great one for novels."

"You are not a great one for anything but grumbling, and poking fun."

"I do not think it makes the bird feel better if the cage has pictures pasted to't, however pretty. Good evening, Papa."

Smith jumped. Lovell had returned on padding feet, a caddy of japanned wood in his hands, and had been standing in the shadows at his side, it was not evident how long, with a speculative look upon his face.

"I see you've met my daughters, sir. Tabitha, Flora, this is Mr. Smith, a man of affairs; just don't ask him what. Well, step in, step in; don't block the door. And just lay what you have in your hands on the tabletop, will you, for I perceive I've made an error, fool that I am."

"How unaccountable of you, Papa," said Tabitha.

Lovell shot her a look, but only said, "Ah, yes . . ."

The card-dealing began again, except that Lovell was, as well as paying down new paper, also whisking back certain bills he had already dispensed, and replacing them with other, similar scraps of print, equally mysterious. This time, he didn't count aloud, and this time, every note marked "Rhode Island" seemed to return to the box.

"What a lot of money you've got, Mr. Stomachs," said Tabitha.

"If it *is* money," said Smith, "and not a printer's foul-papers."

"You'll get used to it. —Papa, you should invite him to dinner."

"I was about to, my dear," said Lovell. "There's your guineas rendered, fair and square. Would ye care to dine with us tomorrow night?"

"Are you sure you want to do that?" said Smith.

"Come now, come on now," said Lovell, with a grin that seemed, from disuse, in need of the oil-can, to ease the rusty motion of his jaws. "Let's not let a poor beginning spoil matters. Our compact is made, sir, and if all goes well—if all goes as you promise—why then, there's no quarrel between us, but the contrary. And you've made landing on a far shore, and you'll thrive the better for a change from hard tack, I'll be bound."

Mr. Lovell could not be said to have succeeded in the paternal note he tried to strike, for "impudent pup" and "lying rogue" are not obliging terms, and do not vanish from conversation, once spoken, without leaving a trace of awkwardness: but the invitation was pressed, and at the first refusal pressed again; until Mr. Smith, having found (at least) much in the house to interest him, at last accepted it. The arrangement made, he bowed goodbyes to Miss Tabitha and Miss Flora, and two minutes later found himself back in the street, having been loaned the prentice Isaiah to bear his trunk.

It was now raining in good earnest, and the kennel was running, carrying city swill and city ordure down the centre of Golden Hill Street. Uphill and inland the narrow roadway dimmed to a windy darkness, faintly broken by lanterns. Isaiah swore, and tried to shift the box higher on his shoulders, to serve in the office of a wooden roof, but the weight sank his feet deeper. He was bullcalf-broad of figure beside the spindly, phthisical merchants' boys Smith knew, and his skin shone with unearthly cleanness, but a Mannahatta youth seemed to share very fully his Eastcheap cousins' taste for flash in the article of clothes. Isaiah's coat had more gold lace on its facings than many admirals' did, though the colour was all paint and not bullion, and his shoes were elaborately double-buckled and pointed in the toes.

"God's bollocks," he said again, shifting unhappily. "Where away, then?"

"You tell me, cully," Smith said amiably. "Where's clean and comfortable, with a decent chop-house to hand, and won't bleed my purse too fast? —Not a school of Venus," he added, seeing a particular light kindle in Isaiah's eye. "Just a plain lodging."

"Mrs. Lee in the Broad Way, then," said Isaiah. "But I hain't your cully, whate'er that be. I don't cotton to your cant."

And he kept a sullen silence as he led Smith over oozy cobbles. It was not a joyous procession, between the half-seen house-fronts, some rising tall in brick and others mere hovels of wood, or black empty lots where animals complained unseen. Everything trickled, gurgled, spattered, dripped; kept up a watery unwelcoming music. The rain drilled in slantwise, as cold as ocean, and almost as immersing, soaking collar and hair, filling ears with icy drams of floodwater, making soused fingers to ache. The few passers-by scurried along at a crouch, holding canvas sacks overhead if they had 'em, and Smith lost his count of the turns through the town-maze that took them to the door upon which Isaiah, after fifteen sodden minutes, knocked. Yet his spirits rose. A task begun is easier than a task contemplated; besides, he was a young man with money in his pocket, new-fallen to land in a strange city on the world's farther face, new-come or (as he himself had declared) new-born, in the metropolis of Thule. And these things are pleasant still, if the money be of some strange kind easily confus'd with waste paper, if the city be such as to fill you with fear as well as expectation. For what soul, to whom the world still is relatively new, does not feel the sensible excitement, the faster breath and expansion of hope, where every alley may yet contain an adventure, every door be back'd by danger, or by pleasure, or by bliss?

Mr. Lovell, to whom few things retained the force of novelty, and who misliked extremely the sensation when they did, as if firm ground underfoot had been replaced on the instant by a scrabbling fall *in vacuo*—was, at the moment the door opened on Broad Way, hesitating in his parlour. Flora was downstairs, commanding from Zephyra the supper that would have arrived whether she commanded it or not. Only Tabitha still sat on the sopha, her hands quite still in her lap. It had been his custom, since his wife died these three years past, to call from time to time on his elder daughter's intelligence, in the same office her mother's had served; but now, for particular reasons, the issue might touch on her own self in terms that made advice unwise to solicit.

"Why do you suppose," he said slowly, "that a young fellow who has money might pretend he does not—or, at any rate, keep it doubtful?"

"*Does* he have money?" Tabitha asked.

"I think so, yes. I *think* the rest is all palaver, confusion a-purpose. Sand thrown in our eyes. Why, though, is what I cannot tell. What do you make of him?"

The same question was asked that night by Isaiah of Jem, at the kitchen fire; and again, by the master of the *Henrietta* of its mate, as the ship rode at anchor, on the swelling black rain-pored skin of the East River.

By morning, the news was all around the town that a stranger had arrived with a fortune in his pocket.

II

As a mason must build a wall one brick at a time, though the finished wall be smooth and sheer, so in individual pieces did Mr. Smith's consciousness return to him, the next day, as he lay in the truckle bed of Mrs. Lee's gable-end bedroom, and assembled the world again.

First, the white ceiling. Then the slow realisation that this was not the dark, damp timber six inches above his nose to which he had woken for six weeks in his bunk aboard *Henrietta*. Then the memory of his purpose; and the whole variorum mosaic of the evening before; and a burning curiosity. The light through the gable window was full sunshine. He jumped out of the bed in his shirt and threw the casement wide—rooftops and bell towers greeted him; a jumble, not much elevated, of stepped Dutchwork eaves and ordinary English tile, with the greater eminences of churches poking through, steepled and cupola'd, and behind a slow-swaying fretwork of masts; the whole prospect washed with, bright with, aglitter with, the water last night's clouds had shed, and one—two—three—he counted 'em—*six* crumbs of dazzling light hoisted high that must be the weathercocks of the city of New-York, riding golden in the hurrying levels of the sky where blue followed white followed blue. The Broad Way, it turned out as he leaned and craned from the window, was a species of cobbled avenue, only middling broad, lined on Mrs. Lee's side with small trees. Wagon-drivers, hawkers with handcarts and quick-paced pedestrians were passing in both directions. Somewhere below too, hidden mostly by the branches, someone was sweeping the last leaves, and singing slow in an African tongue as if their heart had long ago broken, and they were now rattling the pieces together desultorily in a bag.

But Mr. Smith took his time from the hurrying clouds and the hurrying walkers. He splashed his face with water from the ewer, changed his shirt, and threw on his breeches and his coat; descended the stairs in clattering leaps that startled the widow Lee, who was serving porridge and a dish of kidneys to her boarders in the ground-floor parlour.

"Shall you be wanting breakfast, sir?" she asked, with more deference than she was used to show to guests, for the word had reached her too, with the morning's delivery of the milk, that she was entertaining a nabob unawares: a being so overstuffed with guineas that he might scatter them at the slightest nudge.

"I thank you, no," said Smith, scarce pausing; "I shall furnish myself as I go. Good day!" And the hall door slammed behind him as he went.

The singer had departed; the street was all business. Which direction to follow? To the left, Broad Way seemed to debouch onto a green common, with a complication of barriers or fences beyond it, but the flow of the traffic favoured, by a majority, the rightward direction, where the houses thickened, and the heart of the town plainly lay; that was the way the barrows of bread and the milk churns were going, and Smith strode with them, almost skipping. The cobbled roadbed seemed to lie along the top of the gentle hummock the island made, between the two rivers, as if it were following out the course of some mostly submerged creature's spine, with the cobbles as lumpish vertebrae. On both sides the side-streets sloped down, but beyond Broad Way on the side where Mrs. Lee's door stood—the west side, he calculated—there was only one layer of building, backed by a few scraggy shacks: the lanes descended there to an uncertain shore, where rowing boats were drawn up in clumps of yellow grass, and wading birds stalked on mudflats exposed by the tide. The weight of the town seemed all to be to the east. It was there that the openings revealed descents tight-packed with tall houses in the mode of Amsterdam, where pyramids of doorsteps supported mid-air door-ways. Or rather—looking closer—in the modes of Amsterdam and of London intermingled, for the spindle-thin facades of the one style jostled now against the broader haunches of the other. It was from these windings that Smith had emerged in the rain, last night, and it was into these that the barrow-pushers and the costermongers, the merchants in a hurry and the prentices on errands, steadily streamed away from the main flow of the avenue.

But Smith, in holiday mood, followed Broad Way instead, strolling past a square-towered stone church that might've been transplanted (like a rose root in moistened sacking) from any county town of the English shires, and a bowling lawn preserv'd from foot traffic behind railings, a teardrop of perfect green, until the avenue dissolved into a parade ground before a fort, with a blowy esplanade behind, where left and right and all around the bright air showed yesterday's grey expanse of water turned tossing blue in all directions, crowned with white caps. It was the point, the last, the *ne plus ultra* of the island; and the burly wind pumped Smith's chest with tipsy breaths. The silk of the Union flag on the pole within the fort snapped and ruffled, but the fort itself, on inspection, was if not quite derelict then at least distinctly singed, with blackened walls and here and there rooflines broken to bare, scorched rafters. The sentry in the box beside the gate sat head-down, a huddle of red. Only the wooden structure alongside seemed fresh, a contrivance of pale timbers whose function Smith at first could not fathom. A gibbet without nooses? A giant's enlargement of the vermin board where a zealous keeper nails carcasses of owls, weasels, all rivals who presume to hunt the master's game? This board was strung with dark blotches and streamers; rustling congealments Smith puzzled at till, leaning close enough, he saw the fibres the wind stirred were human hairs, still rooted in the parchment-yellow of scalps. There must have been forty, fifty, sixty of them nailed there, and close up, they reeked like bad meat. He stepped abruptly back.

Round to the left, the swaying mast-forest beckoned from behind the houses, and now Smith took the invitation of a street's mouth, and followed into the gullet of the town. Prosperous dwellings, here, with window-glass glinting, and maids swilling doorsteps and stairways clean; counting-houses too, and stalls, and shops; streets a-bustle, heterogeneously, for though the houses were plain as day the domicile of wealth, New-York's answer to the new-pattern'd squares of the West End, the business of the port was running through them, in mixtures London did not see. Wagoners moving boxes, cases, crates, barrels; fresh-landed emigrant families carrying off their all, looking as dazed (no doubt) as he did himself; a coffle of shuffling black men in irons underscoring the street music with a dismal clank. In London the costers would not have cried their apples at the Lord Mayor's door, a goldsmith would not have been in business next to a meagre dealership in marine supplies. There were omissions too, as well as unexpected presences. Smith had instructed his brain to ignore the information of his nose—schooled reflex of the city-dweller, in the face of stinks—and it took a little time for his brain to take the news that there were few stinks to ignore. The vapour from the scalps remained the worst of New-York's bouquet. A little fish, a little excrement; guts here, shit there; but no deep patination of filth, no cloacal rainbow for the nose in shades of brown, no staining of the air in sewer dyes. A Scene of City-Life, his eyes reported. A Country-Walk, in a Seaside District, his nostrils counter-argued. No smells; also, he realised, no beggars. He had been strolling the city's densest quarter for minutes, and yet no street-Arab children pepper-pointed with sores had circled him round, no gummy crones exhaling gin had plucked his sleeve, no mutilated men in the rags of uniform had groaned at him from the ground. He wandered at his ease among strangers who seemed universally blessed with health and strength and moderate good luck, at least, in life's lottery. Not to mention height. He was used, in the piazza of Covent Garden, to standing taller by a head than the general crowd; but here, in the busy bobbing mass of heads, he was no taller than the average.

It was perhaps because of this relaxation of the usual irritations of the street that Smith, without taking notice of it, relaxed in turn the town-dweller's habitual guard, and failed to perceive, as he reflected and considered, that others were meanwhile reflecting and considering upon him. He paused to admire the unloading boats, where an arm of the harbour pushed up among the houses. He passed into a narrow square where printer's devils ran from door to door with bundles of paper, and smiled on enquiring its name and being told it was Hanover Square, for its London counterpart ran less to ink, and more to ballrooms lit by half a thousand candles. He spied a coffee-house ahead, from which came perfumes of hot bread and well-ground beans, and stopping short of it, did what he would not have done at home, or anywhere he had full conviction he trod the humdrum earth. To try to sift from the unruly cram of Mr. Lovell's paper a suitable scrap to command his breakfast, he pulled out in the street his whole pocket-book. Quick as a wink, one of his followers dashed forward, snatched it, and took to his heels up the road ahead.

Smith had had his riches in his hand. Suddenly he did not. Smith gawped. Smith stared stupidly at the empty hand where money had been. And a document besides, which— But there was no time

for that. Smith hesitated—considered shouting "Stop thief!"—
perceived a train of likely consequences—shook his head like a man
assailed by flies—and set off in pursuit himself, silently, instead. His
moment's stillness had given the snatcher a lead of twenty yards or
so already, and though Smith's legs pumped and his green coat's
tails flew out behind him, the goal of his chase was slipping deftly
between backs, round corners, up alleyways. Now the streets of New-
York reeled by, not at a stroll but at a sprint; the same scenes, the
same mixture of familiar and unfamiliar chequered close together
as black and white squares of a chess board, but accelerated, passing
at a blur; in fact, some of the very same route he had trodden the
night before, but now had no time to recognise, as he gasped, and
pounded, and felt the enforced enfeeblement of his shipboard weeks
dragging at his limbs, while the figure ahead, jinking and turning,
weaving and bounding, drew no closer, in fact pulled ahead. The
thief was thin, with long, straight, black hair, and seemingly tireless
legs in grey breeches, and bare dirty feet that twinkled as they rose
and fell: that was all Smith could tell as the distance widened.

Now they were running uphill. Smith, seeing the grass of an open
space ahead, and deducing that every street here must run upward
in parallel to the open ground, whatever it was, resolved on a desperate expedient, and flung himself right at the next cross street,
then left uphill again on the next street over, meaning if he could to
cut the fugitive off at the top. The street was far emptier here, and
Smith made himself squeeze out the greatest pace he could as he
bolted upward (as he hoped) in parallel to his wallet. There were no
more cross streets: no chances to see if his stratagem was working.
Bare walls, poorer doors, empty lots. A hammering heart. Lungs
on fire. The top of the street coming up. Smith threw himself left
once more and gasped his way across to the top end of the original
street, expecting at any moment to catch sight again of his quarry.
He turned the corner.

Nothing; nobody. Nobody in sight at all at this end. The currents and eddies of the town's traffic all flowed other ways, leaving this street, at this moment, as an empty backwater. Just a hundred closed door-ways in the bright morning light, into any of which, Smith saw, realising the magnitude of his error, the thief might have vanished. He could not knock on all of them. He wheeled around. The green space was a ragged common. A cow was gazing at him, chewing the cud in comfortable incuriosity. Any of the bushes might conceal a thief. Then again, they might not.

Mr. Smith put his hands on his knees and breathed; labouring, just as much, to bring his emotions under his control, to stop the indignant working of his mouth, which wanted to form—which wanted to shout—words he would not permit it. When his chest no longer heaved, he smiled, experimentally, at the cow, and if the expression resembled a rictus somewhat, a drawing of the lips from the teeth such as a corpse may perform when the strings of the flesh tighten in death, it was, nevertheless, voluntary, which was the only quality he just then required of it. The cow was indifferent.

Then Mr. Smith walked onto the common, past a cricket-pitch worn to bare dirt at the wickets, past a pot kiln and a charcoal-burner's fire and a flock of sheep, and found himself a spot between trees where he could feel as sure as may be that he was not observed; and there, in the security he had not bothered to assure himself of earlier, he turned out the coat pocket where he had kept the pocket-book, and investigated his resources. As he had hoped, some of the paper bills had escaped in his carelessness, and were loose in there. But not many. He smoothed them out one by one, and counted. Five—six—six shillings and six—and eightpence—and this dirty spill was a sixpence too—and another shilling. Eight shillings and eightpence, in the money of—he squinted—New-York and New Jersey. The flimsiness of the paper seemed altogether less entertaining now. Plus, he remembered with a burst of relief, the small pile of veritable coin, which he had left in a heap at his bedside. Twenty-nine shillings odd, where he had reckoned on six times as much. He calculated. Could he live as he had planned? No. He would live as he must.

When he rose from his hiding place, his smile convincing once more, the road running along the far side of the common struck him as somehow familiar-looking, and a minute's walk in that direction confirmed it. It was the Broad Way continuing in the other direction to the one he had set out in. He had circled the whole town; that was New-York, all of it. The far end of the common was blocked with a palisade, and the Broad Way, cobbles diminished into a cart-track, went out through the barrier at another sentry post. At a venture, he asked if the soldier decorating the ground there with spit had seen anyone; anyone running.

"Migh'er done," he said.

Smith studied the expectant face, and considered the state of his pockets.

"You didn't, though, did you," he said.

"No," agreed the soldier, amiably, and stuck his clay pipe back between his teeth.

III

With what sadder steps, and slower, Smith retraced his way, the reader may imagine; how the faces of passers-by, which had formerly expressed a cheerful involvement in their own concerns, now seemed locked tight, so many declarations of secretiveness and guile, not to be trusted; how the city itself, a few minutes before remarkable and new, now appeared provincial and small, rustic and contemptible, absurd in comparison to any metropolis of Europe, *et cetera*, with a mere delusive shine laid upon it by the morning. Even the savour of fresh bread, once he had returned to the coffee-house, stirred his appetite with less relish. He hesitated at the threshold. He had been out of sight of the window when he was robbed, he calculated. Yet he had run past, and might have been seen. Some customer might have been going in, or coming out, at the critical instant. His catastrophe might have been deduced. Well, well: nothing for it but to spin the wheel, and play.

"Service!" he cried, entering a long low room canopied in smoke, diversified with steam, where men (all men) conversed in a gruff murmur that rose and fell like a masculine sea. At an unoccupied table he bounced into a chair and settled with a wide spread of knees, a confident sprawl of legs, a benignant beaming in all directions.

"Service!"

Heads turned, but mildly, slowly; not—he judged—with that quickness that betokens an interest in a drama resumed at its exciting mid-point. Not as if they were expecting Act Two of *The Wrong'd Traveller*, in which Simon Simple (an *ingénu* from the country) loses his all to a sharper, and must throw himself upon the dubious mercy of Sir Bartholomew Quorum (a lawyer) and Mrs. Spurt (a bawd). It seemed only the slow stir with which any coffee-house registers an unknown come among regulars; fresh supply of another talking head, loud or wise or foolish as the case may be, to be recruited into the great plural organism of the room, which now and again loses a body or gains a body, as people arrive and depart, but talks on, talks on.

"Yessir?" A boy had bustled up in a white apron. "Tea, coffee or chocolate, sir?"

"A pot of the dark Mahometan, no cow juice."

"Yessir. Victuals?"

"Basket o' white tommy."

"Yessir. News-paper, sir?"

"What do you have?"

"*Post-Boy, Intelligencer* or *Monitor*, sir."

"All three, then."

"Yessir. In a moment, sir. May have to wait for the *Post-Boy*, sir. Only one copy in this morning, and it's with those gentlemen over there." —A youngish pair, one bearded and one in horn-rimmed spectacles, laughing over by the window.

"Just the others, then," said Smith. "No need to bother 'em."

The rolls came, smelling of the oven, and the coffee in a pewter pot that London would have called ten years behind the fashion, its sides were so straight and its handle so lacking in decorative folderol. The boy whirled the breakfast in on one tray while he kept two more balanced up his arm; shifted, uncrooked his neck to release the folded pages he'd clamped against his shoulder with his chin; laid them before Smith; spun onward into the next figure of his coffee-house dance. Smith found his appetite returning. He inhaled the rising savours of basket and pot as if they were friends whose shoulders he could throw his arms around, and fell to his meal, munching and buttering, licking crumbs from his fingers while he propped the papers against the pot, and the clatter of plates and speech and the guggling liquid made their familiar music, played *continuo*.

When he had ate his fill, and proceeded from the urgent first cup and necessary second to the voluntary third which might be toyed with at leisure, without any particular outcry seeming to suggest he should be on his guard, he leant back, spread the city's news before him, and, by glances between the items, took a longer survey of the room. Session of the Common Council. Vinegars, Malts, and Spirituous Liquors, Available on Best Terms. Had he been on familiar ground, he would have been able to tell at a glance what particular group of citizens in the great empire of coffee this house aspired to serve: whether it was the place for poetry or gluttony, philosophy or marine insurance, the Indies trade or the meat-porters' burial club. Ships Landing. Ships Departed. Long Island Estate of Mr.

De Kyper, with Standing Timber, to be Sold at Auction. But the prints on the yellowed walls were a mixture. Some maps, some satires, some ballads, some bawdy, alongside the inevitable picture of the King: pop-eyed George reigning over a lukewarm graphical gruel, neither one thing nor t'other. Albany Letter, Relating to the Behaviour of the Mohawks. Sermon, Upon the Dedication of the Monument to the Late Revd. Vesey. Leases to be Let: Bouwerij, Out Ward, Environs of Rutgers' Farm. And the company? River Cargos Landed. Escaped Negro Wench: Reward Offered. —All he could glean was an impression generally businesslike, perhaps intersown with law. Dramatic Rendition of the Classics, to be Performed by the Celebrated Mrs. Tomlinson. Poem, "Hail Liberty, Sweet Succor of a Briton's Breast," Offered by "Urbanus" on the Occasion of His Majesty's Birthday. Over there there were maps on the table, and a contract a-signing; and a ring of men in merchants' buff-and-grey quizzing one in advocate's black-and-bands. But some of the clients had the wind-scoured countenance of mariners, and some were boys joshing one another. Proceedings of the Court of Judicature of the Province of New-York. Poor Law Assessment. Carriage Rates. Principal Goods at Mart, Prices Current. Here he pulled out a printed paper of his own from an inner pocket, and made comparison of certain figures, running his left and right forefingers down the columns together. Telescopes and Spy-Glasses Ground. Regimental Orders. Dinner of the Hungarian Club. Perhaps there were simply too few temples here to coffee, for them to specialise as he was used.

The pair by the window were coming over, still laughing, the one in the spectacles bearing the missing *Post-Boy*. He had a remarkably smooth, white, oval countenance, on which the dark circles of the horn frames made, somehow, a most neatly comic appearance. His hair was the stubble of one who usually wears a wig but is off duty.

"Here you are," said the stranger, tilting a curious look at Smith.

"No trouble, we've finished with it. You are welcome, sir, to all the slender pleasure it may give you." His voice was fastidiously educated and amused. "May I ask—did I just hear you say, 'No cow juice?'"

"It was in the nature of an experiment," said Smith. "I am new-come, and last night I drew a blank with a London word I thought was plain to all the world. So I made the venture of a little coffee cant today, just to see—"

"Oh, you'll have no luck with Quentin there, for he's fluent in every English in which a cupful can be ordered, let alone Dutch, and most other tongues a sailor may bring through the door. French, Spanish, Danish, Portuguese. Latin, if all else fails. *Nonne, Quentinianus?*" he said, as the boy passed by, deep in trays.

"*Sic, magister,*" said Quentin, gliding on.

"Will you join me?" Smith asked.

"If you're sure we don't intrude—" But they were already pulling chairs around, and waving two fingers at Quentin.

"Septimus Oakeshott," said the smooth, pale one.

"Hendrick Van Loon," said the other, pronouncing it with so little Dutch guttural, that Mr. Smith took a moment to find the surname in it. Front of an army; name of a wading bird.

"Richard—" he began.

"Oh, we know," said Septimus Oakeshott. "I'm afraid that everyone knows, Mr. Smith. You are celebrated before you open your mouth. You are the very rich boy who won't answer questions."

"Well . . ."

"Unless, by chance," put in Van Loon, "you *do* answer them?"

"Hendrick's interest is professional," said Septimus, his comical eyebrows raised high on the blank egg of his forehead. "He actually writes for the *Post-Boy.*"

"Not wholly professional," said Van Loon. "My family has dealings with Gregory Lovell, so we are . . . intrigued . . . that you've come, Mr. Smith. But it's true that you're news. And our friend Septimus here is plying his trade as well, in case you were wondering"—paying Oakeshott smartly back—"for he is Secretary to the Governor, and we suspect him of keeping his ears wide open while he sits here in the Merchants."

"The Merchants?"

"As opposed to the Exchange Coffee-House, back that way on Broad Street," said Septimus, pointing a white finger at the wall. "The coffee is better here, and the conversation."

They both gazed hopefully at Smith. He, understanding that he was in the presence of the two powers of Press and Government, albeit their junior versions, gave his most guileless smile.

"I'm afraid I am exactly as advertised," he said.

"How unusual," said Septimus. "*Exactly* as advertised?"

"Yes."

"What, in every detail?"

"Yes."

"A perfect fit with legend?"

"Mm-hm."

Septimus waited, his face exhibiting the glazed patience of a porcelain owl, to see if there was more; but there was not, for Mr. Smith was as patient as he. More coffee arrived, and the silence lengthened between the two ingenuous faces, with Van Loon glancing amused from one to the other, as if spectating at chess; and it was Septimus who spoke first, resuming the vein of his chatter as if no time had passed at all.

"Then you must be a marvel of nature," he said, "quite remote from the usual run of mortals. For I am not as advertised, and he is not"—indicating Van Loon. "You could make a little grammar of it. I am not, you are not, he or she or it is not as advertised. Speaking for myself, I rise in the morning, and it takes all the effort of which I am capable—the thought of my pious father the rector, and my six virtuous sisters—to stuff the billowing sackful of whim-whams, impulses and contradictions back behind my face, and turn myself out for the day as a plausible secretary again."

He laid his white right hand tidily atop his white left hand, on the tabletop. Smith smiled appreciatively, but still declined to come out to play. Septimus tapped the toe of his shoe on the floor. Tap-tap-tap: a foot tutting.

"How disappointing you are, Mr. Smith. I understood you talked. 'Talked the hind-leg off a donkey' was the phrase I heard."

"I prefer to talk myself out of trouble, Mr. Oakeshott. Not into it."

"Do you anticipate trouble?"

"Do you, sir?"

"Never in life," said Septimus. They drank.

"This is really very good coffee," said Smith.

"Yes," said Van Loon. "It comes from the Leeward plantations, and the voyage is probably shorter than you are used to."

"I am not speaking officially," said Septimus. "But if I *were*—if I had my wig on—then there are several categories of thing we would rather you were not. We would rather you were not a spy. We would rather you were not a hireling of the ministry. We would rather you were not a scoundrel, come to spoil the credit of London paper in the city."

"I am not a spy or a hireling," Smith said promptly.

Septimus laughed. You would have thought it would crack the eggshell of his countenance, but his teeth proved as neat and white as the rest.

"For myself," put in Van Loon cheerfully, "well—speaking for myself as a member of the family, not for the *Post-Boy*—we would not mind at all if you proved a scoundrel. Pray, be one. For if you're a fraud, then there's no drain in prospect on old Gregory's funds, and our projects with him are not in danger; but he is treating you at present as the genuine article, and so we shall too, and be glad to dine with ye, and shake your hand."

"Thank you," said Mr. Smith.

"Now, I had better be getting back to the printing-house," said Van Loon, rising.

"Would this be of any use to you?" asked Smith, shaking out the page he had drawn from his pocket, and reaching it up. *London Prices Current*, it said across the masthead, and a date six weeks old.

"Yes indeed," said Van Loon. "Indeed it would. The *Post-Boy* would be delighted. These are fresher by a fortnight than any I've seen."

"Take it, then."

"I thankee. So long, Septimus. See you later, Mr. Smith."

"You will?"

"Oh yes."

He departed.

"Why will he see me later?" Smith asked.

"Because you are dining at the Lovells'."

"And everyone knows this."

"They do. It's a small town."

"Is it? I see streams of people, all in motion, and ships enough to turn Quentin there polyglot."

"True. But the ships come and go again, and the most part of the traffic of souls passes straight through. They walk up from the slips to the streets and are gone; the continent devours them. New-York is but a gullet. Few stay. Will you be staying?"

"For a while."

"Well, if you stay till the snows come, you will discover just how tiny it can be. When the winter takes hold we all huddle in each other's pockets. Colonial snow is a different article from the domestic: altogether fiercer."

Septimus was playing with a tea-spoon.

"Do you really have six sisters?" asked Smith.

"Yes. In Hampshire."

"Hence the name."

"Hence my name."

"May I ask you a question?"

"What, another one? Luckily I am in more of an answering mood than you are. Go on."

"There is a board by the fort, with—"

"Scalps nailed to it. Yes."

"What are they doing there?"

"They are showing how much we love the French. In order to keep the river valley north of here empty of all but those who speak good English—or Dutch—the Government has a bounty on the scalps of settlers *avec un mauvais façon de parler*, and once a year the friendly Mohawks bring down their crop to New-York, and we count out the cash. It's a celebrated local occasion. They march along the Broad Way with their trophies on a pole, and the Governor receives them. I stand on his right. Everybody cheers. You have to remember that here, too, last year was rather tense."

"I would have thought you were well out of reach of Jacobite troubles."

"Would you? Were you in London last year?"

"Yes."

"Doing . . . ?"

"This and that."

"Of course. And what was it like?"

"When the Pretender came marching down on us? A lazy sureness of being secure, till almost the last minute, and then panic so late it was virtually over as soon it was begun. The prince is coming, the prince is coming, the prince is retreating."

"Ah. Well, here it was long and slow, for the lag of the news kept us in suspense for weeks. Weeks of furious doubt if the next sail into the harbour wouldn't be a frigate bearing tyranny on its quarterdeck, and orders for us all to turn Papist on the instant—those are words I heard spoken in this room—and nothing to do about it,

Europe's afterthought that we are, politically speaking, but to abide the issue of the quarrel, while snarling (or worse) at any soul within hand's reach who might be suspected of serving King Louis, from the French cut of their coat. So you see how the appetite would arise for a wholesome parade of savages, lightly blood-dabbled. Besides, we have no theatre."

"Do you not?"

"No," said Septimus. "Not since before my time, at any rate." His foot had begun to tap again, steadily.

"But— Wait a minute," said Smith, rummaging under the coffee-pot for the news-sheets. "Oh yes—what about the celebrated Mrs. Tomlinson, and her rendition of the classics?"

"That will be an upstairs room over a tavern, and Terpie dressed up as Britannia. Terpie keeps the lamp of culture lit, but her helmet will be gilded cardboard, and every time she misremembers a line, she'll give a flash of thigh."

"You don't approve? Peg Woffington does that every time she takes a breeches role."

"Mrs. Woffington gives us the thighs *as well as* the tragedy. I'm afraid with Terpie it's the thighs *instead of*. It doesn't take much to be celebrated here. —I saw her in *The Recruiting Officer*, you know—Peg Woffington. She was marvellous."

"Still is. Do you know she's broken with Garrick?"

"No! When?"

"Two years ago."

"Oh, you brute," said Septimus. "You absolute brute. Really?"

"Yes. How long have you been here?"

"Four years," said Septimus. His brows steepled, and a fine upright wrinkle appeared between them: as eloquent a mark of passion, on a face so Toby-jug-like, so china-smooth, as if he were rolling on the floor tearing at his garments, and raving in wild anguish at his exile. The tapping foot accelerated. Smith took pity on him.

"Let's see," he said. "The news of the Town: —— has ceased to announce his retirement, and actually retired. The *bon ton* have flocked to ——, but —— has closed after six performances for want of backers. The fashion for —— has all gone out, but new in the firmament shine —— and ——. Mr. —— is suspected of taking guineas to allow the Marquess of ——'s tragedy onto the boards. The new man in comedy is one Mr. ——. There: is that better?"

"No. Now I only feel more sensibly the miles of water in between."

"I'm sorry," said Smith. He smiled. "Well, maybe there's my opportunity. I should use my famous riches to build you a theatre. Or an opera-house. Turn impresario. What do you think? Give me an orchestra pit and a red velvet curtain, and I shall make you feel you're in the arms of Aunt England again."

Septimus narrowed his eyes. The foot stopped tapping. Smith, feeling himself looked at closely, and of a sudden in no friendly spirit, found that he had fallen into a close mimickry of Septimus' posture at table, from the folded fingers to the tilted head; which mirror-work, executed in flesh and blood, Septimus perhaps took to be mocking, judging by the pursued distaste of the Secretary's lips.

"Heavens," he said slowly. "What a lot of different cants you do know, Mr. Smith. But that is too blatant to be pleasing, I think. Too gross a tease. And though I may have been out of the arms of Aunt England, as you say, for a dreadful long time, I think I can still tell when I am talking to a little bold face, and when I am not, thank you; to one who is really a dear little Moorfield toad, and one who only counterfeits being so. —And now I had better go and wait upon the Governor. You may keep the opera-house you offer, sir; but by all means pay for breakfast."

"Of course," said Smith, with as little of a detectable pause as he could contrive. "Quentin? Put Mr. Oakeshott's and Mr. Van Loon's victuals to my account, would you? I believe I shall be here most mornings."

"Yessir," said the boy. "Three shillings and fourpence New-York, then, on the slate, sir."

Oakeshott had already left, jangling the bell on the door as he pulled it sharply to, behind him; and Smith, who had coloured, did not hurry as he followed; so he was surprised to find Septimus in fact still waiting, outside, beneath the overhang of the coffee-house's old-fashioned upper storey; hesitantly rubbing or perhaps hesitantly tapping his pointed white chin with one well-cared-for fingertip, his gaze seemingly fixed in fascination on the mastheads of the ships opposite.

"This may be needless advice," he said. "I don't know what game you purpose to play here. I think I don't care to know, unless you force me to take notice. But let me give you a warning. This is a place where things can get out of hand very quick: and often do. You would think, talking to the habitants, that all the vices and crimes of humanity had been left behind on the other shore. Take 'em as they take themselves, and they are the innocentest shopkeepers, placid and earnest, plucked by a lucky fortune out from corruption. But the truth is that they are wild, suspicious, combustible—and the devil to govern. They flare up at the least thing, especially at the least touch of restraint, real or imaginary, which they resent as the most bitter imposition, having known so little of it. In all their relations they are prompt to peer and gaze for the hidden motive, the worm in the apple, the serpent in the garden they insist their New World to be. And thus there are few quicker to get a scent of anything . . . odd . . . about a fellow. Anyone with a particular reason to prize their privacy must work at it assiduously; for London is really a very long way away, and if a person were to get into trouble, there would be very little help that could be expected. Only what is here matters, and *who* is here. The courts are, if anything, more savage than those at home, and even more ruthlessly commanded by party interest. You have walked into a mesh of favours owing, where everybody knows everybody—even if none of them, as yet, know *you*. Do you know that there is a graveyard here, quite as if it were a real town? I think it would be taking your visit altogether too seriously for you to end up in it, don't you?"

A sailor had ascended the foremast of the country schooner nearest in to the dock and was painting it with something out of a pail.

"Thank you," said Smith. "I think."

"Well, I am not sure I am saying it for your good, exactly. But my sisters would like me to have said it. My father the rector certainly would."

In Smith's mind these vicarage figures, who had seemed entirely substanceless, thickened slightly, and for an instant he imagined Septimus as a painfully well-behaved child, playing tidily on the floor while seven high-minded adults stared at him.

"I perceive you are a man of virtue, Mr. Oakeshott," he said, trying for the lightness of their conversation's opening.

"Go away, Mr. Smith. —Achilles!" he called, and a tall African of about Smith's age, wearing livery, with long limbs and a tight knob of a head like the bole of a dark tree, wordlessly unfolded himself from where he had been crouching against the dockside wall, chewing a mouthful of tobacco. He spat into the gutter.

"And shall I see you later, too?" Smith asked Septimus.

"Not tonight. But soon, assuredly, if you stay. Just wait for the dark and the cold to set in; for then, as I say, all the little planets circle closer, jostling for company. Treading on each other's heels. Good day."

IV

At six o'clock that evening, in a clean shirt from his trunk, and with the green coat freshly brushed and pressed—Mrs. Lee having consented to include the care of his wardrobe in a rent on the gable-end room of eleven shillings a week (New-York), at which rate his debts would exceed his resources in a fortnight—he presented himself at the town-door of Mr. Lovell's house on Golden Hill. He was wearing his hair clubbed at the nape and tied with a dark red ribbon. In his hand he held a copy of *The Adventures of David Simple*, by Mrs. Fielding.

The door was opened to his knock by the maid Zephyra, who rather than letting him immediately in stood stock-still in the door-way, fixing on him the same mute gaze of assessment she had bestowed the night before. Chin lifted, black pupils surveying him with no indication of what they found, the light going in and no intelligence of her conclusions coming back out; this stillness lasting only a fraction of an instant, yet already contrasting strangely with the bustle of the hall beyond, where already-arrived guests, strangers to Smith, a family group by the look of them, were chattering and hanging up scarves and hats upon a peg-board. Then she stood back against the wall, and he stepped over the bar of silence she had laid across the threshold. He had seen the hall of the Lovells' house last night in shadow. Now it was cheerfully lit with candles in wall-sconces, and the young wood of the panelling shone ruddy yellow.

"Good evening," said Smith. There was a replying murmur, and heads inclined in nods, but the mother of the group, a short stout busty body with coiffed hair, instead of replying called out through the open door on the opposite side to the counting-house, *"Gregory, hij is hier!"* and Lovell appeared, in an embroidered waistcoat.

"There you are," he said, frowning as he advanced, as if, despite inviting Smith to dinner, he had successfully reduced him to a problem in the time intervening, and were now surprised to find he had remained, also, a tangible man. "Well, come in. Come in!"—this last with a sudden joviality that made the pouching lines beside his mouth jerk.

Smith was ushered into a biggish dining-room, where a fire was burning in the grate, the coals hissing slightly, and in a corner beside it a seated African dressed in livery was tuning up a violin. The guests who followed him pressed curiously behind and the faces of those already seated at table turned all Smith's way as well.

"Friends?" said Lovell. "This is Mr. Smith, my *unexpected* counter-party. Mr. Smith, may I introduce the Van Loons, these many years our good partners in business, and good neighbours. Mijnheer Van Loon, Piet"—indicating a red-faced patriarch with a square visage swagged north and south with white hair, like a king on a play-ing card; "Mistress Van Loon, Geertje"—the rounded and coiffed woman, taking her place at the end of the table opposite to Lovell at its head; "Hendrick, George, Anne, Elizabeth"—the younger Van Loons, ranking downward in age, all paler and slenderer than their parents, but taking from them respectively a squarish jaw and a short upper lip showing prominent top teeth; "Captain Prettyman of Mystic, who sails for us both on the Indies run, and who happens to be in port"—a lean weather-beaten bald-head, rising far enough to duck into a half-bow; "Flora and Tabitha, who you know"—the first smiling at him from a nest of Van Loons at the far end, the latter watching him, chin on fist, from the seat next to the one into which Lovell waved him. Hendrick nodded a greeting, with an air, however, less of sympathy than of anticipation, like one who seats himself in the theatre and ruffles out the tails of his coat as he settles himself for the show. "Now, take your ease, Mr. Smith," said Lovell. "This is Liberty Hall here, you know; no need for party manners in the family." Tabitha snorted.

The violinist launched into the figures of a minuet, and Zephyra came and went with a tray until the table was loaded with the soups and meats of the first course, in silver dishes stowed among the candelabras. Mr. Lovell carved from a grand ham blackened with molasses. While he passed along plates, and exchanged pleasantries,

Smith was able to consider upon the informative and (as it were) strategic design of the plan according to which the diners had been bestowed at table: his own placement amidst the knot of the adult men, where Captain Prettyman and Van Loon senior could rake him from opposite, and Mr. Lovell could contribute enfilading fire from his left, while Hendrick remained just in range should reinforcements be required, and the careful removal meantime from out his conversational reach of all the women except Tabitha, who was presumably considered an armament in herself. Little Elizabeth Van Loon, a solemn eight- or nine-year-old sitting bolt upright in the lee of Piet, he could speak to, but Anne, a sulky fifteen- or sixteen-year-old miss with her mother's curves, was in the fortified maternal zone at the far end, and so was Flora. "Anneke, if you eat that, it will give you schpots," Mrs. Van Loon was saying. "Floortje, my dear, would you ask Joris for the chicken?" Joris seemed to be George, one beyond Tabitha, planted squarely between Flora and any Smithian temptations. He was a skinny, hollow-templed youth, more elegantly dressed than anyone else at dinner had bothered to be; and it was not difficult to guess the reason for his sense of occasion, for he had scraped his chair closer to Flora's, proprietorially, and was loading her plate for her. Of all the faces along the table, his was the only one so unprotected as to show a naked hostility when he glanced Smith's way. Aha, thought Mr. Smith. Very well.

"A glass of wine with you, sir," rumbled Piet Van Loon, filling Smith's glass: his voice, like his wife's, preserving the Dutch that had vanished from his children's. *Ey glarsch off vein.*

"With all my heart, sir," Smith said, pouring for Van Loon in turn as protocol dictated. "To your very good health! And to the company," he added, turning to left and right with his claret glass held up between finger and thumb. "You are quite right, sir," he added to Mr. Lovell. "The change from dining in the wardroom aboard is very welcome."

"A difficult voyage?" said Van Loon.

"No, sir; just a long one."

"Indeed. In these days the journey down to the Leewards is long enough for me. I made the greater crossing once, to study in Leiden when I was a jongeling, and that was sufficient for a lifetime. You would not undertake it without some serious purpose, nee?" Van Loon's periods growled along like barrels on a hard floor.

"Indeed not, sir. There's a deal of water out there to drown frivolity in. But tell me," Smith said quickly, for he feared an instant return of the question he must not answer with either truth or lie, "are you then, sir, a native of the city?"

"Naturally. What else should I be?"

"All the Dutch are," put in Lovell. "They all date back to the old times. Piet is the third Van Loon. He was a ledger clerk in his grandfather's house when first I laid eyes on him, pricing beaverskins for hats. How they stank; it was August. We had some times, didn't we?"

"You were prenticed together?"

"No, no, I was bound to Walton's at that time. Come over on the indenture, and worked a little of this, a little of that. Thought I'd never learn the lingo, and you needed it then, it was Hoogen and Haagen all along the water then. I wheeled in the barrow of skins, and I said to him, 'Tell me your offer in the Queen's English—'"

"'—for I'll not onderschtand it if you gargle it,'" finished Van Loon. It did not seem a very hearty beginning to a friendship, but Hendrick wore the polite smile that attends an anecdote of family history told often.

"And you still trade for furs, sir?"

"No!" said Van Loon, staring. "That was thirty, forty years ago. What," he went on, incredulously, "you don't know on what sort of concern you are drawing your bill?"

"Well yes, sir—Mr. Lovell's sugar—"

"All the same now, practically," said Van Loon. "Separate in name, but we have grown together. The cane plantation, together—a leedle more me than him; the ships, together—a leedle more him than me. He distils, I distribute. Together." *And an injury to him is an injury to us both*, Van Loon did not have to say. Smith glanced at the far end of the table. Flora was glowing—with happiness, but also with importance; sitting next to Joris as if they had been voted King and Queen of the May. Of course, it made dynastic sense.

"And do you prosper, sir?" Smith had meant by this only the polite enquiry that might be answered with an "I thank God we do" or a "Tolerably, tolerably, I thankee." But to his surprise Van Loon took it as sceptical probing of the two firms' credit, which must be answered with a show of convincing detail, and began at once, with an air bordering on belligerence, to paint a picture of loaded hulls bearing New-York flour to the West Indies, and returning freighted deep with sugar, this to be sold up the Hudson as it was or else transformed to rum first; every stage, every transaction, yielding sweet, secure profit, and those profits in turn buying a flood of Turkey-carpets, cabinets, tea-pots, Brummagem-ware toys and buttons, *et cetera, et cetera*, imported from London to retail, handsomely marked-up, for still greater gain; and those yet further profits spreading out to fund an ever-diversifying empire of schemes. Mr. Lovell, not wishing to be wholly spoken for, began to add in remarks as the advertisement proceeded. Captain Prettyman merely nodded and drank. Smith, listening while helping himself to spoonfuls of a curious orange vegetable, found himself struggling against a sense of unreality, that he should be the object of all this testy boasting. The room swam in the candle-light.

He had dined in a variety of places, in his time. At the tables of the Hanover Square in London, with a footman behind every seat, and the ladies chewing in tiny mouthfuls as if the height of their hair might be imbalanced by larger motions; eating catch-as-catch-can suppers in the chop-houses of Drury Lane or Gray's Inn with actors hilarious off duty and students gesturing with their forks; in a cellar in Limehouse, gnawing stale bread. There had been middling, commercial invitations too, where as here family and trade mixed at the table. A printer—a prince among printers—had brought him home one night from the coffee-house to drink milk punch in a tall house in Soho filled with tall, laughing daughters, who all had read more books than he. A tiny silk-weaver of Spitalfields had seated him, a Gulliver marooned in Lilliput, amidst his even more diminutive family, velveteen legs a-dangling, to hear a lengthy grace in French and then receive slivers from the smallest fowl in the world, carved apparently with a pair of bodkins. Each had been a separate cell of the great hive. Each cell, be it ne'er so honeyed or so bare, had had its manners, which could be learned. It had been his study to fit whatever part of the honeycomb housed him. But here—though it would suit him now, far more than before the loss of the purse, to fall in with the merchants' preferences, whatever they might be, or at least not to flout them too scornfully—he must study *not* to fit. He must remain the mercurial, the unreckonable stranger. That being, by long discussion affirm'd, his best safety.

"Property, farm leases, perhaps soon a privateer," finished Van Loon, whose red spades of hands had been continually building, building in the air as he spoke. The little girl beside him paused mid-mouthful and gazed across through the candle-flames with round, steady eyes.

"I wonder that you need worry about me at all," said Smith.

"We don't, jongeheer, we don't," rumbled Van Loon. "We *worry* about the Governor, and his verdomned excise duties. We *worry* about the stupid game of soldiers he is playing at Albany. You are an inconvenience at most." Lovell pressed his lips together.

"What my father means to say," put in Hendrick, turning away from the quite separate conversation that had been going on up at the other end, "is that your bill is no challenge to our resources. All the same—"

"Nee!" said his father, sharply. "We are not there yet, or anywhere close to there. Let us hear some assurances before there is any making of offers. Tell me, mijnheer,"—the swags of beard jutted up at Smith like the prow of a barge—"do you plan to make your home here with us, or are you passing through?"

"Yes," said Lovell, "a good question. Settler, or bird of passage?"

Smith hesitated, apprehending the tumble of conclusions that would be drawn, depending on his answer. When he planned his entrance, he had not considered how much more easily an illusion is begun than maintained; especially in the face of a determined curiosity, which could dispense with the shadings of courtesy when it would.

"That will be decided by the success of my business here," he said.

"You do call it business, then," said Lovell quickly, "and not an errand of pleasure, or of some other sort?"

"I know not whether you would call it so, sir, but I am bound—"

"By instructions? By the instructions of another?"

Tumbling conclusions.

"I—" Smith was beginning, when he felt a sharp pain in his ankle. Tabitha had kicked him under the table.

"Talk to *me*," she said.

"Hello," he said, turning with grateful joy toward the scowl whose pressure he had been feeling for some time on his right side. "How do you this evening, Miss Lovell?"

"Bewitching well, I thank you," she said, "for I enjoy seeing fools struggle."

"Meaning me?"

"You are stuck like a fly in syrup."

"And you are holding out your knife to give me a road out."

"Or to crush you from pity, sir."

"Tell me," said Smith, "do you still hold to your low opinion of novels?"

"It was only yesterday's opinion, and today has not been so rich in incident I'd change it; so, yes. Slush for small minds, sir. Pabulum for the easily pleased."

"In that case," said Smith, fishing out the volume from the coat pocket where he'd thrust it, "will you take my apologies that I have no gift for you, and pass this along to your sister?"

Tabitha took *David Simple* from his hand—momentary contact of cool fingers—and flipped it open to the title page.

"Ugh," she said. Her look of contempt would have curdled milk; and yet she seemed to be acting it, too, to be offering it like a card he should recognise in a two-handed game they were playing together.

"What do you want me to do with this?" she said.

"Pass it along," he said, puzzled.

"Are you sure?"

"Yes."

"Very well." *If you absolutely insist.* Then without a pause, and certainly without looking to see where it would fall, she threw the brown octavo over her shoulder, toward Flora's end of the table. It struck Joris a glancing blow on the side of the head, and flew fluttering downward into Flora's soup-bowl, which fortunately she had emptied.

Flora cried out, Joris jumped to his feet clutching his temple, Mr. Lovell shut his eyes and bowed his head, breathing out hard.

"Tabitha!" he said sternly; or imploringly.

"Cannot you control this . . . this . . ." stammered Joris, in reedy fury. A hard look from his father quelled him, and Hendrick, rising, reached an arm across the table, and took his brother by the shoulder, and pressed him back into his seat again.

"No harm done," announced Mrs. Van Loon comfortably, wiping the gravy and crumbs from the book and setting it before Flora, whose hand she patted firmly. "There, now."

"My dear, we mustn't startle Mr. Smith," said Lovell. "We have all the excitement we need, eh?"

Tabitha sat grave and tranquil, hands folded, as innocent as a cat beside a broken milk-jug.

"Remind me not to annoy you," Smith said to her.

"I will be sure to let you know if you have," said she.

"I don't doubt it."

"So, mijnheer," said Mrs. Van Loon, raising her voice a little to catch Smith's ear, "how are you finding New-York?"

"Delightful, ma'am," said Smith, "and very welcoming to the weary traveller." Casting about for more particular praise, he remarked that the streets were very clean, and the people amazing tall and healthy-looking, by London standards; altogether a well-favoured city. The greatest novelty for him in the prospect, he added, being the regular presence of slaves, English law only uncertainly permitting them, and the trade therefore seldom bringing Africans over.

"Only the profits, eh?" said Lovell.

Zephyra came in and cleared the dishes; returned, in relays, with the second course, arranging vermicelli, fruits, cheeses and fish on the table, with a new decanter of wine, and placing a tankard of beer on the floor beside the violinist-slave; who contrived a cadence with some sound of closure to it, broke off, and drank. Without the music, the murmur of resuming conversation seemed louder, more exposed. It was harder for two independent conversations to be maintained, and soon all the heads at Mrs. Van Loon's end of the table were turned to follow the talk at Mr. Lovell's. The interrogation of Mr. Smith continued; but now Tabitha was participating too, at Smith's side if not on it.

"You must see, sir, what a puzzle you have put us in," said Lovell. "And that it does you little service to have us thus . . . bemused."

"How so?" asked Smith, obligingly.

"Why because, if you will not affirm one of the virtuous possibilities for your being here," said Tabitha, "our minds will race to the vicious reasons."

"Yes," said Lovell. "You make yourself out too frivolous for business—"

"I proclaim I am in earnest—"

"Then, what merchant house do you represent? Or what venture are you engaged in?"

Mr. Smith only raised his eyebrows.

"As I say, too frivolous for business; and if you are a man of wealth, set on some tour of pleasure, no need for hugger-mugger, all being glad to assist where a thousand pound is to be spent. So," continued Lovell, "our natural fear must be, that you are something in the political line, bent on some mischief, the doing of which may redound to our harm. You need but speak, to take the imputation off. An honest man need have no secrets."

"Do you say so, sir? Some honest purposes require delicacy."

"Delicacy!" said Captain Prettyman on a sudden, his voice unexpectedly hoarse and high. "Ye've come to the wrong place for *delicate* people." He seemed to find the word offensive. "Plain men for the plain daylight, that's our preference."

"And me for night's black agent, if I hold my tongue? I assure you," said Smith, grinning, "you may discount me as a politico, for I don't know your controversies here, to meddle in 'em."

"'Night's black agent' is *Macbeth*," pointed out Tabitha, to the company at large.

"I thought you didn't read," said Smith.

"Well," said Lovell, ignoring this, "I am sure you know that the Governor and the Assembly are at daggers drawn—"

"No, sir—"

"—and both sides looking to, let's say, oil up the undecided—"

"No, sir—"

"—for which a thousand pound might be a handy sum. But you know this."

"Sir, I don't. I am an ignorant blank, a *tabula rasa*, a page not smirched with the ink of knowledge."

"Nor's that the worst that may be, when a man creeps into a city in time of danger with a bag of gold. Since King George's War began—"

"Sorry; what?"

"The present war with the French, sir," said Lovell, irritably. "That, you *have* heard of, I think?"

"Perhaps it goes by another name in England, Papa," said Tabitha. "We call all our wars, here, by the names of monarchs; as, King William's War, Queen Anne's War, King George's."

"What royalists you are!" said Smith, lightly.

"Is that intended as a fling at our patriotism?" said Lovell. "I may tell you," he went on, knocking on the table for emphasis with a forefinger, "that His Majesty has no more loyal subjects than us, and that if we object to the dangerous conduct of our idiot Governor, it is not for want of any zeal against the Frenchies, nor against their Papist savages, neither. We hate the Pretender, sir, and we hate the garlic-eaters, and we don't abide their intrigues, not for one minute. No; we only stand by our rights as Englishmen, and ask why the upper Valley must be stirred up to no purpose, and troops garrisoned upon honest men who never consented to them, and never voted funds for their supply. When all know that a standing army is a maggot in the state, a caterpillar feeding on liberties. Sir."

Smith turned to Tabitha, his face a mask of polite puzzlement.

"Governor Clinton has encamped two regiments of regulars at Albany, meaning to march them north on campaign, but the Assembly of New-York will not pass the bill to feed them," she said, concisely. "As we speak, chickens are going missing all over Albany County."

Smith smiled reflexively.

"That is not really a joking matter, sister, is it?" said Hendrick to Tabitha.

"And I am not really your sister, am I?" said Tabitha. "Not *yet*."

"Let us say all this is truly nothing to you," said Van Loon to Smith, talking across their exchange as if it were not happening. "You have not heard our gossip, you are not mixed up in it." *Mikscht opp*. "Everything you know about is far away, back in London."

"Alas, alas, Babylon, that great city!" squeaked the Captain.

"So, why so cautious? Why do you object so much that we should know what you plan to do with the money of friend Gregory, here?"

"Mine, sir, surely; my money, when the bill is honoured."

"True, true: you may say so at quarter-day. But that leaves you still sixty days—"

"Fifty-nine now, sir—"

"—to set our minds at peace. And perhaps to make friends of us, hey? You should consider how much we may be able to help you, with any righteous purchase in your mind."

"Is it the law here, sir, that money must explain itself?"

"Not the law, Mr. Smith, nor even the custom." Tabitha leaned forward into the candle-light, the dark silk of her dress gleaming. "Our grandees go unmolested, I assure you. Mijnheer Philipse can walk up Broad Street without a soul tugging his sleeve and asking what's in his pockets; Mr. De Lancey can rule in the court without the plaintiff saying, 'Now, sir, what's this about the block for lease by Rutgers' Farm I hear you're buying?' Mr. Livingston can take his pinch of snuff in the Black Horse without the waiter asking, 'Wheat or oats for you, sir, this sowing season?'"

"I am not the damned waiter at the Black Horse, my dear," said Lovell wearily. "I am this gentleman's creditor, seemingly. We all are, you included—and are due, if all's square, to hand him a budget for who-knows-what. Which gives us a very natural interest, as I say, in learning what mischief he purposes."

"Yes, Papa. I know. You only *look* like a waiter," said Tabitha, wriggling her shoulders. "But what's Mr. Smith's interest in telling? You must set subtler bait."

"My interest," said Mr. Smith. "*My* interest?" He shot his cuffs and stretched both hands out, palm down, fingers wide as if he were playing octaves, before him, so that all eyes were drawn to them expectantly, and all could see they were empty, and there was nothing between the fingers. "My *interest*"—he clapped his hands hard together, making the company jump—"is all for your delight." And quickly he stretched a long green-clad arm between the candles, to cup the ear of silent little Elizabeth opposite. His hand twisted; her mouth opened in an O to match her eyes.

"*Sihirle, para bulmak!*" he cried. Between his fingers silver flashed. He flipped the coin in the air so it made, briefly, a glittering sphere, and presented it. "For you," he told her. "Precious metal out of thin air."

But Lovell seized Smith's wrist, tilted it and squinted.

"Out of my cashbox, if I'm not mistaken."

Elizabeth looked at her father.

"You may take it, Lisje," he said. And to Smith: "What tongue was that?"

Lovell released his grip.

"Conjurer's gibberish, surely," said Hendrick.

"In fact, no," said Smith. "Turkish. It seemed fitting, since the coin is so too."

"You speak Turkish? A strange knack for an Englishman."

"Just a few words, sir, gained on my travels."

Tabitha, though, had been gazing intently not at Van Loon and her father, nor at Elizabeth, nor even at the piece of money, but at Smith's hands. She tilted her head from one side to the other and back again, as if settling something into place. A flickering smile appeared on her lips, narrower than her sister's, and roseleaf-brown

49

in the shadows at the edge of the candle-light. It was the first Smith had seen there.

"No, Mr. Smith," she said softly, "that is not your interest."

Scarves and coats in the hall; a squadron of departing Van Loons. It was only half past nine; Smith wondered what he was going to do with the rest of the evening. The women had not withdrawn when the meal was done, in the usual way, possibly he guessed because an effort was being made to keep Flora and Tabitha apart. Flora, in fact, was pulling a coat on too: the Van Loons had enfolded her, and were carrying her off to a game of cards in their house two streets away. Tabitha remained at the table while Zephyra cleared it, the men talking around her. "You will call again, won't you, Mr. Smith?" she had said, looking up at him. "Oh, of course," said Lovell, without visible alacrity. "Why not."

"I'm sorry they were so rough with you," Flora said now, in the hall, her face flushed prettily, a tendril of fair hair hanging down. Joris tugged at her arm.

"They comported themselves very reasonably," said Smith.

"Well, then I'm sorry that Tabitha was so very . . . Tabitha."

"She has a temper," Smith agreed.

"She has a demon," said Flora, seriously.

Smith waited at the stairfoot for the buttoning to be complete. The framed thing was in front of him that had sparkled in the dark, the night before. It was not a picture, he saw now. It was a shallow box filled with whorls and loops of some brittle material encrusted with flecks of light. It drew the eye in: coils balanced countercoils in there, curls countercurled around other curls, in minuscule filigree. The colours were mineral. It was like looking into the bottom of a rock pool when the pebbles shine in sea-contrived patterns, or at the floor of a cavern cysted by patient droplets. It was a petrified forest, a hard little, subtle little garden.

"What is this made of?" he asked Hendrick, who was next to him.

"Paper. You haven't seen one before? It is called quill-work. Very frustrating, very difficult. A recreation for clever girls who don't have enough to do. The shiny parts are ground glass, glued on. But you have to be careful. You can easily cut yourself, hey?"

"What do you make of him?" Geertje Van Loon asked Piet that night, in their box bed with the damask curtains. "What do you make of him?" the printer's devil asked Hendrick, inking the pages of the new *Post-Boy*.

By morning the news was all around the town, from the Bowling Green to the Out Ward, that the stranger was a Saracen conjurer, and quite possibly an agent of the French.

2

Pope Day

November 5th
20 Geo. II
1746

I

Had a map been drawn, a week later, of Mr. Smith's movements through the streets of New-York, with a thickness for each path beaten by his feet in proportion to the number of times he trod it, a tangled hydra indeed would have been revealed, with its head at Mrs. Lee's house.

One thick line led to the Merchants' Coffee-House, where every morning he breakfasted, receiving cordial conversation from Hendrick and an ever-increasing number of the regulars, and cold nods from Septimus Oakeshott. Another, still a substantial spoor of ink but slightly thinner, led to Golden Hill Street and the Lovells; another again, to the low streets on the western or Hudson side of the Broad Way, up against the outer palisade of the town, where it then split into a purposeful splay of tendrils, for Smith was deliberately visiting every tavern or gin-cellar or drinking den he could find, and privily enquiring in each one whether such a man might be found as a fellow who specialised in the recovery of *lost things*. In

London such people certainly existed, serving as recognised points of communication between the daylight and the criminal cities, between *bon ton* and flash mob; and to ask for one was to signal plainly that you wished to open negotiations with the thief who had robbed you. But whether it was that New-York lacked this sophisticated convenience, or that he was asking in the wrong words, all he found was sullen silence in the earth-floored rooms he entered, and unfriendly stares from those drinking there.

Meanwhile, certain other threads broader than a single passage marked his route to places where he had begun, as discreetly as possible, to make the enquiries his errand required. Yet entangling these main and subordinate limbs of the hydra—almost losing them in a maze of the finest lines—was a spider's scribble extending everywhere, as if Mr. Smith had made it his systematic business to stroll, unhurried, at least once along every lane, street, dock and thoroughfare the city contained. This was not so far from the truth. Almost everywhere had seen Mr. Smith wander by, whistling under his breath; but nowhere did he lay eyes on any who might have been the lanky, black-haired thief, of whom he had glimpsed only the back view. Perhaps the thief had cut or dressed his long hair, perhaps he was lying low, perhaps he inhabited one of the outer settlements— Greenwich or Haarlem, Breuckelen or Flushing—which Smith had not yet penetrated; perhaps he was long gone along the High Road to Boston, or over the water to New Jersey, with the windfall in the leather portfolio. Perhaps Smith was simply being unlucky, for even in a city of only seven thousand souls, it is possible for two of them never to meet, for them to draw paths of ink that cross, over and over, yet never arrive in the same place at the same time.

His purse grew ever lighter. Day by day, it perceptibly clinked and rustled less. Soon it would not clink and rustle at all, vapour being silent. The most strict economy regulated Smith's spending on necessaries. At least, such spending as no-one could observe, and might draw conclusions from; for nothing could be more disastrous to his credit, he realised, than to betray any suggestion that he needed to pinch pennies, or had access to anything less than inexhaustible funds. If he was to maintain his ability to run up bills he need not settle, until the bill on Lovell was paid at the Christmas quarter-day, it must always appear to be no more than a rich man's whim that he preferred to handle any particular expense with credit rather than cash. So he laid out his slender store of coin and paper where it would make the most open-handed impression: producing it from a child's ear, tipping Quentin at the Merchants, giving with careless liberality when the collection plate came to him on Sunday morning in church. He ate as large a breakfast as would not seem greedy every morning in the coffee-house, on credit, and he cleaned his plate at dinner every night with Mrs. Lee's other boarders, on credit; and in between he ate nothing, and drank only from the public pump, and his stomach griped as he walked and walked. After four days, he had only eighteen shillings left. He needed, he could see, to secure new supplies, and shortly. But *how* was a hard question. Rich men do not sell things, and nor do they ask for loans. In what way does one get money, while giving no sign that the getting of it is any more than the merest indifference?

He hesitated, the first Sunday that he woke in the city, before he betook him along the Broad Way to Trinity. Worship implied expenditure. And he had not always been a notably pious Londoner. He had lain abed of a Sunday morning, with or without company, far more often than he had roused himself. Yet possession of a secret that cannot be shared lends a particular promise to the company of the Almighty, from whom it is declared that no secrets are hid; whose temples we are told are antechambers each facing that light which burns without effort through every human disguise or imposture. Mr. Smith, being burdened, desired to lay his burden down, at least momentarily, especially if this could be accomplished invisibly to those on his left and on his right. And then beyond these private and spiritual considerations there were others, public and prudential. A church might be a stage at which the Lord, as auditory, gazes undeceived; but the congregation also performed to each other. Smith shaved with a bowl and jug, splashed himself with rosewater, and set out.

The bells were ringing, and a fashionable crowd was gathering at the doors of the grey-stone church opposite the western end of Wall Street, when he arrived. Already, thanks to his campaign of walking, he recognised many faces. Not everyone he knew was there, by any means—for if New-York resembled London in the wild variety of churches, chapels, meetings and conventicles it accommodated, hospitable to every sect and shade of sect except the Papists, it differed too, in that here the sectaries made up the majority, rather than being the animated foam beating at the edges of a great calm boulder of Establishment. The Lovells were Baptists, and were to be found at this hour in the meeting-house just around the corner from them on Cliff Street, and the Van Loons were Dutch Reformed. They were sitting in a row in the Nieuwe Kerk on Nassau, the younger ones restless at the prospect of an hour-long Dutch sermon of which they would not understand above one word in three. Trinity was only one church among New-York's thirty-odd churches. Yet, dispute its sway though people might, and resent its sway, the Church of England remained all the same the established form of the entire Christian religion in the Province of New-York, sustained by law, and swaddled in privilege; and Trinity was its chief and central building. It was the King's church, and so necessarily the Governor's church; it was power's church, and also the church of power's intimate opposition; it was pride's church, wealth's church, fashion's church, and also the place where pride and wealth and fashion went to be medicined.

As a well-dressed newcomer, Smith was shown to a pew halfway up the left side of the aisle, a seat not firmly locked into the subtle hierarchies of placement, yet with a grand enough view of the height of the social firmament, at the front of the nave. Over the white wooden box-walls he could see impressive heads, cut off just below the shoulder at about the level where an antique bust would end. There, at the very front, with a peanut-shaped brow and an anxious expression letting down the blue and gold of his coat, must be Governor Clinton, and his lady in lilac silk, and two African footmen with wigs powdered to the colour of icing-sugar to get the maximum contrast of black and white. A row behind, a skinny, sinewy, querulous man with eyebrows like caterpillars and a pointed nose was tapping his teeth, rubbing his lip, scratching his concave cheek, with a yellowed finger; next to him, at his most glazed and impervious, was Septimus Oakeshott, and Achilles the slave alongside. Septimus raised an eyebrow when he saw Smith looking. And then behind *them*, with a whole lavishly-dressed household around him, stood a middle-aged man in plain black who justified the accidental classicism imposed by the line of the pew-top, for he had a massive and statuesque Roman head, finely modelled at ear and nose, like a slightly depraved but very intelligent emperor; and this man was turning, and nodding, and working the room as the Governor was not, directing smiles, and ironic compressions of the brow, and communicative glances, to many faces in the ranked congregation behind him, stirring as if with a spoon the coupled merchants and merchants' wives, officers and officers' wives, lawyers and lawyers' wives. The men bowed, the women dipped and dimpled. His eye travelled over Smith too, and bestowed on him a look of lively curiosity, charm and danger. Seeing where he was looking, the people in the pews behind all looked too. Smith inclined his head.

A band of fiddle, bass-viol, trumpet and hoboy tuned up in the west gallery, a choir of blue-coated orphan boys trooped in, followed by Trinity's rector in surplice and cassock, and a wig whose weight was all in bunched clusters on each side, like ear muffs. On the sanctuary step he turned, and declared in the loud voice required by the prayerbook, "If we say that we have no sin, we deceive ourselves, and the truth is not in us . . . Wherefore I pray and beseech you, as many as are here present, to accompany me, with a pure heart and a humble voice, to the throne of the heavenly grace, saying after me—"

The congregation dropped to its knees, and consequently out of sight of itself. Smith was all of a sudden alone, with nothing in view but the rectangular top of his separate box, and above it the church roof and vacant pulpit: a most effective architectural similitude of the individual soul's necessarily separate and lonely address to the mercy seat. From all the separate souls, in all their separate boxes, lidless before the Lord, arose the grumbling, lisping, rumbling, droning, hoarse, melodious, piping, muttering, murmuring, whispering, bellowing voice of the congregation together, making its way through the utterly familiar words of the prayerbook's General Confession, at once soothing and demanding, ignorable and liable from moment to moment to sink a hook into the soul where least expected. *We have followed too much the devices and desires of our own hearts, and there is no health in us* . . . Whenever an individual lost their place in the flow of the words, lost their attention or paid too much attention, they heard the flow continue over their heads, a roof of sound beneath the roof of wood, made from the voices of the many separate souls combined, but apart from each, and asking no questions when the faltering voice was raised again to rejoin it. What, if anything, Mr. Smith confessed, this history must not tell; and what answer he received, if any, it cannot. The operations of grace are beyond the recording powers of the novelist. Mrs. Fielding cannot describe them; nor Mr. Fielding, nor Mrs. Lennox, nor Mr. Richardson, nor Mr. Smollett, nor even Mr. Sterne, who can stretch his story further than most. Not much redemption is to be looked for, in a novel, when we lean so materially upon the visible and the audible, when the four walls of our domain are: what is seen, what is said, what is done, and what became of it. Certainly, all the heads reappeared again looking none the worse, when the Rector pronounced the absolution. And quite possibly none the better, either.

Mr. Smith, similarly, did not give any outward sign as (it being early in the month, and the church's endless progress through the psalms having reached Psalm 15) the blue-coat little boys, assisted by fiddle and hoboy, asked:

> *Lord, who's the happy Man, who may*
> *to thy blest Courts repair;*
> *Not Stranger-like, to visit them,*
> *but to inhabit there?*

—and the tenors in the adult half of the choir, accompanied by sawing bass, replied:

> *'Tis he whose ev'ry Thought and Deed*
> *by Rules of Virtue moves;*
> *Whose generous Tongue disdains to Speak*
> *the Thing his Heart disproves.*

He prayed gravely for King George to be replenished with the Holy Spirit, and for the Royal Family to be prospered with all happiness. He attended with calm seriousness to the hour-long sermon, not participating in the fan-flutters and glance-exchanges that broke out behind him: although, two rows back, an older woman on the arm of a choleric lobster of an infantry officer had eyes of the deepest blue he had ever seen, almost lapis-coloured. Sober Mr. Smith; reverent Mr. Smith; chaste, pious, prudent Mr. Smith.

In the church porch afterward, he was not completely surprised to find the Roman emperor somehow materialising smoothly beside him, amid the swirl of people, and taking him by the elbow with imperious familiarity, and fixing him with twinkling, cold little eyes.

"Let me introduce myself," he said, "for I mean to take no chance of missing your acquaintance, young man. James De Lancey."

"Chief Justice," said Smith, bowing; for he had worked out the structure of New-York's governance since Lovell had accused him of arriving to meddle in it, and in any case, De Lancey spoke in a voice of legal milk and honey, exercised, expressive, not hard to match together with a courtroom in which he had the unquestionable right to be heard. "I'm—"

"Oh, I know who you are. Up to a point, anyway. An intriguing point. George, I hope this boy is on the list for the King's birthday." Now De Lancey was speaking, with an absolutely undiminished expectation of authority, to the Governor himself.

Smith bowed. Clinton's peanut forehead creased anxiously. He made an indeterminate noise, and bent his head toward Septimus, who was hovering at his shoulder. "Er—?"

"I had not thought of it, sir," said Septimus, shortly.

"Well, you should; you surely should," said De Lancey. Rivers of milk, floods of honey. "And I look forward to it. Gentlemen, Mrs. Clinton; good day." And he swept on, with family, entourage, and (it seemed) much of the congregation following in his wake, bowing and curtseying to the Governor as they passed, but treating him and his party—the sinewy man scowling, Septimus porcelain-bland— as little more than an honorific outcrop in a riverbed.

Smith, not sure of his ground, let himself be carried with the current; and he would have got away entire, if it had not been for a grubby child of nine or ten years, threading his way through the crowd, who that moment thrust a hat under his nose, and cried out, "Penny to build the fire, sir! Penny to burn the Pope, sir! Penny for the guy, sir!" Smith, already five shillings (New Jersey) the lighter thanks to the church plate, cursed inwardly, and with a radiant outward smile stuffed sixpence (Maryland) into the ragged bonnet.

Golden Hill

Strings and gangs of boys, all promising to burn Guy Fawkes, were out in force in the streets that afternoon when Smith made his way back to Golden Hill to take tea with Tabitha Lovell. He was obliged, several times, to dodge as if accidentally up alley-ways, as he heard the collectors' chant.

> *The fifth of November*
> *As you well remember*
> *Was gunpowder treason and plot.*

Down King Street, back up Crown Street:

> *I know of no reason*
> *Why the gunpowder treason*
> *Should ever be forgot.*

Past the mouth of Rutgers Hill, south on William Street, and suddenly north again by way of Bloat Lane:

> *When the first King James the sceptre swayed,*
> *This hellish powder plot was laid.*
> *Thirty-six barrels of powder placed down below,*
> *All for old England's overthrow:*
> *Happy the man, and happy the day*
> *That caught Guy Fawkes in the middle of his play.*

Sidling and doubling back so incoherently that the poor hydra was all scribbled to indistinguishable blackness:

> *You'll hear our bell go jink, jink, jink;*
> *Pray, madam, sirs, if you'll something give,*
> *We'll burn the dog, and never let him live.*

Francis Spufford

We'll burn the dog without his head,
And then you'll say the dog is dead.

The exercise was certainly such, as to fix the street-plan good and
deep in Mr. Smith's head; and when he arrived, panting slightly, on
the Lovells' doorstep, he still possessed undisturbed the twelve shillings and sixpence he had set off with. He hoped that there might
be something to eat inside.

If the Lovells' house, the first time he had seen it, had worn (at
least for him) the dress of mystery, and the second time of hospital-
ity, this visit showed it in a duller mood. Tabitha was sitting in the
upstairs room where he had surprised the girls the day he landed,
with some abandoned sewing beside her. Mr. Lovell and Flora
appeared to have gone a-visiting, leaving her alone in the house
except for Zephyra; who, having fetched a tray with tea-pot and
cups, settled herself by the door and mended stockings, so that the
proprieties were minimally observed. A grey light without promise
painted all the surfaces, including Tabitha's face. It had seemed as
pretty as her sister's, and considerably more interesting, when she
was misbehaving by candle-light; now it seemed tired, and tight-
drawn around the mouth in a way that Smith did not understand,
as if she were continually gritting her teeth. The jolt of animation
that had seized it when he came in had settled back into a kind of
eager ill-humour, a readiness (as he read it) to disoblige, once he
had indicated in what way she might needle him most relevantly.
Perhaps he was not in the best mood either. He was not quite sure
what he was doing there, or what was expected of him, in this sulky
tête-à-tête. There was no little plate of cake or macaroons on the
tea-tray. She poured the tea, and the spout of the pot rattled irritably against porcelain.

"Tell me something," said Smith.

"Possibly," she said. "What?"

"Why did you throw my book?"

"You asked me to."

"No, I didn't."

"Oh? My mistake, then."

"You know I didn't. Really, why?"

"I suppose I assumed that when somebody hands you a nauseating lump, they want it disposed of."

Smith looked at her. "I would like to know," he said—annoyed, as much as curious.

"Why? Oh, you seem disappointingly earnest today. To amuse myself, obviously. I didn't know there would be conjuring tricks later. About that—"

"It seemed a little cruel."

"Did it."

"Yes."

"It made you laugh."

"It did. But still."

"I am not sure I invited you over to lecture me."

"I am not sure why you invited me over at all."

"Well, not to moralise, that's for sure. Your character is slipping, Mr. Smith. Scoundrel or moralist: pick one. I assure you, Flora has squadrons of defenders. Armies. Legions. I had not thought you would turn out to be another."

At this she sounded so unexpectedly woebegone that Smith repented his bad temper; indeed, felt it vanish and promptly could not remember where it had come from. He smiled at her.

"I—" he began.

"God's teeth," she said, looking into her lap, "you remind me of my mother."

"I—What?"

"Never a day she was alive that she wasn't *at* me, prating of kindness." Her voice climbed to a high-pitched foolishness, with much wet mashing and flapping of the soft palate. " 'Oh, Tabitha, how can you? Oh, guard your tongue. Oh, what a thing to say. Oh, Gregory, what have I done to deserve this?' "

"You miss her," said Smith, attending to the downcast gaze and the misery of the shoulders, rather than the nasty vigour of the mimicry.

"No!" she said, so emphatically, and looking up at him with such a jerk that he recoiled from the sympathetic crouch he had leaned forward into. "Not I. The mind of a milch-cow, and the clinging suckers of a squid."

"Look," Smith said, holding out his palms.

"More stage magic?" she asked, after a moment.

"No, just a demonstration. Look: fingers, fingernails, ten grasping digits. No suckers. Hands, not tentacles."

"I see them."

"The mind you will have to take on trust."

"Trust *you*, Mr. Smith? Good heavens."

"But I dare say it is not so different from yours. A little impatient at dealing with fools, a little unwilling to wait to be amused."

"A little cruel, too?"

"Maybe."

"But we are not the same; we cannot be. You don't have to wait. You are a man, and may go where you please and see what you please and say what you please."

"And you cannot? I haven't noticed you hold back much."

"Now you *are* being a fool. I amuse myself because I must. You because, what, it is your whimsy. Or because you are a scoundrel, purposing to rob us. I haven't forgotten, you know."

"Granted that you are a girl and cannot run away and join the dragoons. Granted that this city is not of the biggest. Still it is not without variety. Or curiosity. Mystery, even. I know that after four days. After a lifetime of New-York, I don't see how you can doubt it; or justly call yourself confined, because you live here."

She stared at him. Then she smiled.

"You booby!" said Tabitha. "Have you really not noticed?"

"Noticed what?" said Smith, feeling the first burn of a blush, at he-knew-not-what idiocy, naively committed.

"That every time you meet me I am sitting down? That, damn your stupidity, there is a stick leaning on the arm of my chair?"

There was, now it occurred to him to look. A walking cane with a round metal head, which might, he realised belatedly, be more than an ornament. Mr. Smith opened his mouth. Uncharacteristically, nothing came out. At the corner of his eye, black moved on grey: Zephyra in her corner had turned around.

"So you see," Tabitha said triumphantly, "*confined* is the word. Barring a few painful expeditions, I have fifty years of this room to look forward to. Will you count my blessings for me now? Will you tell me I am lucky in my family? Will you offer to pray for me? I sting and I bite, yes, so those who come close enough to be bitten will not count me altogether pitiable."

"Even your friends?" said Smith, finding his voice.

"I do not recognise the category you speak of," said Tabitha.

Smith considered her, interpreting anew the temper and the bitten lip, the grinding teeth, the contempt for stories of courtship or adventure: which, he could now see, might be pre-emptive, rejection before there was a chance of being rejected. He had been warned, with teeth, away from pity; but he could not afford it anyway. It could not be his concern what the effect on her might be, if payment of the bill should damage or ruin Lovell, if it should in some wise undermine the room in which she sat. This was—it was doubly plain now—not the place for him to play, beyond the necessary play to support the business that had brought him. Not the place for any expenditure of sentiment, beyond the general appetite for life it had seemed fitting for a Mr. Smith to show. Yet an unwelcome compunction was moving in him, sharp-pointed, stitching him through to the spot where he sat, attaching him by thin threads.

"All your life?" he asked.

"No," she said. "Only since I was fifteen. A bad break, from the barrels in the warehouse."

"And, can you stand?"

"Yes," she said. "I can stand *up*, and I can even stand your questions." She pushed herself to her feet, leaving the stick where it stood, and there was no visible struggle, except in the working muscles around her mouth. She was taller than Flora, and not deformed, except that one of her feet, below her skirts, turned in more than it should, and there was something more rigid in the shape of her leg on that side. Zephyra was standing, too, with her hand to her mouth, but Tabitha made a sharp forbidding motion with her hand.

"It is only," she said, "that it hurts."

She took one—two—three effortfully graceful steps across the Turkey-carpet towards him, and swayed. He leapt forward from the chair, and was in time to catch her by the hands before she fell. They were hot, almost feverish. He steered her back to her seat as best he could, their legs moving in time like awkward dancers; and all the while her face was alive with mockery.

"Oh, Mr. Smith!" she whispered. "I believe you have *saved* me."

"I think I should go," he said.

"Coward," she said. And then, as he was sidling towards the door, "I know why a magician claps his hands." Laughter followed him down the stairs, but it seemed to him that it was shame that kept a lazy, lolloping pace alongside. No need to pursue him: he was already caught.

II

Smith broke his economic vows and commanded a meal at the Merchants in despite of the hour, hoping that a solid something in his stomach would counter-act upon the agitation in his cranium. He ate his chop with a kind of defiance. One of the news-papers— not the *Post-Boy*—had reported him, under "Fresh Arrived," as "a *Turkish* Illusionist, richer than *King Midas*, if the Rumor Itself be Gold not Counterfeit." The coffee-room was far emptier than usual, and Quentin missing, replaced by a woman who might be his mother. Beyond the window-glass, the afternoon plummeted into darkness. The darkness was rent by cries, whizzes, and sudden surprising gouts of flame. The New-Yorkers, it seemed, kept the feast of Guy Fawkes grandly, on the large scale. He would have guessed that fervour for it would dwindle away, so far from the Parliament that poor Fawkes had failed to blow up with his gunpowder, but the opposite appeared true. He supposed he might go and see; there was little enough here in the way of diversion or conversation, to quell the memory of recent embarrassment.

The blood flared in his cheeks again, when he came out, but this time from cold. A bitter wind had come in, from off the East River, and licked at his skin as a salamander might, if that creature's legend were reversed, and it lived in ice not fire, with a body of glassy blue. It gave him an appetite for whatever bonfire the collecting boys had scraped together. On the Common, presumably; that was the way the foot traffic seemed to be going, in narrow streets thicker thronged by shadows the farther he went. First a few, darting up as quiet as fishes towards the junction with Smith Street, then more, flitting in from both directions along Nassau, school upon school of indistinguishable citizens, and all strangely hushed, it seemed to Smith, though a species of dull roar seemed to be sounding up ahead.

"Cold night!" he said cheerfully to the street of walkers in general, but earned nothing back but a few grunts and hums; there was even, he had the impression, a slight drawing-back from him, as if he had shown an unseemly levity. The streets of New-York were perplexingly altered in their spirit tonight, and not precisely in the direction of jubilation, or festival ease. The citizens slipped forward in their deft black myriad, unobtrusive, sombre; but the ruddy glare that now spilled back from the street's opening ahead onto the Broad Way threw their shadows back behind 'em, and the shadows told a different story. Twenty foot, thirty foot tall, they flickered in antic motion across the walls of houses; capered, stretched and stilt-walked over red-dyed brick-and-plaster, with spindle-knees and heads elastic. Metamorphosis everywhere: how thorough, how complete the alteration the night effected, he did not perceive until he was carried by the current into the back of the crowd at Broad Way, and could see the sources of both light and noise.

The street was lined along both sides with people stamping their feet. *Thud—thud—thud*, not in time but in sluggish pounding waves. *Thud—thud—thud*, where usually the costers sold and the slaves swept, in civility and melancholy. And to this rhythm, a thing aflame was approaching, from which the shadows streamed. A kind of juggernaut, stuck with many torches, and bundles of hissing, sparking firecrackers; a moving, skirted mass as wide as the road, on which rose three monstrous heads, gleaming in lines of gleeful red where fresh paint had been applied to pates and noses and villainous grins, as if Mr. Punchinello had been enlarged to giant size three times over. And drawing along this mass of carnival wickedness were figures in robes with hoods rising to points seven feet, eight feet above the cobbles, and all seeming, beyond their own natural movement as they tugged on ropes in irregular heaves, to be wriggling and flowing and twisting as the red glare swayed that lit them. It was a spectacle of nocturnal frenzy, gravely—almost silently—executed. Here and there, yes, a child chattered, but the *thud—thud—thud* of many feet drove gravity into the scene like hammers driving nails. Those who had thronged with Mr. Smith to the corner of King Street with the Broad Way were stamping too. The air seemed to be shaking, and their faces seemed to him to wear a common mask, of eager, reverent, anger.

As the hooded servants hauling the juggernaut came alongside, the pointed caps on their heads were revealed to be cones of butcher's paper, and their robes to be bedsheets tied with string. But the tawdry means to the transformation only rendered it stranger, not ridiculous. Smith recognised faces among the acolytes—Isaiah, the Lovells' prentice, Quentin from the coffee-house, a bass and a tenor from the Trinity choir, some of the sullen onlookers from the westside taverns—and each alike was changed, to a swollen straining gargoyle seriousness. Then he saw, on the far side and with the face obscured, a paper cone beneath which writhed out long, straight, black hair, and a body so thin and long that even in the robe it seemed but a coagulate line in motion—

"Hey!" shouted Smith, and tried to push forward. But the thudding and the crackle of the gunpowder robbed his voice of force, and whether by accident or design, the rank of citizens in front of him formed a most effectual fence. As he tried to penetrate it, the stamping feet fell without malice on his shoes, and he would have reeled back had the rank behind not repelled him just as effectually, so he must stay bruised and upright, as tight-packed as a lucifer match amidst a bundle. The straining acolytes and their ropes passed by, and then the slow-shifting body of the fiery mass itself, many cart wheels turning beneath its tacked-on skirt of canvas, and above, in clouds of pitch-smoke and powder-smoke glaring like a furnace, the splotched gilt writing that identified the giant puppets. *The Pope* on the crowned one with the leer of pride. *The Pretender* on the simpering face, with the beauty-spot as big as a plate and the blubbery lips. And last, on the visage of pantomime evil with the protruding tongue, *Fawkes*. Only after the back of the juggernaut passed could the bystanders begin to move into the road and follow; and there was an order of precedence here, rows of citizens already stamping along behind, with two drummers from the garrison in their midst beating a more orthodox time, and ruining it again, boys with saucepans they were banging, and men with old trumpets and bugles that they blew for noise not tune, in bellowing discordant squawks and blasts; and only after fifty feet or more of procession had passed, did the crush slacken enough for Smith to sidle into the road and follow on, seeing the puppets' chariot up ahead now as a slow-travelling blockade, a tight plug of fire and dancing demon shadows creeping between dark walls, with no possibility of over-taking.

But the procession was bound for the Common. When they had inched past Fair Street and the Spring Garden on the east side, and Van Pelt's ropewalk on the west, the pressure was abruptly released, and the narrow parade spilled out into a fan of walkers, all pursuing the bobbing light ahead into the wide darkness. Through these at last Smith could weave his way, and run on, tripping from time to time on tussocks, and casting to left and right trying to get the aco-lytes back in view. But when he came up to the float, he found the corps of the acolytes dissipated—caps removed—ropes fallen—the men all indistinguishably faded into the general assembly—and *that* not open to his easy inspection, for that it had formed, as he found when he tried to cross it, into a thickening ring of bodies, extending left and right as far as he could see around some central eminence buried in the darkness; and this elastic human obstacle proved as unpierceable as before, if slightly more talkative. "Steady now, steady now, keep back, no pushing, sirrah, room enough for all," said the dark around him. All were craning forward, towards what stygian vanishing-point Smith could not perceive. A single figure still capped (but without black hair) walked forward from the stranded car of the heads, a torch detached from it burning upright in both out-stretched arms. A faint contour formed in the air ahead of it, black on black; then, bigger than Smith could have imagined, a mountain where no mountain had been on the grass of the Common, all formed of wood and flammable rubbish, with flanks of discarded wardrobes and smashed cabinets, and ravines in which broken bedsteads gaped, an alp composed seemingly of every old thing, every burnable thing, every imperfect cumbrance of past time the city of New-York could scour from its attics, its middens, its cellars. The acolyte thrust the torches into the base of the mountain. A pause. Then—*crackle, crack*, with a quick dry popping flare of tormented wood—lines of flame began to work their way, zig-zag, through the inward jigsaw of the alp, with pauses for consumption, for gnawing at dense nuggets of mahogany, and rapid advances through fillets of wadded paper, but always up, up, up to the summit: which glowed, improbable high, then seemed to sit on red fire like black trellis-work, then burst at last into a crown of yellow flame. The bonfire was ablaze.

In its brightening light Smith began to see the extraordinary extent of the human ring that stretched around the fire. There must have been a thousand people there, a goodly fraction of the whole city gathered to gaze, with uptilted faces, at the flame-mountain. And on face after face, an expression of a kind of excited fear, as if there were something both horrifying and delightful being released in the increasing furnace roar. As the heat intensified, the damp November ground about the base of the fire began to steam; and the steam was sucked, at the speed of a river running, back across the silhouetted ridges of the grass and into the fire. Where it seemed to transmute, the vapour without any interval becoming the rising, rising lava-flows of orange-gold that ascended the hill of fuel, crinkling and incandescing, with a sound that resembled many distant glass windows shattering. A stippling of black stuff not yet burnt floated like slag on molten iron over the fire's volcano heart. And at the peak the rising orange-gold transmuted again, into rushing gauzy tongues fifteen, twenty foot high, breaking in flickers at their ends into particulate tides of crimson sparks, that pulsed up high and slackened again, as the billows of heat assailed the night sky; pushed into its cold; lost way and sank again. That sky! The fiery glare blanked out the stars, but the very hugeness and extremity of the blaze made the far greater hugeness of the night more palpable, as the sparks recoiled defeated. New-York had gathered to ignite its biggest signal of assertion and wrath, and the intensity of the light and heat only seemed to reveal, for once at its true scale, the immense darkness of the continent at whose edge the little city perched—from this one pinpoint of defiant flame, the thousands upon thousands of miles of night unrolling westwards. For the first time Smith, dizzy with sparks and smoke, lost the comfortable understanding of size he had brought with him from home, and the awe and the fear of the New World broke in upon him. As if, till then, he had been inhabiting a little doll's house, and misled by its neat veneers had mistaken it for the world, until with a splintering crunch its sides and front were broken off, and it proved to be standing all alone in the forests of the night; inches high, among silent, huge, glimmering trees.

The fire by this time was settling back from wild uprush into something more sullen, a hill all crimson-orange, morosely aglow. It made now a very creditable portrait of a landscape in hell, especially since from time to time across the infernal oven-glare capered, or reeled, or stumbled, the black outlines of the fire's servitors. They were dragging forward the heads from off the cart. The Pope was first for the furnace. Two men on each side, they swung him crown and all like a battering-ram, as near as they dared get to the hell-mouth, and flung him up onto the coals. He rolled a little way, and came to rest on his bulbous nose. For a second, his profile remained unchanged, a black exception to the fire; then on an instant it turned all to a flayed musculature of flame, a visage of wreathing scarlet fibres; then another instant, and hollow papier-mâché that it was, it was entirely gone, dissolved to a puff of sparks. A roar went up from the onlookers. For the Pretender, next, the crowd counted in its blundering voice-of-many-voices as the effigy swung. "One-ONE*one*one! TwoTWO*two*two! ThreeTHREE*three*three!"—And as Prince Charles Edward Stuart leapt into ash, an explosion of hoots, jeers, catcalls, whistles. Fawkes went more reverently, being a more ancient and more toothless enemy. Just a count as he swung in the air, and then a happy universal sigh of justice done. He rested on his nape, malicious tongue pointed skyward, and wick'd away to fiery nothing, up it. "God save the King!" someone shouted, and a part of the circled crowd, away on the other side of the bon-fire, attempted to chant it in chorus. But the voice-of-all-voices was separating to a babble of many; the linked arms of the circle unlocked; the strange grave hush disappeared; conversations began; flasks, bottles and jugs began to pass hand to hand.

Smith could have ventured forward now in search of his thief but, clue gone, he did not believe he would locate him at random in the dark of the Common any more than he had by quartering at random the streets of the city. Instead, shivery with more than simple cold, he accepted the earthenware jug coming from his right, and drank a mouthful of what turned out to be new rum, treacly and fiery. No sooner had he passed it on, than a stone bottle smelling of genever was thrust at him, and more, and yet more drink. He took sips, but looking left and right, he saw the rum, genever and moon-shine going down in throat-pumping gulps: serious drinking, such as he had not seen since he left London, and which he had insen-sibly supposed he had left behind on the farther shore, the sozzled, desperate, waver-footed self-obliteration of the gin-cellars a part of all that was poxed and ulcered at home. Yet here it was regular, cleanly-dressed citizens—he would have said sober citizens—who were casting off their daylight selves upon the sulphurous apron of the fire, and drinking, not to be convivial, not to take off the cold edge of the night, but to dissolve as much of themselves as spirits would eat away.

Already the younger prentices had started to spew, and laugh, and try the liquor again; already gestures were growing bigger and rougher, and steps more lurching. The women were not drinking, except a few haggard-looking drabs over in the poorest part of the ring around the fire. The good wives, the respectable maids, the well-dressed ladies were melting away into the shadows, homeward bound, their part of the evening done. The circle rocked, and reeled. One man, receiving his mouthful of spirits, ran with his cheeks distended forward into the zone of intolerable heat close to the fire, and blew it at the coals, so that a line of dripping yellow-blue flame lit on the instant, and he seemed dragonish as he wove back grinning. Cries of laughter and applause; immediate imitation by three or four others dashing toward the blaze, till inevitably one too incapable to manage the trick cough'd at the critical moment and spilled blue flaming gin down his chin and clothes. Louder laughter, and a pause of admiration while he rolled on the ground screaming and beating at himself, before his friends stumbled to the rescue, dragged him back into the shades, and, lacking other resources, pissed him out.

Smith having sipped, not gulped, had the little glow in his belly, not the raging melting demon his neighbours had eagerly imbibed, and now the night was getting rowdy, he judged it best to fade away too. But he had missed his moment, it was past and of a sudden seemingly long past the stage of the carouse when a man might bow out and still be counted a good fellow, for instant offence bloomed on the face of the burly prentice to his right when he refused the next drink, and, backing, he only backed into the hot damp weight of the prentice's friend, who gripped him.

"Wassamatter? Where you creeping off to? 'S Pope Day. Have a drink."

The one in front shoved the bottle at his mouth, like someone trying to push a spoon past the resistance of a baby. The glass banged his teeth, and he got his hands up to grip the neck, before it could knock any out. The prentice didn't want to let go. He was only about seventeen, but he had the same milk-fed mass Smith had seen in Lovell's Isaiah. Smith twisted, and the bottle came free. The boys were very close round him.

"Thanks," said Smith, and took what he meant to be a hearty stage swig; but the base of the bottle was slapped at that moment, the hard rim struck his palate like a hammer, and he choked. The liquor sprayed. This they found very funny, the one behind creaking out a fit of mirth that broke down into hiccups.

"Gotta have a drink on Pope Day," said the first.

"Yuh!" agreed the second. "Birth! righ'! ovva Eng! lish! man!"

"Abfolutely," said Smith, tasting blood. He passed the bottle over his shoulder. "Here you go." As he'd hoped, the hiccupper let go to take it. Smith wriggled left, and stood back from them both. Another step and he'd be away.

"Have a good evening, lads," he said. "This Englishman's for his bed. Hey," he added, beginning to back, "do you know the fellows who drew the cart?"

They weren't listening. The first one was staring at Smith's shadow-dappled face, with the dark line running down from the corner of his mouth, and his neck-cloth loose, as if the backstep into the dark had revealed a strangeness there that hadn't been apparent when they were nose to nose.

"Fuck," said he. "'S him."

"Who?" asked the hiccupper.

"The heathen. The one as is rich as Creezus."

"That you?" asked the hiccupper, muzzily interested, as you might be if introduced unexpectedly to a man with six fingers. But his friend was savouring the discovery more darkly.

"Fuck," he said again. "It's a fucken Papist. A Papist on Pope Day. You gotta lotta front, you evil *fucker*. Standing here! With *us*! You fucker!" He was shaking his head with delight.

"Oi! Lackwit!" said Smith sharply. "Dim your gabber. I'm no more Popish 'n you."

"Jonesy!" shouted the boy. "Simmo! Mr. Higgins! Come over 'ere a minute! Look what we got here!"

Enough. Smith sidled into full shadow, and turned off briskly, yet at a walk, upon the usual city rule that a man who does not wish to be noticed, whether he has picked a pocket or pasted a play-bill where one is not allowed, should never pick himself out by running. Mistake. He had not made above twenty paces across the uneven grass, before the raised voices behind resolved into pounding feet, and a shoulder struck him behind the knees, and he was slammed to the turf beneath a mountain of rapidly augmenting male meat. Frieze against his cheek, his cheek against the cold dirt; the weight of at least two bodies on his back; excited, spiritous breathing. "Got him!" someone cried. Smith was pinned. He tried to flex his spine, but there was no wriggling this time; the weight had him flat out. He waited, having no choice, bundled beneath so much brisket; yet calmer, to tell truth, than he had been a moment since. Smith, when his expedition was in nervous prospect—and when he was corked, contained, forced to bide his time aboard *Henrietta*—had imagined many dismal outcomes to his errand; disasters varied, disasters manifold; and tho' none had quite figured him mobbed by angry prentices beside a bonfire, under mistake for a Jesuit, angry crowds had certainly been enumerated among disaster's instruments, several ways; he had fingered over, in panicky imagination, those cards on which were printed futures where a multitude with screaming mouths dragged him gallows-ward, or pulped him to nothing in a ring of falling cudgels. Yet now, it seemed the maxim was true, that anticipation had been the worser part of the prospect, worse than actuality. As the heap of prentice disassembled, and he was yanked up roughly to his feet with many hands on him, he felt panic drain out of him, leaving a different fluid behind, steady and chill: winter salamander-blood in his veins.

"What have we here?" said a new voice, big but lazy, blustering but comfortable: a kind of plebeian cousin to the Chief Justice's, with the same confidence of being made room for. Here in the deep black space between the bonfire's red domain and the first pale-lit windows of the town, it was not possible to make out much more of the lads that held him than a shifting dark mass of shoulders and heads, and the man they'd turned him to face, as he strolled up, taking his time, was lit only in patches and gleams, with the fire-light behind the fat dome of his head, and distant scarlet picking out the delicate frizzle of his side-whiskers. But it was dimly clear he was wearing stripes for the holiday, broad avenues of lighter and darker silk stretched over his bulk, for if the boys were bullcalfs, he was the full ox. And he smelled of—the new, cooler Smith registered it as one more fact of the situation, plain as an angle in Euclid—animal blood. Steak, black pudding, offal in the mincer. Mr. Higgins, I presume. The butcher come sauntering to see what the butcher's boys had caught. But not to offer adult reproof, oh no; the butcher too was on holiday. And the rest of the dispersing crowd was spreading off in the darkness to its private pursuits; no help coming, there. The prentices had Smith held spread-eagled by his arms. The butcher drew back a fist as big as a pie, taking his time, taking his time. "O-o-o-o-o," went the prentices, on a rising note of pleasure—

But Mr. Smith had learned a thing or two besides the art of patient starvation in the cellars of Limehouse. Left and right he stamped as hard and fast as he could on the toes of those holding him; and as they commenced to jump about swearing, and loosed their hold, he threw himself forward onto the blood-perfumed bulk of the butcher before the fist could pick up speed. It was an awkward, huddled embrace that checked the momentum of the blow at cost of leaving Smith merely draped on his adversary, but all he needed from the posture was leverage; a hand's grip on each bulging shoulder of the butcher's coat, quick, quick, while he still grunted with surprise, and then his own jack-knifing body all the weapon he required to pivot back from the waist and slam his forehead as hard as ever he could into the butcher's nose. The cartilage cracked. A hot wetness splattered Smith's brow. The butcher howled. The butcher fell. Smith's head seemed split with pain itself, and flashes of white internal lightning obscured his sight, but he retained enough of himself to roll from atop the fallen pork monolith, and to try his best to crawl into the confused dark. Legs, shouts, the pain in his head—hands and knees over the tussocks—when he shut his eyes the lightning continued—he had seen the Limehouse Kiss performed but had had no idea it was so grievous for the doer—still he was moving, foot by foot, yard by yard—the stir and the groans falling behind—the inglorious escape of an injured beetle, but even so an escape— And then a hand seized his ankle, a firm and solid and unappealable hand, and he was caught.

It took a couple of panting minutes for him to be hoisted again to face the butcher, for the butcher himself rose only in slow staggering stages, the centre of his face a bubbling black mess, and all holiday humour gone.

"You liddle *bastard*," he said thickly, spitting out dark gobbets as big as garden slugs. This time the fist was inevitable and, swung into Smith's belly, drove the breath out of him as effectually and thoroughly as if he had got in the path of a hammer. Smith coughed and retched. The butcher's shadow-smeared visage loomed close.

He spat on Smith. He hit him again. But it did not seem to satisfy him.

"We wuz only goig ter tiggle yer up a bid," he said fretfully. "No fugging longer." Rummaging in the dark; the rousting-out from the butcher's pocket of something that gleamed as narrowly along its edge as the new moon. A clasp-knife, maybe; extended with professional delicacy in the butcher's quivering, aggrieved hand. "I ab goig," he said, his voice a caress of treacle, "to fugging *fillet* you."

Hesitancy in the group; a palpable in-drawing of breath all the way around the little circle, at a thought so cold and sharp it momentarily cut itself free from the soft fuzz of drunkenness, though it might in a moment more succumb to it, and dissolve back again.

"Master—" began the hiccupper anxiously.

"Shud it," said the butcher. "Tide's goig out. He'll be floading past the Narrows by dawd. No-one'll fide him. No-one'll care. Now take his coad off." The butcher spat black slime; the butcher advanced. Oh well, thought Smith, surprised still to find his grieving all done.

"Gentlemen!" said a new voice: a bright voice, an amused voice, a drawing-room voice, a voice of tea-cups and couplets. "Are we all having fun?" Smith dragged his gaze from the butcher, which seemed as hard as shifting a planet from its course. The gravity of his death had had him in its pull; he was tumbling down, all struggle done. He almost resented the interruption. There stood Septimus Oakeshott at the edge of the group, a sabre hanging negligently in one hand.

"Who's that?" one of the prentices asked.

"The Governor's bumboy," said another.

"This is private business," said the butcher, ignoring them. He seemed to be finding it as difficult as Smith to change direction.

"Is it?" said Septimus. "I do sympathise, for I know myself how annoying our visitor here can be: but I'm afraid you will have to let him go. —Witnesses, you see."

"Nod if you both go oud with the tide," said the butcher.

"Well, then, the other reason would be cold steel. Mine being bigger than yours: that sort of thing." Septimus raised the sword, and the circle parted away from it, as suds do on a basin of water when soap is introduced into it. The hands holding Smith dropped.

Smith cleared his throat. His voice sounded rusty; he had not expected to use it again.

"Mr. Oakeshott, you are very welcome," he said.

"Mr. Smith, you are very *stationary*. Run!"

Smith pulled the green coat that had been half stripped off him back onto his shoulders, and hugged it round him, staring stupidly. The advice was excellent, he could tell, but he did not quite seem able to take it. The running, the grabbing: surely they had already done that.

"Run!"

That did it. Smith turned obediently and lumbered away into the dark; and as his legs rose and fell, as slow it seemed as logs pounding the ground, the strange quietness of the last few minutes went dizzily away. Urgency, alarm, trembling were stirred back into him. A wave of pins-and-needles ran up his awakening calves, thighs, chest, neck. His head hurt, his heart fluttered, he felt the numb turf beneath him again with painful sharpness, and then he was running faster; sprinting indeed, as fast as his legs would carry him, with his arms pumping; bolting toward the welcoming mouth of the Broad Way. Nevertheless, Septimus overhauled him, coming up alongside after a brief interval as if propelled by the rising growl in the dark behind, running in a swift thin-legged scamper, breathing hard yet curiously upright, with a frown on his white face as if his body had carried him away of its own accord and he were, more than anything, puzzled to find himself hurtling disjointedly through the night. He was carrying the sabre pointed straight out in front of him, like a man ordering a cavalry charge in a painting.

"Keep going!" he said. "They're coming!"

They reached the gravelly dirt of the street. Lighted windows were just ahead, but there was no cover to hide in along the ropewalk, nor time to bide the uncertain outcome of hammering on one of the doors, judging by the swell of the noise behind.

"Achilles!" yelled Septimus, and waved with the sword: a blacker streak of shadow slipped out of the dark to their left and disappeared towards the far end of the ropewalk, and the ingress of Nassau beyond. They ran on, panting, along Broad Way.

"Two—corners," gasped Septimus; "two—corners—between us—and them—to lose them—"

They skidded left onto Maiden Lane, running downhill over cobbles now from the whaleback of the island. Quick glimpses of candle-lit chambers, families at table, ordinary life continuing; the sound behind getting louder, becoming diversified with glad hunting whoops, echoing between walls as the followers came off the Common and into the streets; clearly more, many more of them than had stood in the little circle with Smith and the butcher. Neither looked back.

"Small streets—oldest—best—more cover—"

Right at full pelt onto Nassau. Past the Dutch church, where a knot of greybeards were smoking long pipes on the steps, self-exempted from the English madness. Jinking left, right, left in the deserted dogleg alley around the red-brick back of City Hall. Left down the cracked paving of Wall Street, masthead lanterns swaying ahead; Septimus tripping, slipping, his blade grating out a shower of sparks from the rough slabs; recovering himself, gesturing right; them both flinging themselves into an alley that threaded away between the dark bulk of house-fronts. Septimus pressed his finger to his lips. They flattened themselves against the near wall and listened. Smith's blood popped and bounded in his ears. The riverine roar of the pursuit surged, as the city's stone brinks channelled it round some bend, back behind. Then seemed to settle, as if the flood were tossing irresolute, not sure which way to proceed, and might ebb, given a little longer.

"If they just get bored . . ." whispered Septimus. He sheathed the sabre carefully and tiptoed back to the alley's end, and with a hand to shield the lightness of his face, leaned one eye out. One of the Hervormde Kerk greybeards was helpfully pointing their way, clapped on the back as they passed by a mob thirty or forty strong. His pipe ember brightened and dimmed contentedly. The hunters threw back their heads and bayed.

"Oh *drat*," said Septimus.

"Could you not order them to disperse?" cried Smith as the two of them laboured on again up the twisting gullet of the alley.

Septimus laughed. "How?" he said.

The view over the tops of the alley walls as they pelted by was a chaos of lean-to roofs, blind back-sides of warehouses, yards heavy with the smells of trade both sweet and disgusting; even a tree growing a courtyard or two over, where someone was cultivating a garden in a tight embrace of masonry; but no yard, gate-way or recess that offered anything other than a small confined space without egress; any prospect better than continuing to run. So they ran on. The alley debouched into the bend of Bloat Lane, which in turn gave onto William Street. Smith, pounding along next to Septimus' spring-loaded lope, wished most passionately that he were again trying only to avoid requests for sixpence, yet his second wind had come in, and there was a sort of mad exhilaration in this helter-skelter dashing along; a sort of antidote of movement, to having been held, pinned, secured.

At William Street they were, all of a sudden, in one of the city's little domains of wealth and luxury. Tall, handsome houses of the newest proportions; white shutters at windows; candelabra lighting moulded ceilings visible at windows; patient horses and even a sedan chair at the mounting blocks beside the doors, where guests had spent Pope Day far from the bonfire's barbarity. Septimus skidded left, no doubt intending by that means to get onto Duke Street and the shortest way to Fort George, but he halted after two steps and held his hand up. The pursuit was ahead of them, coming round the east end of William Street. Back they went—but the happy baying and hooting was coming from that way too. Intelligently the pursuers had divided, and were coming round from both sides at once, as well as boiling along the alley itself, judging by the way Bloat Lane had begun to pulse and echo. They were not growing bored. They had found their entertainment for the latter part of the evening, and they meant to make the most of it. The only way left open was ahead, up Princes Street, too wide for the preference of anyone seeking concealment, and with the even greater breadth and openness of Broad Street beyond, where public oil-lanterns burned on posts and passers-by on foot and horseback could be seen, of sympathies most doubtful. But needs must, and on the pair of them flew.

However, they had not quite crossed the junction when Septimus' attention was arrested by a whistle from above. It was hard to pick out in the gloom up there, against a night sky of hurrying cloud intermittently rent with stars, but a figure was running in a precarious crouch along the roofline of the townhouse on the corner opposite, waving something in one hand. Smith, groaning inwardly, assumed at first that the pursuers had somehow got an agile spotter up there, to guide them on to their prey from above; but Septimus was waving back, whistling back, and as the roof-runner scrambled over the sloping slates of the first roofs on Princes Street, Septimus was hopping along beneath, sideways from foot to foot, staring at door-ways, gazing up at the sash windows of the floor just below the eaves—the fourth—with an expression of rapid calculation.

"There!" he called, pointing, and the figure stopped against a chimney, and threw down what appeared to be a rope: a rope so short, however, that Smith could not see how it could be of any earthly use. It only hung down far enough to dangle just outside the fourth-floor window Septimus had indicated. With the figure motionless in the dark beside the chimney-stack, and nothing therefore to call attention to it, the rope was virtually invisible, a dark thread amidst the dark.

Septimus seized Smith by the elbow. "Right, in we go," he said—and bounded with him up the marble steps leading to the grand door-way of the house before them, where he hammered furiously on the door-knocker. It seemed hideously exposed to remain there unmoving, in plain sight, while the three hubbubs of the pursuit converged, for the stretching seconds it took for the door to be answered. At any moment the first emissaries of the mob would come view-hallooing over the cobbles. Feet were audible on the stairs inside, though. Septimus sheathed the sabre, drummed his quivering hands on his temples; absurdly adjusted his neck-cloth. Keys turned inside. But as soon as the first crack of light appeared along the door-edge, Septimus shoved with an un-Septimus-like lack of civility, and they burst through into a tiled hall sending a housemaid reeling.

"So sorry," said Septimus to the world in general. "Up!" he added to Smith. "Good evening, sir!" to an astonished, red-faced householder, his mouth an O. "Shut the door!"—over his shoulder to the maid, as they plunged up the treads of a grand oval staircase, elegantly carpeted, radiantly lit, where guests clearly stuffed and basted with dinner were craning out of door-ways. Round and up, round and up; flashes of dining-room, where the walnut gleamed, and of a drawing-room with card party where a flutter of ladies, having withdrawn from the gentlemen, was being teased from the door-way by a moustached officer. "I say—" said the officer, wondering whether he was supposed to perform some gallant intervention.

"Sorry—terrible hurry—" said Septimus, brushing past.

"Excuse us," Smith threw in.

"Your servant, sir—your pardon, madam—coming through—"

"Thank you—obliged, obliged—marvellous party—very kind," said Smith, trying to smooth somewhat the impression they were making, yet helplessly on the verge of laughter at this sudden transition from naked Fear to clothed Society, this dash as quick as a scene-shift from wild black street to domain of piquet and face-powder. The trick was to stay close behind. Septimus progressed upward like an extremely well-mannered fox going through a hen-house. In his wake, feathers, clucking, dismay, uproar—yet he behaved as if he had such a perfect right to push his way through someone else's house from bottom to top, that no-one gathered the confidence to protest effectually until he was well past.

The twist of the stairs tightened; the carpet beneath their galloping feet gave way to boards; a door presented itself with a simpler, barer flight of staircase beyond. Glancing back down the well, Smith saw beneath the spiral of astonished faces tilted up at him that there was a commotion in the hall now, with shouts and banging, but that, judging by the banging, the door to the street had not been opened. Not yet, anyway. Up the next flight. Oilcloth, plain wood, a child's wooden horse: a nursery. Past a nurse with a babe in arms that began, reliably, to bawl. Last flight: up among the caves, servants' bedrooms, grey plaster, cold air, truckle beds. Along a mean corridor, Septimus counting along the rooms on their right. Last room. Door of plain pine. Door locked from inside. Septimus rapped on it. No answer but a faint, sickly groan.

Smith looked back. The temper of the house-noise was altering behind them, now that the hypnotic effect of Septimus' passing was worn off.

"Bother," said Septimus, "I shall have to send them a note in the morning," and kicked the door open with his pointed black shoe.

The woman who had been lying in the bed in the corner with the toothache screamed, or tried to. Her jaw was bound up with a grey clout of rags, and she could only open her mouth enough to emit a high-pitched moan. She clutched the sheet up to her chin.

"Come now, mistress, your virtue is perfectly safe," said Septimus reprovingly. "We are only interested—in—your—" The last words were said in grunts, he having bounded across the room and addressed himself to the casement.

The top half of the wooden sash could be forced down to the mid-point of the window, creating a slot two feet high at about chest height. There, in the darkness outside, the loose end of the rope was swinging down over the guttering at the edge of the roof, just above. Alas, the eaves of the house projected outward, from window-top to gutter, so the rope hung a good yard away, and there was not much length to it, perhaps a scant man's height, and no knot at the end neither, to arrest a pair of slipping feet or (worse) slipping hands. Four storeys down, their pale faces gleaming like bubbles around the edge of a glass of dark wine, the mob ringed the front door, shouting—shouting *through* it, for it had still not been opened, the house having learned caution from Smith and Septimus' first invasion. None of the besiegers were looking up. To them, the eaves of the house were deep-shadowed.

Septimus cast round for a chair. There was none.

"Better give me a leg," he said. Standing on Smith's bent knee, he leaned forward over the sash and wriggled forward, with his stomach as a fulcrum, and his head, chest and out-stretched arms projecting free and unsupported into the night air. Smith gripped his coat as he inched forward. The sabre in its scabbard projected awkwardly, clipping Smith's chin. Septimus' hands found the rope.

"You will forgive the ludicrous posture," said he—and, gripping the rope in both fists as tightly as he could, he wriggled the rest of the way over the sill, a black secretarial seal entering the ocean, pushed off from the window above fifty or so feet of empty air, and swung out to dangle over the street, making a *huff* of effort. His thin legs kicked, his hands slid: but then they caught, and he wrapped himself tight round the fibres. As soon as his weight was full on the rope, he began to rise, and the twisted clove-hitch he had made of himself disappeared upward, with further quiet *huffs* and *mmphs* where he was scraped on the gutter. What seemed only a couple of seconds later, the rope reappeared, empty. An urgent hiss from above: "Come on!"

At this point Mr. Smith made the mistake of pausing for an instant, and looked down, considering how he would have to scramble up and out above the fifty-foot void without a helper behind to steady him; how he would need to throw himself beyond all chance of appeal upon the mercy of a narrow, slippery cord; how much more likely it was than any other outcome that he should tumble screaming through the air, and strike the stones below with a croquillant squelch, in a posture of annihilation. He paused on the brink; and, hesitating, looked back into the room.

But it was no longer empty. Coming through the door-way, three steps away, was the householder, his periwig off and a fowling piece in his hands, with other male guests crowding at his shoulders.

"What the devil do you think you are—?" began his host.

Propelled by embarrassment, and by a prospect of explanations that made the atrocious fall before him seem at least the simpler alternative, Smith scrambled up onto the sash in a kneeling crouch, and before consideration could weaken resolve any further, leapt.

One hand caught on the rope, but the other's knuckles bumped off it, and he swung for a moment over the gulf by the grip of one burning, slithering palm. The mob-filled deep spun beneath his feet, and the indifferent darkness of the continent leaned in, prompt to claim him. —Then his other flailing hand got purchase and up he rose out of the pit, away from the window filled with open-mouthed faces, over the hard sharpness of the gutter, and up to a tiled slope where Septimus and Achilles were pulling, braced against the drop, with teeth bared in effort. They landed him like a fish and dragged him up over the roof-crest and into a leaded valley beyond.

"Better move on a house or two," panted Septimus, and the three of them scrambled up and down and up and down the steep tiled slopes till the noise of the street diminished behind them. Septimus held up a finger, and they listened: a hubbub, still, but not a hubbub rising. A hubbub on the contrary spreading its skirts and settling into a mutter. No figures rising through trapdoors. No battering-ram blows upon the Princes Street door. Perhaps the members of the mob would countenance slaughter on a midnight impulse, but found they could not contemplate house-breaking, without a calculation of daylight consequences. Or perhaps the hot blood was simply cooling. Soon, the sounds from below were those of departure. King Mob melted into his separate parts, and slunk away, restored to the mode of individual existence.

The three on the roof looked at each other. Septimus' face was calm but his eyes were wide, as if the wind had changed and frozen him in a moment of disbelief. Achilles was smiling slightly. After a while they moved again, to an east-facing slope of slates commanding a view of Broad Street's lower end, descending to the docks, and there in a crevice they settled until the streets should become quiet. Achilles had acquired one of the bottles of rum that had been circulating by the fire, and this they drank the greater part of while they waited to descend—it having been agreed that Smith had better come with them tonight into the safety of Fort George—passing it from hand to hand convivially, and without urgency, each one succumbing at times to a quiet spasmodic laughter for which the others required no explanation. At the northern limit of the dark city, the dull red glow of the fire smouldered on, while the shrieks and the pyrotechnical whip-cracks faded away. A man with a ladder came and extinguished the pale lanterns along Broad Street. Over the water, the scattered twinkles of Breuckelen went out one by one, and the cold wind brought faint creaks from the rigging of the ships riding at anchor, borne up to them in chill gusts and eddies, there where they perched, high above Manhattan.

III

The Fort, behind its ramparts and its outer rind of scorched and roofless barracks, turned out far less military in feeling than Smith had imagined, with a refurbished old Dutch house for the Governor extended out into a higgledy-piggledy quadrangle, which by night seemed to possess the peace of a cloister. Or would have done so, had there not been three musty bell-tents pitched on the grass for the sentries displaced by the fire. Septimus' dwelling was a pair of rooms up a staircase in the corner: a sleeping chamber, with bed and palliasse, and a small day-room or parlour-room with a casement window overlooking the lawn, and a sopha losing its stuffing, beside a little fireplace. Here Septimus placed Smith, and left him with a blanket, tho' without conversation. The awkwardness between them that danger and hilarity had dissolved was drifting back into place, like a sediment in a briskly-shaken bottle that, when the shaking ceases, begins at once to float down again. Smith was embarrassed, and alarmed at the dependence he had demonstrated; Septimus was angry at what he had been compelled to do, and anxious about what damage he might (on the morrow) prove to have done, by the escapade, to his standing in the colony; and all for the sake of one who might very well turn out no more than a travelling rogue.

The sopha was too short for Smith, and the mutinous springs beneath its torn velvet pressed lumpishly into his back. But the rum had soaked his consciousness through, and he tumbled off into a confused depth of sleep, accompanied by the pattern of the lumps, which incorporated itself into his dreams, so that at times he appeared to himself to have become a chess board, to be stiffly locked and strenuously divided into squares which (as well as being different colours) stood at different heights. Here there was something which must be put into order; yet though he revisited it again and again, the puzzle remained always still to be done. The different heights were of immense significance. The different roughnesses too. Yet a leftward twist—a kind of siphoning mutual substitution—no—back at the beginning again. Or sometimes, he was a giant slumbering upon the points of a mountain range, poised on nothing but the lumps, and must compose himself to perfect stillness, or he would fall off. Roll from spiky safety into an abyss on all sides. Yet no sooner had the fall begun than he was restored to the uncomfortable heights, with something to do, something to do—

A banging woke him. He startled awake and lay listening. His head ached and his mouth was dry. It was the pit of the night, some cold recess of the small hours. A faint smear of moon-light crept through the diamond panes of the casement, no brighter than the luminescence of a snail. His heart raced. All seemed still, but for the sound. He thought at first of fists hammering on the lodging's outer door—of the mob reconstituted, and back in pursuit!—but it was not coming from outside, and it was a wooden sound, a hard regular knocking. Perhaps a shutter was loose and the wind had risen. Still mazed, still half-stupid, he uncoiled from the sopha, and padded to the inner-chamber door. The moon's trail of reluctant phosphor followed him; not much of that dim, snailish light, but enough to see, when he opened the door, Septimus and Achilles in vigorous congress, the head of the bed striking the wall. They saw him seeing—their motion arrested, both pairs of eyes looking up at him.

Smith groaned, pulled the door shut, and went and sat down by the ash-filled grate with his head in his hands. After an instant's silence, there came through the door the sound of furious swearing, of clothes being frantically pulled on and feet stamped into shoes. Then Septimus burst into the room in a night-robe. He did not look collected, he did not look china-smooth. His skin was blotched with shadow, and his mouth was a writhing black square.

"Good God!" he cried. "Is there no end to your intrusions, you shameless wretch? Must I be punished immediately for helping you? You didn't even have the decency to wait till morning, did you, you little coxcomb. Oh no, straight on with the damned squeeze. Maybe no-one else can tell you for the Drury Lane offal you are, but I can—oh, I can. So, out with it! What do you want? What are you after, you—" But then he stopped, because Smith was not, in fact, sitting with his legs complacently crossed, and a sharp smirk of satisfaction on his face. His face was invisible behind his hands, and his fingers were digging into his temples, and he was making small sounds of despair.

"What?" demanded Septimus, still angry. *"What?"*

"I thought I heard a shutter banging."

"A shutter. I have no shutters."

"I didn't know that! I came in half-asleep. It was an accident. Believe me, I had no desire to walk in upon your—your—"

"You know what it was."

Smith took away his hands. "Do I?" he said. There was, for the first time, a note of defiance or even anger in *his* voice; but his eyes were wet, and gleaming in the moon-light.

"You are confusing me," said Septimus. "You talked like a street-corner molly-boy in the coffee-house; and now you are all weeping innocence. Is this your method of work, to pretend to a shock, that a man may—"

"For heaven's sake," said Smith, "I am not trying to blackmail you. I am not trying to blackmail you! And as for innocence, I can name the act you were engaged in, in six tongues, including gutter Arabic and medical Latin, I thank you. I am quick with languages;

voices too. I pick them up. They stick to me. Sometimes I use the wrong one, in haste. That was what I did in the Merchants—used the wrong tongue to you. And I am sorry for't, as I am sorry now, for blundering in. It was a poor recompense for saving my life. I ask your pardon. There! And if I think the worse of you, it is not because you are a sodomite."

"You think the worse of me," said Septimus. He was puzzled, and cautious, now. He came around, and leant on the mantel, the other hand holding his robe together. "What, you think I am a low fellow, for consorting with a slave?"

"I think you are a low fellow for taking your pleasure where there is no possibility of being refused."

Septimus stared. "Now that," he said slowly, "is a judgement I was not expecting."

"Are you sure?" said Smith. "Is there not a little voice in here"— he tapped his head—"that whispers it to you?"

"Did it look like a rape, what you just saw? Did either seem reluctant?—I cannot believe I am justifying myself to you."

"I am sure you do not need force, to win obliging behaviour from one who is your property."

"Achilles is the Governor's property, not mine. But, what is far more to the purpose, he is my friend."

"I am sure you tell him so."

"He tells it to *me*."

"Of course. Then, what is his name? His *real* name, I mean, for I do not think it is Achilles, any more than yours is Patroclus."

Septimus flushed, but it was another voice that answered.

"Achilles is my real name," said the slave from the door-way between the rooms, where he was standing, wrapped in a sheet. "Once I had another one, yes, and *he*"—nodding gravely toward Septimus—"has asked me for it again and again. But that life is over for me now. I must live where I am, or I will have no heart in my chest. If I called myself by the old name, even just inside, silently, behind the bones, I would be a ghost. And I do not want to be a ghost. I want to be alive. He understands that. You should not accuse him. He is a good man." Achilles' voice was strongly accented with Africa. It was a country voice, steady, self-possessed; and Smith, hearing it, realised what the man's thinness and shaved head had hidden, that he was the oldest of the three of them there, perhaps by twenty years.

"My dear, there is no need—" Septimus began.

"Yes, there is, with this one," said Achilles. "Listen, boy," he said to Smith. "He did not make me do anything. He did not even ask me. I asked *him.* I put my hand on him. He was surprised."

"I was," said Septimus, quietly.

Smith cleared his throat. "It was a free choice?" he said.

Achilles laughed.

"Who is talking about choosing?" he said. He came into the room, and sat on the other end of the sopha. The sluggish moonlight painted dull trails of pewter on him. "Your trouble is, you are afraid," he observed cheerfully to Smith. "You are waiting for the bad thing to happen. You are looking for a little safe place to hide in. But there are no safe places, and the bad thing happens all the time. Tonight they nearly killed you. You were lucky, that is all. Tomorrow, who knows. Every time you can be happy for one half an hour, it is enough." He fumbled a long dark arm out of the sheet, and proved to be holding the almost-empty bottle. He drained the dregs.

Smith and Septimus looked at each other.

"He will not let me plan," said Septimus. "Every time I try to fathom out a scheme for a future for us, he shuts me up. By shutting up himself. His silence is very persuasive. I would like to buy him out from the household and free him, if I could raise the money, but . . ."

"Where would you go?" said Smith.

"London?" A shrug.

"Eccentric Mr. Oakeshott and his butler?"

"You have a madly exaggerated idea of my resources. It was the most the family could do, to place me in a position where I could rise with the Governor, and share in his lustre. But the Governor is not doing well, and there is no lustre to share. If I go home—especially if I quit his service and go home—I can look forward, at most, to a life as a schoolmaster, perhaps as a private tutor. Perhaps a scribbler. Do you remember you mentioned Lincoln's Inn Fields? You must picture us sharing a garret there. —Even that would require me to scrape up a sum that seems entirely beyond me."

"How much— But of course, you cannot enquire," said Smith.

"No, indeed. Not until I could be sure of meeting the price, whatever it proved to be, and to depart without lingering. But wait!" said Septimus, clapping a hand to his forehead with a sarcastic flourish. "How foolish of me! Why, this very evening I have put Mysterious Master Money-Bags in debt to me for his life! He will surely be glad to lend me a modest twenty guineas!"

"Alright," said Smith.

"Al— What?"

"When the bill is cleared at Christmas, I will lend the two of you Achilles' price."

Septimus gazed at him, mouth slightly ajar.

"You sound almost as if you are in earnest."

"I am."

"Do you mean to tell me," said Septimus slowly, "do you seriously mean to tell me—that the money is *real*?"

Smith nodded.

"I don't suppose you would care to explain yourself," Septimus said.

"I would if I could," said Smith, "but I cannot. It is not my confidence I am keeping. But for what it is worth, you have my word. And I will keep my mouth closed on your secret, too."

"Well," said Septimus. He was grinning. "Well! Let me see: if I trust you, and if it proves you are lying, I am a future fool, but if I trust you, and you are telling the truth, I am a past fool for having looked the gift horse in the mouth; and if I do not trust you, and you are not lying, I am a future fool again; only if I do not trust you, and you *are* lying, am I not a fool at all, but only a very disappointed man. Three ways to be a fool, and one sad way to avoid it. I think I must take the foolish step, and hope for the best. If that is agreeable to you, dear stoic," he said to Achilles.

But Achilles was asleep.

"Are you sure this is safe?" Smith asked in the morning, as they prepared to depart from the Fort in different directions, Achilles' face restored to a mask, Septimus' to a state of ceramic polish that made the night seem a dream.

Achilles raised an eyebrow, but Septimus said, "Oh yes. Pope Day is in the nature of a purge, before the enforced proximity of the winter. Not only will you not be threatened: you will find no-one willing even to allude to last night."

"All the same, I think I will buy a sword of my own," said Smith. (On credit, he thought.)

Septimus loped away across cobblestones rinsed by the morning rain, Achilles keeping pace a discreet step or two behind. At the corner, Septimus turned and, backing all the while, cried out, "Shall we see you later?"

"Yes," called Smith, with a pleasant feeling of alliance, "and you can tell me what the story is, about Lovell's crippled daughter."

Septimus' receding visage crumpled with puzzlement. "What?" Smith heard him say. "Neither of Lovell's daughters is crippled . . ." He shook his head and was gone.

3

His Majesty's
Birthday

November 10th

20 Geo. II

1746

I

"I think I won't ask you why you did that," said Smith to Tabitha.

"Oh good," she said, striding cheerfully beside him across a damp pasture half a mile north of the city.

Now she was no longer pretending to limp, her gait was a brisk, long-legged, functional matter, with no sway in it, and no particular grace either. It did not seem to occur to her that how she moved ordinarily might be an opportunity for artifice. Indeed, she struck Smith as being, in some ways, more oblivious to allure, and to how she might appear to another's eye, than any other young woman he had ever met. All her consciousness, all her intent, was in her quick face. Nevertheless, she was in looks today. The wet November air had blown some colour into her cheeks to match the delicate ruddiness of her lips, which she was biting unselfconsciously as she darted upon Smith her sharp, smiling, studying glances. The loose strands of her brown hair were blowing about. Her teeth were very white. They were almost alone. Nothing was visible of New-York above the hedge-rows and half-bare trees but a couple of its steeples. The scene was not wholly pastoral to an English eye, however, for the labourers in the far corner of the field lifting potatoes were Africans, and along the rutted track that the Broad Way had become, rolled wagon upon wagon, far more than would conceivably be chance-met on a country road; and through drifting screens of drizzle there floated snatches of lamentation from the slaves' burial ground, on the road's farther side. Zephyra, pacing behind them, had turned aside to speak in low murmurs to a party carrying a child-sized bundle, wrapped in rags. Now she was stationed twenty feet away, in the shelter of the thorn hedge, with her fist propping her chin, and her averted face as unbetraying as ever.

"Were you terribly angry?" Tabitha asked.

"No," said Smith, "for I never believed you for an instant."

"Liar!" said Tabitha, grinning. "It was written all across your face, in characters an inch high, that you believed me. And pitied the poor cripple girl. The poor—lonely—imprisoned—"

"If I *were* angry, I should never tell you," Smith said, "for I begin to know now how much pleasure it gives you to annoy people. So to tell you would be to oblige you; and you have not given me much reason to want to oblige."

"Yet here you are. In any case, I am sure you were not angry for long. I should think it was probably a relief to you, more than anything else."

This was perceptive. After the initial surprise and fury, Smith had felt in himself a kind of moral relaxation, at the removal from his path of the supposed innocent who might be injured by his scheme, and it was from gratitude at being so released that, a couple of days later, once his self-possession seemed returned, he had sent her a note asking "if Miss Lovell would join him for a Walk"—thus assuring her that her trap had sprung. But now he only inclined his head non-committally. For it was also true that he found himself, generally, less inclined to do anything to oblige her. A savour of anger remained, like pepper, to flavour their relations. His guess was, that this might be the common experience of those who had the misfortune to like Tabitha Lovell. Flora and Mr. Lovell seemed scorched, and wary.

"I hear you had quite a time, on Pope Night," she said, seeing that her previous gambit would draw no more from him.

"What do you hear?"

"Why, that you and the Oakeshott boy broke into Mr. Perkins' party, with a mob at your heels, and scarified the servants, and broke out again—onto the *roof*? Can that be right?—and that Mr. Perkins had an apology in the morning that was so cold and English and peculiar that it left him puzzled if he was being laughed at? All the guests told all their friends, and their friends told *their* friends, and so the story is broad-cast into every ear on the island. There are no secrets here. All is known as soon as done. Except," she said, turning to stare him smilingly in the face, "that it *isn't*. What on earth were you doing?"

"We-ell," said Smith, unwilling to forego the chance to recount an adventure to a pretty and eager hearer, yet tugged at more darkly by the memory of that night's fears, "I ran into a little trouble at the bonfire. I had not understood what a serious, ah, saturnalia it was going to be, and I offended some gentlemen with my manner."

"Imagine that."

"It is a puzzle, isn't it? But I did. And things grew a bit rough, and then I made a mistake and made them rougher by, you know, putting up my fists."

"Ah," she said. "Pugilism, London-style!" And, stopping to face him, she danced a few steps on the spot in the manner of a prize-fighter, which made her look about twelve years old, and sent a very gentle right hook gliding through the air to pause beneath his chin.

This fist, unlike the butcher's, was a slender hollow knot of tubes, like sections of bamboo, or the pieces of a flute. She had tucked her thumb inside: the infallible way to break it, if she actually hit anyone, Smith's Limehouse advisor had told him. He could kiss the pale knuckles with the faint pink flush creasing each, if he lowered his head an inch.

"London-style," he agreed, smiling at her instead, and she withdrew her arm. "But it did not answer. It inflamed them, and there were too many for my heroical efforts. But then—"

"Were you frightened?"

"Yes," he said, surprised into candour. Her face was serious. "I thought I was done for." Speaking these words brought back to present memory the spike in the butcher's hands, and he twitched at the cold ghosts of punctures. "I thought I would—"

"You'd have talked your way out, I'm sure."

"No," he said, still addressing her serious eyes. "It had gone past talk."

"These things always grow in the telling. A skirmish to a battle, a scratch to a severed head. What happened next?"

Was she serious or only eager?

"Go on," she said. "Tell me the next part. —I am glad you are all right, of course."

"Oh, of course," said Smith, struggling to retrieve a light touch, like a man drawing a full bucket back up from a well, and finding the rope longer than it had seemed when it went rattling easily down. "Well—there I was, surrounded by ferocious New-Yorkers—"

"—twenty men in buckram suits, yes—"

"—yes, blood-boltered and savage, every one, with their teeth filed off to points—"

"—for extra ferocity—"

"You know," said Smith, "this is uncanny. It's just as if you had been there. But who is telling this story, mistress, you or me?"

100

"You."

"You're sure?"

"Yes. You—you—you—you—"

"Very well. So there I was, *as* I was saying, in a desperate condition, fending off half these assassins with my left hand and half with my right, throwing them by twos and threes over my shoulders, using such tricks of combat as would make your eyes water, all learned from subtle masters of the East; and yet making no headway against such a press of numbers, when out of nowhere appeared Mr. Oakeshott, the Quixot of Secretaries, fortunately equipped with a hanger, and the enemy fell back. 'Why, Mr. Smith,' he said"— he was giving Septimus, most unfairly, a voice of small-mouthed niminy-piminy exactness—"'I see you are labouring under some difficulties? Will you allow me to assist you?' 'Why yes, you knight errant of the inkwell, you may!' I cried; and so—"

"So you escaped," said Tabitha flatly, and deliberately yawned.

"Yes. I did," said Smith, equally flatly, after a moment, and fell silent.

"And all of this unlikeliness happened beside the fire, on the Common. And then you ran to Mr. Perkins', on Princes Street."

"Yes," said Smith, with a sigh.

"Why did you not run to Golden Hill? We were much closer."

The truth was that in the rush of the flight, Smith had not even thought of it. The Lovells' house—thinking of it now—stood in his mind as a place of effort and exertion, not of refuge. It had not the character, for him, of somewhere that one might seek safety.

"It would not be a friendly act," he said, "to bring a mob to your door, would it?"

"We would have managed, I dare say. But that was not your reason."

"No?" said Smith.

"You were not sure that we would open the door to you."

"I am sure you would," Smith said half-heartedly.

"Are you? Would you bet on it? How much? Would you bet a thousand pounds? For that is how much we would profit, were you assassinated on our doorstep. We might leave you to be mangled there, and it would be all to the credit side of the ledger."

Definitely eager; avid, in fact. She had her eyebrows up, as if she were awaiting something. Indeed, she was waiting, he realised. She was waiting, excitedly, for him to strike back. It was his turn.

"Must we play at this?" he said suddenly. "Must it be Queen Tabitha's War every time we meet?"

She drew back sulkily, and kicked at a piece of rotten wood on the ground.

"You are mocking me," she said. "I do not care to be mocked."

"You care to mock, though; and you invite mockery, so you can mock some more."

"What about you? You only want me to admire you, and to listen to your boy's tales with a girl's wide eyes, because you prefer to be liked. You want us to like you right up to the moment when you take our money and suddenly depart. My way is more honest."

"Assuming I am a villain."

"Till you explain yourself, you *are* a villain."

"You have a nasty sharp eye for other people's weaknesses, Tabitha Lovell. Do you ever turn it on yourself? Do you—"

"Sometimes," she said unexpectedly. "When there is no-one else to fight with."

Smith stopped walking. Tabitha took a further step, and stopped too, her head down, her gaze fixed on her feet.

"I do not have much company," she said. "People do not seek me out, very much."

"Imagine that," said Smith, but gently, surprised into sympathy. "But why fight at all? Why always have rapier in hand?"

"I don't know," she said. "It just seems to come out like that. When

I talk—when I get excited. When I am enjoying myself, it flashes out of me. I *want* people to fight back, you know. I like it when I cannot knock them over; when they do not give up and melt into tears. But mostly they do not. My father avoids me, and Flora is as aggressive as a puddle."

Now she was looking up at him. Now she was in earnest, or seemed to be: brow furrowed in a scowl of puzzlement, brown eyes fixed on his as if he might possess the answer to a question she had not put.

"Well, at least, then," he said with deliberate lightness, "I may know it is not a mark of special disfavour, when you stab at me. If you run me through, it will be just on general policy. You do not hate me in particular."

She blinked, and rallied.

"Why no," she said, "—no more than measure."

They smiled at each other. The drizzle of the day was becoming determined, and soon might be rain. The bloom of moisture on her forehead was gathering into tiny clear beads.

"Perhaps we had better go back," Smith said. "You *do* know your Shakespeare," he added, when they were wandering again back toward the traffic on the road. "Why don't you scorn him, like the novel-writers?"

"I suppose, because he does not tell me lies about things close to hand. I can read about thrones, and kings, and Romans, and yellow cross-gartering, and madmen on the heath, and I have free air to breathe. Theatre is my open window. I don't see what I *do* know, business and money and manners and ordering of beef and sallots, turned all to smirking sentiment and unlikelihood."

"What if Shakespeare is lying to you just as much, and it is only that you don't spend your days with kings and Romans?"

She shrugged. "If so it is a style of lie I don't care about. I don't read *Hamlet* for the Danish news."

"I think you like him because the comedies are full of quick-tempered women with razor tongues. I think you like to hear Beatrice and Benedick insulting upon each other."

"Maybe," she said, laughing. "But you, sir, are not Benedick."

"And you, madam, are not Beatrice."

"True."

"Hammer and tongs," said Hendrick, breaking his fast the day after in the Merchants. "All day, every day. Like a choir of harpies, so that you doubted the report of your eyes that there were only the two of 'em, they made such a room-filling racket. Mrs. Lovell complaining always of Tabitha's unkindness, coldness of heart, lack of tender and daughterly feeling, and what-have-you, but always giving shrewdly fierce blows of her own; and Tabitha proclaiming every minute how she was traduced, confined, misunderstood, and all the while lighting up the curtains with the epithets she threw back. Flora crouching in the corner of the sopha like a rabbit, Mr. Lovell hiding in the counting-house. They were a famous pair of shrews, and the best that could be said of 'em was, that they soaked up the worst of it themselves. Passers-by were not hit except at random, or when one or t'other was alone and didn't have the usual place to sink their teeth. Now that dear Tabby is without her partner in shrewdom—well, you've seen."

"And when did her mother die?" Smith asked, eyeing the bread Hendrick had left on his plate.

"When she was fifteen."

A bad break, thought Smith; an injury that did not heal aright. It is only that it hurts.

"I must say," said Hendrick, getting up, "the family is grateful you've volunteered to put yourself in the way of it. While she is kicking you, we have a quieter life altogether."

104

"And Flora's engagement to George can go ahead without the half-bricks flying."

"Or with not so many, at any rate. So: thank you. It is a noble duty you do, and a better service than one would look to receive from an impostor bent on fraud. If that is what you are. Try to take her *away*, if you are intending to ruin her. You won't mind getting this, I'm sure"—indicating, as he departed, the array of dishes between them where bacon had been reduced to grease, and rolls (mostly) to crumbs.

II

The next day was the King's birthday. Smith had had a pasteboard invitation, in Septimus' handwriting, bearing the Governor's arms and bidding him to dinner, and he was looking forward to it, because he was curious but also because he had, the day before, expended the very last of his store of money. His pockets rustled no more. All he had in them was air.

All over the town lesser celebrations at home were raising a glass to King George, and making the traditional toasts, in a kind of decorous indoor reprise of the patriotic orgy at the bonfire. But the Governor's dinner, having been burned out of his residence by the fire at the Fort, needs must occupy the panelled long room upstairs in City Hall, where the Assembly usually sat. This super-position of two powers, and their two proper territories, made for wariness on all sides. Septimus—still up a ladder when Smith arrived, and trying to organise a mass of red, white and blue ribbons around a decorative lozenge of the royal countenance—was as uneasy as a cat carried into a stranger's house. And the others of the Governor's party, His Excellency included, were little less inclined to twitch and fidget; while the Assemblymen and their wives and daughters, the prominent citizens and *their* wives and daughters, hung back in a murmuring mass.

"I don't think I can get it any better than this," called Septimus.

"Your problem is, you are looking for his good side," said James De Lancey, massive and genial in his judge's black; he alone, it seemed, strolling about indifferent to the fissure in the room. "But King George's good side is the Constitution."

Septimus at the ladder-top nodded stiffly. It was the querulous, hollow-faced man Smith had seen at church who answered, in saw-edged Scots.

"Is that a gene-rr-ous, a co-orr-dial, beginning to the evening? To insult His Majesty's face?"

"Come on now, Cadwallader," said De Lancey easily. "No offence was meant, and I'm sure none would have been taken, even if I had said it *to* his face. By all accounts he is the most moderate and undespotic of princes—that is what my cousin Pelham tells me, from his interviews with him."

His smile was warm yet the group around the Governor contracted as if poked. De Lancey made a bow, and moved on among his constituents.

"Did he mean Lord Pelham?" Smith asked, holding the ladder while Septimus descended. "Is he really cousins with the prime minister?"

"Yes," said Septimus bitterly. "That is one of our problems. Usually, a governor can at least call on his interest in London as a counter-weight, when things get sticky here. It is slow but it works in the end. But De Lancey's connections are better than ours. His cousin is prime minister and, just to set the cherry on the damned cake, his old tutor at Cambridge is this year made Archbishop of Canterbury. Church and State, he has us out-flanked, and as you see, he likes to remind us of it from time to time, to torment us. Right; wine and music."

He wove away between the sidling dignitaries, towards the small slave orchestra tuning up at the end of the room, and the squadron of waiters with trays who had been drafted in from the taverns and the coffee-houses. The banquet had been laid along a single great table down one half of the room, leaving the other clear as a dance-floor; and as the band struck up a minuet, the guests sorted themselves into standers and dancers, the standers receiving a glass of canary and the dancers beginning (amid chatter and calls of recognition) to tread out the measure on the polished boards. They did at the least overlay the division in the company with some animation, and as the couples turned, at first a few and then more, their circular motion gently scoured the partisans out of the corners, and blended them together. The Governor and Mrs. Clinton took to the floor, and so did the De Lanceys, so did the Livingstons, so did the Philipses, so did the Rutgers, so did the Van Loons, with the younger members of their clans following as soon as, in a flurry of bows and curtseys and laughter, they had found themselves partners.

Smith, looking around to see whose eye he might catch, was pleased to spy a mixed phalanx of young Lovells and Van Loons readying themselves, and slipped over to join them. Flora smiled, Joris snarled, Hendrick raised an eyebrow, and Tabitha turned on him a gaze of such amused welcome that his heart startled within him; she was dressed in a dark red silk which became her, and had garnets in her ears, but rather than taking a pleasure in the gown as a new and formal skin, as Flora was with her pink, shifting in it and stroking at the fabric with a fingertip, she stood there inside it as if it were no part of her, like a tall pole which in the wind happens to have become entangled in a cloth.

Smith made a leg to the group in general.

"Does anyone require a partner?" he said.

"You must dance with Flora," said Tabitha promptly.

"No, I shall dance with Flora," said Joris.

"But you promised *me*," whined Anneke, whose grey made her look like a little pouter pigeon.

"I was thinking I might dance with you," said Smith to Tabitha.

"Were you? I am afraid Hendrick has claimed this one."

"I have?" said Hendrick. "Of course. I have. How forgetful of me."

He held out his hand, palm upward, and Tabitha took it. The two of them stepped away into the minuet, turning smoothly and correctly, and no more involved with each other than a couple of clockwork figures.

"You *promised*," said Anneke to her brother. "You know that it is my first time, and that no-one else may ask me if you don't, and you *promised*."

"Oh, all *right*," said Joris, his teeth clamped. "Just . . . just . . ." His finger was pointed warningly at Smith, but he could find no way to disburden himself that would not make matters worse.

"Don't be so silly," said Flora, with unexpected firmness. "I shall be quite safe with Mr. Smith. You know that Tabitha is only trying to annoy you. You and I can dance the next one. Go on!"

"You are determined to enjoy yourself," Smith observed, as Anneke was rotated, beaming, away.

"Yes, I am," said Flora cheerfully, accepting his fingertips and sliding into place next to him, pink and white and fair, and smelling of soap and healthy young skin. When they were facing each other, she did the dips and turns with zest rather than delicacy, feet almost stamping, and when they were in the close turns, she made a very pleasant armful. As her breath quickened, her bodice rose and fell, and the tops of her breasts grew flushed.

"Yes, I am," she said again. "Tabitha wants to dance with you, and you really want to be dancing with her, and neither of you are getting to do what you want, because she would rather be spiteful instead; and I just think that is stupid, so I am going to have fun no matter what. I am going to dance with you, and I am going to dance with Joris, and I am going to dance with anyone else who asks me. —You're good at this, aren't you?"

"Two years with a fashionable dancing-master," said Smith, seeing again the waxed floor of the *salle* in Covent Garden. *And another year trying to wring shillings from the skill by teaching it*, he did not add. If Flora had been in respectable society in London, she would have seen that his movements had become more flashy than was strictly gentlemanly: the noble art corrupted into a show that would please at a distance. Joris and Anneke passed, Anneke stepping on her wincing brother's toes; De Lancey went smiling by, a victory column in deft motion, and nodded to Smith.

"I don't think it's very flattering to be called *safe*," he complained to Flora, essaying his best glance of flirtatious menace. She laughed.

"But I am safe with you," she said. "I may not be clever like Tabitha, but I am not an idiot, you know. You think I'm pretty, but she is the one you're interested in, Mr. Smith."

"In that case, you could call me Richard, surely," he said.

"When the bill clears," she said, comfortably her father's daughter.

At dinner he was placed three-quarters of the way towards the top of the long table, in what was evidently the tail of the Governor's invitation list, with Septimus opposite him, and the great men of the colony clustered together to his right, where he might have the pleasure of overhearing their collisions, yet was plainly not bidden to participate. The Van Loons and Lovells were far down the lane of white linen. Half a dozen different conversations were rattling on between: leaning to look, he received the performance only in dumbshow, quite soundlessly, of Flora laughing, and settling herself in state with the folds of the pink silk around her, and both Joris and Hendrick leaning solicitously in, to confirm her rights in acting the princess on this royal evening; and Tabitha, finding no purchase for mischief in this impervious happiness, sitting bolt upright on the other side of the table, looking isolated and even a little lost. He raised his canary glass to her, but her gaze was fixed on some inner horizon, and she did not see.

The dinner, as it must be on this night, was roast-beef. And of course, as the sides of the beef were carried in on trenchers, to cheers, sizzling and brown and scarlet, each a goodly fraction of a cow, the orchestra struck up, as it must, "The Roast-Beef of Old England," and the company roared out loyally:

> *When mighty roast-beef was an Englishman's food*
> *It ennobled our veins, and enriched our blood;*
> *Our soldiers were brave, and our courtiers were good . . .*

—the Assemblymen vying in volume with the Governor's party, to prove they were of no less devotion, until the table's head was all wigs and wide mouths and glittering eyes in the candle-light, the rough music dissolving at the last chorus into a general laughter.

"James, may I carve you a slice?" asked the Governor reedily, a spot of colour in each powdered cheek.

"Why, George, I don't mind if I do," rumbled De Lancey, passing his plate; and the treaty was sealed in dripping and gravy.

Septimus, who had been watching with the stem of his glass pinched between a whitened finger and thumb, exhaled; and directed his attention across at Smith instead, with the air of one allowed for a minute to go off duty. Smith was cocking an ear to the conversation on his right, and glancing as if compelled down to his left; but most of all he was chewing the largest mouthful of beef that he could decently take in, and trying not to salivate on the table-cloth. Septimus, intercepting the direction of the glances, smiled at him.

"Do you know," he said, "I have them both—both the Misses

Lovell—down for roles in my play; I mean the drama we put on to beguile the first part of the winter. It is *Cato* this year. Should you like to take a part?"

"Maybe," said Smith, swallowing. "Is this in the nature of private theatricals, then?"

"We-ell, not strictly; we do not take money, for that would waken the city's puritan doubts, and make 'em think acting not a fit recreation for their sons and daughters, but we do show it before such a public as wants to see it. It was formerly in the Fort, with an audience chiefly from the families of the garrison, but this year I have procured for a night the use of the old theatre on Nassau Street, which is usually a lumber store, there being no players to turn it to its proper purpose. Come; it will pass the time; let me tempt you to be a Roman."

"Are they any good?" asked Smith, with a motion of his chin to the left.

"Well; Miss Flora more than Miss Tabitha, strangely enough, for she has it thoroughly in mind to be a heroine, if she can, and she cries out the lines with relish, if not with subtlety. While Miss T understands the piece, but carries herself like a reader of it, who has been deposited on stage by chance, with eyebrows raised at the absurdity of it all."

Smith laughed, since he could picture this entirely.

"Alright," he said. "Who may I be? Portius? Marcus?"

"You know the piece! Excellent. No, for you I had in mind Juba— the Numidian prince?"

Smith hesitated, but Septimus, who was sawing at his own beef, did not remark it. I have not cultivated caution up until now, he thought. It is no part of the plan to be cautious, but rather the opposite, he reminded himself.

"Very well," he said out loud. "But I am surprised at the choice of the play."

"Why?" said Septimus. "It is a guaranteed crowd-pleaser, here, as a matter of fact. No other piece comes close, for it tickles all the themes that New-York loves best. Liberty and virtue, virtue and liberty. Sometimes I think that if I could train a parrot to say those two words, we might run it for the Assembly, and get His Excellency one reliable vote at least, that way."

"What's that?" said the middle-aged man on Smith's next right, roused by the naming of the Assembly. "Liberty an empty cry? No surprise, coming from you. Don't listen to this popinjay. Precious trust. *Sacred* trust. Finest flower of the Constitution. Greatest glory of 'n Englishman. Smith!" he said, sticking out a paw. His brow was a solid black bar, surprising beneath his wig.

"Yes?" said Smith, puzzled, taking the hand.

"No—Smith!" said the man, irritably pulling free and stabbing at his chest with a finger. "You?"

Septimus sighed elaborately. "William Smith, meet Richard Smith," he said. "Richard Smith, meet Master William Smith, lawyer and historian—himself an ornament to our Senate of Lilliput."

"Lilliput, is it?" said the Assemblyman. "If you patronised us less, you superior little court-worm, you might get more co-operation."

"I might patronise you less if we got any co-operation at all," snapped Septimus. "You might pay the Governor's salary, for instance. Or mine."

"It is our ancient right to vote *all* spending," said the other Smith.

"Ancient, is it?" put in the cadaverous Scot beside the Governor. "Funny, then, that we never-rr heard of sich a thing, till last year-rr."

"Purse-strings to the people, or kings grow insolent. Ancient, yes. Old as the Saxon moot."

"Och, the Saxon moot," said the Scot deprecatingly, making of the word a derisive little hoot. "A wee bit misty a source for a legal doctrine, d'ye not think? When in braw black and white, it's clear-rr that for the hale sixty year-rrs of its existence, the Assembly of the

Province of New Yo-rr-k has rr-ecognised its duty to finance the basic, I say *basic*, fabric of gov-err-nment!"

"The power is there. Acted on or not acted on: still a power. I've read the records, Colden; know 'em as well as you; probably better. Surprised you'd want to shine a light in there. Never mind rights 'n duties. Dirty hands! Dirt in the land grants, dirt in the customs. D'you want it dug out? Do you? Do you?"

The Governor (who was staring appalled at this outbreak of brushfire) tinkled frantically with his spoon on his wine-glass. The table stilled; first at his end, then in a spreading imperfect wave, till almost all heads the table long were turned his way in expectation, and the slurp could distinctly be heard of a fat gentleman at the far end securing his last mouthful of gravy. The Governor rose to his feet, glass in hand.

"Gentlemen!" he said, "—and ladies, of course. My Lord Mayor. Learned gentlemen of the Bar. Honourable members of the Council and the Assembly. Our gallant defenders from the garrison. My fellow citizens of this fair city, and my fellow subjects together of the Sovereign on whose birthday we are glad to, ah, meet. It is my duty, yes, my very pleasant duty, to recall to our minds the blessings of the past year, and our many gracious deliverances from dangers domestic and foreign, and to propose that we give thanks, with loyal heart and voice, yes, with heart and voice together, *for* these our many blessings, and solemnise them indeed, as is only fit, on this special day of the year, by together raising our glasses, and saying: the King!"

"The King!" echoed the table, in one ringing near-shout. Smith, who was not used to these festivities being executed with such fervour, had his wine upraised, but his mouth open in surprise rather than loyalty, and added no sound to the toast.

De Lancey rose smiling opposite the Governor, his own glass ready.

"Here's a health unto His Majesty," he said, "in whose person we see secured the majesty of our laws, the assurance of our rights, be we ne'er so high or so low, and the freedom of our Protestant religion. The King! Queen Caroline! And Prince Frederick!"

"The King, Queen Caroline, and Prince Frederick!" cried the company.

"Indeed, yes indeed," said the Governor, once the wave had crashed past and subsided into foam. "How right it is, that having, ah, drunk to the person of His Majesty, we should conclude, yes, as we always do, by drinking to what he represents. Ladies, gentlemen: civil and religious liberty!"

"Civil and religious liberty!" intoned the table, solemn now, and with somewhat of the air of a congregation making a response in church; as in church, too, subsiding after this moment of high seriousness into a slightly uncertain contra-moment of awkward muttering, as if they scrupled to put against such a sentiment anything of too-great ordinariness, yet hoped, at the same time, to scramble down off the pinnacle as quick as may be. Smith, seeing the Governor still standing, wondered if he would launch the company into the new anthem that had concluded almost every play in Drury Lane, this past year and more. But it seemed that the fashion for "God Save Great George Our King," to the music by Mr. Arne, had not yet crossed the sea, for the Governor had a different purpose.

"Now we have a treat in store," he said, clasping and unclasping his hands. "St. James's Palace is far away, and yet we are privileged this evening to hear one of the famous Birthday Odes with which His Majesty himself is, ahaha, regaled on this day. Performed for us by our very own Mrs. Tomlinson!"

Septimus' wide eyes and startled brows declared transparently that this was not an element of the entertainment upon which he had been consulted. The porcelain of his forehead humped itself, indeed, into a pained white wave that stayed there, motionless, baked-in, glazed, as on ripples of applause and even catcalls, there walked past the table toward the orchestra the woman with the remarkable blue eyes whom Smith had seen in church, dressed in grey tights and a kind of tabard, wearing a cardboard helmet and carrying a trident not much larger than a toasting-fork. Her eyes were the rich colour of lapis lazuli, or of the warm sea of the tropics in that state where the turquoise of the shallows is just darkening to the purple of the deeps, and she had heightened it by painting the lids and the skin around with a blue kohl, giving the effect on wrinkling skin (she was not young) of a jewelled rope coiled around the greater jewels. But few of the men, at least, at table were confining their attention to the brilliance of her gaze, her Grecian nose, her red-gold hair, *et cetera*; for Mrs. Tomlinson was one of those women blessed, or cursed, by the combination of prettiness of feature with voluptuousness of body. She was not fat, it must be clearly stated; she still possessed by some standards an excellence of figure; but she curved to the point of grossness, or perhaps just over it, in every respect in which a woman can curve, from calves upward. Her bosom strained the material of the tabard, and her thighs rolled in round magnificence as she paraded unhurriedly by. Except for those, like Septimus, disqualified by nature from the admiration of this species of abundance, the men the length of the room watched her hungrily, and their womenfolk, with a more narrowed gaze, watched them watching. Once, Mrs. Tomlinson might have had a fresh, or ingenuous, charm. Now—said the judgement of the women's gaze, at least, upon her six-and-forty years—she trembled, like a plum already fermenting, about to burst in a mess of juices.

Arrived among the musicians, she spoke briefly to the cellist, who commenced a series of deep scrawling figures; and with this as audible backdrop, and the dark faces and shining wigs of the band as a visual one, she turned into profile, and struck a pose, one leg extended behind her, the trident (or toasting-fork) extended in line with it in front.

"Of fields!" she declaimed ringingly.

> *Of forts! and floods! unknown to fame!*
> *That now demand from Caesar's arms a name,*
> *Sing, Britons! tho' uncouth the sound . . .*

It was possibly the worst of Mr. Colley Cibber's notoriously awful odes, the one, three years old, hymning King George's personal valour on a German battlefield. Yes, here came the rhymes of "Seligenstadt" with "defeat," and "Dettingen" with "joyful strain." Here came the martial blasts from the Poet Laureate's personal wind machine. Septimus was all wince. "Oh God," he murmured, through unmoving lips and closed teeth. "Oh God. Oh God." James De Lancey was feeling the need to clear his throat, rumblingly, every few seconds. The stares of the Assemblymen seemed fixed, if not on the spectacle in general, then in particular on the way the pose bunched and elevated, beneath the rising hem of the tabard, the muscles of Mrs. Tomlinson's magnificent arse.

But Smith shut his eyes to hear better. He could hear the layers in Euterpe Tomlinson's voice. He could pick out the last traces of the Essex or perhaps Suffolk she had come to London speaking once, long ago, when, he'd bet, she'd been a Peggy or a Liza, determined to make her looks yield her a future. He could hear the careful lessons someone had given in breath and voice production, in instant grandeur and synthetic elegance, and how they had been taken to heart, and held close as recipes for destiny; and he could tease free, with his eyes closed and the absurdities blocked out, the gallant consciousness that that wished-for destiny was passing, or had passed, and stranded her here, on tour for ever. The poetry was awful. But she was doing it rather well. She was hitting the consonants finely, dealing neatly with the persistent hiss of Cibber's s-fixation, and opening the verse out wide—all you could do with it, really—into a kind of warm, generous vacuity. She was, in short, a professional, and listening to her Mr. Smith felt, for the first time in New-York City, a curdling homesickness.

> *Ye Britons! blessed in such a race,*
> *Alike secure in arms or peace,*
> *What can your happiness annoy,*
> *Unless yourselves yourselves destroy?*

She managed to give the last words a sober thoughtfulness that conjured, for just an instant, the illusion that the Poet Laureate had actually been thinking when he wrote the line. There was a hush, rather than applause. Smith opened his eyes, to find that she had turned out of profile to fix her audience with a dark-blue gaze of warning, preposterous but oddly authoritative and compelling: the sternness of Pallas Athene, plus tremendous cleavage. She dropped her head, dowsing the blue lanterns. Then there was clapping: not tremendous, except at the mid-point of the table where one of the red-coated officers was whamming his hands together, suffused with pride and delight, and his fellow lobsters were pounding him on the back, as if Major Tomlinson were the one to be congratulated. But it was respectable applause, none the less, some of it even contributed by women. A creditable harvest, considering the unfruitful ground, thought Smith. He added some of his own.

Septimus looked at him as if he were mad. "Oh no," he said. "Another one La Tomlinson has taken by the cods? Say it isn't so."

"Septimus," Smith said, "why do you insist on making yourself obnoxious?"

"You are a fine one to talk on *that* score."

"But you have a place to stand, here. I don't see—"

"Do you not?" said Septimus, signalling with his eyebrows, for William Smith was listening interestedly.

"Alright. But there is, I assure you, a difference between us; though I may not be able to put my finger on it at this moment. You know," Smith continued impulsively, "you could do worse than to have her in your play."

"What!" cried Septimus. "You said you'd read the piece! There are but the two women's parts in it, Cato's daughter and Lucius' daughter; two chaste, innocent, virtuous, high-born maidens, of tender years and of good family. Spring flowers in their earliest bloom. Tell me, Smith, tell me: what is it in that description that reminds you of Terpie Tomlinson?"

"It doesn't matter," said Smith. "She would speak the verse well."

"She has no *taste*!" hissed Septimus, leaning forward. "She is a—a lustful *joke*, to the people here. Just *look* at her, Richard. She is the epitome of every low jest you ever heard about actresses. Don't you think?" he added, almost imploringly.

"Doesn't matter," said Smith again. "You are the director. You have taste. You tell her what you want, and she'll do it."

"Oh, I'm sure she is very . . . *pliant*—"

"Not what I mean. I mean she is trained, and she will take direction. If you can convey to her mind what you wish your Marcia or your Lucia to sound like, she can create it for you. Did you not hear that, in her voice? There is proper expertise there. Come on, Septimus: she made people clap for *Colley Cibber* . . ."

"You're serious."

"Of course I am. I don't know who you have in mind for the other parts, but I am guessing that talent may be a bit thin on the ground—here in Lilliput—and she is a real actress. You can't afford to neglect an obvious asset."

Septimus opened his mouth, reconsidered, and said instead: "What about the way she looks?"

"Drapery. Wrap her up in something big and white and flowing that makes her look like a statue, and come up with a staging where she mostly stands still, so people notice face and voice."

"Drape her, eh?" said William Smith, who proved to have been listening. "Oakeshott's budget may not be big enough. You'd need a lot of cloth, to get round Terpie. Interesting, though; interesting. 'S that your *professional* judgement, Mr. Smith?"

"My . . . informed judgement," Smith said, suddenly careful.

"Alright, I'll think about it," said Septimus. "Since you urge it. But I am surprised you would be happy to push one of the Lovells out of her part, I must say."

Distracted by the lure of the familiar, invigorated (almost intoxicated) by the beef in his empty belly, awakened again only the moment before to a different anxiety, Smith had not in fact considered the matter from this point of view at all. Suddenly a likely and unwelcome consequence struck him.

"Wait," he said, "I—"

A large, smooth hand took a proprietorial grip on his shoulder.

"Mr. Smith," said James De Lancey, standing beside him. "We are making up a party at cards. Won't you join us." There was no question-mark in his sentence.

All along the table the party was granulating into separate groups. Some of the younger guests were, once more, dancing, while others were making their way, farewell by farewell, towards the stairhead and the door; a sediment of older and for the most part public men, on the Assembly side of the question, were precipitating themselves out of the banquet's temporary solution of irreconcilables, and pulling small tables out from beneath the unifying table-cloth, to create little islands where they might sit, and smoke, and politick.

Towards one of these De Lancey led Smith, followed by Smith-the-lawyer. The Governor's party seemed to be preparing to quit the field, while Septimus had darted off somewhere in the direction of the orchestra—only, Smith hoped, to make some arrangement concerning the music.

He had expected to be introduced, when De Lancey descended on a parcel of grandees in silk and gilt at the nearest table—all drawing on long clay pipes, for a rustic note, rather than taking snuff in the London manner—but instead the Chief Justice made a circular, scattering motion in the air, giving one of his vulpine smiles, and the sitting tenants all obligingly rose and departed, with nods and significant looks, leaving him in vacant possession. It was apparently a tête-à-tête De Lancey had in mind, to what purpose Smith did not know: just himself, Smith, and the lawyer, who it was clear now must be that evening's deputed crony, set to keep De Lancey's eye and ear upon him at the dinner.

"Well, now," said De Lancey, settling himself opposite Smith, and folding hand upon hand on the tabletop to make a white hill of knuckles. "What will you take, sir? A pipe, a glass of madeira, a little brandy? No? You must take your ease, you know, for the business part of the evening lies behind, and ahead is all pleasure-garden."

"Are you sure you don't have that the wrong way around, sir?" said Smith.

De Lancey laughed, a resonant chuckle that affected his eyes not one whit.

"Fetch us some cognac and three glasses," he said over Smith's shoulder to Quentin, who proved to have been floating there, silent and ready. "I mean to unburden myself, at any rate, young man. You see?" he said, unbuttoning his collar. "Entirely off duty." He lifted his wig from his head and hung it on the back of the empty chair beside him. His scalp proved to be shingled in fine silver hairs. The sight of his naked head was no more reassuring than the sight of a tiger settling in comfort in its lair.

"I have been wanting to talk to you," he said. "The whole city is debating the mystery of your intentions."

"I protest, sir," said Smith, trying for the same light dominance of tone. "There is nothing mysterious about privacy; and simple privacy—"

De Lancey was holding up a finger.

"Spare me," he said. "You have given many proofs already, from what I hear, that you mean to say nothing to the purpose, so let us omit the nonsense."

"'S friendly with Oakeshott," offered the lawyer.

"So I observed," said De Lancey, tilting his gaze. "But is that policy, or taste? The sign of a side being chosen, or mere happenstance? I doubt you will enlighten us, Mr. Smith. Will you?"

"No, sir. I don't see any reason why I should."

"Indeed. And there's the reason, d'ye see, why I said I would talk *to* you. I do not expect aught from you tonight, saving some pretty noise, but I *will* be assured that you have heard me out. —We'll do it over cards, though; like civilised men. Have you cards, William?"

The attorney produced a well-worn pack from the pocket of his coat, the corners waxy with use, and held them out in tobacco-stained fingers. De Lancey cut and shuffled, not as if he were used to the exercise, but as if his hands were independently performing it, and he were an amused spectator. The waiters were dowsing unneeded candelabra, and the room was growing darker, drawing in about the remaining tables where candles were lit.

"What's your game, Mr. Smith? Brag, pharaoh?"

"Whist, if anything," said Smith: for he had read Mr. Hoyle's book, and applied it with some success, at odd moments in the green room, for a penny a point.

"Really?" said De Lancey. "Mine is piquet. So we'll play that. You know the rules?"

"Of course," said Smith, more stoutly than he felt.

"Good, good. I think with three of us, we'll play for the pool. Guinea ante each, every hand; loser sits out the next hand; whoever wins two hands in a row takes the pool. Agreed?"

"Agreed!" said William Smith, so fast that Smith felt certain sure he and De Lancey had contrived the terms beforehand. He felt a pit yawn open beneath his feet.

"Gentlemen," he said, easing his chair back, an inch, two inches, "I regret that till my bill clears I am not in funds to back my play at such a . . . rate." The last word, despite himself, came out audibly pinched by his surprise.

"Tush," said De Lancey, warmly. "As if we wouldn't trust you for it. William, pass him a page of your memorandum book, and a pencil. You can put in notes-of-hand for your stakes, Mr. Smith—with all the will in the world." Once more looking over Smith's shoulder, he made a come-hither gesture with two fingers, and Smith felt whoever was standing there propel his chair forward into place again.

"We should cut to see who the bystander is, for this first round: but William, I have a whimsy to play at once, and a mind to take young Mr. Smith here as my opponent, if you've no objection? Very good. Then we shall simply cut for the deal. Jack for me. Eight for you. You have the deal, and I am the Elder hand—the order of play conforming, for once, to the order of nature. A coincidence not to be counted upon. Stakes for all three, please, gentlemen."

It was apparent from his humour that De Lancey meant, at least, to entertain himself—an expansive and an *expensive* humour, Smith feared. He scribbled the unavoidable promise on a scrap of paper, and pushed it forward. The lawyer laid on top a yellowed clutch of colonial bills. The judge reached into his weskit pocket, and spun onto the pile, gleaming and ardent, an actual guinea. Smith eyed it. There must, of course, be any number of gold guineas circulating in a commercial city, though he had himself laid eyes on none since he parted with his own. He reached for the cards, and dealt, what he was sure he remembered rightly, twelve cards each for himself and De Lancey, with the remaining eight of the pack spread face down in a line between the two of 'em.

Now, it will be most necessary for the reader, in comprehending what followed, to possess a thorough and secure understanding of the rules of piquet, which shall therefore be explained. The play of the game, is in the taking of *tricks*, yet the greater part of the scores are won in the bidding that precedes it, as for *tierce, quart, quint*, of *sequences*, or *trio* or *quatorze* of *sets*— But wait, before that again comes the announcing of *points*, which must be most decisive, unless one player have *carte blanche*, at the outset, which is quite another thing, and then there is the declaration (at the right moment) of *picque* or *repicque*, one of which is worth thirty and the other sixty, though which way around is knowledge gone to the devil this moment—and there is *capot* too that has not yet been mentioned, and other scores beside, very particular ones, which alter according as the player is Elder or Younger, this governing the whole complexion or character of the game, unless— Wait—wait— alas the explanation is bungled, but it cannot be recalled and started over again, for the game has begun. We are out of time, with little enlightenment secured. Still, the reader may now find himself in as bemused a position as Mr. Smith; which is, to be sure, a kind of gain in understanding.

James De Lancey (Smith was not at all amazed to discover) liked to discourse, or even orate, while he played, the needful exchanges of the game being uttered in, as it were, the chinks or crannies of his oratory. Since it had been indicated so plainly that no nonsense from his own mouth would be welcomed, Smith felt himself at liberty to concentrate (which was indeed most needful for him) on the cards, and to supply only on his side the functional utterances.

"Do you know why I prefer piquet? Why I give it my suffrage among games? Because in miniature, with a pasteboard monarch and a pasteboard court, it offers the situation that most closely resembles the situation of political life. At least, political life as it appears if one is in the midst of it, paying close attention, with a clear mind. Five hearts."

"Good," said Mr. Smith.

"*Quart,*" said De Lancey.

"Equal," said Smith.

"Ace," said De Lancey.

"Good," Smith conceded.

"I mean," De Lancey went on, "that it poses us the problem of being nearly, but never quite completely, informed. We see *almost* the whole of the picture, but never absolutely the whole of it. Look at the table—*picque*, by the way. There are only thirty-two cards, and they are all there in front of us. Between your cards and my cards, and what we have seen when we exchanged, we can deduce virtually the disposition of the entire pack. Yet not quite; never to a complete certainty. And in that little space of imperfection, chance reigns, playing havoc with our plans. —The rest of the tricks to me, I think: yes, yes, yes. We can calculate the outcome in detail if you desire, but it is surely plain enough that I have won?"

"Yes, sir."

"Then on we go! William, your turn. Stakes again, if you please."

Another scrap of scribbled paper, which would mean, if the judge won a second hand in succession, and consequently the pool, that Smith now found himself sunk two guineas beneath the nothing with which he had begun the evening: in a hole two guineas deep. Another crumpled wad from the lawyer. From De Lancey's pocket—another identical glitter of bullion. The Chief Justice turned to face the lawyer, but he still kept up the river of talk, and he still directed it all at Smith, barring the necessary to-and-fro of the game.

"Cutting for the deal: queen," said William Smith.

"Ten," said De Lancey. "You are Elder, and away language flies from truth. —So chance is a power, sir, which every wise man must acknowledge. The largest conditions may be the consequence of the smallest circumstances; may be chosen by none, but determine in the end the fate of all."

"Four clubs," said the lawyer.

"Not good: five spades. Take our present impasse between Governor and Assembly, here in the province. Why do we have the Governor so effectually, so gloriously hamstrung? Because of an unseen chance."

"*Quint,*" said the lawyer, chuckling. "True; none could foresee he'd be such a ninny."

"Good. —But I mean further back, Mr. Smith, and more remotely, more randomly. Because the common law of England says that a freeholder of twenty acres shall have a vote, and because the rule was applied in this Province of New-York unchanged, unaltered, with no intent in the world that anything might come of it. Sets?"

"*Quatorze.*"

"*Very* good. The luck is with you now, William."

The lawyer led to his first trick, the Justice declared his five spades, and the rest of the play proceeded with no more sound than the well-greased shuffle and clip of the cards going down.

"And yet here," resumed De Lancey, "almost any man who cares to, may take up twenty acres, for the mere claiming of them, and defending of them, and sweating for them. And many do. And in this manner, forty or fifty years have passed, till it comes to seem, to the generation that possess the province now, both English and Dutch, that a vote almost must be the perquisite of every adult man, if he be a proper man, if he respect himself—and all without a principle involved, without an end in view, though now it *has* come to pass, we start very readily to discern principles in't, and ends it may come to serve, after all. Till we commence, Mr. Smith, and all by chance, to grow into something, of all things, like a Democracy. We are become Athenians, by accident! Thirty, forty, fifty-two, fifty-three. Victory to you, William, though narrowly. Young man, the game returns to you."

They ante'd up again, all three. Smith was no longer surprised that De Lancey should flip real gold from his pocket. The pot had grown to a little heap; a heap certainly worth six guineas, discounting his own paper contributions. He was endeavouring to simulate a civil attention to the political sermon De Lancey seemed to think he must pinion him in place to hear, but in truth Smith's attention was distracted more and more by the money, and by the thought of all the bread and oysters and necessaries of the flesh it might represent. *I am but a temporary tenant*, declared the beef in his stomach. *By morning you will feel me no more. Your regular vacuum will succeed me.* It had occurred to him—what no doubt has occurred to the reader long since—that a pile of money obtained by gambling is one of the few forms of gain that is compatible with the presumed indifference of a rich man. It may be got easily, sounding no alarms in the onlooker. —If it can be got at all. Cutting for deal with William Smith, he drew only a nine, and his heart sank. But the lawyer cut only an eight. Mr. Smith was Elder, with all the greater advantages of the lead. He swapped out such cards as he was entitled to, and made such other manoeuvres as he was entitled to (and which the poor account of the game above has sealed inscrutably from the reader) and gazed at his temporary kingdom; nodding and smiling as De Lancey talked on, and praying inwardly, and trying not to tremble.

"Six hearts," he said.

"Good, damn your eyes," said the lawyer.

"*Quart.*"

"Equal. Queen?"

"King."

"Have you had much to do with political men, yourself?" asked De Lancey.

"Little enough," said Smith, shortly.

"But something?"

"I thought you were resolved to take no notice of what I said, sir."

"I only wish to see that you have that minimum of experience required to understand me, young man: that you are not an entire idiot. In the Greek sense, of course."

"In fact I have dined with your cousin, sir," said Smith, nettled, and paying no attention to the subtleties of *idios* in Greek; nor mentioning, either, the many yards of table-cloth lying between when he had, in the technical sense, sat at table with Lord Pelham.

"Really?" said De Lancey. "At Laughton?"

"No, at another place," Smith said.

"Well, then, I proceed with confidence," said De Lancey. "Play on, play on! Now, sir: this power of chance must reign most strongly when the table is most evenly balanced, in politics, as well as in piquet. Small perturbations have biggest effect when all hangs finely between one thing and t'other. When the scores are almost level, and the single card you had not anticipated turns up where you had not expected it. As there, in that trick, for instance: ouch. And as here and now, Mr. Smith, in this city and at this juncture. If the Assembly have enough votes (but only just enough) to deny the Governor his means to make war, and to deny him too, what is the usual resource of government, a supply of money to bribe and to treat and to persuade sufficient of the electors to shift a seat or two in his favour—why then, sir, if a stranger should appear, with a mass of cash that seemingly he may dispose as he wishes, then *he* may be the little chance that sways all. That swings the game. Ah, this one I see you must score out in detail. Do not forget the *capot*. And the winner is—? My condolences, William. In I come again."

The judge rubbed his hands in an expression of enthusiasm so palpably insincere, so entirely disconnected from his look of forensic intent, that it seemed a wonder the hands were connected to him at all. This time, when the stakes were presented, he paused with a fourth golden disc held between thumb and forefinger, and turned it, so the candle-flame made the guinea blaze and dim, blaze and dim.

"Yes," he said, "I had these of brother Lovell. Who understands plainly where his interests lie. Cut for deal. Jack? Let's see. Oh dear: King, and thus I am Elder again."

Smith gripped his cardboard court tight. It was not impossible, as Younger hand, for him to impede Elder sufficiently to prevail, and gain the second win, and the pot. But it was very improbable. Had Mr. Hoyle written of piquet as analytically as he had of whist, Smith would have been able to give an exact number to his scanty chance.

"Five clubs," said De Lancey, comfortably.

"Good," said Smith, wretchedly.

"*Tierce.*"

"Not good!"

But De Lancey was holding up the interdicting finger again—tilting it—pointing it—into the shadows at Smith's left.

"A lady to speak to you, I think?"

He and the lawyer gazed with unhurried interest where Tabitha was standing at his elbow, clasping her hands together. The other politicos turned at their tables to survey her. There were smiles and muttered comments. She was very much the only woman at the smoking, gaming end of the hall. Smith felt a flash of resentment, that he should needs feel concern at such a thing. He found it hard to drag his attention from the printed red and blue and black in his hand, in which his immediate destiny seemed all encoded.

"Yes?" he said, glancing up. "This is not a good moment."

"I'll be brief," she said. "I have spoke to the Secretary, and he says my part in the play is gone, and why. I had not thought—" she said, and stopped, a struggle in her voice such as to penetrate, finally, all through the atmosphere of piquet. He looked up properly. Her mouth was clamped in a thin line. "I had not *thought*," she said again, winning back her control of herself, "that you would use what I said, about what the theatre means to me. I did not think you would. But it was a good move," she said. "It was a very good move. I shall remember it." And she grinned at him like a carpenter screwing a clamp wider open.

"Tabitha, wait—" he said. But she walked away. He tried to push back his chair, to follow her, but the same unseen human obstacle behind was holding him in place.

"I have not finished," said De Lancey. "Look back this way. Look at me. Bring back your mind. The stranger I was talking of? If such a man should appear, would he not be the subject of the most intense concern? Would it not be a matter of the most pressing import, if he should seem to be becoming, on the swiftest terms, an intimate of the Governor's suite? Would it not be most urgent, that it should be made clear to the *boy* in question, that his own fate, in just the same way, is trembling between alternatives? Depending how he conducts himself, Mr. Smith, he may with a few small steps in one direction or the other, put himself either in the way of making his fortune, or else just as easily ending it, in some unpleasant accident. Two destinies, sir, very nearly placed. One of gold, or at any rate of golden gratitude, for you know now how rare the veritable metal is. And one of lead. —Or of broken ice. Or of a long drop. —Have I spoke clearly enough? Am I understood?"

"Yes, sir," said Smith, transfixed. "I assure you, in all honour—

I am nothing in that line. I am not a bag-carrier for the ministry. Or a piece of left-hand aid dispatched to the Governor."

"I'm delighted to hear it," said the Chief Justice, regarding him ironically. "Of course, if you were, you would say the same. And if you were a Walpole-ite, seeking a safe home across the sea for some of the spoils of the late ministry—the same. And if you were the Jesuit or Jacobite some take you for—the same. When you deny all possibilities, this denial can carry no more surety than the rest. But I thank you." Watching still, considering still, De Lancey seemed content to continue indefinitely, watching and considering.

"I was saying, not good?" Smith offered—the game having turned suddenly to the least of his anxieties.

"Oh, as to that," said De Lancey, with an imperial smile, laying down his hand, "I find my cards are so poor I must resign. The pool is yours. Go on," he said, when Smith still sat, confused. "Take your winnings—and consider your position. Go on," he repeated. "If you hurry, you may catch her yet."

And Smith left the room, to the sound of male laughter. But though he hurried through the streets all the way to Golden Hill, none of the parties of revellers he passed was the Lovells or the Van Loons, and when he reached the house, the windows were dark. He did not knock.

"What do you make of the boy?" De Lancey asked William Smith later, with the brandy bottle almost empty.

"What do you think of him—Oakeshott's friend, I mean?" Terpie Tomlinson asked Major Tomlinson, propped up on three white pillows. But Major Tomlinson did not reply, except in the most liquid terms, his mouth being full at the time. (Why, what was he drinking? Nothing.)

By morning the news was all around the town from Trinity

Church to the Bouwerij that the stranger with the money, however he had come by it and whatever he purposed to do with it, was himself assuredly an actor.

III

The lawyer's stakes at the table turned out to be not even colonial notes of the usual baffling variability, but certificates drawable upon a tobacco warehouse in Virginia, and Smith presented one without much hope, the first time he tried their use as payment. But it was accepted without demur, at fifty-five per centum of face, New-York's merchants seeming all to maintain within themselves a register of values for every conceivable money-substitute they might encounter. Wampum, tobacco bales, rum by the gallon: it was all money, in a world without money. Between the tobacco tickets and his own pointedly-returned guineas, Smith calculated he now possessed enough to reach Christmas in relative ease—if he could avoid being knocked on the head for spoiling De Lancey's game against the Governor, or offending in some other role pressed upon him, or falling victim to a misadventure entirely unsuspected.

Relieved therefore of the fear he would starve, yet supplied with new matter for alarm, Smith over the following days watched from his vantage point in the Merchants as the city rose to a frantic zenith of activity. One of the two peaks of the New-York year, said Hendrick, bawling explanations in the suddenly far more crowded coffee-house: the other being the moment in late spring when the fleet returned from the sugar isles with the harvest aboard, and every trying-house, refinery and distillery would belch sweet smoke, and the air would burn with caramel. For this, though, the first and outward pulsation of the city's commerce, every ship in the harbour, every keel belonging to a Mannahatta merchant house, must be crammed to the gunwales with the products of the farms up-island and up-river. Land in the tropic Indies being too scarce to expend on any crop save the precious cane, the slaves who grew it, in the Barbadoes and Jamaica, Saint-Domingue and Demerara, were fed on flour and biscuit and dried peas from the provinces to the north. The slaves died in prodigious number, but there were always numbers still more prodigious from Africa to replace them in the great machine, and so the owners kept on buying, and eagerly, all that the Province of New-York could grow for their sustenance. Naturally they paid in their own crop. Wheat out, sugar back. So the traffic along the Broad Way, and in Broad Street and Maiden Lane and every other street that gave entrance to the docks, thickened to the point of deadlock. The laden carts and wains Smith had seen coming in through the fields beyond the stockade became a continual procession, a bumping, lurching, swaying, slow armada on wheels, advancing inch by congesting inch through every cobbled chink in the city's fabric that was wide enough (and some that proved not wide enough). Carters swore, horses jibbed and shat, loads slewed. While, on the water, river-schooners from up the Hudson and coasters from all along Long Island and Connecticut, and wherries plying across from Jersey, brought in cargoes of sacks that way, to be raised from one hold to another at the dockside on creaking cranes. A hundred wooden arms moving at once; a hundred sets of cries of Way and Ready and Ware Below; an orgy of transhipment. Carpenters in all the cross-trees, hammering; new spars of resin-smelling pine rising up to them in slings; sail-makers sewing; cordwainers paying out the perished pieces in old rigging and filling in with new manila; an aerial chorus of knocking and banging going on into the night, night after night by lamplight. And into the city, too, flowed all the sailors who would crew the voyage. Tars by trade who farmed at home for the summer months, and younger sons from the Hudson settlements shipping out to earn the wherewithal to set up in new fields and houses of their own, and assorted hopefuls and wanderers and chancers of all descriptions—all these, thronging the taverns, and roaming the night streets in jovial gangs looking for entertainment, and filling out every lodging-house that had bedding or floor-space or attic-space to spare. Mrs. Lee extended her breakfast table by three more wooden leaves, and was kept running with trays of porridge. Since all these new guests were swiftly informed in whispers of Smith's riches, he was fronted, as he left the house each morning, by frequent requests for loans, and offers of part-shares in schemes sure to make both him and the promoters a fortune by spring.

At Lions' Slip, just below Golden Hill Street, Captain Pretty-man watched over the stowage of the Lovells' and Van Loons' three Indies vessels, giving orders in authoritative squeaks, as if a lean ship's rat had risen up into the stature of a man. But Smith heard nothing from Tabitha. Having failed to find her and explain the mischance within the first couple of days, he had resigned himself to receiving some piece of ingenious nastiness in return, by message or by letter or in person, but nothing of the sort arrived, and as the silence lengthened, his reluctance to breach it on his side, and get visited on him whatever she had prepared, grew the more solid, these motives of cowardice or self-protection holding the field unchallenged in the absence of the sight of her face, and of what he had seen in it. He began to tell himself that the careless slight he had given, had been in truth a stroke of luck, and that there was an accidental wisdom (which perhaps De Lancey's philosophy would approve) in being extricated from a difficult connection with an acknowledged shrew. Yet, a peculiar compunction prevented him from asking Hendrick, any morning in the Merchants, how she did; for he had heard with what unaffection she was regarded in the family, and did not wish to salt the wound he had inflicted on her, by exposing the knowledge of it to Hendrick's likely laughter.

"Fallen out with my dear sister-in-law?" said Hendrick, and Smith only shrugged.

After ten days had passed, rehearsals began for Septimus' *Cato.* Mijnheer Van Torn's old theatre on Nassau Street turned out to be a simple box of a space upstairs, made by knocking through three of the narrow row-houses there, and very dusty and dark and cumbered by lumber it was. Powdery flotillas of moths rose from the decayed velvet curtain when it was touched. Smith and Septimus and a gruff lieutenant from the Fort by the name of Lennox, who was playing the part of Cato, had to begin by clearing timber off the stage, and unblocking the nearest pair of windows, so that the actors might see one another. Smith had half expected that Tabitha would make this the occasion for some exquisitely-calculated piece of sabotage or subversion, and appear alongside Flora with a heckler's arsenal of weapons ready: but Flora came alone. Alone, that is, except for the glowering presence of Joris, who sat on a baulk of planks in the half-dark like a spindly monument to disapproval. Flora paid him no attention. She was cheerful with Smith, chatty to Septimus, and so ingenuously pleased to be there with Lennox that he unbent to the extent of several smiles. The one she was wary of was Terpie Tomlinson; and Smith watched, fascinated, as Terpie in turn made it her special study to win Flora's confidence. She had come dressed in a dark respectable gown, buttoned up to the neck, and she sat very still until you forgot she was anything but a face and a pair of moving hands, and she took as the limit upon what she might do or say, Flora's own behaviour. She even copied, though Smith was sure Flora did not notice it, Flora's own gestures. Using only voice and hands she appeared to become another girl of seventeen, just as reassuringly confined by the proprieties, and just as forthrightly innocent—but perhaps a little shyer, requiring to be drawn out. She delivered her lines in the first read-through with a colourless clarity that had Septimus nodding with approval, but Smith thought he could guess what her final performance might be like. By the end of the rehearsal she and Flora were giggling together.

But no Tabitha. The month of November settled into chill mists, like an old sopha sinking down on its springs. Day upon day, the cold winds off the river stirred slow grey tributaries of fog between the houses, through which the crush of traffic loomed, and darkened as it loomed, as if becoming more solid with each approaching step. The fog contained and muffled the cries of draymen, squeak of wheelrims, hammering from aloft, *et cetera*, as a jewel-box with a cushioned lid presses all within into the smothering clasp of velvet. In the Merchants, at breakfast, Hendrick reported without any prompting or enquiry that Lovell and Van Loon senior were mired with business in the counting-house, and did not emerge from it now save to eat and sleep. Septimus, in the same place, attempted to gossip of the latest stratagems in the Assembly, and Smith, mindful of listening ears and the judge's threat, closed down the conversation. In the fog on the Common, sword on his belt, he paced from tree to tree getting his lines by heart.

> *A Roman soul is bent on higher views:*
> *To civilise the rude, unpolished world,*
> *And lay it under the restraint of laws;*
> *To make man mild, and sociable to man;*
> *To cultivate the wild, licentious savage*
> *With wisdom, discipline, and liberal arts . . .*

At the end of every line he stamped his foot. At the end of every speech he stamped and turned. The clamorous fog bore away his efforts and judged them not at all remarkable. It did pass the time. But no Tabitha. Ships were sailing, now, full-laden; dipping away into the hushing veils of white beyond the wharfs, as if bound for nowhere rather than the Indies. But others seemed to take their places without intermission, and at each next successive dawn—with the sun if glimpsed at all as a blue-green yolk, washed over by milk—the awkward frenzy went forward unabated. And no Tabitha.

After the third rehearsal, Septimus took him to a bath-house he had not suspected the existence of, on William Street. The steam was welcome, for the perpetual fog was beginning to make him cough. Hot and wet and smelling of birch, it drove through all the passages of his nose and chest into which the mist had insinuated its clammy fingers, and purged it out in a wholesome sweat. When first invited, Smith had imagined the steam-bath might be a place of ill-repute, as the bagnios were in Covent Garden, at home, and (while taking the invitation as a compliment) had wondered in what scenes he might find himself. But this one, stuffed as it was with sailors baking themselves clean before they embarked, was wild and licentious in no wise; seemed in fact a place of almost aggressive virtue, where men in crowded ranks squeezed together upon the wooden shelves of the hot room, and talked busily the while of the harvest they had brought in that autumn, and their plans for the voyage to come. Septimus, bolt upright in a blue towel, was entirely his public self, rather than the impassioned figure of the bedroom, though the genial roar of the room allowed for a reasonable privacy of speech.

"I was wondering," said Smith, passing the dipper, "whether at the performance, you mean me to put on black-face, for Juba?" This was a point he had particularly considered.

"God, no!" said Septimus. "For these purposes, you are to consider yourself the fairest-skinned African who ever lived. *North* African. African like the Barbary States. African like St. Augustine."

"*Semper aliquid novum ex Africa.*"

"Yes, exactly. Nice, safe, classical Africa."

"He is played dark in London," observed Smith.

"To be sure, but it would not answer here, even if you were

painted up in the most obvious boot-polish, I promise. For Juba loves Marcia, and Marcia loves Juba. And decent society here is *most* clear about where Eros may not visit."

"Even if he does," murmured Smith.

"Especially if he does," said Septimus, more *sotto voce* still. "In fact," he went on, regaining volume, "I've been thinking, *à propos* Marcia. —I might switch around her part and Lucia's, and have Terpie play her, instead of Miss Flora. Should you mind? I know you and Flora go nicely together."

"No, no, that would be fine with me," Smith said. "But why? Are you displeased in some way with Terpie as Lucia?"

"Never in life! She is as good as you said she'd be, and I owe you a debt for getting me to put down my prejudice and see it. But I must still guard against, um, accidents of perception."

"And you've found one?"

"I think so, yes. When Lucia says, of Marcia's brothers, that she longs 'for neither and yet for both'—I think, if Terpie is playing her, that the average dirty-minded New-York gentleman in our audience—being, you know, still filled unlike me with the popular prejudice *in re* actresses—will not be able to forbear to, well, to—"

"What?" said Smith, grinning.

"Well, to picture Terpie as the filling in a kind of Roman sandwich. I foresee snickering."

"Fair enough," said Smith.

And hence at the next rehearsal he found himself opposite Terpie Tomlinson rather than Flora. Though constructed so generously in terms of proportion, she was not, on the absolute scale, very large at all: her head only came up to his chin. As she gazed sternly up at him, without breaking character either as a stoic virgin of ancient times or as a nice young girl playing one, she lowered the eyelid nobody else could see from their positions on the dusty boards, and winked at him. But still no Tabitha.

By 26th November he had persuaded himself that his bruising encounters with the elder Miss Lovell had been merely an early interlude in his visit to the city, now thankfully concluded; a brush with a nasty (if uncommon) girl from which a misapprehension had fortunately delivered him, before it could interfere with his errand. Indeed he was so firmly persuaded of it that he revisited the question several times a day to persuade himself of it again, whenever the temptation grew too strong, to send a message by Flora, or by Hendrick, or to hammer on the street-door at Golden Hill until he was let in. Policy, self-preservation, self-respect, all argued for abiding by Tabitha's silence—which, by now, he did not expect to see broken.

So he was considerably surprised, that morning, when stepping out of Mrs. Lee's front door into more of the perpetual murk, he found himself greeted by the surly countenance of Isaiah, the Lovells' prentice, pressing a note into his hand; and opening it, discovered himself invited, in Tabitha's handwriting, to take a cruise with her up-river in the Lovells' lugger, to fetch the last loads of the cargo. Invited to join her at Ellison's Dock on the Hudson side, that day—that morning—now. There were no reproaches. "You may be glad to quit the Glue of Vapours for a Day," she wrote. "I am sick of it Myself." Smith thrust a random scrap of money-paper from his pocket at the startled prentice, and took to his heels.

Ellison's Dock was a wooden pier extending far out over the mud, from one of the tumbledown lanes west of the Broad Way, to give sufficient draught at low tide, and walking out on it now, into the coagulated grey curtains shifting above the river, seemed to remove one from the firm land without promising arrival anywhere else. It was silent out there, with the incoming salt-flow from the ocean swelling the sinews of the water but not breaking its glassy skin. Only the tiny purling of water against the piles could be heard. Smith wondered nervously if, at the end, he would find some street bully procured to push him in unobserved, but no, there in the fog was the lugger fat and broad and high-riding, creaking at its mooring-rope and bumping against the dock with the force of the moving tide, and its rigging ascending into unseen conjecture a few feet up; and when he called, and peered forward through the damp rope-work, there was Tabitha on deck, muffled up against the weather but bright-eyed, among Prettyman's small crew, and Zephyra hanging behind her, blank as ever, for the sake of the proprieties.

"I am so sorry—" Smith began, as he scrambled aboard.

"Oh, shut up," said Tabitha, slapping his arm. "Watch this."

They slipped the mooring, and the water carried them immediately out and away, with the steersman on the rudder merely nudging them to an angle on the swollen face of the tide. The swirling fabrics of the fog parted and sealed around them, placelessly, in grey limbo for a minute or so, and then suddenly parted for good. Suddenly, they were out of it altogether, drawing clear of a cloud-bank that lay long and curling to the right, stretching as far ahead and behind as the eye could see, with the whole city of New-York—in fact, the whole island of Manhattan—presumably buried inside it. Over on the left side, the Jersey shore too was lost behind another cloud-wall. The sky, though still cloud-covered, was higher and lighter and wider and more open than any he had glimpsed in more than a week. They were travelling up a lane of dull silver, wide enough to engulf the river Thames several times over, with all the solid geography round about apparently abolished on the instant; moving with a kind of effortless ease upon the moving bosom of the river, though not in solitude, for the silver was scattered with a gliding array of lighters, fishing smacks, long-boats and larger vessels, all catching the tide upstream. The sailors hoisted one triangle of canvas on the lugger, which scarcely even swelled in the damp still air but lent a kind of heft to the pull of the rudder, and lit their pipes.

"Magic!" said Tabitha. "I thought I owed you for the coin trick."

"That was free."

"So is this. Nearly, anyway. You can't expect me to pull a whole ship from your ear, without a bit of preparation."

"Where are we going?"

"Not far. Only to Tarrytown, to load up Cortlandt flour, and then back on the ebb this afternoon." She leant far out over the side and hung there, looking ahead to the vanishing-point where whites, greys and river silver met. Smith was content to gaze at the back of her head, where her hair was escaping again in tendrils from the silver pins securing it, and above her muffler, as she stretched, he could see the tendons moving in her narrow neck.

"You must let me explain properly what happened, about the play," he said.

"Must I?"

"I would like to, please," Smith said, still addressing her hair. "For it was an accident, and not a manoeuvre in Queen Tabitha's War, at all."

She blew dismissively through her lips but turned to face him, glancing as he spoke at his forehead, at his shoulders, at his chest— all around him, yet not quite at him.

"I was distracted at the dinner," he said. "Plays and players and play-houses are something I . . . know about; and when a piece of my own world floated into view I grabbed it for the pure pleasure of not being at sea any more in an unknown place, among unknown people; and applied myself to the question of Septimus Oakeshott's play as if it were just a question, a conundrum with no consequences; and I did not remember at all what it might mean to you, till it was too late; and I know it does not reflect well on me that I should manage to forget entirely the concerns of a friend, but at least I wasn't aiming—"

"You talk a *lot*," she said.

"Especially when I'm nervous."

"Why should you be, if I'm your *friend*?—You'll have to excuse me. I haven't said much for a fortnight. Father is deep in the books, and Flora is gone. My mouth is rusting shut."

Smith glanced at Zephyra. Evidently Tabitha did not categorise her as company, or as a source of conversation. It was true that he himself had not yet heard her speak.

"You could come to the rehearsals," he said.

"No."

She still had not looked at him straight on. Her eyes kept up a flickering dance of avoidance, around and about his visage. He could almost feel it: a tickling, wary, dry, velvet-light attention, as if he were being visited by the scouts of a bee-swarm.

"Tabitha, why are *you* so nervous?"

That stopped her. The brown gaze locked to his. The bees stung.

"Why do you think?" she said, fiercely.

This was a statement capable of several meanings. Mr. Smith tried not to assume the one that was most flattering to a young man's sensibility, but he did not altogether succeed. In fact he felt a little swelling of heat and satisfaction behind his breastbone. *There is no need*— he began to say, in his head, but stopped himself before the words reached his lips. Slow down, he told himself. Remember all the impossibilities. Remember what you must do. Remember what you are. Remember everything. Patience.

He smiled at her instead. She scowled, and shook her head like somebody trying to clear a blockage from their ear.

"Tell me where we've got to," he said.

"Spouting Devil Creek," she said, pointing to the right, to where the cloud-bank was breaking up along what seemed to be a side branch of the river. "The top end of Mannahatta."

The Hudson was narrowing, and through the cloud on both sides, glimpses of much higher bluffs were appearing, steep and wooded and dark, and tinted also with a mysterious dim red. The tide was carrying them up into a valley as deep as a canyon; the current within the tide was drawing them rapidly in toward the right-hand shore, until a wall of hillside was scudding by close enough to reduce the mist to mere streamers and tatters, and Smith could soon see, tilting above him, a continual blanketing thicket of bare trees in spidery grey filigree, all strung with tresses of dead creeper, the strange colour explaining itself as a kind of autumn tinge in the bark that (repeated a millionfold) made the whole wood glimmer faintly maroon. The rocks at the Hudson's edge were drawing a little too close for comfort. Two more of the sailors joined the steersman to lean hard on the tiller. Smith and Tabitha moved out of the way, and fetched up together against the right-side rail. Creaking, groaning, the lugger's prow came round, and they eased back more comfortably offshore, into the deeper channel; but Tabitha and Smith stayed, side by side, at the rail, looking out. The strange noiseless flight, the unexpected height and grandeur of the scene, the colour unknown in all his previous experience of country views, lulled Mr. Smith into an awed, almost an enchanted state, and perhaps something of the same quieting effect operated on Tabitha, despite the familiarity of her home river, for her agitation seemed to be soothing away. She too seemed content to gaze at each new sight the thinning mist disclosed.

"I can't tell you how glad I am to be out of the town," said Smith, after a time.

"I thought you were a city animal, through and through," said Tabitha.

"True, I am," said Smith. "But—not meaning any offence by it?—New-York scarce qualifies."

"And London does, I suppose."

"Oh yes. London is a world. —No, a world of worlds. Many spheres all mashed together, to baffle the astronomers. A fresh planet to discover, at every corner. Smelly and dirty and dangerous and prodigious. I wish I could show it you."

"You love it."

"Yes—or I love what it has been to me. New-York, compared, is small and tidy and amazingly much all the one thing, when you get used to it, and you see the same faces over and over."

"Yet here you are instead."

"Yes."

"Because you love running away, too. Even more," said Tabitha with satisfaction, like one who completes a theorem, and now has the whole knowledge of something tidily tabulated.

"How do you know that?" said Smith, startled.

"It's obvious."

"Is it?"

"Yes!"

"Well, I hope it's only obvious to you."

"My dear man," said Tabitha—a phrase which in her mouth sounded like part of the borrowed equipment of a little girl playing house, as much as it did an endearment—"there is a whole school of thought about you, that holds you to be a banker's clerk, or a scrivener's prentice, who has run off with a bill from the master's desk."

"But I'm—I'm not—"

Mr. Smith had had so little practice, lately, in explaining himself, that now, when he wanted to, he stumbled.

"It was in London I did my running away," he said, trying to collect himself. "If I was to run away here, I would go *back*."

"I don't understand," said Tabitha, who looked as if she did not want to.

"This is my dutiful self you are seeing," said Mr. Smith. "My attempt at duty, anyhow."

"Smith the hero," said Tabitha scornfully. "Smith the valiant."

"Must you always interpret me in the most unfriendly way?" he cried. "I do my best to think the best of you!"

Hearing their voices raised, Captain Prettyman was staring Smith's way, with no friendly expression on his face. Tabitha raised a quelling palm in the Captain's direction, and he subsided. Smith felt an abrupt and uncomfortable consciousness that he was with Lovell's daughter, aboard Lovell's ship, among Lovell's men.

"I mean it," Smith said. "Here I must wake every morning, and stay in the same place all day long, waiting. My feet itch to be moving, and I ignore them. I hate confinement; *hate* it."

"You would not be very happy as a girl, then," said Tabitha, "if you regard a few weeks of idleness and play-acting as an intolerable burden." But she put her hand on his shoulder, and kept it there. "Hush," she said. He could feel the moment of hovering and hesitation, as it arrived; and the way she pushed through it; and the way it seemed to call on resolution, in her, to do so. Which made it seem the more valuable, to him. Even through his coat and his shirt he could feel what he had noticed when she had caught at his hands, before—that Tabitha's blood ran hot, a little hotter than the ordinary, as if she were all the time in a dry, hectic fever. He imagined what it might be, to feel the furnace burn of the whole red-pale-brown length of her against his skin. —Yet the touch on his shoulder was steadying. The heat of it, coming steadily through his clothes, smoothed him like a flat-iron. "Hush," she repeated.

"Alright," he said. "I do not wish to give scandal."

"Good," she said. "They say this part of the river is like the Rhine."

Indeed, they had passed the narrow point, and the river was broadening, and broadening still, to an immensity that astonished him, and all of it visible now, for the mists were fading or withdrawing, into distant cloud, hanging above far shores of grey and russet and brown forest, and lines of crags. The impetus of the tide was lost in the width of the water, and they drifted onward, only, across a surface as steady as metal, as well as having its colour, while the crew hoisted more sail, to catch the little cats'-paws of breeze that came wrinkling and dabbing the water, scuffing the water as they touched it, from silver into pewter. The reflection of cliff and forest came and went in bands, where the breeze blew or did not. They watched together. It was a sight to make all human scurrying seem minuscule, and still it was a grateful sight, in its contagious peace: a sight, it seemed, to lay the phantoms of mistakes not yet made. Slowly, the lugger got enough way on her to begin a long curve, aimed at a point as yet invisible on the right-hand shore, ahead.

"Bigger than the Rhine," said Smith. "Bigger and grander." He cleared his throat. "Homer compared to a sonnet, I swear. A canto laid up against a couplet."

"You've seen the Rhine?"

"Yes. —Yes!" he insisted, when she squinted sceptically. "I have done the whole Tour. I have received the education of a gentleman. Why else do you think I needed to run away?"

She clicked her tongue at him.

"It's not a temptation you feel, then?" he asked. "You don't ever want to rise up from your chair, and walk down the stairs, and put on your coat, and step out of the door onto Golden Hill, and just *go*?"

"Where would I go to?" she said.

"Anywhere," he said. "You have a whole continent to choose from. Look at it. You could land anywhere on that shore, and just walk away, under the trees."

"Do you know what is under those trees?"

"What?"

"Nothing, Smith. More nothing than you can possibly imagine. You come from England: you think there will be villages, and roads, and inns to stay in, and there are not, hardly. Just hundreds of miles of bare branches, and dead leaves, and valleys without names. You would lie down and die in it, if you went in without knowing what you were doing—which you do not. You would freeze, or starve, or be scalped; all alone."

"I was not suggesting doing it alone."

"People are different," she said. "They differ even in their mad ideas, Smith." She took the hand off him, and he felt the patch of himself where the contact had been cooling, painfully, towards solitude. Tabitha hugged both her arms around herself, and lowered her chin into her scarf. "I find the idea of stepping off the edge of the world . . . terrifying," she said. "Going flailing down into empty space."

"It is worst the first time you do it," he said. "Then you find that you can find your way. You find that there is enough in you, to manage."

She only shook her head in the scarf.

"Besides," he said daringly, "I think it might be good for you. What else is there here for you?"

"The family. The business."

"Apart from that?"

No reply.

"I think," he said, "that you may be the kind of dog who bites because she is chained up."

He expected her to laugh, or to flash out at him, or to do both. She did look up, but with a melancholy kind of trouble in her eyes.

"A lovely analogy: I thank you," she said. "But what if I am the kind of dog who bites because it pleases her?"

"I don't believe it," said Smith.

Tarrytown was another wooden pier with a couple of muddy streets behind it, and beyond them a shelf of land a couple of miles wide, given over to fields, before the steep bluffs rose, at the valley's rim. Sacks and crates were waiting, piled on the pier, and loading began at once. Tabitha had some call she must make, as the daughter of the house of Lovell, and he wandered a little way inland while she was busy, along a deserted lane. She was not quite right about there being nobody in the woods, he saw: up on the top of the ridge the faint smudge of smoke from a fire was rising into the grey sky.

When he strolled back, he found her in urgent talk, at the pier's end, with Prettyman and another man—an agent, or factor, perhaps, who was stuffing papers back into a case. She broke off, seeing him, and strode quickly over, bidding the men to stay behind with another of those quick hand-chops of command. Smith was so happy to see her face—found her face so important a luminary, in the dimming grey expanse of the day; so unlike the rest of the lumpish indifferent matter of creation—that he did not pause over the look of stricken resolution upon it. He merely added to his elation an impulse of comfort, and a buoyant surety that, with a little perseverance, he would be able to ease her anxiety, whatever it might be.

"I think you should stay here," she said.

"What? Why?—You've changed your tune," he said, half-laughing in a suspicion of an imminent joke.

"There *is* an inn," she went on, still apparently in earnest. "You could stay a few days—try the lie of the land—breathe deep—give the city a rest. You said you wanted to."

"Just now? Tabitha, I was romancing," he said, grinning for two. "Not that I did not mean the invitation, most earnestly"—in case he was accidentally banishing a future happiness—"but . . . but . . . it would not answer. I am, truly, bound by duty, till my business is done. Then I am yours for any escape; for anything."

"Shut up!" she said. "I didn't ask for that. —You're sure?"

"Yes!"

"Very well, then: come along, we're sailing." And she turned on her heel with a snap, and led the way back aboard the boat.

Smith had imagined that there would be time again for serious speech between the two of them, on the return leg to New-York; but as well as a hold full of sacks and a deck laden with casks, the lugger had also taken on a moderate clutch of New-York-bound passengers, from Dutch farm-wives carrying baskets of eggs to several more would-be sailors for the Indies voyage, and a talkative attorney, up, he said, from Baltimore to view the northern colonies. Smith and Tabitha were parted by the casks and the crowd, and he spent the journey back into fog and darkness on the ebb tide, obliged to lob back the attorney's conversational sallies; and thinking wonderingly, where he could betwixt the distractions, as young men are likely to do in these circumstances, how very ordinary and general and unremarkable a destiny it must be, how predictable a part of the universal portion of mankind it is, to love and to feel oneself beloved; and yet how astonishing it seems when it happens to you, yourself; what a stroke of glorious, undeserved, unprecedented, unsuspected luck it turns out to be, that you should be permitted, in your own person, to share in the general fate. It was not until the end of the voyage that she squeezed her way back to his side. They had entered the Manhattan cloud-bank again, and were sounding their way in to the dock with halloos, amid a gloom still darker than before.

"Smith—" she began.

"Richard," he said. "I think you could call me Richard."

"If you insist," she said. The curiously stricken look had gone, and she was animated again. More than animated; almost frantic, as if she was bursting with some news. "Richard, the *Antelope* docked last night—"

"Who are these people?" he interrupted, for Ellison's Dock had swum up out of the murk, and the shadowy group standing at the end of it had the unmistakeable look of officialdom, of worldly powers about their duties.

"The beadle and constables of the Out Ward," she said. "*Antelope* came in last night without any copy of your bill. You are a fraud; you are detected. If you had been abroad in Manhattan today, you might have heard the news and slipped away, but I have made sure you did not. We have *got* you, Mr. Smith. You are caught. I have caught you!"

On her face there was a writhing mixture of triumph and shame, horrible to see.

4

A LETTER

to the Reverend Pompilius Smith

New-York, 1st December 1746

Sir:

You have warned Me so many Times, of the Dangers of the
World, for such as Us, should We but stray one Step beyond the
Bounds of our Safety, that You will not be surprised to discover
(after so long a Silence) that my present Accommodation is a Gaol.
Not, however, one of the common Bridewells of London, where
You may expect Me to have tumbled, after the Misadventures You
predicted, when I quit the Patronage of Lord ——, and declined to
submit Myself tamely to the Connection He had devis'd for Me at
Oxford, in the perpetual Role of Hanger-On to his Son. Instead an
Ocean lies between: my Confinement is American. I find Myself
lodged in the Debtors' Prison of the City of New-York. Which is,
to particularise less grandly, an Attic of the Town-Hall here. The
Apparatus of the Courts, as of the Government, is all conducted
upon the Floor beneath. At present I am detain'd upon the civil
Suit of my Land-lady and some Merchants and Victuallers with
Whom I had run up Bills; but a Date is set for my Trial upon

a criminal Charge of Fraud, in the Courtroom below, and if all continues to go ill with Me, as Events seem presently determin'd to do, I shall within some Days pass irresistibly downward through the whole Building, for the criminal Prison is in the Cellar. And though my Fate after that would comprise a brief Excursion to the Common, it would in a manner of speaking be downward still. Fraud, as I have been informed with vengeful Grinning on all Sides, is a Hanging Offence. So if found guilty, my Destination would be swiftly Subterranean.

I confess, Father, that were it not for this Consideration, I should probably preserve the Silence between Us that has lasted since I declin'd Oxford, and the petted and protected Future that would have followed it, by departing His Lordship's House in Grosvenor Square, through the Scullery Window. It gives me no Satisfaction to confirm the Judgement which You long ago made, of my Recklessness. Yet I would not desire to quit this dangerous World, without ensuring You receive some Account of your Son, and to tell Truth, there is some Comfort in addressing You thus, for I am Nineteen Parts in Twenty wretched, many Things upon which I had counted or hoped, having misfir'd, or proved flat contrary to my Hopes and Understandings of Them. And as my Pen scratches on, between the bare Walls of Lath and Board, and the Noise of the World's Business floats up on ever colder Air, to the two unglaz'd Dormers with which my Apartment is provided, I discover in Myself too a meagre Satisfaction, in being able to talk to you at whatever Length I chuse, without You interrupting Me—without it being in your Power, to raise your Voice, or clap a Hand to your Temple, or to declare in your Pulpit Manner, the Strictures of God's Word upon ungrateful Children. I am not in your Study now, but You in Mine. I may say what I like, while Paper and Ink hold out.

For These I am indebted, to my remaining Friend in this Place, Mr. Oakeshott. He is much puzzled, having but recently decided upon my Honesty, by this Sign that (perhaps) I am now after all not to be relied upon. He does not know, whether He was fooling Himself before, or whether He would be a Fool now, to continue even in so generous a State concerning Me, as Doubt. I exasperate Him: which as You see, is the Mode of my Relations with much of the World, and not just with You. But such is Mr. Oakeshott's Make, that He cannot forebear the Attentions of Charity, having once suffered Himself to feel a Connection. You would recognise and approve Him, Father, in some Things at least. He too is a Child of the Parsonage, inculcated with Principles of Benevolence and Magnanimity that work in Him most comically, whether He will or no, despite a sharp Tongue and a mordant Temper. He saved my Life three Weeks ago, in a Fit of Annoyance. I wish I could give Him better Recompense. —All these are Deductions made in His Absence, for He has not visited Me Himself, but sent his Man Achilles, with a Basket containing some Provisions, and the Means to write this Letter.

"Is he very angry?" I ask.

"Oh yes," says Achilles, cheerfully. "All the People are telling Him, He has made Friends with a Rogue and a Thief. The Governor scolds Him; then in the Coffee-House They laugh and say, look, the Governor's Side is the Side for Thieves and Rogues."

"Oh dear."

"He uses stronger Words, Sir."

"Will you tell Him how grateful I am, for—" and I indicate the Basket, which I can see has Bread, and Cheese, and Apples in it, all bought no Doubt on Oakeshott's Credit, He possessing little else to share. Achilles has not actually passed it through the wooden Bars of the Apartment yet, but holds it teasingly close.

"Maybe I wait till he is more calm."

"Alright. It is very kind of Him," I say, endeavouring not to reach out. (I have not eaten for a Night and a Day at this

153

Moment, it being impossible to adopt the usual Expedient of
Debtors, and commission the Turnkey to go to the Merchants for
my Meals. Having sued Me for the Amount of my existing Debt
to Them, They are inclined to feed me no further. And this is the
general Judgement. I may go empty-stomach'd to the Gallows, in
the Opinion of New-York.)

"He is a good Man," says Achilles, turning upon Me his small
neat Visage, and a smiling Gaze with Intent flickering in it,
like a Snake's Tongue. He has said it before, but now there is
a protective Warning in it. Achilles too is angry, I understand.
Perhaps more furious than His Master, for what am I to Him?

"I know that."

"Yes, Sir. And you, Sir? What about You?"

I am enough your Son, not to answer that Question with an
easy Affirmative. I shrug. Achilles shrugs in return, with a Twist of
his Mouth, and hands me the Basket.

"Well," he tosses out, departing, "here is the next bad Thing for
you, coming along quick, like I said."

So I dine on one Slice of the Bread, and a Corner of the
Cheese, and an Apple; and in the Morning, I breakfast on a Heel
of the Bread softened in Water, and another Corner, and another
Apple, and I resist the Urge to fill my Belly with more, since I
do not know how long I must endure on These alone, and thus I
keep Body and Soul scraping along Together. I pray, most gravely
I assure You; and I write This, and the Practice of it saves Me from
incontinent Howling. For the most Part.

There is little to be found otherwise within these Walls, of
Recreation. The Turnkey, a Mr. Reynolds, having so few Clients,
scarcely looks in upon Us, and I have had Nothing of my sole
fellow Captive, in the wooden Cage across the Floorboards,
but Groans, issued from a malodorous Heap of Blankets. He
is (reputedly) a decay'd Soldier of some Sort. I can tell by my

own Ears and Nose that the last Part of *His* Debt to the good
Merchants of New-York, He certainly incurr'd in Liquor.

I watch the slow Progress of the Daylight in the Windows,
and I wait, trying to extract some Pleasure in the Snail's Pace of
the Hours, from the Reflection, that if (or when) I step up to the
Noose a Week hence, I shall at that Time wish very earnestly that
I might exchange the Situation for mere Sorrow and Boredom
and Hunger, in a comfortable Cell. But I do not wait well, when
I must sit still—as You will recall of course, from Our thousand
Collisions upon this very Topick, and the thousand Sermons
You have given me, and Whippings too, to recommend the
Necessity of Patience, whilst I wriggled and writh'd and chaf'd.
You would think, Father, if you could see Me here, that I have
learn'd the Lesson, for to the exterior Eye I sit good and patient
indeed, upon the Floor, with my Back to the Wall and my Knees
up as a Writing-Desk, and Mildness adorning my Countenance.
But within I rage, and shout, and kick. There is One, of course,
from whom I would desire a Visit more than any Other, were
her Purpose in coming nothing save to gloat. But I am not such
a Fool, as to ignore the third Demonstration of her Ill-Will
toward Me. Fool Me once, fool Me twice, and I retain my Smile
of foolish Hope. Fool Me three Times, and a stupid Suspicion
stirs eventually in Me that my Feelings are not returned. I have
not the Heart, to render more fully the Mistakes I have made
in this Respect. Suffice it to say, that I mistook Malice for Wit,
and a lively Interest for a kindly One. And yet, She seem'd at
Tarrytown—no; no. No, that Way lies my Chance to become a
four-fold Fool. With some People, I learn, there is no Mending
of Injuries, for there is no Wish to be less than scarred. I am sure,
that if I explained Myself to You, You would unfailingly observe,
how mad in Me it was, to have entertained any Hopes, placed as
I am upon this mad Errand: yet believe Me, that it would point a

diverting Moral, and make at least a sour Specimen of Comedy, if You could behold how I, who makes such a Boast that I do what I chuse, found out at Expense the common Knowledge of Mankind, that You do not chuse where You bestow your Heart. Your Heart bestows Itself, will-you-nill-you, in the Midst of other Business. —Perhaps You would not laugh, Father, but regard it as the Beginning of Wisdom.

I can hear the cries of the Costers upon Wall Street, below; and the calling of the Hour; and lately, now the Day darkens, a Dialogue between two waiting Chair-Men, upon the Chances of a Horse they favour to run at Flushing, named Royal Roger. Merriment, and bawdy Jests on the Subject of this Name. But I could make Nothing distinct of the Voices coming up directly through the Floor, from the Court and Assembly. They were too muffl'd, and Business down below is now prorogued, to judge by their Dwindling. It is a melancholy Reflection, that only a few Days past, I was dancing across that very Floor, and there receiving the Solicitations (albeit more terrifying than flattering) of the Powerful. I am imprison'd today, in gross Proximity to my swelling State of yesterday. The Judge, who yesterday cajol'd and threaten'd Me in case I should meddle against Him in the highest of Politics, will tomorrow frown on Me, as the Prisoner at the Bar. You would take from This, a Lesson in the World's Untrustworthiness—a Model of how slippery our Estates are, within It; how scantly possessed, on how weak a Security—and therefore, how much to be clung to, lest they slip from our Fingers. But I hold the Opposite. I take it as a Maxim, that One must skate on, though the Ice be thin; skate as fast as may be, as if the Footing be secure, even if it proves not so.

Talking of Ice, it is passing from chilly to freezing, in this Room. When they brought me in, the Day before Yesterday, a rheumatic Fog swaddled the City, but it has cleared. A Turn of the

Seasons seems come, a crisping and clarifying Advent of Winter. I
have the Suit of Clothes I stand up in, including my Coat, I thank
God, but no others to put on. The Air has hardened and stilled.
I smell the Smoke of Wood-Fires—not Seacoal, for They have
none—rising undisturbed in straight Lines from the Chimneys
of the City. Not from this Chamber, though, for We have no Fire
nor Fireplace. The Sky, clear blue in the Windows this Afternoon,
now descends a Ladder of blue Shades, travels a Spectrum as
lucid as Water yet blackening toward Ink. There will be Frost on
my Blanket in the Morning. My writing Hand is growing Numb.
I had better stop, for the Shade of the Window is now a Blue
it were a Work of Casuistry to distinguish from Black, and the
veritable Ink on my Page floats and glimmers, a dimming Ghost
of the Alphabet.

The next day. I had meant, at the Returning of the Light, to
begin the Work of explaining Myself to You, so that You might
understand, how I find Myself in Trouble here, so far from Home,
and might be persuaded, perhaps, that You need not be entirely
asham'd of Me, despite the Appearances of the Case. I image to
Myself You reading This, as I write It, so clearly that, although
it will be some Months hence that the Pages come into your
Hand, wither'd from the Salt Sea and smelling of Onions from
the carrier's Cart that brought it You from Blandford, the Words
seem to fly straight from my Mouth to your Ear. "The Dead yet
Speaking"—as it says from the Mouth of the Skeleton on the
Title Page of Fuller's Lives of the Divines, which is just behind
your left Shoulder as you sit in your common Stance of Reading,
with four spread Fingers of your Hand supporting your Forehead,
and your Little Finger curl'd. You see how I know You, though
We were a Torment to one another. And I suppose I torment You

now, for the last Time, with this News. I imagine you rising up, having finished the Letter, and folding It away as neatly as ever, and walking next Door to the Church-Yard, as long and black as ever in your Cassock and Gown, to communicate the Intelligence of It, at my Mother's Grave. You will think Me very stupid, that I had not consider'd, until the Forming of this Picture upon the Eye of my Mind, how alone my Death will render You. You have always occupied so great a Place in my Mind, that You seem'd to be, in Yourself, a Platoon, a whole Company of Men, as unsolitary as a Crowd. Father, I am truly sorry for this latest Grief I afford you. Believe Me, if I could, if it were in my Power, I would take this Paper on whose other Side You seem to sit now, whatever the Months and Miles between, and tear a Hole in It so cunningly, that I might fold It out into a Door in the Air, through which I could step, and at once be at Home with You. —Even if We quarrel'd but a Second later.

But my Longing—my Apology—my Design of Explanation— are All interrupted now, at Intervals of no more than Thirty Seconds, by my Fellow Prisoner across the Way. The Dormer on his Side faces due East, and as the Sun of December topp'd the Roofs of Wall Street, brilliant tho' without Warmth, it sent a golden Finger poking at his dirty Nest. The Blankets writh'd; He kick'd, He rose, a foul'd and filthy Anadyomene. The Night's Excesses roll off Him in sensible Waves, yet seem to have slough'd from his Mind. At least, They are no longer depressing It to Silence. If He is fuddled, it is vivaciously so. He has a Nose swollen to the Likeness of a Piece of Crimson Fruit, ornament'd by as many black Pores as there are Seeds upon a Strawberry; and a Skin of sunburn'd Leather otherwise, much pock'd and mottl'd; and verminous Hair as long as his Shoulders, depending from a bald Pate; and a Pair of Eyes so crusted and blood-shot They would deserve to be made an Epithet by Homer, yet bright,

and lively, and designing. I was puzzl'd, as to why I found Him
familiar, and then realiz'd, that He was the first living Sample
I had seen in New-York, of that Type of wreck'd Humanity, of
floating human Hulk, so commonly to be found in London, in
Gin-Cellars, and in Penny Lodgings of the lowest Kind. I must
have grown Here more rapidly tender of Stomach than I realised.

"Boy," He said, with a significant Nod, when He found Me
gazing at Him, and proceeded to his Toilet, of Spitting, and
Scratching for Lice, and Pissing in great gurgling reeking Volume
into his Pot.

"Good morrow," said I, Company after all being Company, no
matter what Charm it seem to lack, and I being mindful of the
long Hours I had passed yesterday without Diversion. "How do
you find Yourself, today? I hope your Head is not too sore."

"Well, ain't You the cheerful little Perrokweet," he answered,
showing me a brown-toothed Grin. "Wery polite. —It'll take more'n
a few Pints of Bumbo to keep Me on m'Back. To in-ca-passy-tate
the Capting." If He has ever been the Captain of Anything, then I
am the Apostle Paul. "Got any Prog over there, Boy? Kelkashose in
the Victuals Line?"

I looked reluctantly at my two Apples, and threw Him one. He
caught It from the Air with an Arm as dextrous as a Monkey's.

"'S that all You got? Well, needs must," and He proceeded to
eat it whole, Core and Pips and All, at last grinding away the Stem
between his snaggling Teeth, and belching reverberantly. "Bumbo's
a Lady on the Way down," He said, smacking his Tongue to his
Palate like a Natural Philosopher eagerly collecting a Specimen,
"but she in't Half a rough old poxy old Bitch when You comes to
wake up with her. Like Vinegar," said He, exploring. "Vinegar as
has had a Rat pickled in It. And I have et of our Brothers the Rats,
when Commons was short, so the Comparison, as You educated
Fuckers would say, is exact. So. Whatcher in for, Boy?"

"A Misunderstanding."

"Aye?"

"A Misunderstanding over some Papers."

"Papers, eh? Oh, 'Papers' is wery broad—anyfink from fiddling a Cargo to running a Book. What's your pertickler Mischief, then?"

I hesitated, and He began to cackle furiously.

"Oh, don't mind Me! Ne'ermind, ne'ermind, I'm only funning. I know what You done. Ev'ryone knows what You done. A thousand Pound for an arsewipe Bill you writ yourself! Handsome! Wery bold and handsome! Why think small, eh?"

"What about You?" I said, judging it better to turn the Conversation.

"Me? I'm a Regular, I am. This is my u-shual Chamber. Only, They don't bring Me in because of any Misunderstanding. They brings Me in when They understands all too clear there's Nothing in my Pockets no more. But don'tcher worry. I'll be out again in a Day or two, soon as Somefink dirty needs doing. I'm in Demand, I am. They know where to find Me." He winked one Oyster of an Eye, and tapped his Nose. "Unlike You, poor little Bugger, on your Way to the Hemp Jig. Shoulda started smaller. Ne'ermind, ne'ermind. We'll make the Time fly. Got any Cards?"

"No."

"Ah well. Any Baccy?"

"No."

"Ain't you the Misery, then? You wanna stir your Spirits up a Bit, Boy. No use drooping all over the fucking Floor now, eh? Too late now! Should've thought of That before. Live while You live, that's the Motto. You wanna feel the Blood moving. Tell you what. Have You had any Quim since You got here? There's a Nigger Gel on Cortlandt Street, Lips like Cushions, sucks like a Bilge-Pump for Sixpence. She—"

But I will spare You the Rest of his nasty Tirade, which however He did not spare Me, not one Jot or eager Detail or bright-eyed relishing Sound. It was a special Boast of his, that on his last Visit he had cheated Her of the Sixpence. The Animal Spirits seem to burn in Him undiminished by the Corruptions of his Flesh, as if, in Fact, his Weaknesses and Diseases had worn away not his Lusts, but all Checks and Restraints on Them; had only crazed the Pigsty's Walls, and let out the Pig. He wanted Me, when his Tale was done, and He was chuckling, and cracking his Knucklebones, and rubbing at his Cods, to pay Him back in Kind. I confess, I felt a vile Temptation, for a Moment, to pay back not Him but She in whom my Hopes are disappointed, by counterfeiting a lewd Story of her, and launching it via my Cellmate (who I am sure can hold Nothing back) into the Gossip of New-York. But my Despair is greater than my Anger, and the Thought of this, an Instant later, filled Me with a lurching Despondency near to Tears; and I replied instead, that I had a Letter to write. Sounding, I am sure, like the milkiest and most prim of Innocents, when in Truth I like my Share of the Pleasures of the Flesh as much as any Man.

And this I thought would terminate our Conversation. But the worst of my Cellmate is, that He proves One of those People with no inward Resources for Solitude at all. Having settled on Me to be his Entertainment, He is at Me continually. "Boy," He says. "Boy. Boy. Boy. Boy? Boy!"—on and on, until I answer. "What?" I say. And infallibly, every Time, he will reply, "Nuffink," and hoarsely chuckle, and seem to fall silent; and then resume, as if obliging Me with his Thought, "But what about—?" What about a Riddle, a Story, a Jest? What about satisfying his Curiosity in a million Particulars? "You'll like This," He says, and as He says it, eyes Me knowingly. When I grit my Teeth and try to be agreeable, He accepts It. When I show Signs of Impatience or

Antipathy, and try to turn Him off with short Answers, it pleases Him I think the More, as if He revelled in my Discomfort, and took a Delight in Smirching his Hearer's Ears against their Will. I should be able easily to turn and manage such a Conversation, having myself enjoyed many Varieties of low Company, and myself sparkled for a Wit in the Salons of the Gutter, and learned largely in Them of the Types of Humanity: but Today I cannot relax to It, I cannot find the Vein, I am too sad. I feel too a kind of Compunction caused by your Presence; even your paper Presence, at a great Remove. It seems I am in *your* Study, after all. I repel Him but feebly. "I must write my Letter," I say. "Whassit about? Whatcher saying? Who's it to?" He asks at once. A Nurse-Maid I spoke to, once said the Care of an Infant could become a kind of Torment or Madness, if You were alone, and must find new Matter to distract the Child every Minute; and that it was necessary then to guard against sudden, surprising Rages in your own Breast, dangerous to the Child. I thought Her then a little Dangerous or Lunatick by Temperament, that She should make such Difficulty at a simple Task. But now I understand Her in Full.

At about the end of the Morning, judging by the Traverse of the Sun outside, after a Passage of Time excruciatingly prolonged and sub-divided, his Temper grew more raw, and his Hands began palpably to shake. I judge that the receding Tide of the Bumbo had crossed the whole Zone of Lucidity in Him, and begun to expose a painful Need. He fell from Enquiries to Insults, and thence to Shouts. He rose on ulcered and vibrating Legs, and gripped the wooden Bars, and began to rage, in fevered Denunciations, at Me and at his Keepers and at many a Jack and Sue unknown to Me: a Development which I welcomed, as requiring less Participation on my Part, though I did not look forward to whatever frothing Fit the next Stage should bring. I

turned my Back and tried to fly away in Fancy. You may figure my
Surprise, when Reynolds the Turnkey responded to this ranting
Summons, and, climbing up the Stair to our Attic, seemed in
a fair good Humour over It. "Ho there, you Monster," he said
amiably—more amiably than He had been to Me—"is it Time
already for your Bottle?" And thorough the Bars He passed, as
if by absolutely accepted Arrangement, a black glass Flagon of
Spirits, which my Neighbour seiz'd and gulp'd at, with pulsing
Throat. "There now," said Reynolds. "Settle down now, like a good
Monster."

There was more here, than I understood, but I was glad of the
Mystery all the Same, for obediently the Rage was converted to a
trembling and reverential Suckling, at the very Rear of his Cage,
and thence to a renewed Stupor in the Straw, gloriously silent save
for a saw-toothed Snore. I might pity his Infirmity, was I not so
heartily grateful.

And so He has remained for two—three—four blissful Hours,
and I begin to collect Myself, and to win free of the Trembling He
induced in Me, and to gather such Calm in Me as is necessary for
Explanation. Now: You must know, Father, that I am not come
here in New-York, in any Spirit of idle Adventure, but rather,
to do a Duty such as You will respect once I expound It, at the
Request of—

But I have a Visitor. When Reynolds told Me so, and I heard
the light Feet of a Woman upon the Stair, my Heart leapt: but it
was not She, for whom I discover in Myself even the Willingness
to be gloated upon, but instead the African Maid of the House,
Zephyra, looking powerful Wary. She trod, as if She did not trust
the Floor, and She station'd Herself at the furthest Extremity of
my Cage away from my Neighbour's. This was to speak to Me
in Privacy, I first presum'd, yet then must admit a Correction, by
judging of her Tension as She turn'd her Face away from the other

Cage, and the flickering Glances she gave from the Corners of her Eyes, as if a Danger lay behind Her. Which seem'd to Me excessive, for though He was assuredly noxious, as I had Reason by now to know, He was safely penn'd.

"Hallo," I said, and then unable to repress a Hope, "Have You a Message for Me?"

"Yes," said She, and her Voice, which I had never heard before, prov'd deep and full of Vibration, like the String of a Violin-Cello. She lean'd in close, giving me Occasion again to observe, what uncommunicating Pools of Dark her Eyes were; and said with hush'd Emphasis:

"Mewura, wo ne gyefwo a me twen no?"

I blink'd, feeling Myself of a Sudden teetering on a dangerous Edge. "What?" I said.

"You do not understand Me," She said wonderingly. Then again, but bleakly and flatly, this Time: "You do not understand Me." A most woeful and grieving Look of Disappointment fill'd her Face for a Moment, before, almost more woefully, It was flick'd away by a great Effort of Will, drawn back as if It had never been, behind her customary Blank. A Door had open'd, and as quickly clos'd, upon a Room in which something Desperate transpir'd. A Tragedy, but of what Sort, there was no Time to determine.

"What was that?"

"Nothing."

"But—"

"Nothing," she said. "I make a Mistake. Sir." And at once She turn'd away, and made to sidle off towards the Stair, with her Face averted.

"Wait!" I cried, louder than I had meant. "Please, wait." She paus'd, but did not come back. "I regret," I said, "that I cannot—answer You—as You desire. As I see You require. But—please—would You tell Me, how your Mistress does?"

"What you doing," she said. Do-ing. The Syllables were separate, the -ing rumbling and humming on her Palate. "If you not—" She stopp'd again. "I think You a crazy Man."

"Please?"

She tightened her Mouth, by that Act making a perfect Miniature of ironic Scorn.

"Please?"

Zephyra sigh'd.

"She sit and she chew she Lip and stare. She more mad than ever. She want to sit all alone, but her Father say, no: now there no Thief to watch and catch, she go with Miss Flora. So she sit now mostly at Van Loon's, and chew she Lip there." Are You happy now, you Fool?—her Face added, transparently.

Neither of Us had observ'd, that my vile Companion had ceas'd to Snore. He had, however. More than that, restor'd by the black Bottle, he had awak'd with his Animal Spirits return'd to rampageous Life, and was rear'd up, clinging to the criss-cross Mesh of the Cage, with his Tongue hanging forth, glist'ning, and his scrawny Hips thrusting in similitude of the Act of Love.

"Black Meat!" he cry'd with hoarse Relish, staring at Zephyra. "Wery dark, but that don't signify, if You have the Taste for It! If you wet your Yard in—the—Pink—of—it!" Each of the latter Words, accompany'd by a Thrust, the Disarrangement of his torn Breeches showing his Excitement all too clearly.

"Shut up," I said.

"She's in pup, though, but that's no Matter. That's Prime—for bigger Teats and fatter Haunches. Come here, Darling. Come over here, I got—Somefink—for—You—"

"Shut your Mouth," I commanded, or rather entreated, having no Way to enforce any Command: in any Case, entirely in vain.

"Don't listen to Him," I said to Zephyra, who was cowering, again with that same strange excess of Fear, for One who was

165

securely cag'd; as if in Him she fac'd a Tiger, rather than Vermin. "Don't be afraid. He is vile, but pitiful."

"He is *sasabonsam*."

"I don't know what that is."

"No," she agreed, bleakly.

"Tell me," I said, while He went on shouting, trying to draw Her back towards Me with my Eyes, like two People caught together in a Storm, "are You truly with Child?"

"Yes."

"Who is the Father?"

"Who You think."

"Mr. Lovell?"

"I sleep down in Kitchen. When Girls sleeping, I hear him Feet come creeping on the Stair. He says, Come here Girl, come here you Bitch, I am lonely."

"Does Tabitha know?"

She shuddered.

"It will be alright."

"How it be 'alright'? How?" Then, in a Rush, as if her Disappointment were a Liquid that must spill, the Jug being shaken: "I think you Lord Eshu. He know all Language. He make Trick, like You; He change, like You; He both Kind, any Kind, like You. He know the Trick that make the weak One strong. I pray to Lord Eshu and Lord Jesus. I say, help Me, change Me, save Me. You come. I think You come for Me. No; You just a crazy Man. A stupid Man."

Upon which she turn'd in earnest, and swirl'd off down the Stairwell as rapidly as Ink down a Drain, leaving me with my Cellmate's Cries of Disappointment, which rather than diminishing then, only changed Key, and mounted to a quivering Rapture, for He was Frigging himself. I sat down on the Floor with my Back to the Operation, that being the only Means by which I could even pretend to shut It out, and awaited its Termination in Gasp and Squeak and Spatter.

"You are disgusting," I said quietly, in the Snuffling afterward. I spoke to a Point in the Air a Foot or so before Me, but He heard.

"Am I?" He said, seeming highly delighted at this Compliment. "Oh, I am, Boy, am I? Yes I am, for I do offend your delicate Nose; yes I am, for You are so clean; yes I am, for all *your* Thoughts are righteous; yes I am, for my Shit smells, and I don't deny it; yes I am, wery disgusting, for I turn Myself inside out, and show in the Day what you do at Night. Oh, I am. I am, I am, I am, I am I am I am I am I am I am I am I am—"

There was such a Species of Malignancy, in this Repetition, as I cannot rightly convey; Something, so insinuating and so tireless, so happy in the Degradation of its paltry Flesh, that I could almost, in my desperate State, believe It the Work of a Spirit sent to torment Me, a Spirit but hous'd in the derelict Body of my Companion, and working it (so to speak) mechanically, jerking its Limbs to dance by pulling with Glee upon Strings, spewing Repetitions of Filth from its Jaw by cranking a Lever. Such were my Thoughts, at any Rate, there being no Corrective to Fancy, for Me to take a Hold on, while the Taunting continu'd, it seeming not to weigh with Him, what He said, so long as He kept poking at me continually with Speech. At length He grew bor'd, however, of addressing my Back, which I kept firmly turn'd to Him. He try'd, to throw Straw at Me, but it would not fly across the Space between the Cages: and so He return'd to his first Means, of securing my Attention.

"Boy. Boy. Boy. Boy. Boy—"

But it gave Me Pleasure now, to think I was denying Him Something that He wanted, and I was enabled, for a Time, to ignore Him. He grew obsequious, He grew plaintive, He grew beseeching.

"I can be wery good, if I puts my Mind to It," He said. "Come, Sir, don't deny Me a Trifle of Company. I can suit Myself to your Innocence, see if I can't; suit Myself to You as neat as any Tailor, Ha Ha. I can be all Sweetness and Light, I shall talk of Sweethearts and not of Cunts. Come, Sir. Come, Boy. A little Talk. Just a little Talk. Won't the Time fly faster, if We talk? A little Talk, Sir. A little Civility. A little Parlay-voo between Unfortunates. Between Brothers, Sir. Between Brothers in Adwersity, Sir—"

"I am not your Brother." You would have reproved the Sentiment, Father, on Grounds of Theology, but in any Case it was a grievous Mistake to say it aloud, for He chuckled with Satisfaction, and immediately his Grovelling vanish'd, or rather metamorphos'd.

"Ain't You?" He said. "Well, that's a Relief, then, a powerful strong Relief to my poor Sensibilities, ain't It, for who'd be a Brother to a prim Prick-Drip like You? Who'd own You, you Milk-for-Spunk? You Pox-Ooze. You Flux-Breath. You Cockless Pretender. You walking Hole. You Piss-Puddle. You—"

"Reynolds!" I shouted, discovering that it was possible, to be converted in the Twinkling of an Eye, without at all anticipating It, from an apparent Calm to a shaking Fury. (Or rather, perhaps, a shaking Compound of Fury and Fear.) I was up, and rattling the Bars, and shouting for the Keeper, before I rightly knew what I was doing. He came, after I had shouted for a Minute or two, with heavy Feet and a heavy Frown.

"Can You not silence this Moon-Calf?" I cry'd. "Can You not give Him a Kick to quiet his Nonsense, before I lose my Wits with listening to Him?"

"What!" Reynolds said. "Kick the poor Monster?" He look'd across at the other Cage, and there lay its Inmate, curl'd peaceably upon the Floor, as if He had never mov'd. I almost doubted It myself. "I had as soon give You a Kick, Jackanapes," He said, "for You are the One who is giving the Trouble. Shall I?"

"No, Sir," said I bleakly after a Moment, observing his Brawn.

"Then don't give Me Cause to fetch out my Keys."

Straightway He was gone, my Tormentor rose from the Straw, grinning like a Jack o' Lantern with all his brown Teeth.

"*That* won't work, Boy," He said. "You're stuck with Me, You are. Now I've thought Me, since You won't be civil, of the wery Story to treat You right for It; to medicine up your Disrespect. And hey hey, It's a true 'un. All the better, eh? For so You may jes' picture It, as I tell It, and know It happen'd, but five Years back, in this wery Place, in these wery Streets, on our lovely Common, where I'm sure You po-litely stroll'd, You Puppet, while You was po-litely purposing your po-lite Robbery. But This ain't polite; no. This has got some Gristle in It; and some Marrow too. Well: You have noticed, ain't You, that the old Fort where His Nibs lives is the Worse for Wear? All scorch'd up like a half-burned Log. Now the Night that happen'd I was drinking in Hughson's Tavern, over by the River, and about the Middle of the Candle a little Welsh Bugger (His Name I can't recall) puts his Head in the Door and cries, Lively boys, there's Somefink afire. We tumbles out onto the Cobbles, for to get a Look-see, though the Frost was hard and biting, and to be sure, there's Sparks in the Sky, and a red Glow like Hell's Locker had sprung open, beyond Trinity Spire. 'Tis the Fort for Sure, said Caesar, a Nigger belonging to Vaarck the Baker; and Sarah Hughson, the Tavern-keep's Lady, She holds up her Hands, like one warming Theirself, and says, There's a Hearth I'm glad to see lit, and there's all the big Houses too on Broad Street might burn, for Me. She being angry because Hughson her Man was in Chokey downstairs here, for receiving Goods. I remembers the Words, for I give 'em in Court later. Well, We laugh'd, and We went back in and drunk a Toast or Three to

Fire. They was jolly Fellows, in Hughson's: Caesar and Prince who was John Auboyneau's Nigger, and Newfie Peg who lodg'd there with Caesar's Brat. Prince and Caesar, They call'd Theirselves the Geneva Club, for They lift'd Barrels from out the Warehouses, to sell 'em to Hughson, and that's why the Gin was cheap, and no Fuss when You puk'd. Peg was Caesar's Girl, but you could have her for a Shilling, or for a Glass, when the Thirst was on Her. Jolly Fellows, yes, and many a Jolly Night the Capting had with 'em. But in the morning—"

I had no Notion whereto this Story was tending. Yet perhaps it tended somewhat to my Relief, for though the Monster had seem'd to threaten Something by it, He now was winding Himself, I judg'd, into a Labyrinth of Foul Anecdote, where He might wander reminiscing till He lost Wits and Lucidity again for the Exercise, and I hop'd might leave Me be. I hop'd it most desperately, for I still trembled. Moving soft so as not to disturb his Flow, and nodding from Time to Time, I ventured to sit down and privily took up my Pen again.

I am writing in the Straw now while pretending to listen. Father, another of the short Days is darkening, and the Air is gathering up again in Stars and Splinters the Ice the Morning melted from it. It seems hard if I must pass this remaining Portion of my Life in the Lap of another's Delirium.

"So, Some said the Frenchies done it, and Some said 'twas the Spaniards, come to put the Pope upon Us; but Most agreed, in a Panick, it must be the Niggers done the actual Deed of the Burning; and Mr. Horsmanden, as is Recorder and Justice along of De Lancey, He sees This, and being a quick old Screw for Anything to an Advantage, He says to Himself, I'll make Somefink of This. And He snatches up Caesar and Prince and a Dozen more besides, and in the Court He says, a grand Conspiracy, Gents, a heinous and dastardly Plot, and don't the

170

People love It. Well, I see which Way the Wind is blowing, and when it comes my Turn, to go Witness, I does my Best to dish the Niggers too, and give 'em a few shrewd Blows in the Telling, of how They laugh'd at the Tragic Sight."

"What, your Friends? The Jolly Fellows?" I said, incredulous despite Myself.

"Oh, You *is* awake. —I'll awake You in a Minute, I'll be bound. —Yes, Caesar and Prince and the Others."

"You did not think that, perhaps, being their Friend, you might stay your Hand?"

"Ain't You simple, then! No, it don't do to be too pertickler in this World. You must take your Pleasures where You find them; a Drink and a Joke one Day, and the Next, whatever the Day brings. I never thought I owed a Fellow a Debt, that We shared a good Time; nor He, Me; so best to get in first, before He can get at You. Anyway. Prince and Caesar and the Niggers, They go down, a-course; and Horsmanden says, Gents, We must have special hard Punishments, so all the World may mark. And Prince and the Others, They must be burned on the Common, slow, but Caesar, says Horsmanden, since that He purposed to set up as King, must be broken on the Wheel. Which the People was wery satisfied with: You could hear Them growl, in the Court. The only Problem being, that Nobody in New-York knowed the Trick of It, not Peters the Hangman, not Nobody. And when the Call went out, does Anyone know how?—why, not a Soul replied, there being, Boy, Things as are wanted to be done in the World, which Few want the doing of, no Matter how fierce they growl. Well, thinks I, a Chance for the Capting, and foolish not to take it. I'll do it, I says, for I have seen it done in the Brazils. (Which was nearly true.) So, Boy, picture Me on the Morrow, out upon the Common, with poor Caesar truss'd to the Wheel of a Wagon, and Me furnish'd with a Crowbar, and also a Barrel of Beer, for to wet

my Whistle with while I work'd, which I took wery kind, it being
likely to be a lengthy Job; and a Crowd round about me, eager-like
yet hesitant, glad the Lot of 'em that 'twas to be my Hands on the
Crowbar. Good Morning, says I to Caesar. Friend, says He, won't
You give Me a Ding on the Head first off, and let Me out quick?
Sorry, says I, We must give 'em a Show. And I grins at Him, for
what is Life without a little Pleasure in't? But though I speaks so
confident, I am to speak true working by Guesses; They have give
Me a Book, a Surgeon's Book, with a Map of all the Bones, but
the Capting has never been much of a Reader. Says I inside my
Head, well, let us commence Operations with the Shins, for They
are near the Surface, and will make an easy Target while I gets my
Eye in—"

"I don't want to hear This."

"Don't You? Don't want your Medicine? Then You are Plumb
out of Luck, Boy; for You *shall* hear it, every word the Capting
chuses to medicine You with. I swings the Bar—"

I cover my Ears, I sing with all the Force of my Lungs, I crouch
in the Dusk and try to crawl away into this Trail of Ink, but I
cannot block it out. Night comes, but He goes on remorseless,
with no End in sight, either of the dreadful Story or of the poor
screaming Victim it concerns—for there are, says the Monster,
one hundred and fifty-six Bones in the mortal Tower, and He
means Me to hear of the clumsy, patient, methodical Splintering
of them all, running in at my Ear like a Venom, churning my Guts
till I spew (to his high Satisfaction) into the Straw. "Then come
the Ribs," He says.

Father, I can hardly see to write. His ruin'd Countenance bobs
in the Dark, talking, talking, with cheerful indifferent animal
Glee. I do not understand how Anyone can be so lost, so content
to be devour'd by Impulse. This may seem a strange Declaration,
from One who deliberately lost Himself in London, with

Nothing in his Pocket, but the sad Truth about Me, Father, is that however low I wandered, I always knew I could come back. I would return and stand conceal'd behind the Park Trees opposite Lord ———'s House, sometimes, in those first Weeks of my Wanderings, and just look upon It. And having seen It was still there, with a Door that would open to Me at the Price merely of a few Recriminations, I was enabled to trudge away again. Though sometimes the Temptation was strong. You see, I have never doubted my Safety. Such was the Reason for my Impatience, at all your Proclamations of Danger.

I remember the Moment—as You purposed I should never forget It—when You bared your Arm and, seizing Me, drew up the Sleeve on Mine, and laid it besides yours on the Table, and bade Me attend to the Colours of our Skin. Yours, a Brown like well-milked Coffee; Mine, for it was Summer, a faint yet insistent Amber. "This is our Destiny," You said. "The Lord has given it Us, and We must find his Grace in It." And You drew for Me the liveliest Picture you could, with all the Resource You were wont to dedicate in Sermons to rendering Hell-Fire, of the Cruelties awaiting Me on account of that Colour, were I not careful. Of Slaveries, Plantations, Chains, Whips, Floggings, Burnings; of a whole World of Terrors lying, as You made It sound, just beyond the first Milestone on the Road out of the Parish. You represented to Me, that my only Safety was at Home; my only Passport, in the wider World, the Protection of Lord ———. I was I suppose Five Years of Age, and I ran to my Mother to hide my Head in her Apron, the Whiteness of her Arms round Me seeming then a Kind of Promise of Exemption, a Freedom from all You had named. "He must understand, Martha," You said, when She protested. But I would not believe, not then, not later, that We had no Choice but to hide Ourselves. Or that the Chance of You having a Slave for a Father, and my having One for a Grandfather, must be a perpetual Doom upon Us. Or that We must forever accept from Lord ———— a Kindness precious near to Ownership. I would not believe You. Your Fear, I said to Myself, was a Disease of your Soul, individually. I would not catch It. I would not consent to be afraid.

But now I am: oh, now I am. I hate this City. I hate these People. I should never have

(Here the letter breaks off unfinished.)

5

Sinterklaasavond
(St. Nicholas' Eve)

December 5th
20 Geo. II
1746

I

"So they just let you out?"

"They didn't have much choice," said Smith indistinctly, with his mouth full of bread. Hendrick and Septimus had been breakfasting at the Merchants when he came in, wild-looking and unshaven and (to tell truth) not savoury of smell. But neither were uncivil enough to mention his state of disarray, being besides desperately curious and surprised at his reappearance. "It seems," he went on, swallowing, "that *Sansom's Venture* came in this morning at first light with the other two copies of my bill in the mailsack together—there'd been some error in London, and the one meant for *Antelope* had missed the tide—and presto! on the instant I was converted from a fraud and a public enemy into a wronged man. Lovell came running to City Hall with the papers in his hand, and a gaggle of my creditors strung out behind him like the tail of a comet, and gave me, oh, you should have heard it, the angriest apology in the world, every word pushed from his lips with pain."

"You're speaking very loud," put in Septimus, with a warning look, for Mr. Smith was announcing his story as if speaking to the whole room; and indeed, most of the room was listening to him, with greater and lesser efforts at dissembling it, while he stuffed himself from the basket of rolls, and waved for more with scarecrow urgency.

Smith smiled breadily and nodded, and dropped his voice, but it was clear that he was not much concerned; that he was content to let New-York know, starting with the roomful of gentlemen before him, that the roles were reversed, and that Lovell's credit now lay in *his* hands, if he chose to complain of his treatment. "Well, then," he continued, "the keeper unlocked me, and all the others at whose suit I'd been held thronged around too, telling me how sorry they were, and pressed back on me all that had been sponged, against my debts. My *supposed* debts," he reminded the room. "My sword, my purse of money, my welcome in this fine establishment. Mrs. Lee wanted me to know that she would change the sheets on her garret bed, in honour of me, and that there was beef-pie for supper tonight. At which, I confess, my mouth began to water, and I departed City Hall upon a velvet cushion of protestations, and so came here."

"Well, you are welcome back," said Hendrick, awkwardly.

"Am I?" said Smith. "That is good to know. For I *am* back, and I mean to stay back, and it is about time that your family repented of its cat-and-mouse games, and we fell to business, I think."

"I see that Mr. Lovell is not the only angry one," said Septimus.

"Me? Never in life!" said Smith, giving them his familiar beam of amiability: only now with a ragged carelessness, a desultory approximation, like a man who briefly raises a mask on a stick to his face but cannot be bothered to line up the eye holes. Septimus and Hendrick glanced at each other involuntarily, to share the dismay that each for different reasons was feeling.

"For my part, I am sure you have been ill-used, and I am heartily sorry for it," said Hendrick carefully. "But I ask you to remember that we worked, as we must, by the appearances of the thing; and that it was a chain of accident that set you in gaol, and not any . . . malignancy on our part. No-one in the family bears you ill-will."

"No-one?"

"Not my father," said Hendrick, swallowing, "nor Gregory Lovell, nor me, nor any of us concerned in the business you have with us. I see that Tabitha has bitten you hard enough to draw blood, and the bite is presently festering, and again I am sorry for't; but a bite from her is not policy from the houses of Lovell and Van Loon; it is in the nature of a curse, that lies in the first place on us, but which it seems we cannot help sharing. We did speak of this? But you seemed then to be enjoying the poison."

"Also," put in Septimus, "you did seem too to be enjoying the doubt you put them in, that you were here to rook them. Come on, Richard. You played at being a fraud, unmercifully. You *flirted* with it. It is not so strange if people believed you."

"*Et tu, Brute?*" said Smith. He closed his eyes and scrubbed with his fingertips at the sockets, which Septimus and Hendrick, following the motion, saw were stained yellow with lack of sleep. The freckled skin over his nose was waxy and transparent. "True," he said, with his eyes still covered. "I think my stoicism has taken a dint, gentlemen. Excuse me."

"Then, will you not give us one more chance?" said Hendrick, pressing his advantage. "Let us make amends. There is a Dutch festivity tonight, at the house, and I think you should come along."

"You're joking," said Smith. "It is only an hour or two since, that you were all content to see me hanged: and now I am to be your guest?"

"You should think of this as a restoration of the way things should have been, all along."

"I am not an actor in a farce, that I may spring back in through one door, the instant I have exited through another."

"No, no," said Hendrick. "This will be a feast day. We shall bombard you with marchpane and St. Nicholas-rhymes, and sweeten you into forgiving us."

"You will all sit in a row and scowl at me, seriatim."

"We will not. I undertake it. There will be no scowling, no recriminating; no-one there who is not on their feast-day manners."

"Seriously?"

"Seriously. I swear to it: no unpleasantness, even if we have to gag Tabitha, and lock her in the cellar. Come, what do you say?"

Smith covered his mouth with his hand and gazed at the table-top, pitted with saw-marks from knives, and names gouged in the wood by idle hands. The moment lengthened. It was not clear if he was thinking, or refusing, or simply drifting off into reverie.

"Mr. Smith?" said Hendrick. No answer.

"Richard?" said Septimus.

No answer.

"It will not be you that Uncle Lovell is most angry at," Hendrick said, cunningly.

Smith transferred the hand from his mouth to the tallowy division-line at the centre of his forehead, and clawed at it. His gaze lifted.

"When I came in the door," he said wearily, "I had the most straightforward resolution in the world, never to take anything from the pack of you again, except your money. But it seems I cannot abide by it. Oh very well, then; very well."

"Excellent!" said Hendrick. He had plainly learned that cardinal rule of selling, that you should never linger after the bargain is struck, for he rose at once to his feet. "I shall come and fetch you from Mrs. Lee's at six this evening, after you have had a chance to sleep and bathe. And now I had better go to work. Quentin! Fetch Mr. Smith a plate of chops, on my bill, will you?" He left, grimacing a smile.

"He is a good son," said Smith to Septimus. The coffee-house was emptying around them, at the call of the desk and the counting-house.

"He tries to be, in what he can, to make up for the ways in which he is doomed to disappoint his father."

"Ah," said Smith. He yawned. "Tell me, am I grievously offensive to the nose?"

"Yes."

"I had better go and wash off the stink, then, and get some clean clothes."

"Eat your fill first." Septimus hesitated. "Was it . . . very bad? I understood that the debtors' portion of the prison, if not the dungeon below, was quite clean."

"It was fine. Lovely straw, pleasant views, informative company."

"Well, I am sure I have no desire to pry."

Smith groaned. "Sorry!" he said. "The basket was a God-send, and I was more grateful for it than I can rightly say. I hope you have not been too embarrassed on my account. Achilles said you had been."

"Not to worry," said Septimus. "For having participated in your downfall, I now participate in your resurrection, and may wipe the smirk off several faces. Look, here come your chops."

"I am almost dribbling at the sight of them. —You remember the warning you gave me, at first? About the—the—*nature* of the city? I . . . had it confirmed. In sickening abundance."

"I thought something must have happened."

"Bastards, all of them," said Smith, speaking in a fierce undertone to his plate. "I will punch the next one who mentions liberty."

"You know, London has gaols," said Septimus gently. "Newgate is a darker pit and a deeper by far, than the little cellar here. More die at Tyburn tree every season, than have hanged here in all the years of the city."

"And been scalped? Or burned? Or . . . broken?"

"Oh. You have heard *that* story."

"At least at home, they do not pretend to clean hands and righteous hearts."

"I know I have been away a while," said Septimus, "but I am almost positive I remember there being liars in London; and hypocrites too, more than one; and girls who proved a disappointment to boys who loved them."

"It is not that! At least— It is not *all* that."

"I make sure of it," Septimus said. "Not that I am any expert." He made a ball of bread and pushed it in a circle before him with his forefinger, like the titan Atlas manipulating with ease a very small planet. "You know, if I find anything to praise here, when they go to such lengths to make my life miserable, you may perhaps believe it? I had a visitor, a year after landing; a grand connection of my father's bishop, come to survey an inheritance he had come into, down in the Virginias. And it puzzled me, why I found I so disliked his manner of speaking to me, more than any here, more than any number of Van Loons or Van Rensselaers, or William Smith in his cups, or Judge De Lancey at his most self-satisfied: till it came to me, that he addressed me, as a matter of course, as a Secretary, with all my nature that it was needful to know comprised in that title. And I realised I had grown insensibly used to being treated, even by my enemies, as a man, with my nature all to be proved by what I did and said. He used no more toward me than the ordinary condescension of the great, and yet I found I resented it. I found I had gained the liberty to resent it. And that is a real liberty, Richard."

"Unless your skin is African."

"True."

"They would bludgeon your true love to jelly for speaking the wrong word."

"They would bludgeon him in London for sixpence in his pocket, or for stepping up the wrong alley. Look, dear man, I must go to work too. Sleep soon, won't you? You are missing several of the usual layers of *your* skin, and I do not think you are quite safe for company yet."

"Goodbye," said Mr. Smith. "Thank you, Septimus. Oh—how is the play?"

"Suddenly improved now that you, and not I, are playing Juba again. We have only four more rehearsals, so restore yourself, do. Eat, bathe, *sleep.*"

As Mr. Smith walked slowly towards the William Street bath-house, his stomach loaded to the point of a moderate nausea, his own thoughts taking the greatest share of his attention, he at first confused the quietness of the streets with his quietening mind. But it was not so. New-York was quiet because it was, suddenly, far emptier. A good half of the businesses had their shutters up, and where there had been busy mobs converging on the waterfront, his footsteps now rang out almost solitary on the cobble-stones. While he had been imprisoned, the city had passed its great autumn climacteric. The sugar fleet had departed, and with it the whole frantic mood of the last weeks. The sailors, the country merchants and farmers seeing their stocks safe aboard, the buzzing projectors with their plans for instant profit, all had made their farewells; and the citizens who remained were locking down and bolting up for the winter. The city was shrinking in on itself, as Septimus had predicted. It was stoking up its stoves and sitting closer to 'em; it was drawing up its furs around itself. And not a moment too soon. The bare sky at the eastern street-ends, where the masts had thronged, had in it today a bitter green pallor, the unmistakeable colour of impending cold. On the shadowed sides of the streets the frost of the night was not melting, even at noon; and in the maze of little alleys up toward the Broad Way, where the low sun did not shine directly at all, ice already held the whole dim territory. The air there was as still and as chill as it had been in the ice-house upon Lord ——'s estate, when Mr. Smith was dispatched into it one day to fetch a block for freezing a pudding, and found a buried winter reigning there underground, dark and silent, patient and permanent, lending iron rigour to each breath.

And when he awoke in the dark that evening between Mrs. Lee's clean sheets, blinking and confused for a moment, he found that outside the cold panes of the dormer, the first snow was falling. Tiny flakes like feathered dust were floating out of the unlit night above into the unlit night below. He opened the casement and leaned out. On the skin he had steamed and scrubbed, pinpoints of cold prickled, as if winter were beginning without delay to tattoo its map upon him. All along the dark avenue, to left and to right, the powdery fall was already furring the cobbles with a thin grey nap like velvet, and rimming them white along all the crooked lines between. Everything seemed slowed to the speed of the descending snow. A holy expectation reigned in the thickening air, and passers-by walked as if they did not want to disturb it. Only a small party, coming from the mouth of Crown Street opposite, made any noise. They were singing something, and carrying a small lantern on a pole which lit the flakes to swarming gold in a small globe around itself, and touched the edges of their faces—the line of a hat, the scroll of an ear, the filaments of a beard—with shadowy gilding, like statues in an ancient shrine. They crossed the road. Smith, lulled and fascinated, shivered in his shirt and watched them come closer; closer *and* closer, till they were arranged in a semicircle directly below him on Mrs. Lee's own doorstep, and were knocking at her door. A moment later her voice could be heard calling up the stairs for him.

He came down slowly, and took his time wrapping himself in scarf and gloves and cocked hat, for he was in no hurry for the magic theatre he had glimpsed from above to dwindle into a parcel of Van Loons. But when he opened the door, and found himself indeed confronted in the flurrying glow of gold by Hendrick, Joris, Piet with little Lisje tucked beneath his arm, a face or two he didn't know, and, nodding at the end, Jem the clerk at Lovell's, all with expressions of effortful goodwill, they seemed to remain transformed by the advent of the snow; to be still their own grasping, dangerous, anxious selves standing there, that is, but brought by the weaving flicker of the flakes into a new, patient, unearthly solemnity. What Mr. Smith's face showed, or didn't, emboldened Hendrick, who beat his finger in the air for time and said, "One, two."

> *Sinterklaas, goedheiligman!*
> *Trek uwe beste tabbard an,*
> *Reis daar mee naar Amsterdam,*
> *Van Amsterdam naar Spanje,*
> *Daar Appelen van Oranje,*
> *Daar Appelen van granaten,*
> *Die rollen door de straten.*

As soon as they had finished the lyric in Dutch, they went on without a pause and sang it in English, a little more heartily this time as the younger ones ceased to stumble.

> *Saint Nicholas, good holy man,*
> *Put on thy tabard, best thou can,*
> *Ride clad in it to Amsterdam,*

Francis Spufford

From Amsterdam to Spanish lands,
With oranges then fill thy hands
And pomegranates bring to me
That roll the streets at liberty.

Lisje's nose was as pink as a sugar pig's, and she was blinking when
the snow blew into her eyes. Despite the mention of liberty, Mr.
Smith did not punch anyone. He clapped his hands; or perhaps his
hands clapped themselves, commanded by the strangeness of the
night, and by his instinct to rally any uncertain performance.

"Is there an answer I must give?" he asked Hendrick. He meant
to sound sardonic and self-possessed. Instead his voice came out
almost reverential.

"No, no, just come with us, and help us sing it again at another
door or two."

So Smith went along, in the moving sphere of gold, helping to
smudge the grey velvet underfoot with a trail the sky commenced to
fill as soon as their feet had moved on, crumb by crumb, feather by
feather, and lent his tenor when the next door opened, and the next,
and first a couple and then a whole Dutch family, ready-dressed for
the night, stepped out to join them. There was no small-talk, only the
muffled tread of feet and the hiss as snow fell on the hot tin of the
lantern. New-York was not so big that Mr. Smith could by any means
lose himself, but the streets seemed altered in the fine, silent swirling, and he did not attend to the exact path of the Nicholas-night
pilgrimage. They might even have passed City Hall. The Van Loons'
house, where he had never been, took him by surprise: a tall old
fortress of the Amsterdammer type, with stepped gables, but tonight
illuminated at every window by candles stuck in oranges, and
wreathed around the sills and sashes with green branches of pine. It
seemed a castle of lights, a magnet to draw their own lantern home
through the snow. The children gazed up at it, bespelled.

"Right," said Hendrick, and handing the pole to his father to hold, trotted up the steps to the front door, *crunch-crunch-crunch*, and hammered at it. When it opened, and Geertje Van Loon wide in bright silks stood there, with Flora and Anne crowding behind her to see, a myriad of little flames spangling the dark hall, it looked as if a treasure-house had opened, a winter cavern set with jewels, and an air laden with spices flowed out. One last time at the foot of the steps they sang *Sinterklaas, goedheiligman*, and the three hostesses listened with hands clasped. But that was it. At the last note the snowy silence collapsed into a genial roar, and all the singers surged up to the door chattering and laughing nineteen to the dozen, to kiss and be received.

Smith, feeling the spell broken, felt too the sullen grasp of his resentment closing again, and hung back, wondering if he might sidle off, but Piet Van Loon put a hand in the small of his back and propelled him firmly upward to the threshold, before slipping past and in. Mrs. Van Loon put out a hand. He meant to bow over it; instead, she drew him against the powdered slopes of her bosom, and bussed him explosively on each cheek. *"Prettige Sinterklaas,"* she said firmly, as if prescribing a medicine, and passed him on for the laughing imprint of Flora's lips and the anxious nibble of Anne's. "Happy St. Nicholas," they said. "Go in, go in." Flora was in looks, and in her element as well, apparently: suffused with busy excitement, a fair tendril of her hair come loose from its net of pearls and bouncing by her mouth as she spoke. Stationed authoritatively at Geertje's shoulder she seemed settled into place as the house's elder daughter already. The contrast with the put-upon girl he had seen through the upstairs door a month before was marked. It occurred to Smith that the short time he had passed in the city stood for a whole epoch to Flora. Some of what she had wanted, she had gained, while he did her the unwitting service of distracting her sister. She was well launched out into her career of change, and if

Joris was not quite the cavalier of romance, he was the means of replacing the sharp words of the Lovells' long room for her, with this shrewd domestic enchantment, this easier household where the conversation did not bristle with traps.

"Richard, you're staring," she said, sounding perfectly happy about it: as if, in fact, receiving his stare was helping to make her cheeks glow. "Go in! The saint is coming in a half an hour, and there is food and drink everywhere, but the men you'll find upstairs, smoking."

The Van Loons had cleared their main rooms to accommodate the party. Only the blue-and-white-tiled stoves in the corner of each could not be removed, being built into the walls, and these seemed too to be the last traces of Dutch taste in the furnishing. Paint, wallpapers, pictures—all were smartly in the latest English fashion, or at least the latest version of it that had reached New-York. By the light of many candles a crush of prosperous people were exchanging the news, here and there in Dutch but largely in English, and trying to moderate the appetites of their children, who were reaching their hands over and over into baskets of flat little biscuits offered by the Van Loons' servants. "Wim, Davey, leave some room in your stomach for when Sinterklaas comes. You'll be sorry if you're sick." Smith took one for himself. It tasted of cinnamon and orange peel and, surprisingly, black pepper. He was wished the joy of the feast many times as he worked his way up the stairs, either absently, as the mere compulsory custom of the night, or with a nodding, beaming significance that suggested a closer connection of the family, primed by Hendrick to please. After a while he started saying it back, and by the time he reached the first-floor landing he had the pronunciation of *prettige Sinterklaas* about perfect, thanks to his quick gift with tongues, though he still had no clear idea of what was being celebrated, or of what the saint's arrival might entail, not having happened to pass through the Low Countries in December on his Grand Tour.

On the landing a room to the right was filled with all the exiled chairs, and on them smiling ancients discoursing gummily together, but on the left a closed door declared that a domain of private business lay beyond. The African footman stationed there was expecting him, and ladled him a steaming silver beaker of orange punch from a grand silver tureen on a side table, before turning the door-handle and bowing him into a seam of blackness. Smith passed from treasure-house into cavern. He could feel the dense softness of a Turkey-carpet underfoot, and smell tobacco smoke thickly compounding with the spices, but in here the only lights were the four little stumps of candle piercing oranges at the windows, and the dull red-gold coals of a fire. It was so dark, it took him a moment to sort and establish the shadowed forms of what must be Piet Van Loon's study, with its desk and globe and tall armchairs by the overmantel. If the room had been a print, it would have been one of those cross-hatched unto Hades by the burin, line upon line, ink upon ink, till the figures are lost in a frenzy of gloom. If it had been a painting, it would have been one of those ancient daubs smoke-blackened till the viewer must guess at subject and setting from the few ambiguous streaks remaining, and decide according to taste whether it depicts a battle or a serenade, a tragedy or a cucumber-lodge. His hosts were waiting in the chairs. Piet, Hendrick, Lovell, the embers of three pipes coming and going in the black with their breaths. No: Piet, Hendrick, Lovell, and *Tabitha*, beyond the others in the far corner, twisted in her seat to avert her face as far as might be from the closing door. He knew her by the faint gleam along the narrow shoulder hitched up against him. The twisting line there, it was impossible he should fail to recognise. He would have recognised it on the moon; where there would certainly have been more light.

"Sit down, jongeheer," said Piet. They had left him a place facing outward from the fire, towards the flames along the sills and their quivering doubles in the glass, and the thin snow falling beyond the glass. Tabitha was almost behind him, and quite out of view. His nerves quickened at the thought of the elaborate malice she would be nourishing in the darkness. The sounds of the party throbbed remotely.

"I didn't think you Calvinists had saints' days," he remarked.

"Only this one," said Piet.

"A bit gaudy for you, isn't it?"

"We're a long way from the synod of the Hervormde Kerk," said Hendrick. "We can afford to be lax. Sinterklaas has grown much bigger since the Governor started holding his St. George's dinners, and the Irish and the Scots societies got going with St. Patrick and St. Andrew. But," he went on patiently, a man obliging his family in what he could, "you didn't come to talk about that. You wanted to get down to business. Here we are."

"Yes," said Lovell around his pipe stem. "And I'll bite my tongue and not say a word whose fault I think it is we've danced about the matter so damn long to no purpose: but, yes, here we are. Your bill is good. We'll call that established fact. Now, how will you take it?"

"What do you mean?"

"We mean, that quarter-day is but nineteen days off, and that we must agree what properties you'll take your seventeen hundred and forty pound New-York in, for doubtless a deal of haggling—"

"I think I am owed an apology first, am I not?"

"You've had it," said Lovell. "You've had it from me, and as I understand it, you've had it from Hendrick here too, and that's both houses covered."

"It isn't your houses I'm owed it by," Smith said; his attention, his rancour, the quiver of his sinews, all concentrated with galvanic sensitivity upon the dark chair behind his left shoulder.

"Oh, God save us from pride-offended youth. Well, we reckoned on that too. Tabitha, apologise to the boy."

Silence.

"Tabitha, you know the necessity of this."

Silence. Lovell huffed a sigh. He stood, and the thud that followed suggested that he had kicked the chair in the corner.

"Tabitha!"

A thread of a whisper: "I apologise."

"There," said Lovell, breathing hard. "Piet, excuse the insult to your furniture."

"Granted," said Piet.

"Now. If we may, please God, dispense with any more of this spoony mumchancing: what will you take the bill in? Speak plain at last. We can offer you a three-fourths share in one of the spring sugar cargoes; or a stake in our privateer a-building at Mystic; or a choice of city properties and building land; or rum to a quantity to be decided. Or one of the farms. Or some piece of another of our enterprises. What d'ye favour?"

"None of those," said Smith.

"Very well," said Lovell, after a fractional pause. "What, then? Name it and we'll find it."

"Tobacco, for instance, we can get you at better than the spot price," said Piet. *Der schpot prysch.* "Better than wholesale, even, if you deal through our friends in Baltimore."

"Slaves?" said Smith. "Can you make me a bargain there?"

"Surely. But quick or slow depends on what kind of hands you have in mind. The city markets are run low for stock in winter, and they mainly provide for household work, that being the demand hereabouts, and all seasoned and broken for the country, able to speak the lingo, and so on. If you wanted labour to set up as a planter, you'd need to look south. But that'd be no hardship. We have a friend in Savannah would look you out whatever you needed in that line, at a keen enough price—"

"What about a wench for the cold nights?"

A longer pause, and ice in Lovell's voice. "Smith, my daughter is present."

"I had not forgot it," Smith said, and waited, but there came no interjection from the corner. "Anyway, you mistake me. I was merely curious. Gentlemen, you are too elaborate. I don't want to take my bill in human flesh, or as a thousand gross of pincushions, or in barrels of lard neither. Call me old-fashioned, but I prefer money. I want cash."

Lovell and Piet both began speaking at once, in raised voices. Pief's basso calm prevailed over Lovell's tenor indignation.

"We have explained"—*eckschplayned*—"that there is not cash money in the city of such an amount. Here the money is figures in the ledger only. When it is time to settle, we do it with assets. When in Rome, jongeheer, when in Rome? You do business here, you must do it our way."

"Must I?" said Smith. "The law is of another opinion, I think. I paid in cash, and if I want cash back again, it is my right to have it."

"But anything you want to buy, we can get," said Lovell. "Where's the difference?"

"Privacy," Smith said.

"And why do you need to be private?"

"Well," said Smith, steepling his fingers, and making of his voice a confidential murmur, "Let's say . . . that perhaps I have been commissioned by a certain gentleman—a certain *very distinguished* young gentleman, of, shall we say, German family—who desires, on terms of strict anonymity, to visit his . . . *estates* in the New World; and requires the way to be made ready for him, with a household befitting his station, yet with great discretion. A house, a carriage, an equipment of staff; yet all to be muffled in deep secrecy. Deep, deeper, deepest secrecy. The most regal of discretions." At each syllable of this farrago of nonsense, he expected a snort of derision from the corner, yet none came.

"Do you mean," said Lovell, hushed, "that you are acting for Pr—"

"No," said Hendrick flatly. "Listen to him. He is just amusing himself."

"True," said Smith. "Prison must have put me in the mood for it."

"You little blackguard—"

"Don't let him bait you so easy," Piet said to Lovell. "We must still settle this. And it *is* his right in law to ask payment how he likes."

"How am I supposed to find seventeen hundred pound in cash?"

"Oh, I don't expect it in gold," Smith said. "I have learned better than that. Any pile of paper will do, as strange as you like, so as it is negotiable; —and does not come from Rhode Island. Pay me in dead leaves, I care not, if they will pass in trade. But *how* is your problem."

"Banyard's will not pay for my sugar till spring."

"But then, if I have it right, in cash themselves, you having settled your balance with them by paying me?"

"I suppose so; theoretically."

"Then borrow until then," said Smith. "Or sell something. Or beg. Or steal. But in nineteen days, I want cash."

"There is none."

"What, in no drawer, closet, chest or cubbyhole of the entire colony? You disappoint me. And I believe you would disappoint Judge De Lancey as well, who promised you'd oblige me lavishly, if I forebore to meddle."

"I see you do not purpose to mend a friendship at all," said Hendrick.

"I have not yet heard the words to make me want to!" said Smith. Silence.

"We might perhaps be able to offer a per centum over value, if you would settle for payment in kind," said Piet.

"Really?" said Smith. "How much?"

"Six per cent?"

"Nonsense. Twenty."

"Ridiculous!" said Piet, but there was beginning to be a general relaxation in the room, when a noise that had been swelling on the stairs outside for some time rose to a bursting point, and the door flew open in what seemed to Smith to be a blaze of light, admitting a confused throng of persons, with, at its head, a mighty bulk of red and white and palpably false beard, brandishing a candelabrum.

"St. Nick am I, with bulging sack," roared this apparition.

> *Come to judge twixt white and black:*
> *Twixt vice and virtue make I choice*
> *And give to goodness its reward.*
> *I praise the virtuous, at this time,*
> *And pay back wickedness, in rhyme!*

Smith, who had half-risen, dazzled, made out appraising little eyes he recognised between the white flax moustaches and the red hood. His silky politic voice expanded to a booming bellow, it was plain who was in the robe: the saint was the judge, Sinterklaas was De Lancey. Smith wondered if, on St. George's Day, he turned out to delight his constituents as the Red Cross Knight. Or possibly as the dragon. The soot-smeared sprite holding out the sack at his elbow was William Smith. Around them crowded curious faces. Whatever the saint had done downstairs, the onlookers were looking forward to seeing it happen again up here.

"Welcome, good holy man," said Piet from his chair.

"You find us not in the harmony we'd hoped, Sint Klaas," added Hendrick.

"Is that a fact?" said Sinterklaas, peering sharply into the shadows. "Then, well come or ill come remains to be seen, for my sack bears punishments as well as sweetness, and words to sting as well as words to bless, for such as cannot agree. Ho. Ho. Tell me, Black Peter, my faithful helper, whom have we news for first?"

"For Hendrick, son of the house," said the lawyer, reaching out a folded slip of paper and a little packet wrapped and ribboned. The saint cleared his throat, raised his candles to light the paper, and declaimed:

Hendrick, thou good and duteous boy!
To both thy sire and dam giv'st joy!
Yet on thy clean sheet spills one blot—
One virtue's missing from the lot!
In bachelor joys too long you've tarried!
It's getting late! You should be married!

General laughter. In the flickering candle-light, Hendrick smiling gamely.

"Do we give him his cake?" the saint asked the jury at his shoulders.

"Yes! Yes!"—and the little package was passed across.

"Next, Gregory Lovell," announced the sack keeper.

The saint took the slip, and beetled his stuck-on flax eyebrows as he read it over. "Brace yourself, friend Lovell. Ahem—"

Across the sounding seven seas
The waves sustain thy argosies;
Treasure's heaped up by the shovel
By sage and prosp'rous Greg'ry Lovell.
Why then, upon your golden head,
Wear you that thing like mice long dead?
Is it your plan to make us puke,
Too mean to buy a new peruke?

Groans of outrage, cries of approval. Lovell, dim in the yellow-stippled blackness, arranging his features in a grin of vinegary goodwill, but unconsciously touching his offended head. No snicker, no sound at all, though, from Tabitha's corner.

"The verdict goes against your wig, sir. But boys, girls, ladies, gentlemen: does the man beneath it deserve his Sinterklaas cake?"

"Yes!"

"Very well. Black Peter? —And surely we must now have greetings of the feast for the master of the feast? Yes, yes, here we are. *Een Sinterklaasgedicht voor Mijnheer Piet Van Loon*, with our grateful respects, and the pious hope he will forgive us."

> *Dear Piet is famous for his board.*
> *With generous hand he spreads abroad*
> *Meats, sauces, dainties, sweets: the most*
> *We see from any New-York host.*
> *But should he maybe for his health*
> *Eat slightly less of it himself?*

The watchers whooped, but the saint spoke over them. "Nonsense!" he boomed. "Who writes this stuff? Mijnheer, as one well-sized man to another, I advise you to glory in your stature. Roll through the world with pride! And yet"—undoing the ribbons on Piet's sweetmeat with nimble fingers—"I think I had better eat this one myself. Hmph. Mmm." Laughter; Piet's belly shaking at the joke, in (as it were) comfortable discomfort. "So much for the easy part of my task," Sint Klaas boomed on, wiping his mouth, "when Sinterklaas has old friends to commend, familiar faces . . . and familiar *vices*, to smile at as the winter comes and we draw our circle close. But what will my sack have in it for a guest unknown? Black Peter?"

Smith, knowing himself not part of that circle, rose to his feet warily. He did not want to receive the saint's judgement, whatever it was, at De Lancey's feet. He could see that this ceremonious clowning had been supposed to furnish a cement for the agreement they had expected to reach with him, but what present they were trying to give him, what balm they thought they could offer—he did not know. The judge stepped forward, the candelabrum a crusty anchor for streaming ribbons of light, and held it so that the two of them were looking at each other through the flames, with all the world dark beyond. The judge's real eyelashes were a sandy pink, like bristles in pigskin.

"Had us disappointed for a while there, son," he said quietly; "thought we'd wasted all that consideration on a nobody. Steady there, hey? Play your part, hey? You mean to dance on the rope, I conceive, not dangle from it."

He raised his voice back to the jocular blast required of the saint.

> *Alone and bold, mysterious Smith,*
> *You wander far from kin and kith:*
> *Thy manners wild, thy actions tame,*
> *As if thou schemest, but in game.*
> *By accidental ills assailed—*
> *Misjudged, accused, arrested, gaoled—*
> *You endured in Christian meekness*
> *Showing forth your soul's true sweetness.*
> *Quick to forgive, when made amends,*
> *You turn your adversaries to friends!*

This verse could not give the satisfaction of confirming a known character in Smith, Smith having none to confirm: but it drew a very pleasing and pathetic picture, with the different satisfaction of surprise about it, and so when the saint then clapped his hands together, to show what the reaction should be, the jury at his back and in the door-way obligingly joined in a ripple of applause. Sinterklaas indicated by a lift of his beard, and an opening of his hands, that Smith might reply if he wanted to; but Smith only smiled, tightly, and the saint turned away with a swirl of his robe, candle-stick held high.

"Black Peter," he said, "there remains one more in the room, does there not?"

"There does."

"Has she deserved a gift from Sinterklaas?"

"She has not. For she is a very froward, meddlesome, mischievous soul; a bad daughter, and a curse to her acquaintance; a notorious shrew and scold."

"What have we for her in the sack, then? A switch, a whip, a lump of coal?"

"Harsh words, good holy man. Words to sting her for her offences, and to offer recompense where she has offended."

A paper was passed, and the saint began to inflate himself within his robe for the oration, the bolster at his waist moving upward in a lump as he took breath; yet Smith was suddenly paying him little heed, for as Sinterklaas had turned towards Tabitha's chair, the candles had at last illuminated her, and shown him what the chair contained, and it was not at all the mocking, self-possessed creature that he had all this time imagined. Curled up on the seat, with her knees drawn up to her chin, she was indeed twisted as far away from the company as she might turn: but not laughingly, not in a posture of proud refusal. She seemed clutched in on herself as an animal is who curls tight against pursuers, who presents brittle spines or creaking plates of horn because it cannot contend with the world by any more active means. The flames made her look yellow, but she might have been so anyway, without them, for her skin seemed wizened into a mummified dryness on her bones, with dark shadows practically amounting to bruises under her eyes; and she appeared to have shrunk, to have thinned past slenderness to a dry, jointed angularity. She did not look well, or young. In the sudden glare of light from the candles she only stirred and winced sluggishly, like a wasp left over from summer. The same momentary glare seemed to accomplish an entire revolution in Mr. Smith. It has often been observed, how our desires take strength or force from having a minute dash of repulsion curdled into 'em, the fruit no doubt of our fallen state. Now desire ceded to repulsion altogether. The soft expansive wish to reach for her, with mouth, with tongue, with hands—the bare-skinned greedy gentle unprotected urge to hold, stroke, suck, coddle, transfix—recoiled in alarm, as if he had been wishing to kiss (indeed) a creeping wasp in winter, or a crab, or a furr'd and feeler'd moth. He had believed till that instant that he hated her, but to hate a strong enemy, full of resource and will, is to continue to admire, after a fashion, especially if what you hate you also find beautiful. Now, rather than a girl who made mischief from an excess of spirit, a wicked lively freedom, it seemed he saw a being miserably compelled, venomous and yet helpless; self-stung, self-poisoned; unequal to the catastrophes she caused.

> *To set thy virtues down in song,*
> *Miss Tabitha, would not take long.*
> *Had I a nag as bad as you,*
> *I'd sell her carcass cheap for glue,*
> *Had I a dog with such an itch—*

Smith felt his anger shrivelling away to ash inside him. What was there in the chair was too small for the great feelings it had stirred: too ugly for love, too ingrowing for passion, too negligible for hate. But not too small for pity. If it was wretched to care for her, it must be still worse to be her.

"Please, stop," he said.

"What's this?" said the saint, baffled.

"Please, enough."

"Don't you want your cake from Sinterklaas?"

The saint peered from face to face for guidance, the verse still poised.

"Stupid," muttered Tabitha into the upholstery.

"Can you not stop this?" Smith said to Hendrick.

"Mr. Smith is very tender-hearted," said Hendrick, discovery in his voice, and something like glee. "I think Mr. Smith wishes to renegotiate. Six per cent," he said.

"What?"

"Six per cent."

"Ten," said Smith, but not as if he meant it.

"Six," said Lovell.

"Six," rumbled Piet.

"Alright," said Smith. He reached for the paper in Sinterklaas' hand. Hendrick nodded. The saint made him tug on it before he released it, grinning. Smith crumpled the poem in his fist, and threw it into the hot coals of the grate, whose crackle could be heard in the room's sudden hush. Everyone was looking at him—the Van Loon men and Lovell, De Lancey, the mob at his back, even (slow as a serpent) Tabitha. On the window-sills wax had puddled and run on the oranges. "But you must give me a few days to think how I take it," he said, and pushed his way out through the room, and down the stairs between the prosperous men and women and the children gnawing marchpane, while the buzz of speech resumed behind him, and the saint began to laugh.

Outside the fine flakes fell in patient multitudes.

II

It was still snowing in the morning, and by noon the streets of New-York had turned a solid white Smith never saw them lose for the rest of his stay. Then the sky cleared, the mercury dropped, and the promise of cold the green sky of St. Nicholas' Eve had made was fulfilled with a vengeance. From the north came airs so hard with frost that Smith's exhalations froze on his pulled-up scarf in icicles as he crunched gingerly to rehearsal, and the skin on his forehead tightened as if it might snap. All who could, kept indoors. Out on the East River, the pulse of the tides between Manhattan and Breuckelen swept more and more hesitantly, with more and more weight of tinkling, lumpish obstruction, until the reaching fingers of ice growing out from each shore met in the middle and locked, and the water between the city and Long Island became a hummocked, granular plain, into whose depths you could look and see swirls of grey brine and glassy freshwater fused together as still and rigid as in the heart of a child's marble. Thicker and thicker grew the ice-sheet. When the clouds returned and the temperature rose, the ice ran too deep to weaken. The snow—this time falling in fat, tumbling clots, as if the stuffing of furniture were being tossed over the balconies of heaven—only laid a soft, thick dressing atop the ice, smothering the prospect in indistinguishable white on white, except where the Hudson still tore an iron-coloured path out toward the leaden harbour. The city's houses became a congeries of specks, perched on the white edge of a white shore: the white tip of a continent layered in, choked with, smoothed over by, a vast and complete whiteness. Undaunted, the city's people reappeared, once the sharpest bite of the cold was past, in furs and beaver hats (and foot-cloths for the poorest). After the briefest pause, the mails to Boston and Philadelphia and Newark resumed, whisking in on sledges drawn over the white roads by horses helmed in steam. Which means of mobility, the rich of the city also favoured for their own pleasure and use. The Philipses, the Van Rensselaers appeared in sleighs big enough to seat six, eight, ten persons; Chief Justice De Lancey drove in with a fine rasp of runners to the sittings of assizes, from his farm out in the Bouwerij, while little boys ran alongside shouting. The snow of streets was rammed by feet, drilled with holes where passers-by had pissed, and printed by horses' hooves in confused stanzas of c's, n's and u's. When the sun shone, loose handfuls of crystal hissed off the rooflines in prismatic eddies.

Meanwhile, Smith concentrated on the play, there being little else on which he could fix his attention with pleasure. Every day, he received a note from Lovell demanding a decision as to the nature of his payment, which he ignored. Otherwise, his only contact with the family was Flora, the Merchants having been shut during the extreme of the freeze, which made it easy to avoid Hendrick.

"It is a terrible waste of everybody's effort," she remarked severely, when first they met in the icy barn of the upstairs theatre on Nassau Street, "if *someone* is so selfish, that he will not fall in with what has been prepared to please him." Her pretty pink lips, now chapped with the cold, were squinched together in disapproval. "Honestly!" she said.

It was not apparent to Smith, whether she blamed him most for failing to enjoy the come-uppance designed for Tabitha—or simply for not appreciating the party—or more commercially, for being difficult where the interests of the clan were concerned. Her manner did not invite questions, and in any case he was not inclined to ask any. She had demoted him from "Richard" to "Mr. Smith" again, and when she needed to address him in the business of the play, did so with what she meant to be a lofty coolness, though it leaked annoyance. It was a good thing that she was no longer Marcia, required to fall in love in the piece with Juba, but instead the noble Lucia, her heart divided between Cato's sons. These two were played by a couple of genuine twin brothers her own age, sprigs of one of De Lancey's supporters in the Assembly, in town for the winter; and she took to Lucia's dilemma in relation to them with such innocent alacrity, such a frank wholesome delight at the situation of having two suitors, that the lewd suggestion Septimus had feared was completely dissipated, but Joris gave up glaring at Smith and glowered at both twins instead from where he invariably sat watching the rehearsal, hunched up in fur like a dyspeptic bear.

While Smith had been in prison, the production had crossed the elusive but distinct line between the early stage of rehearsal, where the nature of the production is still to seek for, and experiments are welcome, and that later stage where the effect to be aimed for is essentially agreed, and it would be a distraction and an annoyance to the other players, to introduce any very significant new idea. The lines were almost all learned, a coffin-maker on John Street with a sideline in fancy painting had been commissioned to produce a backdrop of columns and ruins, and breast-plates and skirts were in hand for the men. Pig's blood for the death scenes was on order at the butcher. In a way, Smith welcomed this settled state he returned to, for it made much easier the task of fitting in with a group who (apart from Terpie Tomlinson) were all amateurs. They must not be too sharply pulled-away-from, for fear of rending the shared fabric. It was already a little awkward that, after a scene was done, and they all stood waiting in the indoor dusk of Nassau Street, hugging themselves and stamping, Septimus would have many remarks to make to the others, much advice to urge upon them, but to him and Terpie would only say, "Very good, Mrs. Tomlinson. Admirable, Mr. Smith."

But he was sorry for the chances he had missed to influence the fabric's weaving; especially since it seemed clear to him that in one respect Mr. Addison's tragedy of Roman virtue was presently tangled, knotted, snarled, drawn into an unsightly bunch.

"So, how did it all strike you?" Septimus enquired that evening with a careful carelessness, as they sat in the bath-house, now almost empty, and let the heat melt the ice out of their bones, take the crystallised kinks from fingers and toes. The roof of Smith's mouth felt like a raw cushion, yet the sting was delicious compared to the air outside. They had some rum in a bottle between them on the bench.

"Very tolerably."

"Yes?"

"Yes!"

It was true, too, with the grand exception he had in his mind.

"You're not disappointed by Lennox?"

"Not in the least. I mean, he could not be called a natural actor, but Cato is a part to be played on one note, and he has it secure, it is a bell he can ring again and again. When he talks about duty, and dying for your country, and so on, there's conviction in his voice; he sounds like a man who means it. And he growls along steadily through the verse. No; rough sincerity will not fail of its effect, I think you'll find. You should probably prime him to expect applause for 'Remember, O my friends' in Act Three, and to stop and wait while it dies, or he'll speak on through, and lose some."

"Very well."

"Have you remarked, though," added Smith, grinning, "that he's taken to heart the comparison of Cato to Mount Atlas?"

"What do you mean?"

"I mean, whenever he comes on, he gets to his mark, and he plants himself like this"—Smith got up to demonstrate—"one foot here, *bam*, and one foot far-removed over here, *bam*."

"Lord, you're right. You think he's making himself more . . . massive—"

"—mountainous—"

"—*triangular!* Good God, he is, though, isn't he? On account of his looks, probably, wouldn't you think? Which all agree are . . ."

"Stony?"

"Craggy!"

"Hail the man-mountain! Pass me the bottle."

"There you go."

"Hail!"

"Hail!"

"And Terpie's good too, of course."

She was. Having first established herself as young, pure and high-minded, she was now painting upon this severe white surface the innocent upheaval of first love; its fright, its fluttering, its undefended convulsions of feeling; with such tender touches of nature, as stoic Marcia lost her self-control, that the spectator quite forgot on what a slab of preceding illusion this new illusion rested.

"But?" said Septimus. "For I sense a 'but' coming."

"Your Sempronius won't do. He puts out no passion at all. The play becalms whenever he speaks."

It was essential to Addison's design in the play that Cato be flanked by two figures of equal weight. Not the statesman's two sons: they only provided a romantic subplot, and a contrast between a cool and a hot head, as the great Roman waited in Utica for the tyrant Julius Caesar to arrive and extinguish the last flame of liberty. The piece advanced instead by the difference it made between, on Cato's one side, Juba the African prince, a barbarian who wanted to be a Roman, and on his other his supposed ally, the wicked senator Sempronius, a Roman who behaved like a barbarian. Sempronius endeavoured to hide his villainy yet out it came in the excess and savagery of his language, and in the end he displayed it pure, purposing to carry off and rape Marcia while dressed as Juba. Thus, when the false Juba encountered the real one in Act Four, and they fought, and Sempronius was killed, this combat proved the play's contention—that at root the civilised virtues were matters of the will and soul, and not of blood. They were elective, freely to be chosen. The skin was not the character. Anyone could be a "Roman." Anyone who cared enough for liberty could be great Cato's inheritor. Pre-eminently of course to Mr. Addison, Britons, they being the famous citizens of the present world's empire of liberty; yet his message ran on wider, without respect to nation. Unfortunately, the gentleman who must embody the half of this conceit, who must plausibly portray a bag of furies writhing in the skin of a legislator— was a country uncle of the Philipse clan, incapable of representing any fraction of it.

"Come now, he is not so bad," protested Septimus.

"Come, yes he is; and you know it."

"He speaks the pentameter very correctly—which you always make a great point of?"

"Indeed he does; and he beats time comfortably upon his waist-coat with his thumbs as he goes, to make sure of it. And he is entirely an amiable soul besides, as is witnessed by the way he beams at us, when anyone else on stage is speaking. But the nasty libertine in the mask of virtue is nowhere. He does not speak him, act him, or (I am convinced) even imagine him. What were you thinking of, in casting him for your villain? Had you a fainting spell that day? A fit of the mulligrubs?"

"He is the right age," said Septimus defensively, flipping a drop of sweat off the end of his nose. "He is the right age; he stands straight; he speaks clearly; he was willing. This was accounted very full qualification for the role, you know, before you came along and commenced to raise up expectations."

"I am not spoiling it for you, am I?" Smith said, smitten by a sudden compunction.

"Never in life!" cried Septimus. "No, no, never think so. It is a pleasure to see how much better a thing we may make of it, with your help. —It is a pleasure to be *shown*, how the results I admire from the boxes are achieved on the stage. A privilege, even."

Smith looked down, embarrassed, but Septimus did not see, since he too was studying the floor between the pale knobs of his knees.

"The truth is," Septimus went on awkwardly, "I had in addition a political motive in casting old Philipse, for he belongs to no party in the ruckus over the Assembly; so if he were the villain, I could not be suspected of any satirical fling. I would not be saying that either side, the Governor's or De Lancey's, was a false friend to liberty. I was avoiding a danger."

"But now you have avoided Sempronius. He is not there at all."

"Cannot the success of the rest carry him along?"

"A villain is hard to do without. —A fight scene is hard to do without, if it is meant to tie off a whole department of the story, with a satisfying clash. You saw what happened today, when we tried to rehearse it. He died like—like—"

"Like a man sitting gratefully down in an elbow-chair, because he has a touch of indigestion. Yes. Damn it, yes."

"Would he mind very much, being replaced?"

"Probably not. He is only doing it to oblige. I think he would as happily spectate. But the point is moot, when I have no-one who knows the part, to replace him *with*."

"What about doing it yourself?"

"Oh!" cried Septimus, after a fraction of a pause. (A fraction with a very low denominator.) "What an excellent plan! Who could possibly find matter for satire, if the *Governor's Secretary* plays a notorious enemy to freedom? Is a grinning, cackling, hand-rubbing monster?"

"I see you've given the part some thought. Not sure about the cackling, though . . ."

"Richard! Be serious!"

"I *am* being serious. You know the words—you know everyone's words—and I think you could be good. You could do Sempronius with a surprising fire. I have heard you lose your temper, remember; I have heard you roar—and the contrast with your usual precise appearance is most striking and horrible."

"Why, thank you."

Smith sighed. "You know, it is not an insult, to an actor, to say that he can find some unpleasant quality within him. The assumption of the profession is, that everyone has every quality in 'em, and the trick is, how to find the needed one."

"You really think I could be good? —I don't for a moment think you are taking seriously what consequences may follow; you just like to get your own way. —And I've no more idea than poor Philipse how to fight on stage, you know. I only know real sword-play."

"I can teach you! Nothing easier!"

"Oh, Lord. I suppose you know your business. Pass the rum."

When they shambled out at last onto the snow-crust of William Street, in a moonless night a single degree of blue removed from black, and gimleted with the steel points of stars, the shock of the cold hit the freshly steamed and softened flesh of their bare faces like a slammed door. It rocked them on their unsteady heels. Smith crammed down his tricorn and yanked up his scarf. Septimus, who was wearing a complex flapped cap of many layers on his shaved head, fumbled the buttons closed under his chin. Achilles, seeing them emerge, came out of the grog-shop opposite carrying a lantern.

Smith was so full both of rum and of his thoughts for a whirling, exhilarating to-and-fro with wooden swords, that at first he paid little mind to the swinging light drawing closer, or to the swaddled long-boned small-headed figure crunching paternally across holding it, with a resigned look for the state they were in; or to the other dark-muffled shape that slipped from the same door-way at Achilles' heels, and flowed away at once down the shadow-walled pale-floored gallery of the street, like a shadow itself, or like a streamer of black ink twisting in water, flying over long spaces of untouched snow between each light footfall. The loose, flying run was somehow familiar. And the long, straight hair. It was— With a distracted, a stupefied slowness, Smith recognised, or was almost sure he did, the thief of his portfolio on his first morning in the city.

"Hey!" he shouted, and set off to run after; but Septimus somehow clumsily contrived at that exact moment to jostle into him, and to get his foot tangled between Smith's, so that instead of flying in pursuit, Smith just went flying, and measured his length with a powdery thud on the snow, face first. Septimus and Achilles crowded close, all solicitude.

"Stop him!" he said, spitting out snow.

"Who?" said Septimus.

"Him! Him!" said Smith, trying to point between their legs. But the figure was already gone. "He stole—"

"What?" asked Septimus. They helped him up.

"My money. Some money. From me."

"That's terrible. When? Recently?"

"No, when I arrived."

"Well, alas, I am sure it is long gone now."

"But you must have got a good look at him," said Smith to Achilles, collecting himself a little. "He was just behind you."

"No," said Achilles.

"I didn't see anyone," said Septimus. "Did you, old thing?"

"No," said Achilles.

"But he was just *there*," said Smith. "You must have seen him. He came out with you. He was only a step behind you."

"No," said Achilles.

"In fact," said Smith slowly, stumbling over again through his memory of the previous minute, "you were *with* him, weren't you. Together. Weren't you? I'm sure you were."

"No," said Achilles.

"Come on, who was that?"

Smith began to press forward, carrying his insistence close into Achilles' face; but Septimus put an arm in his path.

"Richard, stop," he said.

The voice was muzzy, but the arm was definite. He smiled at Smith, and Achilles joined in with it. It was on both faces a friendly smile, an encouraging smile; yet with a patronage in it, a patient confidence of being in the position of power here, that startled Smith considerably. Thanks to the play, and Septimus' deference, he had grown used to thinking of himself as holding the patron's position. He felt a tremor of alarm.

Septimus brought up his other gloved hand, and with both, began to brush inaccurately at the snow clotted into the wool of Smith's coat-front.

"You must allow me to know my business, too," he said kindly. "And I promise you, there was absolutely nobody there. Absolutely nobody for you to be talking to, do you see? Absolutely nobody it would do you any good to meet. Trust me upon this point. Now, Richard; now, you terrible persuasive fellow; you and I have drunk too much, and I have committed myself to something I am going to regret in the morning, and assuredly"—some shushing and sliding in the s's, there—"it is time to say farewell. Without saying anything else to make life more complicated than it is already, don't you think?"

"You should both be in bed, that is for sure," said Achilles. "The frost tonight is not safe for foolishness."

"You see! Farewell! Good night!"

He planted on Smith's cheek a neat, dry, Toby-jug's kiss, and clasping rather at random at Achilles' shoulder, was led away by him without looking back. Smith remained shivering in the silent street, with its hard meniscus of white creeping up the cold bricks on either side, and the few lights showing in windows seeming deep-sunk, dim embers inaccessible behind many ice-layers. It was certainly time to move. As he trudged to Mrs. Lee's, meeting no-one, a slow confused revolution took place in his ideas, the planets within him grinding sluggishly into new positions relative to one another, and new suspicions taking form according to the angles of vision thus revealed. He began to consider, what he should perhaps have considered before, that a person who gathered intelligence for the Governor—as Hendrick had actually told him Septimus did, as plainly as possible—might do more than simply listen in coffee-shops; that the plan of the enmity between the disputing factions in the city of New-York might have depths of detail he had not perceived; that the partnership of Septimus and Achilles, with its proficiency in handling swords and ropes and rooftops, might have wider applications than he had guessed.

III

Mr. Smith upon stage was a different creature, with all the impulse shaken out of him. Whether he moved fast or slow, he moved deliberately, almost ceremoniously, with an impersonal grace of gesture. The white lead wrought a similar change to his face, as the little tongue of Terpie's brush licked it over inch by inch. His caramel freckles vanished; the readily-colouring individual skin beneath; the mobile eyebrows; the lines of laughter and surprise around his eyes. In their place she drew the ideal slender black arcs of a male lead's brow-lines part-way up his forehead. She added no beauty-spot, because Juba was not a fop. She drew, over the whited-out outline of his real mouth, a smaller mouth in carmine. Fierce brushing, fierce tying and a dense dredging of powder turned his unruly red-brown hair to a tidy whited-brown like a sugared date. His face had become an expressive mask, ready for the display only of selected, intended emotions—surely as far from betraying a natural truth as could possibly be required for a performance as an albino prince of Africa.

Terpie being the possessor of the only complete equipment of make-up for the stage in the whole city, she painted everybody's face during the waiting hour before the performance, on the afternoon of the 15th December, which was the Monday of the third week in Advent. Septimus had agreed to pay for the replenishing of her store, and she was generous with it, sitting on a stool in front of each of the cast in turn, gazing intently with her lapis-blue eyes at the effect she was making, and touching her teeth with her real tongue while she touched the faces with her brush. For Septimus as Sempronius, she drew on the jagged wrinkle-lines and jowl-lines that conventionally signalised age, and added muddy smears of rouge for choler. For Cato, she applied thicker brows, and a pair of lines at the corners of the mouth, for determination. Herself, she did last, in front of a piece of mirror held by Septimus, laying on a mask identical to Flora's, from rosebud-carmine mouth to delicately girlish brows and lashes, except that for herself she omitted the faint blush of rouge on the cheeks, Marcia being after all a cooler soul than Lucia. All the while, they could hear the chatter and scraping as the audience came in, carrying chairs from home as requested. They were in the side store-room of the theatre, there being no curtain to raise or wings to lurk in: only, when the moment came to begin, a plain walk out from the store-room door onto the bare boards in front of the one set, facing the sudden sea of curious faces, and the row of candles in tin cups burning on the edge of the stage, which they must be careful not to kick over.

First out, and all alone, came Smith to speak the prologue by Mr. Pope, traditionally the task of the actor playing Juba. He stalked to centre-stage and gazed at the audience, and what in a more proper theatre would have been a mere gesture, aimed conjecturally into the blackness beyond the footlights, was here a real piece of looking, with the same pale winter light as yet painting the whole length of the room, and all of it mutually visible. There, murmuring and breathing together and warming one another with their shared breath, sat substantially everyone he had met since coming to New-York: the Governor and his household, Major Tomlinson and his brother officers, the Assemblymen and their families, De Lancey and his grandee cronies, the Rector of Trinity, the Van Loons and Lovells all in a row with Tabitha's pinched face helplessly drawn up by the spectacle, the coffee-drinkers of the Merchants, and going back and back on stools and benches and eventually standing, the middling and lesser sorts of inhabitants, including Mrs. Lee, and Quentin the waiter, and the murderous butcher of Pope Night, and a host of prentices eating nuts, and even (right up against the back wall) a line of the city's slaves. A crowd halfway to becoming familiar to him, after only six weeks. But he made himself a stranger to them. He began so quietly, so much as if he were talking to himself, and the lines were coming to him as he thought of 'em, that his whole body of hearers involuntarily leaned forward to hear him better, though his voice in fact carried easily to the very back; and then, having as it were secured their confidence, while he mused aloud upon the notorious power of tragedy over even the hardest heart—the tragedy of the least deserving, the tragedy of mere hapless humanity—the white-faced clown before them began to move, and to reason with grander, bigger, more formal gestures, and to speak with quickly-mounting intensity of rhythm, like a white snake weaving before fascinated barnyard chicks; until, abruptly, he struck a pose as lavishly eloquent as the statue of an orator, and spoke the turn in his argument with the voice of a trumpet.

> *Here tears shall flow from a more generous cause,*
> *Such tears as patriots shed for dying laws:*
> *He bids your breasts with ancient ardour rise,*
> *And calls forth Roman drops from British eyes!*

And the rest he delivered at full oratorical pitch. He had them; their eyes followed him, magnetised, as he stamped and turned, and boasted of great Cato, whom they were about to behold. "Who sees him act," he cried, "but envies every deed? Who hears him groan," he groaned, "and does not wish to bleed?" Smith had from the crowd before him none of the sense of reticence or sluggishness you get from an audience that does not desire to be moved, and must be gentled into it by touches, against its inclination. These wanted it, and were off their marks and sliding fast and free into emotion without resistance, without restraint. Perhaps, therefore, he shoved them along more roughly than he would have done upon the London stage—where, in any case, he had never been of such eminence as to play the lead. They were persuadable, and he persuaded them. They wished to feel, and he obliged to the top of his bent.

The effect lasted through the, frankly, rather humdrum expository scene that followed, in which Cato's sons kindly laid out the political situation, and carried the play safely through into the meat of the drama, which succeeded it. They liked the girls, both Lucia's bright, happy advocacy of love, and Marcia's stern denial of it. Far from snickering at Terpie, they listened rapt. They approved of Juba, and nodded gravely as he explained that, instead of rendering him into some indoor milksop, the virtues of civilisation would set the stamp of self-control upon his manliness. Cato, they applauded whenever Addison gave him a speech of defiance, which was almost every time he opened his mouth as Lieutenant Lennox played the part, feet wide apart, fist banging his chest, growling the lines. "It is not now a time to talk of aught, But chains or conquest, liberty or death!" Roars from the room.

But they hated Sempronius. Smith had had time only to talk Septimus through the character once, and it had been their agreement that Septimus would treat the traitor senator as something like the stock figure of the hypocrite, turning one way to smile, another to mutter out his bile in soliloquies. But when, on his very first entrance, he declared himself Cato's secret enemy, and virtue's, they booed him like a pantomime villain; and after a moment of dismay and hesitation, in which he glanced reproachfully at Smith, Septimus decided to play up to it; played up to it with increasing relish, growing pantomimic himself, skulking and sneering, winking and cackling, making of his soliloquies insultingly direct speeches to the audience, in which he encouraged and solicited their hatred; drew it forth; flirted out further reserves of it. "I blame you for this entirely," he whispered to Smith, as they passed one another in the store-room door. "So, stop having fun," Smith whispered back. Septimus had particular fun, he judged, in delivering Sempronius' extravagantly fake paeans of praise to liberty, and having them reliably jeered by the New-Yorkers. "A day, an hour of virtuous liberty, Is worth a whole eternity in bondage"—Septimus' head winsomely on one side; catcalls. Smith had hoped that there might be at least some frisson of consciousness and discomfort when Sempronius ordered his own rebel troops to be "broken on the rack, Then, with what life remains, impaled and left, To writhe at leisure round the bloody stake." No chance of that, however. Sempronius was by then the voice of assured evil, and all his savageries could be comfortably condemned without reference to any sins on the onlookers' part. The onlookers looked on and hissed. Tabitha did not. Less poisoned-looking now, infused almost against her will with the life of the occasion, she was sitting up and glancing fascinated—deeply entertained—about the faces of the hissers, as well as at the stage. Harvesting ironies, Smith was sure.

When the time came for Sempronius and Juba to fight, Septimus and Smith circled in a series of flamboyantly clashing parries, and clinches sword to sword, nose to nose. Septimus had declined, in rehearsal, to fall in with Smith's suggestion that he should at one point jump into the air, while Smith's wooden foil swept under his feet. Ridiculous, he had said; much too likely to go wrong. But now, caught up in the pleasures of villainy, he overacted his share of the combat fearsomely, and managed to flick a candle with his sword-point into the front row, where it was fortunately caught. Puncturing the bladder of pig's blood under his costume, he died in a gush of crimson; then rose to his elbow, gave a death speech of owlish excess with his painted eyebrows raised, and did it again. Cheers.

It was a tribute to Terpie's skill that, discovering his body dressed as Juba a moment later, and mistaking it for Juba's, she was able to wrench the mood back to seriousness. Having, from the opening of the play, glided rather than walked, and moved her arms like marble come to life—now she jerked, trembled, widened her eyes, bit her fingers. The audience quietened, stared, pitied her. "O, he was all made up of love and charms," she mourned, and she seemed like great Cleopatra herself bewailing Antony, not like Addison's faint, efficient copy of that queen. The pity of love squandered, mislaid, overlooked, ill-fated, was made present, trembling, in the room. Then Juba himself entered, and all was righted. "O fortunate mistake! O happy Marcia!" More cheers, of a more benevolent sort; cheers of willing belief and relief. The same willingness to enter in seriously marked the response to the final act, with its sombre tableaux, first of Cato's elder son displayed to his father in another heroic welter of blood, then of Cato himself, nobly extinguishing himself as the last light of Roman freedom guttered out. Deep hush. Sighs. Sobs! Leaning from the store-room door, Smith was surprised to see a generous, general weeping grip the room. Damp eyes everywhere. The butcher at the back cramming his big fist into his mouth, a pair of visiting gentlemen from Virginia blowing their noses, De Lancey himself wiping one eye with his finger. When the cast lined up for their curtain call *sans* curtain, the clapping was thunderous and long-sustained, with particular peaks for Cato, for Juba, for Marcia, and (with hooting) for Sempronius. They were a hit.

• • •

After the dinner in the Black Horse for the cast, with bumper upon bumper of congratulatory punch ladled out, and a bottle of veritable champagne produced, and Major Tomlinson swollen at Terpie's shoulder like a proud tomato, and Flora forgetting to not smile at Smith, and many toasts exchanged—Smith and Septimus sat in the steam at William Street again, laughing quietly. But there was constraint between them as well as jubilation. Septimus was beginning to feel the fretful aftermath of his elation. Smith was wondering how much he might count on the friendship between them.

"That feeling!" said Septimus. "It's extraordinary, isn't it?"

"Yes."

"As if you held intimate converse with a whole crowd all together. As if you might stroke 'em, tweak 'em, tickle 'em, strike 'em, all as one beast . . ."

"As if all shared one circulation of blood, yes."

"And you feel them, and they feel you; and yet the you they feel is not quite you—not, you know, you simple, you veritable—but a you whom they decide upon."

"The part did run mad away with you, tonight."

"I have never felt anything like it."

"You made me an entire speech, when first we met, about the power of seeming, and how it was not to be relied on."

"Yes; I suppose; but that was seeming *opposed* to being; seeming with the real, animal life beneath. This is seeming striking inward into being. The artifice stronger than the animal. Not a lie, a change!"

"Septimus—"

"I wonder, will they let me put Sempronius off, tomorrow? Will they always be seeing him, a little, when they talk to me? Always hooting at him?"

Smith could have assured him, conventionally, that a play was only a play. That a crowd filling a theatre in a city must be worldly enough to tell the difference between the actor and the role. But he had seen enough of the temper of this city, by now, not to be sure that this was definitely the case.

"Septimus, the other night. —That light-heeled wraith who prigged my purse. If I understood you rightly—"

Septimus sighed. "If you had understood me rightly, you would not be asking questions. You saw something you should not have done. I asked you to trust me. Can we not leave it there?"

"The thing is"—doggedly—"I have a particular reason for asking. It is not the money. There was a paper with it—"

"No!" cried Septimus, standing up, indignant, milk-white and bony. "I will *not* discuss this with you. It is not in your sphere. You must just trust me, when I say, that in this case what you do not know will not harm you. Lord knows you require enough trust in return."

Smith looked at him.

"In any case," said Septimus more gently, "I must go. Achilles will be waiting for me. There are not many places we can go together, you know. We have to do all *our* celebrating in private. I will see you before Christmas. You will still be here then?"

"I must be. For my bill."

"Of course. Well, I will be back by then. I must go up-river tomorrow, and try to mend matters as best I can with the regiments waiting there; but I will be back on the twenty-second or the twenty-third. Good night, my dear. That was sublime as well as silly, and I thank you for it."

A gleam of a porcelain smile, and he was gone, leaving Smith alone in the steam. He could be heard in the next room, dressing and latching his shoes; then doors opened and closed farther away, and there was no further sound at all.

Smith, melancholy, solitary, presumed he was the last customer in the bath-house. But he found he was in no hurry to exchange it for the colder solitude of the streets, or for the room at Mrs. Lee's, which had taken on few of the qualities of a home, or even of a very substantial refuge. Since his time in the gaol, it seemed the winter wind blew where it willed through every structure in New-York. He poured another dip of water onto the stove, from the barrel, and with a sputtering hiss it seethed instantaneously to vapour, descending from the planked ceiling in a thick grey mist that first burned and battered at Smith's pores, dragging out new sweat in a sheet over his skin, then coiled and drifted more languorously, in luminous haze around the lantern, in slow hanging twists and tendrils. He could scarcely see a foot but he did not mind. He had playing before his mind's eye, on his mind's stage, his view from the store-room door as the audience shuffled out, bearing their chairs. Terpie had been scrubbing at his face with a vinegary rag, to take off the greasepaint, but over her shoulder, through the door-way, between the shapes of those departing, he had seen how Tabitha had stood hesitating; lingering, while her family around her impatiently tried to hustle her away; still looking at the empty stage with a baffled expression, as if she had discovered in herself something else that needed saying. Something surprising. She is a goblin, he reminded himself. There is something very wrong with her. But the imprinted picture persisted regardless. He shut his eyes and could still see it. The sweat trickled down. The hot stove popped and fizzed. Such was the power of the association of ideas, that when he heard footsteps, and a woman's voice, and his eyes flew open again, startled, he almost expected it to be Tabitha standing there. But it was not: it was Terpie Tomlinson, only as high as his shoulder but as bare as Eve, leaning against the door-frame, and waiting to be admired.

"I haven't got to play the *ingénue* for a long time," she said. "I wanted to say, thankee." The voice beneath the elocution turned out to be not a flat Essex drawl, but a warm burr from somewhere in the West Country. Or perhaps that was just another voice left over from the stage: a friendly milkmaid, chosen to please.

Mrs. Tomlinson, naked and lightly steamed, was all rosy curves. All cream-smooth skin puckered and stippled and flustered and whipped up, by the heat, into mobile rashes and foxings of colour. Her noble bosom, uncovered and unsupported, spread wider than her ribs, and jostled out into heavy, rich, pendant udders, whose general blush concentred in fat raspberry-coloured nubbins thick as thumbs. Her wide hips, canted out to exaggerate a swell already near the limit of the probable, spread from her narrow waist like a lyre. Her belly dipped into a crease touched with brownish-pink at her navel, then swelled out again, descending, into a lesser hill, and a lower yet, valleyed and russet-lipped, tangled with springy hair where the steam collected and dripped. —How hard it is to describe a desirable woman without running into geography! Or the barnyard. Or the resources of the fruit-bowl. As if flesh itself, bare vulnerable flesh-of-our-flesh, were not enough, considered merely as itself, and we could not account for its power, without fetching away into similes. I do not want to write this part of the story, and am quibbling to hesitate. —The grave beauty of her face seemed to contradict the lush abundance of her body, yet both were true of her, and in truth contradicted each other as little as any two qualities whatsoever happening to be possessed by an individual: the contradiction existing only in the expectation of an onlooker who had presumed a whole woman would conform to a single impression. Who, finding she didn't, might if sufficiently led by his loins, choose to interpret the double impression as an extra piquancy. And the effect of the years on Mistress Terpie? Let us be painterly. Let us say, it cannot be denied that the line of beauty had wavered, wandered, thickened in her, with time. Where before there had been the perfect serpentine bow of the river there was now the braided spread of a delta. But magnificence blurred is still magnificence.

Smith, looking at what she showed him, looking at her confident smile, felt at first a kind of defeat. He had not contrived the situation. It was flat contrary to what he had, that moment, been wearily desiring. He saw at once vistas of disappointment and embarrassment, if he said no, and of complication and embroilment, if he said yes. And of course a betrayal. But a betrayal of what, really? There seemed, one scant second later, a perversity, a negligibility, a bare, thin, almost contemptible unlikelihood in what he had just now been contemplating, and wanting, and dreaming of, compared to the rich certainty of what was being offered by Terpie. As if, to continue faithful—even to consider continuing faithful—to his actual passion, would be to prefer a will-o'-the-wisp, a sour vacant mouthful of air, over a mouth to kiss, a willingly opened body in which to find at least the sensation of a home in the world. He liked to choose. He liked to choose. He was a man who chose for himself. When had he last been able to do that? He was sick of waiting on choices not his own. And as he stared, and moments passed—not many, by all external calculation, but enough to be felt, when no response is arriving to this kind of offer—he noticed, what he had been too dumb-struck to see before, that there was anxiety quivering around Terpie's lapis eyes, despite her smile, and quivering more there by the second. Though he was sure she had many times laid calculated waste like this to men, it might he realised be some while since she had last dared it. She might be inwardly quite unconfident whether this coup-de-l'oeil still worked, at forty-six. Suddenly he saw in her boldness a kind of sluttish courage not a million miles removed from his own willed shamelessness in every New-York room he'd stepped in. She was blatant; so was he.

Smith grinned. " 'He bids your breasts with ancient ardour rise,' " he said.

"You may stick that right up your arse, Master Smith," said Terpie, in the cool, pure little voice of Marcia.

"Well, I think I'd rather—"

"Maybe later, if you're a good boy."

She swayed into the steam-room: a foot away, six inches away, into his reaching hands. He held her spectacular haunches. Her damp, flushed skin was warm, and very solid. He blew gently and experimentally on the corrugated dull-pink skin around one big nipple. It tightened and swelled. She shivered.

"I don't s'pose you're staying?" she said.

"No," said Smith.

"Only we could do good work together."

"I can't."

"A lot of things. Real theatre. None o' this tableau nonsense."

"I really can't."

"Oh well," she said. "Then there's no reason to be careful, is there."

Mr. Smith could think of many reasons to be careful, but only one he cared to mention.

"What about the Major?" he said.

"What he don't know, won't hurt him." She ran her hands into Smith's wet hair, and he—

But why always Smith? Was it necessarily true, that because she seemed to *him* to be the ripe, round, straightforward antidote to the complications of his hopes, the scene looked as simple through her eyes? Was she not taking the greater risk here? Did she not have to set aside cautions, sorrows, hopes, fears, loyalties, to permit herself the role of the plump and ready siren in the steam-room? Have we not heard enough already of Mr. Smith's desire, and seen Mrs. Tomlinson quite sufficiently as he did? Should we not, at least, pay a little attention to Terpie's view of him, lounging like a freckly satyr on the wooden benches, grinning at her with a young man's lazy sense of entitlement now the surprise of her gift had faded; grown almost all the way into his strength but still long-limbed, with the knots of bone at his knees and his elbows giving him the lingering gawkiness of a foal; with the film of sweat on his chest, and his curls thickened to dark emphatic coils with water drops at the end; with the last unremoved traces of the paint around his eyes rimming his gaze in black depravity; with his wide mouth laughing, and his cock lolling? No, not lolling any more. Stirring, as she filled her hands with him, to her pleasure and his.

The reader may imagine the occasional mismatches of desire or of endurance caused by their different ages. By the differences, at times in what followed, between twenty-four-year-old impetuousness and forty-six-year-old patience; between twenty-four-year-old directness and forty-six-year-old guile; between twenty-four-year-old muscles and forty-six-year-old backache. The reader may imagine, as she knelt on the bench *en levrette*—a technical term Terpie had learnt from a French gentleman, meaning *with your bum in the air*—that the pleasure of a boyish lover's deep wet rooting inside her did not entirely cancel the pinching of the skin of her knees between the wooden slats. And yet the two of them made for themselves, successfully, that little encompassing sphere of sensation which seems while it lasts to be, if not a home in the great world to be relied upon, at least a little world in itself, outside which not much matters, for a while. And yet, they arrived together, if not at rapture, then at those melting convulsions which come as close to it as you may, where gratitude and mutual greed are all you have to furnish the place of trust.

She took him in the bath-house. Having crept with him, whispering, up Mrs. Lee's stairs to his bedroom, she took him again in his bed. She slept the night with him there. She woke first, in the grey snow-light of Tuesday morning. Finding that one of the costs of age was soreness after greed, but unwilling yet for the adventure to be over, and the reign of consequence and perhaps remorse to begin, she roused him with her mouth; and when he woke too, climbed comfortably atop him nose to tail, to work at her leisure on the young tree of flesh in her mouth, while he guzzled among sopping coral folds.

It was unfortunately at this moment that Flora, who had mistaken one of the muffled sounds they were making for an invitation, stepped into the room with a letter in her hand that Tabitha had prevailed on her to carry. Confusion; astonishment; fascination; the dawning in her equable face of a kind of rancorous glee. She dropped the letter and fled.

6

A LETTER

to Richard Smith, Esqr., Mrs. Lee's, The Broad Way

Golden Hill, Monday night

Smith—which seems tho curt the Name that designates you
easiest in my Head—I am not accustomed to People being
kind. A Cynic would say no Doubt that I make sure I get little
Opportunity to get used to it, being so pre-emptingly nasty
Myself. I find It hard, even to pay a close Attention, to any gentle
or tender Signs of Intent, for my Mind runs on swift ahead into
Abrasions and Contradictions. It is, for me, like listening to a very
faint Sound, to attend to Kindness. Yet you have repeated the
quiet Sound, till even I take a Note of it. I have mock'd you, teas'd
you, fleer'd at you, trick'd you, and done my best to trap you: and
you have return'd, for all these sad Jibes, only a patient Suggestion
that you wish me well. That you think me a Creature not reducible
to my wanton Urge to Annoy. I do not know what to do with
this Kindness—this unwarranted good Opinion—on your Part.
I am not sure at All, since we are speaking Truth here, that I like
it. It has for me the Savour of Danger. It seems to beckon me
into empty Places, where I will likely find Nothing to sustain me.

Nine portions out of Ten in me, or maybe Ninety-Nine, desire to Mock again; to defend Myself by stamping on it like a Bugg. Yet it seems an Honour due to you, for your Kindness, and perhaps an Action of Hope towards Myself, to ask what the Tenth part of me, or the Hundredth, wants. I saw you today acting Juba, and acting him passing well, tho Addison is not Shakespeare, and you were therefore endeavouring I thought to stand tall under a low Ceiling: but no Matter, I am not setting up for a Critick. I thought to Myself, what a Fool is Marcia, to require such hearty Kicks from Circumstance to tell her what she feels for Juba. A due Respect to her own Independency, a Willingness to take a Fraction of the Risks her Lover took, should surely have moved her sooner, to interrogate her Heart. If I can learn Patience from you, Smith—if I can struggle and succeed and for an Hour lay aside my old Friend Spite—will you come again, and drink Tea with me, and see what new Thing we may find Courage to make room for? Your uncivil T

7

O Sapientia

December 16th

20 Geo. II

1746

I

When a log that has lain half-burned in a winter fire is struck suddenly with the poker, a bright lace of communicative sparks wakes on the instant. The sullen coals shatter into peach and scarlet mosaic, with a thin high tinkling sound, and pulses of the changing shades pass over the surface in all directions with rapidity too great for the eye. So was it when the news of Smith's disgraceful liaison was suddenly released into the town.

Within hours, the intelligence that the English actor had been caught in spectacular debauchery with the celebrated Mrs. Tomlinson had run from ear to mouth to ear all the way from the Fort to Rutgers' Farm, from the frozen East River to the black surge of the Hudson. That it spread so fast may be attributed to its easy translation into several varieties appealing to different minds, yet equally satisfying and destructive in all of 'em. Moralising: that one of the wicked creatures of the stage had been caught *at it* with another, a harlot old enough to be his mother, all natural prohibitions no doubt having been overthrown by their practice of godless imposture. National: that all England was a cauldron of filth, and one just arrived from thence would necessarily bring with him the taint of it. Artistic: that the passion displayed yesterday between Juba and Marcia had proved veritable, which was not a surprise to anyone of discernment who had been in the theatre, for indeed you could tell at the time that there was *something in the air*. Envious: that the little pup from London had had the crack at Terpie many a man wanted. Envious in a different style: that he was a pretty fellow, and right to see a lad might learn a thing or two from a friendly widow, or with discretion a wife, but that he must be lacking in the headpiece to settle for his education on such a trollop. Political: that the boy new-come with all the money, who'd seemed to veer elusively between the parties, had surely now just fumbl'd, or stumbl'd, or f——'d his way onto the side of the Assembly, by publicly cuckolding the Governor's officer. Delicious approval; delicious disapproval; a fire of winter scandal blazing up delicious hot.

At least, for those who were not privily concerned in it. Terpie felt the burn first. Disengaging without tenderness the moment the door slammed behind Flora, she dressed at speed with her face set, swearing under her breath. Her only farewell to Smith was a grimace, and a kind of savage, suppressing pat at the air in the direction where he lay groaning with his head under the pillow. Then she was hurrying through the snowy streets to the watch-room in Fort St. George where Major Tomlinson would be sleeping off the port of the night before. She had read Flora's face, and she was grimly confident that she had a disaster to outrun, and must wake her husband, and confess the news to him herself before anyone else could tell it him with laughter in their voice; and must abide *his* anger and humiliation, and try if she could see the way to call on him for the understanding he had promised her, toward the irregular ways of the stage, when he had been wooing her at the stage-door in

Covent Garden as her last play failed. But that had been years ago; and they had followed his posting to America; and the promise had gathered dust unused, lapsing into a mere ghostly hypothesis of an indulgence, fading away to both their contentment. She had liked him, and his companionable ways, and his indifference to there being no prospect of children. A little shiver from men's eyes on her, that had been enough. Until the boy, the damn'd boy, turned up. She took a deep breath when she reached the Fort, and did what she must.

Smith, meanwhile, decided to conduct his wretchedness in private, still under the illusion that he had no more to contend with than having driven off Tabitha again for sure just when she dared to reach for him.

He hid in his bed till a writhing dislike of his own nakedness drove him out of it. Then he found the letter. Then, putting together the contents of the letter, and particularly its praise of his patience, with a vivid viewing upon his inner eye of what Flora must have seen as he lay voluptuously smothered, he began helplessly to laugh, and presently to weep, and then to laugh and weep together. He washed his face, and dressed. But when he stood ready for the world, the very thought of having to rebuild a front of charm, and to carry it through an icy town containing the Lovells, made him feel abruptly too tired to keep his sore eyes open. He lay back down and pressed his cheek into the pillow as if it might open and admit him. He fell into sleep as into a cold river, full of glassy slow-twining currents. He shivered as he lay in the tangled sheets, and clutched his hands into his armpits, but clung to unconsciousness for as long as he could make it last, rolling himself back in, and under, sleep's thick surface whenever the currents threatened to strand him on the brink of waking, and consequences. It was not until the winter dusk that he found himself irretrievably awake, and crept out, and drawn by an urge for refuge crept along Broad Way to Trinity for the evening service. He joined in wanly with the General Confession, but the words seemed remote to him and of no conceivable application, and when the choir sang the antiphon of the day, in praise of the divine wisdom "sweetly ordering all things," he felt welling up again the earlier combination of laughter and tears, and must bite his sleeve till it went away: so that, altogether, his recourse to the comforts of religion could not be called successful. The Rector looked sharply at him as he departed, but he had his head down and did not mark it. Mrs. Lee had her mouth open to speak to him when he returned to the house, but he swept obliviously past, and did not mark it.

He was not even immediately disabused in the Merchants at breakfast-time the next morning. The emptying-out of the city entailed a wider separation in the coffee-house between the remaining regulars, as they came in puffing and stamping and calling for refreshment. Though they may have glanced at Smith, and Quentin regarded him with cocked head and a bright speculative eye, none yet crossed the gulfs of empty table and chairs to speak; Smith, made imperceptive by unhappiness, ordered his usual rolls and coffee, and even made a spasmodic essay or two at the old game of bowling languages at Quentin to see if he could field 'em. Then Septimus came in, pale, swift and intent.

"There you are; you idiot," he said.

"I thought you'd gone!" cried out Smith delightedly.

"I nearly had. I was virtually on horseback, when I was called back to a staff meeting."

"Well, I am very glad to see you—"

"Are you? I am not very glad to see you, because the meeting was convened on your account. There is something maddeningly predictable about the way you procure disaster, Richard. It is like someone winding a clock, as methodical as that, only this time instead of a key into clockwork, you stuck your cock into Terpie."

"Oh. You know about that."

"*Everyone* knows about that."

"I am afraid I have made a fool of myself," Smith said, with that species of self-condemnation which imminently expects to be comforted by a friend's disagreement.

"Do you think so? —I must say, I thought your tastes were subtler, your appetites less gross. For that matter, I thought your heart was given elsewhere."

"Don't; that is the worst of it. That just when I was resigned to all that coming to nothing, and was, you know, indulging myself, thinking it did not matter—"

"If you tell me your heart is broken on this particular morning, Richard, I will just say: what, again? Perhaps you should be more careful with it."

"She was very . . . pressing. Terpie, I mean."

"You poor dear. You poor defenceless darling."

"No; very well; no. She was *there*. And she seemed to be offering satisfaction without complication. And she was very tempting. Come on, Septimus. She *is* very tempting, if you are at all that way inclined."

"No she isn't. She is like a caricature of a temptation, drawn with such mad hyperbole that anyone with any sense would know better than to act on it."

"Perhaps we are out of your domain of expertise," said Smith, puzzled yet picking up some heat by friction.

"Well, I certainly don't want to be having this conversation. Lord knows I would rather be picking my way through a frozen forest with an icicle depending from my nose. I would *infinitely* rather be safe on my way up the valley, with only wolves and wild Indians and delicate diplomacy to contend with, than be here talking to you about Terpie's tits. I wish to God I had never listened to you and included her in the play."

"Septimus—"

"But out of my expertise? Let us see: hmm, *no*. Because to be caught in flagrante with Terpie is not a strictly private problem. You have made a scandal, you idiot, to keep tongues wagging on the entire island till the spring thaw."

"You'll excuse me if by now I don't care very much for the flutterings of these people."

"*These people* are my occupation. And my neighbours. I rise and fall in their judgement. I live in their gaze. I don't know how many times I have to explain this to you. You are not in London. *You are not in London.*"

Septimus was hissing at him across the table, a Toby-jug with a pressure of steam inside it.

"You have explained quite sufficiently; I need no more explanations from you," Smith said, drawing back.

"I will spell it out for you anyway. You have put horns on the head of Major Tomlinson. Therefore you have put 'em by implication on the head of the Governor and the whole administration of the colony. Everyone is laughing."

"I am not."

"Of no consequence—whether you are, or not. Of no consequence—what you meant by it. You have dishonoured us. You have made us ridiculous. You have given us a slight that must be answered. The Major cannot challenge you, or he would lose what little's left him of his dignity, but the meeting was clear: you must be challenged."

"Well, I thank you for the warning," Smith said stiffly.

"You misunderstand me. This is not a warning. This *is* the challenge." And Septimus reached across the table and slapped him hard across the face. The table lurched and the coffee-pot capsized, sending the dregs in black streams into his lap.

"You will meet me tomorrow, early, on the Common, for a *rencontre d'honneur*," said Septimus ringingly, for the benefit of the whole room, "or stand convicted in all men's eyes of a contemptible cowardice, as well as a contemptible incontinence, not worthy of the name of a gentleman."

Smith gaped.

"You should secure a second, and have him deliver a note of your reply, in writing, to the Fort."

"Who would I ask?"

"Anyone who is laughing," cried Septimus. "You have pleased as many people as you have wounded. —Gods, you have me looking after you, even now; you have a hideous knack for it. Stop. Solve your own difficulties."

To prepare for any duel is a melancholy business. Far from concentrating the mind—as it was observed, at about this time, that the expectation of being hanged on the morrow may do—it caused Mr. Smith's thoughts to skitter, without purchase on the grave matters at hand, like a kitten on a pane of glass; or, which would be more appropriate to the place and season, like a man flailing his arms as he endeavours not to fall, on an ice-slide. He could neither forget, for a single instant, what was coming, nor attend to it properly. He acquired a second for the duel, by the mere process of remaining dumb-struck in the Merchants once Septimus had swirled out. This was a gentleman attached in some way to the Assembly's cause. In what way, was explained to him, yet he did not retain it, or even the gentleman's name, although some time passed in the coffee-shop in notional conversation with him, during which it became clear that his supporter was hoping for payment in the coin of lubricious detail, of bedroom gossip. Smith did not provide it. At least, he thought he did not. At least, after a time, the gentleman was gone. In the same way, he began another letter to his father, to be opened in the event of this new New-York death, and discarded it scarcely begun, incapable of the fixity of purpose required to carry through an explanation. He discarded, without beginning at all, projects for letters of apology to Major Tomlinson—to Terpie—to Septimus. For a letter to Tabitha of persuasive reasoning on the subject of the poor synchronisation of hearts. No, for a letter of abject pleading. No, one of angry defiance. No. Skittering still, fizzing with inward anxiety, he made his way back to Broad Way, where he was thrown out of his lodging by Mrs. Lee without particularly noticing it, she very probably making some choice remarks about respectable houses and those who abused them, he (of a certainty) making little response except a vague and distracted smile. He carried his trunk to a far more expensive and more grandiose room at the Black Horse, which he told himself the extra premium on his bill he had negotiated with Lovell would easily cover—unless he were dead tomorrow with the bill unpaid—this provoking a new skittering spiral of thoughts he could not complete, upon the subject of his errand, and his responsibilities, and the promises he might have broken by a contemptible incontinence. And whether he deserved the name of a gentleman. And whether he desired it. And what else he might call himself. And how afraid he was. And his father; and Tabitha; and Septimus. On and on, reeling dizzily through his head, in a whirl of fragmentary self-reproach, and worry, and disbelief, and annoyance, and renewed self-reproach. There may be persons in whom the possibility or certainty of approaching death induces a firm and vivacious grip on every remaining second as it passes. But Mr. Smith was not one of these. For him, even the prospect that at a certain minute after dawn the next day he might cease to be, leaving the morning to go on without him, seemed to infect every passing instant in advance of the event, as if he were already part-dead, and hence already part-dislodged from the calendar. He was far less resigned than he had been in prison. Perhaps he had used his store of resignation up. Between the burgundy velvet curtains of his new bed he turned, and turned, and fretfully turned again. He might be killed, he might be injured, he might conceivably be able to defend himself to the point where Septimus judged that public opinion was satisfied. No terms had yet been mentioned for the duel: whether it would be to first blood, or *à l'outrance*. (Another technical term from the French, meaning *till you turn up your toes*.) He did not even consider the possibility that he might win. He had no desire to hurt Septimus. But it was more than that. He had, once upon a time, received some part of a gentleman's training at sword-play, but it had never been used in earnest, and had been overlaid since by its flashing theatrical equivalent, good only for winning applause. He only really knew stage-fighting.

II

The part of the Common chosen for the duel was at the western end, away from the town, towards the pot-bank and the poor-house. The snow had melted back to a ring of scorched turf immediately around the kiln, but otherwise lay a foot deep, and where they were had been trampled to a compacted strip, dirty-white and crunching, bumped and socketed by the refrozen prints of boots going to and fro. It was a clear, cold dawn, with an intermittent icy breeze blowing, and a transparent flush of colour in the east, beyond the pale steeples of the snow-bound city. By this period of the winter a regular traffic of merchandise across the frozen East River had been established, and from the slight rise of the Common, black dots of humanity could already be seen out in the jumbled ice-field, slowly dragging sacks and boxes toward the city along a winding route where the going was smoothest. They seemed as remote as mites, and few other specimens of humanity were present. The cold and the hour had kept away most onlookers. Apart from the party assembled for the combat, a few curious paupers had come out from the poor-house gate and were standing in the snow in their foot-cloths, waiting to see what there might be to see, with Achilles near them, much better-dressed in the Governor's livery, yet keeping the distance apt to his servile status. The nearest sentry had stepped over from the palisade to watch, with his arms hugged tight round him under his greatcoat, and clouds of exhaled breath steaming out of him around the thin trickle of smoke from his pipe.

Everyone wore a grave, somewhat church-going expression, even Smith's improvised second, who seemed sobered into timidity by the reality of the occasion, now it had arrived. Lieutenant Lennox, acting for Septimus, was as grim as Cato as he checked that his principal's blade and Smith's sabre bought on credit were of a length, and secured the agreement of the parties that, on account of the cold, they would not strip to shirt-sleeves in the usual way, and might fight in their coats. Septimus' face was as hard as china as well as as white; and a lizard would have seemed less impassive.

"I take it that there is no possibility of compounding this with an apology?" asked Lennox for the sake of form.

"None," said Septimus instantly.

"Very good," said Lennox. "Then the quarrel must be submitted to the arbitrament of arms. To first blood, or to the greater extremity?"

"To satisfaction," said Septimus.

Smith, seeing in the obscurity of the term a faint glimmer, said at once, "I agree."

"Very well," said Lennox, after a fractional hesitation. "Gentlemen, step back; ready yourselves; commence at the fall of the hand-kerchief; break at the command 'Break!'"

Smith stepped back, until perhaps twenty feet separated him from Septimus' stare. The fervid confusions of the night had gone: he seemed to be breathing in clarity with the bitter air. His feet were cold, yet had fallen into the fencer's position without him choosing it, ready for the dance. His friend unsheathed his sword: he unsheathed his, and held it before him, awaiting his cue. The kerchief dropped. They advanced.

Smith adopted the first guard, or *guard of prime*, with his hand *pronated*. Septimus, seeing this, struck fiercely at his unprotected head, which Smith countered, but barely, with a rattling move into *tierce*. Septimus disengaged with a rasp of steel, and lunged lower, in *seconde*. Smith replied in *quarte. Quinte! Sixte! Prime! Seconde!*— But really, this is useless, and no more enables the reader to see the battle, than if I shouted numbers at you; which, indeed, I appear to be doing. The truth is, that I am obliged to copy these names for sword-fighting out of a book, having no direct experience to call upon. I throw myself upon the reader's mercy, or rather their sense of resignation. Having previously endured this tale's treatment of the game of piquet, and of the act of love, they may with luck by now expect no great coherence in the reporting of a sword-fight. And yet it must be rendered somehow as Smith experienced it, panting, with blade skreeking against blade and the snow dragging at his feet; and the formal beauty of it too, for if you had had no stake in the outcome, and hovered just above, as disengaged as a seagull from the good or ill of the parties, you would have seen an order in the stepping, the leaping, the gathering, the falling-back, fit for the muses. Elegant, desperate, ridiculous, willful spectacle of mortality! Come, we can do better than a stream of Gallic numerals.

The essence of stage-fighting is, to achieve a series of clashing parries, as noisy as possible; and though the parties usually co-operate in this, with their blades coming together in this place or that place in the air, by agreement; yet Smith, whisking his sword at what always seemed the last possible moment into the un-agreed path of Septimus', at least had half the familiar task to execute. So long as he did not try to attack, but only countered, and coun-tered, and countered, he found he could (just) keep off the whistling onslaught, at the price of being driven back, and back, and back. Soon they were off the trampled pathway selected as the ground, and Smith was backing into deeper snow toward the spot more or less where the great bonfire had burned, but where now a surface whipped to peaks like dirty egg-whites let through each foot into floundering softness. Smith was wading backward into it, slowed as if by molasses, his sword-arm wavering with his balance; yet Septimus laboured under the same disability, and his attacks too were retarded and as it were thickened, both moving to a slower rhythm. Even so, the impetus was considerable, and they temporarily left the seconds and onlookers lagging behind. Smith, for the moment finding he still possessed fingers, limbs and head all intact, seized the chance of this peculiar privacy to say, or rather gasp: "Did it really. Have to be you?"

"Would you rather," panted Septimus, "that it had. Been someone. Who was trying. To kill you?"

"Do you mean you're not?" said Smith, forgetting to step back. Septimus' steel, scarcely deflected, cut past his ear so close he felt the cold of it razoring by, like a concentration of winter itself, a wicked grey finger of the ice. He could imagine that if it touched him, he would crystallise around the wound.

Septimus disengaged, took a half-step back, caught his breath.

"I really am very angry with you, Richard," he said, not loudly. "I am severely tempted to cut off your ears just to make a point; so keep your guard up, for God's sake. But no, I am not. The idea is to contrive some safe piece of humiliation."

"Oh," said Smith. "I see."

"You don't approve? I am open to the alternative." The seconds were lumbering up.

"No—no—please—proceed. Is there anything I must . . . do?"

"It will all be done for you," said Septimus grimly, raising his sword again. But then, in a rapid mutter, in the last seconds left them: "You could work your way round to the left. No, idiot, *my* left. Watch out for the briar!"

Cut and parry, cut and parry, slash and clash. Septimus drove Smith round in a loop, back to the flattened strip whereon they had begun; Smith, his movements a trifle hectic and approximate with relief, tried his best to play his part properly, and indeed the slashes at his guard still came with alarming verisimilitude. A few more onlookers had gathered, drawn by the prolonged music of metal against metal. "Skewer him, Juba!" cried one of these, having apparently recognised the duel as some sort of reprise of the play's battle; but Smith was very conscious that he was, by now, putting up little of a show. Sweat was trickling down his back, the sword seemed to be gaining in weight with each movement, and he hoped that whatever Septimus had in mind, he would do soon. He took it as a considerable mercy when Septimus, glancing left and right and clearly judging his audience to be adequate, interrupted the sequence of blows. As if suddenly forgetting what he had been about, in fighting with Smith, he withdrew his blade and absently inspected its tip, like a man who finds the cheese has unaccountably fallen off the end of his toasting-fork: the whole leisurely performance exuding a speaking disdain for any conceivable peril that might be afforded by his hot, heaving opponent. —An enemy so pitiful, said the gesture, that it was safe to ignore him at will. Unlike Smith, Septimus, though breathing hard, was still cool, unruffled, collected, precise. He flipped his point down again, and planted it in the snow at his arm's length, so the weapon become dismissively pacific, a steel walking stick on which he happened to be leaning at an elegant angle, rather like one of the more balletic-looking woodcuts of the French king. The onlookers tittered uncertainly.

"It seems our seducer here," he declared, "is more apt for the bedroom than the battlefield." The titter grew louder and more confident. "In which case, he is surely . . . overdressed."

The sabre flowed up again into his hand seemingly without effort, on the instant a tool of war once more, and he cut towards Smith's side at waist height with a demonstrative rapidity that made it all too clear he had been only toying with him till now. Smith's feeble, late parry he easily eluded, and Smith felt a bright line of pain scored across his hip, as Septimus sliced neatly through the band of his breeches, his drawers and (to the depth of a scratch) a curved arc of his skin. Deprived of buttons on that side, his breeches sagged down. This is going to end with me bare-arsed in the snow, Smith realised. A whoop came from the direction of the poor-house, the nature of the entertainment having revealed itself. Septimus acknowledged it with a bend of the head and a graceful rotation of the fingers on his spare hand. Then he prepared to do it again on the other side.

Smith knew he might as well wait stock-still while Septimus concluded the comedy, but some point of pride, some residuum of stubbornness, made him lift his blade into guard, to at least attempt a lurching counter. But with his cloven clothes impeding him on the right, he threw his weight clumsily onto an advanced left foot, while Septimus was still poising himself like a matador, and discovered with his toes, under the snow just there, a patch of ice as slick as glass. His foot shot out from beneath him; he pitched suddenly forward, his sword still held out before him. Septimus, not expecting this stumbling lunge any more than Smith had, had no time to do more than to snatch his own blade out of the way, lest Smith impale himself on it as he fell.

It seemed Smith's point had passed harmlessly between Septimus' legs, and as Smith scrambled to his knees, his face again snow-caked, his sword lost beyond his reach, he was already giving a grin of furious embarrassment and apology. But a spot of dark red appeared on the grey silk at the top of Septimus' inner thigh, then expanded in the blink of an eye into a soaked red circle big as a saucer.

"Ouch," said Septimus.

Another blink, and the circle stretched into a waterfall-shaped stain down to his knee. Another, and blood ran out in a glossy cascade over his stocking.

"Break!" cried Lennox, and ran forward. The Lieutenant, knowing what he was seeing, in a trice had Septimus on his back on the snow, and was tugging off the crimsoned, already sticky breeches, to get at the gash right up in the white hollow of Septimus' groin, between the tendons, where a jet of dark blood as fat around as a fence-nail was pulsing regularly. Smith stared stupidly. Lennox pulled off his own neck-cloth; studied it; discarded it as too short.

"Something for a tourniquet," he roared. "Scarf? Shirt? Something! *Now!*"

A muffler was passed. Lennox wrapped it round Septimus' leg as high up as he could, and twisting the loose ends together at the outside of the hip endeavoured to tighten it. But the hurt to the artery was so high up that there was no room above it where the flow might be squeezed and arrested. Twist and grip as Lennox might, the blood still came oozing, trickling, very soon streaming through the folds. The muffler served only as a bandage, and a bandage was quite insufficient to the force with which the blood was leaving Septimus. Lennox's hands were scarlet.

"Ouch," said Septimus again. He did not cry it, he did not groan it, he did not wail it; he still uttered it, controlledly, as a word, but this time through gritted teeth, with great conscious effort, and a victory over a proximate panic in it.

Achilles, coming up fast with a great double-armful of fresh snow, elbowed Smith out of the way, and throwing himself to his knees began, with Lennox's help, to try to pack a mass of snow hard into the wound, as a species of frigid barrier where the blood might clot. They pressed and leant and heaved and struggled for leverage, but through each hopeful tight-moulded cold poultice they balled around his leg, the crimson came creeping, white crystals turning inexorably to burgundy along an advancing front, until there was only a white fur left sprinkled atop dark pink, and then the whole thing melted to wine-coloured slop. It looked like one of Lord ——'s ice-house puddings, thought Smith, sick and dizzy: except for the smell, the hot salt smell, the butcher's-shop smell. The flow began to slacken, but not for any reason to be rejoiced over.

Smith found himself at Septimus' head. His eyes were wide and rolling, like a frightened horse's, and a very shocking change had come over his skin. It had turned to a dingy grey, with yellow in it, as if not redness but his accustomed whiteness were leaving him; as if what he was losing in gouts were his polish, his lustre.

"Look what you've done to me," he said, in a voice without force.

"I am so sorry," said Smith.

"All I had to do was run you through and go home for breakfast. Ridiculous. Ridiculous. I look like a warning of the dangers of childbed."

And indeed, he lay now in a spectacular claret-stained circle on the white of the Common. A crow had flapped in from somewhere, interested, and was being kicked away by the sentry.

"I am so sorry," said Smith again. "None of this was my intent."

"Who cares what you intended. Come closer."

"What?"

"Come down here. Come. Now."

Smith bent low and Septimus turned lips the grey of charcoal toward his ear.

"You have to free Achilles," he whispered. "I need you to make sure of it."

"I don't know if—"

"On your honour. Swear."

"On my—?"

"Swear. Swear. You owe me a debt. And him. Swear."

"Alright."

"On your honour."

"On my honour."

A slight grey nod.

"You will find your pocket-book in my sea-chest. With your secret safe inside it. Good heavens, Richard. Aren't you full of surprises." The ghost of a smile. "I think I am—"

"Yes?"

"—taking New-York too seriously . . ."

Then Achilles, abandoning at last the fruitless labour, pushed Smith aside to take his place. Their conversation, Smith neither could nor wanted to overhear. There was not time for much of it. Lennox was saying the *Nunc Dimittis*. Achilles' face was indescribable.

The sentry gripped Smith so warmly and surely round the shoulders that he took it for a comfort, until the beadle arrived across the corrupted snow to arrest him for murder.

III

"You're fortunate," said William Smith the lawyer.

Smith opened his mouth to laugh at this, but nothing came from it but a kind of hoarse bark of air. They were talking in the cells beneath City Hall, Smith having been assigned this time to the criminal prison below, not the civil prison above. Between the fit of shivering in which he had been led off the Common, and the hours spent waiting in the dark, icy little hole below Wall Street, he seemed to be catching cold.

"No; fortunate; 'tis true," said the lawyer, correctly interpreting his incredulity. "In many manners, I'd say; but at least in this, that tomorrow's last day of Michaelmas Term. Court won't sit again till

January. But the judge'll make room on the docket for ye tomorrow. So you've but the one night in here, before the trial."

"Before I hang, you mean," croaked Smith.

"Half the town wants you swinging, true; half doesn't. Half that doesn't, sent me; you should like your odds the better."

"Why?"

"Causes improve, with good counsel. —Or did ye mean, why'd they send me?"

"Yes."

"Chaste stars, boy, isn't it clear by now? Perhaps your wits have froze. Here," said the lawyer, "have a swig on this." He drew from his inner pocket a flask which, as he passed it, became the brightest thing in the dim blue glow from the snow-choked grating out onto the cobbles of Wall Street, up at the extreme top of the dungeon's wall. The silver captured the little light in a frigid gleaming clot. The liquid inside, however, burned as it went down, cutting steaming tributaries through the dull ice of Mr. Smith's misery, and exposing rawer territories beneath, of guilt, and fear, and despair.

"Better?" asked the lawyer, looking at him head tip-tilted, with a kind of satisfaction. "Now: there are two causes here. What hurts one, speeds t'other. You have put horns on the Governor, near as dammit; you have pinked out his Secretary, who was also his spy-master. He loses, so we win. You have chose your side."

"I did not mean to."

"No? No matter, to us. As the judge said: if the boy won't serve one way, he will serve another. 'Tis worth our while to point the moral, that opposition prospers. 'Tis worth the court's ten minutes."

"Ten minutes?"

"At eleven o'clock tomorrow. Between a larceny and a libel."

"Ten *minutes*?"

"Oh. You've not seen many felony trials, I'm bound. That is the usual length, or a bit over."

242

"It does not seem much, to decide a man's life," Smith said. "Or to give justice on another's death."

The lawyer shrugged.

"Well, time's limited; docket's full. Ten minutes in the eye of justice is more'n many a poor soul'd have, that lives in tyranny. Besides, jury's been sitting a fortnight; fretful now; jaded. Best not to bore 'em with any long proceeding, hey? But I believe this may tickle their palate."

Smith did not seem receptive to this species of good cheer. He sat snuffling into his steepled fingers.

"Come now," said the lawyer. "You do not *want* to hang, do you?"

"No," said Smith.

"Then, less doleful, if you please. Enough melancholy; to business."

"Should I not be melancholy? I have killed my best friend in the city. —My only friend."

The lawyer's eyebrows beetled up, and he bestowed on Smith a very curious glance.

"Surprising," he said. "Surprising; interesting. Won't do, though. Don't repeat it. Oakeshott's death is admitted, you see; cannot be denied."

"I should think not," said Smith. In his mind the red circle spread again—had not ceased to spread.

"Yes; but, the consequence is, penitence won't serve. Might sway a sentence; won't fend one off. You require to justify the death; not mitigate it."

"Duelling is illegal anyway, isn't it? Am I not condemned already, for that?"

"Ah, but who challenged, eh? In the nature of a challenge *by* authority, d'ye see? Therefore, to spare authority's blushes, fact of the duel to be set aside. And there's the opportunity, there it lies: fight's conceded as an affray, and the jury may find you blameless in't, if they like our story of its cause."

"Can we not tell the truth, that he died by accident?"

"Accident? How, by accident? You were fighting with swords, boy; violent intent by definition, on both sides."

"But Septimus was not trying to kill me, only to chastise me."

The lawyer paused, and made a kind of chewing motion with his closed mouth. Again, the curious glance.

"How do you know this?" he asked.

"He told me so."

"When? Before the fight?"

"No, during it."

"Did anyone overhear it?"

"No . . . No."

"Well, thank heaven: or you'd be dished, neat and sweet. To stick him after he said he meant no harm? Culpable homicide. Worse: dislikeable homicide. The law admits truth, sir, in one style only: witnessed. What was not witnessed did not happen. That is the greatness of the law. That is its guarantee, sir: against the whimsy of the tyrant, against mere regulation. The common law finds truth in cases. Is a breathing thing, sir. Is a free creature, sir. Forms law from men's lives; doesn't crush men's lives, under forms of law. Takes authority, from the freedoms of England, not from the dictates of power. —And there, you see, for you, luck sews shut the jaws of disaster. Wasn't witnessed? Didn't happen. But 'accident'? No; don't want talk of that. Law's a tussle, d'you see, to decide on a story; to settle an explanation. Was you to say, with all the goodwill of the court,"—here the lawyer winked—"that, what, you made an unlucky cut at Oakeshott—"

"My foot slipped."

"Did it, so? —But no-one can swear as much. —That all that blood was mere mishap: well: there'd be disbelief, boy. There'd be disappointment. A jury wants a tale proportioned to the occasion. Not a mess of accident."

"Life is a mess of accident, I find."

The lawyer smiled at him, and clucked his tongue.

"No, no, not in the law, it ain't. Not in the *end*, I mean. When a man is dead, sense must be made of it; and it might as well be sense as serves the living, for it won't serve the dead, nohow."

"So I must tell some cock-and-bull story? Concoct some convenient lie?"—Smith saying this with a bitter emphasis.

"A lie, never," protested the lawyer, seeming truly shocked. "And if you did, 'twouldn't serve you. For all the witnesses must say their piece, and who knows what they'll say? Can't predict it, can't control 'em: can give a little turn to it, maybe, on cross, but that's the limit. *Your* power's only, to tell the story the jury likes best: will want to pick *out* from the mess of stories, and believe, and turn into the verdict. What then? You know what then. You're an actor, 'tis no puzzle to you. The court's your stage, tomorrow; to be believed, there, requires you to be believable. You need to tell a likely story; a probable story; a satisfying story. Even if we wander a little, to make it so."

"You want our second fight," said Smith with a dull helpfulness, like his theatrical advice to Septimus, only issued from the remote bottom of a well, "to please the audience as the first did. Only with real blood."

"Yes! You have it. That's the mark to aim for; precisely. Now, why do young men fight? From anger, of course; there's a motive likelihood don't strain at. Hot blood. Impulse. Reckless impulse, even. Carried off by it. Same impulse you bedded Terpie by. Fire in the loins! Not creditable? But credible. Explains itself, don't it. Just look at her. Most have. Teats like a prize heifer. So: Smith *furioso*, eh? Then to colour up fury—"

"Wait," said Smith, putting up a chilled hand to arrest these points the lawyer was making, with accelerating taps of forefinger on palm. He wanted to say, that to boast in this wise of his offence, to blazon it in the jury's eyes that he'd sinned the sin they all wanted to, was surely to compound it. He wanted to object, that there might still be fragments of worth adhering to his name, which it would be better not wantonly to blast and blacken, especially in the estimation of one person. But to observe the professional enthusiasm in the face of William Smith was to be reminded that to receive confidences is the office of a friend. And the only connection of that nature he had had in the city;—well. The red circle spoiled the snow once more. His eyes were sore. The viscous matter stuffing his nose oozed into the back of his mouth like an oyster that will not be swallowed. He took refuge in quibbling.

"Wait," he said. "I thought I was a meek and patient pilgrim?"

"What?"

"The character you fixed on for me, in your St. Nicholas-verse, which you pulled from the sack. My character for virtue." There was a kind of self-gnawing pleasure in saying this; in having got a good mouthful of his own arm, and biting well in.

"Oh: no. That line is quite exploded. Not of further use."

"But is there not a contradiction? Can you bruit out one idea of me, one week, and a different one the next? And be believed?"

"Easily," said the lawyer, with a slight testiness, for he had reached his peroration, and he was as fond as any man of gaining an effect he'd planned, for all that he laid out his words in as grudging a row as if each cost him a ha'penny. "Easily, because in law you may shift your ground without prejudice. You may say in succession: I was not there. If I was there, I did not strike him. If I did strike him, it was not fatal. If it was fatal, it was done without malice. You see? And in any case, we'll keep, as it were, a little moral nugget from St. Nick's Night. For all we need, to colour your fury to perfection, is to make it righteous. And lo and behold, what comes in now very happy, but Oakeshott's own character?"

"Scrupulous. Generous. Kind."

"A tool of power. A notorious spy. A—"

"No," said Smith.

"You don't know what I'm going to say."

"Yes I do. And I'll not insult him."

"Insult him?" cried the lawyer, grinning. "You cannot *insult* him, boy. He's dead. You skewered him, remember. 'Tis too late to hurt his feelings."

"I can refrain from pissing on his corpse."

There was a silence.

"*Very* cold in here, boy," said the lawyer, "and I've no mind to linger, much, for there's a warm room waiting upstairs for me, with a brazier burning. You've a night in here, whatever; and then you've a short walk home, or a long drop. There's your choice. There's the only choice to work your mind upon. You may take the help you're offered, or refuse it; but you shan't pick how you're helped, for you ain't paying the piper. You may live, or you may die. An' you choose to live, you'll help us paint Oakeshott in whatever insect shade is convenable. You'll say, yes, the creature offered to put his hands on you; yes, he said he'd let you live, on the Terpie matter, if you gratified *his* nasty appetites; yes, you was driven to a righteous disgust by the foulness of the bargain. And struck back. And in a lucky stroke, slew him bravely, as he deserved. *Sic semper tyrannis.* And sodomites too."

"No."

Another silence.

"Don't ye have a preference for breathing? Things to do? Matters to attend to, for which you crossed the ocean? Plans; a thousand pounds to spend?"

Prodded out with a stick by the lawyer from the hole where wretchedness had consigned every consideration but guilt, there came to Smith the thought of his responsibilities. The errand he needed to be alive to fulfil. The promise he had made Septimus: which he needed to be alive to fulfil. These were, were they not, other real *oughts* to set in the balance, against the *ought* of guilt? Quickly, greedily, the preference for breathing which by nature he of course possessed, seized on these; urged them on him; tried to scuttle inside them like that species of soft crab which must borrow harder shells for its house—

"Ah! Aha!" burst out Smith, triumphantly. "I cannot, can I? Even if I told this sick tale to perfection, what would they think it was but a ploy to save my neck? There is no-one to testify to it, but me. No way it can be witnessed, for it never happened. It is a useless stratagem, as well as a monstrous one. There!"

"Well, as it happens, a witness has come forward," said the lawyer.

"What?" said Smith.

The lawyer called for the gaoler, and very shortly, a horribly familiar apparition was standing at the door of the cell, transmitting even through the gelid air a reek of piss and dirt.

"No," moaned Smith.

"Oh dear," said the apparition, grinning. "Don't you want the Capting's help?"

In those days, it was not yet common for a prisoner in a criminal trial to be represented by counsel. The common wisdom was, that any innocent man should be able to quit themselves shortly of a false accusation, by their own efforts. Yet after the conversation in the dungeon, William Smith did not feel it quite safe to let this prisoner direct his own defence, cross-examine on his own account, *et cetera*; so when, at eleven o'clock on the morning of the 19th December, the clerk of the Court of Judicature announced *Rex v Smith* as the next case, the lawyer was beside Smith as he came sneezing and streaming to the bar. He had been permitted to warm himself for half an hour in the gaoler's room on the ground floor, and given a basin of snow to scrub his face with, and a clean shirt had been brought from the Black Horse for him; but little fever-squalls of shivering ran over his skin, plucked and pinched at it, and his nose was red, and he made frequent trumpeting use of a handkerchief, and altogether was a predominantly crumpled and pitiable sight.

The room in which the court sat was the great chamber of City Hall's upstairs floor, in the centre range of the building, with the bar running across the middle of the floor, the seats for grand and petty juries ranged to left and right, and the judge sitting in splendour before the lion and unicorn, facing outward to the tall windows and the balcony onto Wall Street, from which flowed back in today a bright white snow-glare. It was the room next door to the one where Smith had celebrated the King's birthday and played at piquet with the judge, and it was just as crowded. But with this difference: that today, from the jurors craning round with their brows beetling to get a first look at him, to the judge in scarlet and gold and a wide-bottomed enormity of a wig, to the fascinated crush of citizens and slaves just behind him, every single one of the spectators was male. Smith had dreaded the gaze of Terpie, dreaded and hoped for the sharp perceiving face of Tabitha. This sudden wholesale absence of the entire sex seemed to him to bring to the room a kind of alarming single-mindedness, like the rough company gathered for a prize-fight or a bear-baiting.

"Where are all the wibbid?" he whispered.

"Persistent sort of dog, ain't ye?" the lawyer replied, out of the side of his mouth. "You must just button your breeches. Win or lose, you ain't a fit subject for decent company, any more."

"I didn't—" began Smith but, sneezing, gave up.

"*Rex versus Smith*, on the charge of murder," called the clerk again, and the chatter stilled. "Silence in court. Prosecuting for the plaintiff, which is to say His Majesty, Mr. Colden. Counsel appearing for the prisoner, Mr. Smith. —Mr. *William* Smith, that is."

Colden, touching the bar with two bony forefingers a few feet to the left, was the irritable Scotsman the lawyer had jousted with at the King's dinner: clearly the two of them were in the nature of an inevitable pairing, an opposition almost ordained by nature.

"What a surfeit of advocates, when usually we manage so well with none," remarked De Lancey. "It would have been politer of the Governor, I think, and shown more respect to the independency of the court, if he had been content to leave the prosecution to me. But, very well. I remind both you gentlemen, that the depositions of the witnesses are not to be interrupted. Examination may have its time, but will not be allowed to exceed it. And I do hope I may be allowed to get in an occasional word, in my own court." His voice was as regal as Smith imagined it would be, restored to the proper setting for its majesty: grand, and with the seal set upon its grandeur by a faintest trace of amusement, in which absolutely no other party whatever was invited to participate.

"I am sure no-one imagines we could stop you, my lord," said Colden, indifferent whether he was invited or not. He turned, and pointed one of the two fingers and his long nose as well at Smith. "We char-r-ge, that on the eighteenth day of December the prisoner did most bloodily and maliciously, upon the Common of the city of New Yor-r-k, by means of a sword str-r-oke, deprive of life Mr. Septimus Oakeshott, late Secretary to His Excellency, the Governor of the Colony of New-York."

"Prisoner, how do you plead?" asked De Lancey.

"Nod guilty," said Smith after only the minutest pause. De Lancey nodded, the clerk wrote, and the rapid settlement of all the prisoner's worldly affairs, and Septimus', swung into its course.

Colden first called the coroner of the Out Ward, who attested that he had sat one hour ago upon the inquest into the death of Septimus Oakeshott; that the cause of the death had been exsanguination, from a wound to the upper leg of one inch long and three inches deep, which had severed the femoral artery; that the wound had been dealt by a sword's-tip; that the manner of the death was therefore certainly by violence.

"Prisoner, m'lud," said William Smith, whose forensic style proved no more roomy than his private one, "wishful to save time, happy to agree, manner of death. Further to state, he caused it. Only, in self-defence. One question: any other marks found on body?"

"Of what kind?" asked the coroner.

"Of misuse. Of habitual vice."

"No, none."

"Hmph. Yet, seem to remember, heard lately, on the stage: 'I must dissemble, and speak a language foreign to my heart.' Who was that? Ah: Oakeshott." The lawyer's version of Septimus playing Sempronius was a miniature of hissing wickedness.

"I trust," said Colden, "that counsel for the prisoner is awar-r-re of the difference between drama and reality?"

"You're not planning to arraign poor Mr. Oakeshott for overthrowing the Roman Republic, are you, William?" asked De Lancey. Laughter in the court. "No? Good. But time presses: move along."

Colden called Quentin, the waiter of the Merchants' Coffee-House, who testified that he had seen Oakeshott and the prisoner quarrel, and Oakeshott strike the prisoner in the face. He could not witness to the nature of the quarrel, the room being noisy, but the prisoner had seemed surprised, on being struck; had been to all appearances pleased, on Oakeshott's first arrival, and much taken aback, by the development of events.

"So, you would not say, equal anger on both sides, your opinion?"— counsel for the prisoner, cross-examining.

"No, sir. Mr. Oakeshott was the angry one."

"Did the prisoner hit back, when he was struck?"

"No, sir."

Colden to Quentin, on rebuttal: "Might not the behaviour of the prisoner be very naturally accounted for, as the confusion of a wrong-doer, who till that moment had believed himself secret?"

"It might, sir."

Colden then called Lieutenant Lennox, whom he described as having "come upon" Smith and Septimus fighting on the Common. (Smith's own second had secured his non-involvement in the trial by quitting the city at speed the day before.) Lennox said, he could certainly give the reason for the quarrel, Secretary Oakeshott having expressed to him—which was by the by the general judgement of the Fort—a very reasonable moral horror, at the behaviour of the prisoner, who was a contemptible little rake, in dishonouring a brother-officer's wife. No doubt it was this ungentlemanly action by Smith, in betrayal of every obligation of honour and friendship, that had led to the sword-fight. He had not endeavoured to stop the fight, because it was plainly impossible to, the prisoner having disdained to apologise, and Mr. Oakeshott being understandably set on getting some satisfaction for so gross an abuse. When Oakeshott was injured, by a chancy cut to the groin, he offered what aid he could, but the blood was letting at too great a rate. It was a dreadful scene; and a dreadful consequence to the prisoner's indulgence of a low appetite.

"Severe words, hey?" said William Smith. "Harsh terms, an actor dallying with an actress? Young blood, running high; stage, known for it; lady, that matter, known as—"

"The lady is *an officer's wife*," rumbled Lennox.

"You must not interrupt the questions put you, Lieutenant," said De Lancey. "But you are quite right; there is no need for this proceeding to blacken further reputations."

"Apologise, m'lud," said William Smith. "Lieutenant—this fighting, 'to satisfaction'? Usual term? Familiar term, in fighting, your experience?"

"No, sir."

"Aha. *Un*-usual, then. *In*-ordinate. *Out* of proportion. Cruel streak, maybe, in Oakeshott?"

"I never saw a sign of one."

"Was he not known for a mocking tongue?"

"He only mocked the King's enemies."

"The King's enemies. *The King's enemies*," repeated William Smith, relishing the phrase. "Not the Governor's, hey, but the *King's*. Very fair. Tell me, Lieutenant: do you see anyone here Oakeshott would include, under that head?"

"No, sir," said Lennox with a struggle, gazing all the while with helpless honesty at the Chief Justice. Laughter.

Colden to Lennox: "Had Oakeshott injured the prisoner at all, by the time the fight ended?"

"He had not, despite many opportunities, the prisoner being a poor fencer. —He had just laid his blade on him for the first time, to cut through the band of the prisoner's breeches, when the fatal blow was struck by the prisoner."

"To cut through the band of his br-r-eeches? Might Mr. Oakeshott have been intending to visit on the prisoner, not bloodshed, but some salutary lesson?"

"He might, sir."

Lennox was dismissed, and Colden called Corporal Prothero of the ——th Foot, the soldier from the sentry-booth. Who quickly declared, that he had observed the fight in its early stages from a distance, but had closed to no more than a few yards by its end; that he had recognised the prisoner's cut to the groin immediately as a killing stroke, and had secured him, so he might not run off.

"Seen much sword-work, have ye?" asked William Smith, on cross.

"Yessir, a fair bit."

"Was they even-matched, your opinion, the two going at it?"

"Nossir. The gentleman in the grey trews, he was considerable the better."

"Meaning, Oakeshott. And the prisoner here?"

"Flailing like a novice, sir. 'Twas a wonder he weren't cut up already."

"Why wasn't he, d'you think?"

"I thought he was playing with him, like."

"Playing with him: hmm. Cat and mouse. And the blow to the groin that ended it: a lucky stroke?"

"Yessir, most probably."

"A desperate stroke?"

"Mebbe, sir."

Colden, rebutting: "And when Oakeshott was lying bleeding to his death, did the prisoner try to render him any help?"

"Not as I saw, sir."

"Did he express any rr-r-emorse? Contrition? Did he say, oh no, what have I done?"

"Nossir. He just stood there, mazed."

After which, Colden called on the prisoner.

It would be a great exaggeration to say that Mr. Smith had been at ease up to this point, but the trial had been running along its horrid course without his help, and he had gripped the polished wood of the bar with his cold fingers, and let the words echo in the high room, and slide by him while he waited, passive and even a little lulled. Now the attention of the courtroom was suddenly and entirely concentred upon him, as if a piece of folded white paper, lit bright as snow, had abruptly opened up to reveal him standing tiny at its middle point. (He was perhaps by this time already running a fever.) They were all staring at him, curious, grave, eager, hungry: a mass of mouths and eyes. He had, of course, thought through what he was going to say—what he was *willing* to say—and had endeavoured to persuade himself, that this might be a performance in which he spoke what the script required, while reserving a portion of himself still honest, free in its guilt. Yet he found, as he began his deposition, that this was not the way of it, at all. To remake himself as Septimus' victim, he discovered, was not a single decision to lie, once taken and then behind him, but a resolution to be taken again and again, a bolus to be constantly re-swallowed, a staircase of many steps, down each of which he must push himself separately. Other descents to Avernus might be easy: not this one, apparently. He had thought he should aim for insouciance—the Fop at Bay—or at least as much insouciance as a man can show who must blow his nose periodically; but what came out was a sort of hoarse, hangdog defiance.

"I was sitting in the coffee-house when Oakeshott came in and hit me"—honk—"right across the chops. Without any warning. I was considerably surprised. It seemed he objected to a recent"—honk—"*adventure* of mine, which I certainly didn't mean anyone to know of, or be upset by. I always heard it wasn't a gentleman's part to tell. It seemed a private matter to me. I don't know why he took on so; I am a stranger here. It made me angry. I am a student of the passions"—laughter—"I mean on the stage; and I suppose I have as much choler in my temper as any man, but I have never had any trouble with the law. I met Oakeshott again the next day on the Common, early, and I confess that when he proved still offensive and unreasonable, we quickly had swords out, for my blood was up, and his must have been too, or he would not have pressed me so. But I regretted it very soon, I can tell you; it was an impulse I wished to take straight back again. For"—honk—"he proved far deadlier a swordsman than me, and he was in earnest. He wanted more than just to give me a scratch. He would not be satisfied, till I was gravely injured. It was the most I could do, to defend my life. I am no Juba, off the stage, I promise you," said Smith to the jury, who to his disgust nodded in return, several of them. "He pressed me back and back; I believed myself at his mercy, and was indeed reduced to desperate strokes by the end, little more"—honk—"than slashing and stabbing and hoping for the best. I was astonished when my last lunge reached him. I did not know the location of the femoral artery, for I never heard of it till today, not being an anatomist." Laughter. "If I had known, I could not have pierced it a-purpose, not being at all sufficient a fencer. I did not mean to kill him, but only to preserve myself. *I did not mean to kill him.*"

This last repetition, he had not pre-meditated. But as the only part of Smith's testimony he actually meant, and (as it were) the last projecting piece of the drowned continent of conscience, the words jumped from his mouth despite him, with a ragged intensity quite unlike the rest of his speech. I have broke character, he thought with a hazy professional compunction. The cheerfully murmuring court-room was struck almost resentfully to silence. De Lancey, who had been solicitously turning his gaze from side to side the while Smith was speaking, to keep watch like a good shepherd on all the moods of his flock, the golden twists of the carved lion and unicorn behind him gleaming out alternately upon each flank of his wig—stilled; and rested upon the prisoner instead a narrow, considering, wholly serious gaze. Colden, perceiving the change of atmosphere, seized upon it instantly.

"It was a very gr-r-rotesque end you visited upon Mr. Oakeshott, was it not? A slaughter-house scene, more fit for the death of a beast, than for a Christian man?"

"Yes, sir," said Smith, swallowing. "But not one I intended."

"Was it not? Was not this whole spectacle of spilled blood the fruit of your concupiscence? Are you not responsible for it?"

"I did not ask to fight. I did not begin the quarrel."

"Is not the weight of this honest man's death upon *your* soul?"

"No," said Smith.

"Is it not?"

"He has answered the question, Mr. Colden," said De Lancey. "Do you have anything else to ask?"

"One thing, my lord. Prisoner, you said you had never been in trouble with the law—were you not imprisoned for debt in this very building, not a month ago?"

"Upon a misunderstanding," said Smith.

"Amicably resolved?" asked De Lancey.

"Yes, sir," said Smith.

"Good," said the judge. "Counsel for the prisoner?"

"Shook you, hey—Oakeshott's death?" said William Smith. "All that blood?"

"Yes, sir," said Smith.

"Very natural. Not a soldier; not a swordsman; not accustomed. Shock. But, scene not of your choosing, hey?"

"No, sir."

"And sometimes, spilt blood, justified. Sometimes, spilt in a noble cause. 'Remember, O my friends, the laws, the rights, the generous plan of power delivered down from age to age, by your renowned forefathers so dearly bought, the price of so much blood . . .'" As the lawyer growled Cato's lines from the play, his usual staccato periods serviceably lengthening out, the room's murmuring undertone of pleasure was restored. He had safely converted the crimson puddle back to rhetoric. "So much blood," he repeated, more musingly. "Honest man's blood? Remains to be seen. Did you," he shot at Smith, "see Oakeshott again, between slap in the face, Merchants, and fight, Common?"

This was the last of the downward steps required of him. Smith wrestled, writhed, struggled, but found himself still floating above the needful tread on his internal staircase: he produced nothing audible.

"Mr. Smith?" prompted the lawyer.

"I must say," interpolated Judge De Lancey smoothly, "that it confirms my doubts about this novelty of bringing in counsel, when a man refuses to answer his own advocate's question. You would not see a man refusing to answer *himself*, now, would you?" Laughter. "Yet we are told, that this new situation is the equivalent, in law. Prisoner—the question once posed, we must hear a reply from you. Prisoner?"

"Yes," said Smith, dismally. "Yes, I saw Septimus again. That evening, at the William Street baths."

"And what happened then?" pursued the lawyer.

But this time Smith's mouth would not open at all.

"Ask the court's indulgence, m'lud," said William Smith. "Testimony not essential for defence's case; covered by another witness. Understandable delicacy on prisoner's part. Will be made clear."

"Very well—" began De Lancey in his voice like unrolling brocade; but Colden, sharp, incredulous, Caledonian, spoke at the same time.

"*What?* Ye'll tolerate such . . . such palpable *nonsense?*"

"'My lord,'" said De Lancey. "Pray remember, Mr. Colden, the courtesies due to the bench. And remember too, that what we *tolerate* here is at the discretion of the good people of New-York, at whose command we sit; and is not to be abridged or usurped, sir, by any other power whatever, be it never so mighty."

Applause.

"Yes, my lord," grated Colden.

"Now, finish your case, please, if you've no-one else to call. Time marches."

"The case for the Crown is simple," said Colden. "It needs no rr-r-efinement. This travelling mountebank here"—indicating Smith—"of whom we know nothing, except that he sings and nae doubt dances, and shows himself to fine advantage in white-face, and likes to help himself to other men's wives, has by his own simple admission caused the death of the Governor's Secretary; a valuable young man, a serious young man, a skillful young man, known to you all, and I remind you, a servant of the very same lawful power as is manifested here, in this very courr-rt. And all for no reason that has been adduced, save a pettish and careless wrath. The servants neither of His Majesty, nor of His Majesty's honest subjects, are to be cut down at whim and left weltering in their blood. That's all."

"Thank you, Mr. Colden," said De Lancey. "William, call your witness, and let's be done."

Smith's counsel called, of course, his late cellmate, the monster who had tormented his ears with horrors. He seemed equally familiar to the crowd in the court. As the Capting grinned his way to the bar, exhibiting a gape variously cracked, gapped and stumped, and billowing before him like the vanguard of an army his cloud of stench, the bystanders stirred and made room for very self-protection: yet, except for the slaves, did so with nudges, nods and a kind of anticipatory relish, as of people promised some repulsive yet assuredly diverting spectacle. The Capting acknowledged their recognition with little becks and turnings of the hand to left and right.

"Well!" he said, established before the bench. "It is a pleasure, to rid myself of a matter, what has been wery heavy on me since I chanst on it two night since. I was in the William Street stews, when I hear the sound of argyment, and putting my head round the corner, what do I see but this feller here"—rubbing at Smith's sleeve between finger and thumb—"holding off that long, pale, sickly molly-man, Oakeshott, who is after him, to kiss him, or dandle him, or wuss. And *he* says, 'No, no, hands off, I'll have none of your japes.' And Oakeshott says, 'Let me have my will, you pretty fellow, or it will be the worse for you, tomorrow.' And he says, 'What do you mean?' And Oakeshott is laughing, and he says, 'I'll be bound you knows how to play the lady's part well enough, don't you be coy. You are an actor, it is all the same to you. I'll have you at both ends, or I'll slit your gizzard tomorrow and nobody the wiser, for

I am well in dibs with the Governor, and you are gutter leavings compared to the likes of me.' But this one says, 'It is against nature, and I'll have none of it. You may do your worst.' Then Oakeshott is wery angry, and he throws on his clothes, and out he goes, cursing most ugly. You would not think such a milk-and-water looker knew such terms. He says—"

"Enough," said De Lancey, who seemed not to be enjoying this as much as some. "We have the gist. Mr. Colden?"

Colden's long face had by this time passed from astonishment, to outrage, to a kind of bleak amusement.

"Do you agree that it is contemptible to slander the dead?" he asked.

"'S not a slander if it's true," said the Capting, grinning.

"Very well, remind me: where did this alleged conversation take place?"

"In ve William Street bath-house, like I said."

"Two nights ago?"

"Like I said."

"You took a bath, two nights ago?" Colden, with his long fingers, scribed in the air between him and the Capting an oval, a cameo setting, to frame for the jurors the ingrained ooze of the Capting's countenance. "And yet the experience has left you mir-r-aculously untouched."

Laughter in the court, which De Lancey joined in with.

"I saw them from ve door-way," protested the Capting sulkily. He did not like the laughing; his mouth twisted, and he looked nine parts in ten malignant.

"I *see*," said Colden with heavy sarcasm.

"He has answered," said De Lancey. "Any questions from the prisoner's side?"

"Yes!" burst out Smith. "I have a question! How—"

"Prisoner at the bar," said De Lancey. "You can be represented by counsel, or not. But you cannot be half-represented. (A maxim with some political application, by the by.) You have elected to be spoken for; so you may not speak. William, *final* remarks."

"M'lud," said the lawyer. "Jurors: we have here, ordinary young man. No better'n most. Maybe a little worse'n some. Likes to whore and misbehave himself. No choice for a son-in-law. But any man can be liberty's friend; for liberty is every man's. And when power holds out a bargain to him—vile bargain; vilest of bargains—does he take it? No. He fights. And by a lucky chance, he conquers. Juba slays Sempronius. *That's* all."

"Seventeen minutes," announced De Lancey, looking at his golden pocket-watch. "Disgraceful. Not a precedent that must be allowed to stand. Mr. Foreman, can we at least proceed immediately to a verdict?"

The jurors' heads craned, strained and pulled toward one another, muttering and murmuring, like a stook of wheat being gathered by a string. Then they fell away from each other again.

"Not guilty, my lord," said the foreman.

"Hmm," said De Lancey. "No; I don't think so. Not if you take proper account of the prisoner's acknowledged hot temper, or hastiness. Mr. Colden is right. Whatever the circumstances, whatever the provocation, we cannot have our disputes settled with blood in the streets. There must be some mark of guilt, in proportion to the seriousness of the event. Pray, reconsider. Quickly."

The jury muttered once more.

"Guilty of manslaughter, my lord," reported the foreman.

"Excellent. Clerk, write it so," said De Lancey. He cleared his throat: a premonitory noise, a ritual noise, a musical noise. He fixed Smith with his expressive eyes. "Prisoner at the bar," he said, "you are to be branded on the thumb, in token that you have taken life, and to advertise to others your culpability, your life long. Sentence to be discharged immediately by the sheriff's officers." *There*, said his eyes. *Is that not as you desire it?* And he gave Smith a bestowing nod. "Next?"

Smith was indeed so strangely relieved that he had been allowed to be guilty of something, that he suffered himself to be led away through the crowd in a meek daze, back to the sheriff's room from which he had issued forth; and it was not until an iron was heating in the brazier there, that the physical aspect of the punishment became real enough to give him uneasiness; but with a cheerful force, the sheriff's two bullies had already taken an immovable hold on his arm, and were stretching it out across the tabletop.

"Ready?—I would look away, sir, if I were you. 'Twill only take a moment."

Which it did: though that moment was far easier to look back upon or even to look forward to than it was actually to pass through, when the glowing M was pressed in, with a hiss and a smell like roasted pork, and the skin shrivelling back like wax and the meat of his thumb scorching, and the heat seeming to lance right to the bone. Then they clapped his hand into the very basin of snow they'd given him to wash with, still only half gone to water, and wrapped his used handkerchief considerately around the burned and melted flesh, where it throbbed and blazed, a red star of pain attempting to constrain his whole attention to the news of itself.

"Sir? Free to go now, sir."

He tottered out onto the landing, where he found that the stairwell, and the open hall below where the snow had drifted in between the arches, was full of men applauding him.

"You see?" said William Smith, taking his unhurt arm. "No reason for melancholy at all."

A kind of impromptu party had been convened, in the upstairs room of the Black Horse: a gathering of the senior men, and supporters, and admiring hangers-on of the judge's faction, not to scheme any-thing of substance, or to decide anything, but just to lay eyes on each other and celebrate a victory before the moiety of them who had had court business scattered out of the city. They floated in and out as the short winter's day (almost the shortest of the whole year) closed in icy darkness, the snow in the street outside dimming in the window-glass to the merest glimmer, while the pane thronged with reflected flames, and with faces jovial, chuckling, roaring. De Lancey himself came in when the last cases of the Michaelmas Term had been settled, and the room re-oriented around his black bulk and his fine face, where he stood in high good humour, lis-tening far more than he spoke. Smith had been anchored by the lawyer to a chair beside him, up against the panelling. Not much was required of him, this being a triumph about him, rather than for him. He was its visible pretext, that was all, and he felt himself good for little else. Between the flushes of his mounting fever, and the dull thought-suck of the pain in his hand, and the certainty that there was nothing better to be thought or remembered if he *were* rid of these bodily distractions, he was content to be fully occupied sitting hunched in the heat from the fireplace, clumsily drinking from a glass of brandy in his left hand that was never permitted to run dry, and holding up the bandaged other one at command, to have it saluted or commiserated over. He thought blearily that those in the room, exchanging their strenuous tokens of goodwill, were like a troop of baboons he had seen in the menagerie in Stamboul. Or rather he did not think it—nothing so deliberate. The remem-bered hooting and patting and petting of the apes rose in his mind and merged with the present laughter and the clinking of canary glasses and the display of teeth, and all swayed together like the flames of the fire. *And what am I?*

But when Gregory Lovell came in to pay his respects, and saw Smith fixed in his place, he came directly across to beard him.

"Well," he said, "if you'd hanged, that'd have been a thousand pound saved, and my life a deal simpler. Still, good luck to you, I suppose. But now we'll have no more prevaricating. I have you; I'll hold you till I hear an answer. Six per cent for goods—and how'll you take the money?"

So Smith told him.

Lovell stared, and then cackled.

"Not so particular after all! I thought we'd see the back of your damned fastidiousness in the end, but this! All the blether, all the mystery, all the smart looks down your nose at us, and you were—well; wait till I tell Piet. He'll laugh till his guts ache. Alright, then. Seventeen hundred and thirty-eight, fifteen and fourpence New-York, plus six per cent consideration for foregoing cash, is eighteen hundred and forty-three pound one shilling, New-York, or near enough. I'll send you over a note of hand tomorrow which you may carry with you to spend, as soon as you get it, and your other little sums owing, you may tell them to direct to me. And we're done. That's it, Mr. Smith. That's our business concluded. No need, if you please, to present yourself on quarter-day. We'll consider that ceremony discharged, for I've a powerful desire never to set eyes on you again."

"Would you tell Tabitha—" began Smith, his tongue thick.

Lovell held up a finger.

"No," he said. "No, no, no. No messages from you to any of mine. You will stay away from my daughters, and my house, and my business, and my friends, and everything of mine. You may do well enough in this company, but you are spoiled meat for daylight society, I can tell you. Not a door on the island will open to you. We let you in, and look what happened, you pox on legs. William," he added civilly, nodding to the lawyer, and went.

As Lovell passed De Lancey, he drew him into speech for a moment or two, and he must have conveyed what he had just learned, for as the merchant left the room, De Lancey turned to Smith, and directed on him a look of paternal disappointment, with a rumpling of the eyebrows, as if to express surprise that Smith had led the town a dance for such a very dull reason. He rang on his glass with a spoon.

"Let's have a toast, lads, before the season parts us and we all go our ways," he declared. "What shall it be?"

"Confusion to the Governor!"

"Nay, to all tyrants!"

"To our ancient rights!"

"To the wisdom of the law!"

"To the free men of the jury!"

"To the charms of Mrs. Tomlinson!" said a coarser wag, and there was a laughing masculine groan, generally sustained.

Smith, in the lull of sound following, said something indistinct; and both the connection of ideas from the mention of Terpie, and the recollection that he was for today the mascot of their cause, made an appetite to hear what the dissolute little rascal had to say, especially among those who had had no direct acquaintance with him.

"Stand up, boy," urged a hubbub of voices. "Out with it, out with it, we'll hear ye."

Smith wobbled upright, by the wall, and held his glass out, stiff-armed.

"To Septimus Oakeshott!" he cried, in a loud, miserable, belligerent voice.

This was found tasteless and incomprehensible, once it was clear he was not going to add anything of a lighter nature, anything by way of a pleasantry. There was a tutting and a growling of disapprobation, and when he blared it out drunkenly again—and again—and went on doing it, there was a turning away, a detaching and departing, with curses and shaken heads and backward looks at him where he stood staring at the fire and waving his bandaged hand. It continued until the party was dwindled down to nothing, and Mr. Smith was left completely and entirely alone.

IV

Smith took to his bed. The domestics of the Black Horse kept their distance; there were no knocks upon the door, no offers of a doctor or solicitations to shave him or feed him. The side of the bed seemed the height of an Alp. He levered himself up on his left arm and fell forward upon the covers, shaking and shivering. The project of getting his coat or his shirt off over the burned hand defeated him, and he only kicked his shoes free before rolling himself as best he could in the blankets, in a kind of sausage with the hurt arm sticking out beside his head. Drawing the bed's curtains was beyond him, so the winter dark and the patter of snow flowed in unimpeded from the icy window-glass of the room, and the pale winter day leaked in in the same way, and the dark again, while he lay helpless. He plummeted into sleep as into a deep abyss, and the mattress seemed to lurch under him as unsteadily as the deck of a ship, and sometimes the tube of blankets was as hot as a furnace, and sometimes he was so cold that his teeth ached and chattered. Abyss, ship, furnace, ice-house. Ice-house, furnace, ship, abyss. There was no comfortable way to stow the thumb upon the pillow, or beneath, or beside it, and as he rolled, it would be rubbed or caught, and send slivers of pain spiking into the hot or cold turmoil of his dreams: for fever had him, and made him work, and all his rest was netted with branching pathways along which he must labour, effortfully trying to count spilling masses of powdery things, or remember momentous catalogues whose heads obliviously ate their tails, or to persuade animals into boxes without sides or bottoms. Ship, ice-house, abyss, furnace. Lord ——, his father, Cadwallader Colden, Mr. Lovell, all berated him. De Lancey laughed, rich and slow, and his laughter wound richly and slowly in twists onto a bobbin. Tabitha presented her back to him, and when he turned her by her shoulder, why, the front of her was her back too. Septimus bled again. "Save the snow!" roared Lennox. "Not a minim of it must be lost, for we can bundle it back inside him!" With Lennox and Achilles, he pushed the crimson slush through an aperture in Septimus' leg the size of a rabbit-hole, and Septimus swelled out till his buttons burst, into a wine-coloured snow-man, only still with Septimus' natural head atop it, speaking wittily from grey lips. Furnace, ice-house, ship, abyss. Around and around: none of the dreams once, it seemed, but all repeating on a loop of variations, as if some kapellmeister of fever were driving them through an endless fugue. He baked and he froze, interminably. He opened his eyes on the room bright or dark, and it seemed only one chamber of an uncountable spawning of chambers, jelly-walled. He slept on, shaking.

As he slept, Achilles chipped out a grave in Trinity churchyard, softening the iron earth with burning lamp-oil. To passers-by on Broad Way, the little blue flames crept and glowed as if a will-o'-the-wisp were loose in the night among the tombs. As Smith slept, Septimus was buried, and the Rector of Trinity read the service from the Prayer Book over the black rectangle in the white snow. The 20th December slid through walls of jelly into the 21st; the 21st December through tropics of heat and cold into the 22nd.

But there came a lucid waking eventually, unlike the others. Smith opened his eyes upon a renewed winter night, and discovered the bed level and steady beneath him. He could not see anything, and he had no idea what hour or even what day it was, but he felt himself for the first time prosaically present, and the night (though cold) prosaically separate from him. His thumb hurt. He was rackingly thirsty. He unwound himself with difficulty from the bedding, got his feet upon the floor, and felt about in the black room, bumping against furniture and dislodging small objects. He found a jug and ewer on a sideboard of some kind, and drank most of the flat dusty water in the jug. He could feel it going down him in a grateful wet tide, triggering his body's next need, which he relieved by pissing into the ewer; or, mostly into it. Then he felt his way back to the bed, and was able to dig down and climb between the smooth sheets. Sorrow and shame reminded him, undeliriously, of their presence, but they would wait; he banished them on a promise of attention later, and dropped back into an unconsciousness that was, in comparison to what had gone before, all delicious, all cool.

Then it was daylight, and he lay upon a pillow the light revealed to be smeared with dried blood. He was filthy too. He could feel that his limbs all over were sticky with the exudate of the fever. He stirred his legs beneath the linen and they seemed thin and fragile. He was as weak as water: but his mind was as clear as water. He looked up at the canopy of velvet, and listened to street noises: muffled speech, the trudge of feet in snow, sledge-runners hissing, the snorting breath of a horse. It was another morning when Septimus was not in the number of those awakening. It was another day when Septimus was dead, and it would be followed by further days when Septimus was dead until the end of the world.

I am not near as clever as I believed, he thought. I imagined that I was playing a deep game, by rules all of my own making, and so I wandered without attending into other games already begun whose rules I did not wait to fathom. I have blundered again and again. I brought Terpie into the play, and roused up her desire to be what she used to be. I let Septimus try to protect me from the consequences, and instead made sure they were visited all on him. I made his memory an object of contempt. I gave one party a weapon against the other, when I did not mean to take sides. And Tabitha! I meant to woo Tabitha, and she tried to trap me. I meant to leave her alone, and it called out of her an experiment in trusting me, which I crushed. Blunder upon blunder; nothing but blunders; half a hundred blunders. —It will be observed that these realisations were coming rather late, and that Mr. Smith was annexing for himself all the blame in the neighbourhood; but perhaps wisdom is always wont to arrive late, and to be a little approximate on first possession. —All this while, he thought, ever since I left Lord ——'s house, I have exalted in my mind my precious sovereign will. I have told myself, that the greatest thing in the world is to preserve my power of choosing for myself. I have made sacrifices for it. Indeed I might say I have made sacrifices to it. I made an idol, I built an altar, and I have poured out on it— He stopped himself, but the snow still crimsoned on his mind's Common. —I came here with a secret, and I have used it to persuade myself that I may be careless here, as careless as I like, on the argument that, if they knew what they do not, they would have no care for me. But it seems I have mistook.

He gritted his teeth and unwrapped his thumb, to look upon the mark of his mistake. The crusted fabric of the handkerchief had glued itself to the leaking wound, and he must tease the cloth free, but what was beneath was less disgusting than its covering. The ball of his thumb was swollen and clubbed, but the shallow M burned in it was beginning to scab, and there was no sign of infection creeping down into the hand. The wound had been cauterised as it was made.

He could not go back and make amends. He could not vindicate Septimus with a raised glass, or bring him back to life with a drunken gesture. He could only—what? What could he do? Go on; and try to be wiser; and keep future promises better; and avoid future mistakes. He must keep faith with the purposes for which he had come, and endeavour to discharge in something more like honour all he now found himself pledged to. And beyond that, just try to see what might be restored if— No, he told himself, this must be undertaken without indulgent hopes, or sweetening thoughts of lucky chances, unearned rewards, happy ends. There was enough to be doing. More than enough, if he was to be ready by Christmas Day. He closed his eyes, and set himself to compose a list of everything he must arrange; and when the tasks were all in order, he got up, wobbled to the door, stuck his head out into the hall-way, and bawled with a reasonable imitation of insouciance for a bath, and hot water, and bacon and eggs.

The first item on the list, though, proved the hardest to accomplish, and he was still struggling to begin it when he had much of the rest done and stowed away. The Governor's household declined to oblige him in any way whatever, on any subject. His request to collect a possession of his, that he had left in Septimus Oakeshott's room, was rejected with contempt, and his suggestion that he might offer to buy the late Secretary's slave was treated as both grotesque and suspicious. When Smith presented himself in person at the gate of the Fort, to see if he might make more headway in speech than in correspondence, the sentries, who had clearly had instructions, absolutely refused to admit him; and when he persisted, they glanced up and down the street to check if anyone was looking, and then when no-one was, they punched him in the stomach and threw him across the cobbles.

"Bugger off, mate," said the sergeant. "You ain't wanted."

The ruination of Fort St. George by the fire, however, had left its wall more a notional or administrative barrier than a physical one, and Smith, judging that he had no alternative, found it quite easy, deep in the dark night of the 23rd, to approach from an angle not overlooked by the gate, and to slip in quietly over a collapsed baulk.

The snows had smoothed the rutted confusion of the courtyard, and drifted around the three bell-tents pitched there, no doubt warming the soldiers sleeping inside. There were no lights in the tents, just one window lit yellow upstairs in the Governor's house, where maybe a night-sentry sat outside his door. Smith picked his way, with the smallest crunches he could, along the shadowed side of the court to Septimus' stair. He was not sure what he would do if he found the door locked, except to try to force it with the least noise he could contrive, but in the event the latch lifted easily, and the thick mass of iron-bound wood swung open onto a space as dark as Smith had expected, if not quite as cold and abandoned-feeling. He pulled the door to behind him, and waited for his eyes to make a little more sense of the faint gleam through the little leaded window, it being most impractical to strike a light. Gradually, the single undifferentiated black modulated to shadings of black, and he could see under the window a pile of Septimus' clothes and gear, with a metallic something on top reflecting in spots that might be his scabbarded sword. On the opposite wall, by the door into the little sleeping chamber, a scant difference between dark and dark resolved into a square shape that perhaps was the sea-chest Septimus had mentioned. Smith took one step towards it, and Achilles, who had been waiting motionless in the blackest black behind the door, leapt onto his back and bore him to the floor with his hands gripped round Smith's windpipe in a strangler's hold.

Smith choked and scrabbled at the boards for purchase, but though Achilles was not very heavy, he had his weight high up, pinning Smith's shoulders, and the long thin fingers round his throat had a practised force.

"It is kind of you to come," he hissed in Smith's ear. "Because, if I go out to find you, they say: he has hurt a white man. Tear him to pieces. But now you come sneaking in here in the dark, I can kill you, and they say: well done, faithful Achilles. Good servant. You protect your master's house."

Smith produced a guttural rattle.

"What you say? Can't hear you, boy."

271

Kkhglggkh.

"What do you say to me, eh? What you want to say? What is your new idea now? What do you try now?"

He seemed only angrier, but to Smith's surprise the questions proved not purely rhetorical. Achilles loosened his grip: not much, but enough to open a straw's-width passage for air, and to part again by a trifle the walls of singing night that had been closing on Smith's consciousness, and to permit a croaking answer.

"It—was—an accident," he managed.

Achilles banged his head smartly on the boards.

"Of *course* it was accident!" he cried, if it is possible to cry in a whisper. "You think you can hurt him on purpose? You? Never! You . . . you . . ."

He hammered the floor with Smith's forehead again, but he did not tighten the neck-hold. He seemed to need to converse. It occurred to Smith, amid thuds and coloured stars, that Achilles could with far more swift and straightforward effect have just stuck a blade between his ribs, if he had desired only a sure revenge. But a cooling corpse cannot hear what you tell it.

"No—one—to—mourn—with," he guessed.

"You!" repeated Achilles, in a voice so congested with fury and sorrow, and by the need to hush them, that he sounded almost as choked as Smith. "You take him from me, and look at you! Nothing in you is strong. You kill him through his kindness. He *pity* you. You are a bag of wind. You say what they tell you. You understand nothing. You don't know what you are. But look what you take from me! Look what you *take!*"

The last word was a wail, a roar, that lost itself in desperate constriction. Wet drops were falling on the back of Smith's head. Achilles stopped heaving Smith up in order to pound him down, and for a moment was all slack weight upon him. Smith thrashed his legs sideways—heaved—rolled left as hard as he could, and contrived to get an elbow underneath him, and a hand spread on the floor to push. It was the branded hand, which was no more than he deserved, and it hurt like fire when he shoved with all his might upon the out-stretched thumb and fingers, but it got his face off the floor, and sent them both rolling right over clumsily leftward till they hit the wall, Achilles' back taking the force of the collision. Both gasped. Smith was able to surge up onto hands and knees; Achilles regained his grasp, but only of Smith's shoulders, and tried with twists and throwings of his weight to drive Smith back down, but now he lacked the impetus that had first bowled his opponent over. Now, as they struggled, the advantage of Smith's greater bulk was felt. Now, it was bullcalf against spider, though the spider be never so much more subtle, and Smith was able heavingly to turn, and to drag both their weights across the room on all fours, back towards the window-ledge, and the glimmer of Septimus' sword-hilt in the dark, with Achilles trying to brace his legs to arrest them, and to kick out Smith's knees from beneath him. Step by heaving step, and as they gaspingly traversed the dark room, Achilles started talking in his ear again: this time, as if he were talking to himself.

"What I am now?" he said. "What I have left? I was Fulani. I was guard of the Emir. I was *hafiz*. I was husband. I was son. I was father. All gone; start again. I was lover. I was friend. I was older brother. I was soldier. I fight again, I think again, I breathe again. I ride in green forests. I sit with the chiefs of the Hodenosaunee people. I walk on mountains white men never see. All gone. All *gone*. All gone *again*."

He was fighting less hard with every word. Smith, reaching the window-ledge, was able to claw up it, to rear up till he was half-standing, and without too much difficulty to throw off Achilles' spindly, long-limbed weight. And to grab and draw, in the dark of the room, Septimus' sword.

Achilles picked himself up, and stepped with dignity towards

273

the blade. Smith could tell by the dim liquid shine of his eyes that he was weeping, and the crumpled line of his shoulders showed his age.

"And now," he said quietly, "I know too much business. Too many secrets. They won't keep me here. Soon they sell me south, to tobacco field, to iron mine. But I can't begin again. I don't have it in me. It is too much. Two lives is enough. So." He turned his gaze up to the ceiling and held it there.

"I don't—" said Mr. Smith—and had to stop, and rasp and cough to clear his throat—"I don't desire to kill you. I don't desire even to hold this. I mean if I can never to hold one of these again."

Achilles looked down. Smith was offering him, not the point, but the hilt of the sword.

8

Quarter-Day

December 25th

20 Geo. II

1746

Whether Christmas Day were an occasion for work or for play was, at that time in New-York, a matter of denomination. The followers of the established church kept the feast, with green branches in their houses and logs upon the fire, and bunches of sweet-smelling rosemary, and so did Lutherans and Moravians. But the Quakers, the French Calvinists, the Dutch Reformed, the English-speaking Baptists and Presbyterians, all signified their dissent, and their scornful judgement of the feast as a Popish mummery, by treating the day as one for ordinary business. That year, it fell on a Thursday, and you might have made a reliable chart of the affiliations of the whole city, by marking which shop-fronts were barred and shuttered, and which were defiantly opened, with lanterns lit, clerks at desks, merchants ready to sell, and tailors ready with their needles, despite the cold, and the grumbling of prentices, and the mere trickle of customers. It was cold indeed, with a renewed boreal bite in the air, and a hard slippery crust on the snow very grateful to sledge-runners. Ordinary walkers slid and cursed, and noting the cast of colour in the north-eastern sky, resolved to be back in shelter as soon as may be. The counting-house on Golden Hill was open, the Lovells being Baptists. Isaiah hung miserably over the fire, having been given nothing to do but brew up hot pearl for the occasional callers who came by to make or receive a quarter-day payment; Jem, in gloves, scratched away at the reconciling of the account books, the movement of whose figures from column to column embodied the real flow of money in the city, since there was no solider form for money to take; and Gregory Lovell, dipping his quill in the same well of black slush, sighed as he tried to figure on scraps of waste paper, not for the first time, how the plans of the firm for the year to come might be as little crimped and savaged as possible by the sudden vast hole in its capital; how Lovell & Co. might best survive the depredations of Smith.

Smith, however, went to Trinity to welcome the Christ Child. There were iron stoves in there glowing red with generous heat, and banks of the best yellow beeswax candles in blazing radiance, and the smell of wine mulling to fete the congregation after the service: but the verger, scowling, packed Smith into the obscurest pew behind a pillar at the back, where the indigent, the muttering and the strange were housed. It had been a question to struggle with, whether to admit such a notoriety at all, but this particular flagrant sinner, far from flaunting himself, was pale and subdued, with purple bruises fading on his forehead. You surely cannot turn away a sinner who may be repenting. Not at Christmas. Not while proclaiming goodwill toward men. You may only hide him. Smith, behind his pillar, was relieved not to be seen, and not to see the great in their array up at the front, where the choir were carolling "Adeste Fideles," and the Governor's mouth opened and closed like a fish, and the Tomlinsons sat like two statues of wretchedness, and De Lancey was manifesting gravity enough to perturb the orbits of the planets. He did not go up to receive the communion, perhaps because he did not dare to walk through the company, or perhaps from compunction. The tablets of the law were displayed on the church wall where he *could* see them: and of the Ten Commandments, he had by his count recently broken at least three. He closed his eyes and pressed his fists to his forehead and prayed. For what, I know not. And when the service was done, he slipped out unnoticed, wearing a new fur over his green coat, for he had much to do; and meant to have it all squared away before his last conversation in New-York, so that he might be able to depart immediately, no matter how it turned out.

It was two o'clock before he was ready to knock, as quietly as may be, upon the street-door of the house at Golden Hill. He had glanced around the corner: the counting-house was still stubbornly open for business, and the occupants engaged. When Zephyra opened the door, he pressed his finger to his lips, and darted straight past her, running on silent feet along the hall and up the staircase, past the windows where again ships' masts were swaying, past the cruel little gardens of quill-work, trapped in their boxes, to the landing from whose shadows he had first seen the Lovell girls.

Tabitha was sitting alone, grimly sewing, a hardly-touched plate of food beside her.

"Oh look," she said. "It's the killer. What do you want?"

Smith, returning instantly to the state of irritation which was so easy to forget when out of her company—the sensation of a few grains of grit always between the teeth, something niggling or scratching at the skin—saw that she was in better looks; not as supple and rose-brown as when they had walked together in the rain, or as bold and illuminated as on the way to Tarrytown, but not shrunken and dried-up in malice either. She no longer reminded him of a winter wasp. She must have been eating, at least a few meals. Her skin was restored, her wrists were not such sticks. But she seemed, for her, unusually cautious, rather than combative. She had stood up, when she saw him, and edged back, behind a low table, toward the mantel-shelf.

"I came to beg your pardon."

"Really? What for? There are so many things to choose from, now."

"I thought we'd agreed to treat the older offences as squared, and to sink them into oblivion."

"No, no," she said. "That was before you took up with your gross doxy, in the public square, where all could see; before you declared to the world that you would rather be rolling in blubber. Since then, all your sins are fresh again."

"That is certainly how they seem to me."

"Is that so?" she said, politely. Her voice was effortfully calm. She did not fly out, she did not catch fire, she did not frown or grin. She compressed the muscles around the mouth and raised her eyebrows as if that was needful to keep her eyes steady. "Go on, then: say what you must."

"I am . . . sorry I hurt you. I am sorry I betrayed your trust."

"There is no trust to betray. Your amours are your own business."

"You were just beginning—"

"Not any more. That is all gone."

"If I could explain to you, how very much what happened—no, what I *did*, with Mrs. Tomlinson—was a piece of cowardice—or, of impatience—or—of succumbing to the greed of the moment, a *shallow* greed, and stupidly sacrificing for it—something— something more—"

"I don't want you to explain. I don't understand you. I don't want to understand you. You have said what you came to; now, please go away."

It seemed as cold in the room as on the street outside. Smith, looking at her white hands twisting together, understood that she was frightened. That he could not appeal to some resigned, if out-raged, sense in her of the stupid things humanity was wont to do, in the grip of desire, and men proverbially; that what had happened had fallen, for her, quite outside the scope of the game, and perhaps outside of her experience altogether. If only she would fight, he thought. It seemed dreadful that such a fierce soul would not.

"I am also sorry," he said, as gently as he could, "that you found out in the way you did, through Flora. I am sure she did not tell it you very kindly."

"If you had heard the things she said!" cried Tabitha suddenly, her voice going high and wobbly. "She was so *pleased.* She said—such things to me—"

Smith thought for a moment that she was kindling, that the familiar fire was returning, on this more familiar ground; but Tabitha bit off what she had been going to say, and clamped shut her mouth. Smith hesitated.

"Well," he said, like a man spitting gin onto hot coals, to try to rouse a flame, "she had a lifetime of mockery to pay back, didn't she?"

Her eyes rounded indignantly, but she did not ignite. Animation stirred in her face; and faded back into fear.

"No doubt," she said. "No doubt"—wavering upon her way at first, but steadying as she went, into a voice to close accounts, formal and decided. "Now please go away."

"I am going away. I am leaving New-York."

"Good."

"I mean, now. I am leaving New-York now."

"Good. Goodbye, Mr. Smith."

Smith gazed at her, and she returned the gaze, whitely level. He looked an appeal at her; a question at her; a beseeching incredulity at her. *That cannot possibly be all?* But her miserable, resolute, still gaze repelled them all unmoving, like a pane of glass against which snow-balls thump. There seemed no way, from here, to reach the things he had thought his soul required of him to say before he left, no matter how ridiculous he made himself thereby, or how much she might scorn them.

In desperation, he smiled at her, foolish and huge and heartfelt, and made his best bow, and walked from the room.

He was through the green-painted pine door-way and descending the first stair before she spoke.

"I know why magicians clap their hands," she said, as if she couldn't help it.

Mr. Smith froze in place upon the staircase.

"Do you?" he said.

His eyes prickled. He turned, with infinite slowness and precaution, and came back to her where she stood in the long room in the same manner, as if approaching a bird on a bough that would take wing at the slightest startling movement. He made sure he stopped at a good distance.

"And why is that?" he said.

"To keep our eyes busy. So that we should not see something else."

"You are right. And do you know what it is I did not want people to see?"

"No," she said. "No, I don't." There was the faintest flush of frustration in her voice.

"Would you like me to tell you?"

"Yes," she said: the same emotion, stronger, almost amounting to an edge. *Yes, obviously. Yes, you idiot.*

It seemed to Smith that he had her on the frailest, slenderest hook imaginable, made only of curiosity; like a fish-hook of ice, ready to shatter at too much force, or to melt at too much warmth; but that he might play her back all the way to safety on this hook, to the safe shore of her happiness and his own, if only he were subtle enough, if only he were wise enough, if only he had limitless time. But he did not have limitless time.

"I will tell you in five minutes," he said.

"What?"

"I will tell you five minutes after you leave the house with me."

"You want to be out in the street, for this great secret?" she said, not understanding.

"No," he said. "I mean, I will tell you if you come away with me. If you put on a coat, and pack up a bag, and leave the city with me; for good; now."

"Did you—did you not understand what I said to you, a moment gone?"

"I did. I just didn't believe it."

She stared. The fear was plainer again, yet not quite dominant in her face; exasperation vied with it, and something else, startled and very tentative.

"I know you," he said. "At least, I believe I do. You have instructed me of your nature. The lessons were painful, and the pupil was stupid, but I learned in the end."

"And what am I?" she said, trying for scorn, yet arriving closer to entreaty.

"A bird and a cage. Not a bird *in* a cage, as you like to imagine: that is sentiment, that is you indulging yourself in the pleasure of conceiving yourself a victim, and being warranted by it for any amount of clever poison. No, you are yourself the cage. It is not made of your circumstances. It is made of your passions; which, by the way, are very nasty ones. If you were happier, you would be ashamed of yourself. But the cage is small, and getting smaller as time goes by. It is too small for you already, and there is a bird inside, who requires to be let out."

"If this is your idea of a love-note, Signor Smooth, I am not surprised that you end up taking your pleasures in the sty, with the sows."

"It is my idea of the truth."

"How do you even *dare* to offer me this stuff? You! When you have blundered and battered your way around, from the moment you have arrived. And now you are going to set up for a truth-teller? Do you not know how ridiculous you are?"

"Yes. Yes, I do know how ridiculous I am. It has been brought home to me, I assure you. And you are right about the sty: I have rolled in shit in this city. I have had my soul stripped naked, in this city. What further can I lose, by telling you what I think of you? Besides, you like it."

"'I wonder that you will still be talking—'"

"'—when nobody marks you,'" finished Smith. "But you are not Beatrice and I am not Benedick, as we have already established. And you do like it. Listen to yourself. Your voice has got its strength back. Look in the mirror. Your eyes are bright again. I accuse you of enjoying yourself, right now."

"I am not."

"You are smiling."

"I deny it."

"Of course you do, Mistress No. You are the queen of denials, rebuffs and contradictions. But you like it, alright—"

"No—"

"You do; you like being matched. You like playing with someone who is as quick as you, as clever as you, as rude as you. Don't you."

"Yes."

"Aha!" cried Smith, and crowed comically like a cockerel: but quietly, so as not to be overheard from downstairs.

"You fool," said Tabitha, with a kind of undeniable fondness.

"Yes. —The trouble is, you think I'm insulting you. You think we have begun the game again; and we have not, I don't have time. What I am telling you is, you like being known, for it makes you feel less lonely—and I think you are the loneliest person I have ever met. And I am trying to tell you that *I* like *you*."

"Despite all the flaws I have, according to you?"

"Despite them; because of them; who knows? I like all of you. I like the bird and I like the cage. I like the polished mind and the rough tongue. I like the tearing claws and the warm hands. I like the monster and I like the girl."

"I do not like myself very much," said Tabitha painfully.

"I know."

"Since you came I have been very . . . confused. —You make me angrier, you know, because I cannot win very easily with you, so I have behaved worse with you than I think with anyone, even my mother; and then I feel worse about it than with anyone. Is that good? Can that be a good thing? It is a relief when I can just hate you."

"You should try the experiment of seeing yourself through my eyes."

"What would I see?"

"Beauty. —And rage, and bitterness, and solitariness, and a very foul temper; but first of all, beauty. You make everything else in a room look dull. Your face is more alive than anyone else's, to me. All the other faces are dirty windows, to me, smeared with chalk and street-spatter; yours is clear through, to the soul behind. —And I know the shape of your mouth by heart. I know the colour of your eyelids when they are closed. I know your long legs and your careless walk. And what I do not know, I would like to learn; all of it, for many years, gently, greedily—"

Too much. She had been coming closer to him, stepping wonderingly in, as if he had some small flame in his hands she might warm herself at: but now she blushed, the rose-brown going to glaring unhappy carmine, and she drew suddenly back.

"That's enough," she said nervously. "Stop; that's enough of that. What are you asking me, Smith? What are you proposing? Be plain."

"I am asking you to come out of the cage. The door is open."

"No; no! I don't want to hear it in pretty figures. I am a merchant's daughter. We sell cloth and rum and metal goods. We ship grain. We lend at interest. We buy mortgages. We are not poets. You want me to—run away with you? And be—what, exactly? Your wife? Your mistress? An entertainment for the road?"

Smith hesitated again. He was impeded by the reflection that, if she came with him, and five minutes later as promised he explained himself to her, she might by no means then agree to stay with him. He was sure of his own intentions, but he was not so sure of her that he could rule out her being horrified. It was difficult to make some-body a declaration of honourable devotion, when you were con-scious of this conditional check to it, so near a prospect; this no that might follow so hard on the heels of a yes. And what would he do then? Would he leave her at the last house in New-York, at the gate of Rutgers' Farm or at the snowy crossroads in Greenwich, after an engagement of five minutes' duration? This stumbling-block, this awkward juncture at which he was trying to elicit trust without yet bestowing it whole-heartedly himself, he had contrived to glide over, in his planning, without examining its difficulty too closely. Yet here it was, arrived at. —Perhaps he must take things by stages.

"As . . . my friend, to begin with?"

"Oh, your *friend*," she said, with a relieved derision. "What an anti-climax. What a very small delivery after such a mighty labour."

"I meant to suggest, that you would be protected; honoured, as a friend; that nothing would be expected of you, at *all*, until you knew the whole truth; till you were able to consider without, um, prejudice, the proposal I would *like* to make you. To be making you *now*. Tabitha, I *want* to say, just, m—"

"Heavens, how your eloquence has flown out the window all of a sudden," said Tabitha, ignoring the later parts of this speech. "You know, your reputation for protecting your friends is not very good, lately. It is a dangerous business, being a friend of yours. Do you think I would end up dead in a ditch, too?"

"I promise—"

"Where are you going, anyway?"

"I . . . can't tell you."

"I *see.* How tempting! I might end up dead in a ditch on the way to Trenton; or dead in a ditch on the way to Philadelphia; or, maybe—"

"Tabitha—"

"—or *maybe*, dead in a ditch on the way to Boston! Wouldn't that be exciting? I have always wanted to go to Boston!"

"*Tabitha.*"

He held her with his eyes, and she steadied somewhat, though she was breathing fast. They seemed to be going backward; he seemed required to make his most delicate declarations as she skittered away from him into hostile gaiety.

"What?"

"You will be surprised, if you come with me, yes: and perhaps you will be shocked, and the—complexion of things—might seem very different to you, from what you had expected; but I swear, I swear to you with utmost seriousness, that you would not learn anything about me that made any essential difference to what you know of me now. I am as you see me. You may trust what you know. Please, trust what you know."

"I don't see an occasion for trust," she said. "I see a resistible invitation to ruin myself. I see you asking me to make a mad gamble with my future. You are a felon, and a liar, and a mountebank, and careless with those who love you. And you have been unfaithful to me with that *slug* of a woman before we even begin."

"Those are all true," said Smith. "But they're not the reason you hesitate, are they? Not really. The real reason is that you're afraid to let go of what you know, even if you don't like it; even if you hate it; even if it won't let you breathe. Come on, Tabitha. I dare you. The world is wide. The cage door is open. Come out. Won't you come out?"

"I don't know," she said in a tiny voice. She had wrapped her long arms around herself, and was looking at the floor.

"What is there for you here?" he said, coming closer. "Nothing. Nothing but the chance to make trouble; and that isn't enough for a life, you can't make a life out of that, can you? Come away. Bring your temper and your tongue, and come with me, love."

"I don't *know*," she said, louder, with a dry intensity, with an anguished deliberateness, as if she could not let go of not letting go.

He took the last step and put his hands on her shoulders. He felt them shifting, warm and live, the whole slender quire of bone and muscle and spirit that composed her, moving articulate beneath his fingers, trembling. She looked up at him with big astonished eyes, and it seemed to him that her trembling was between possibilities, that she stood irresolute on the brink between two different lives; not strong enough, he thought, to decide to jump, yet too strong to let herself be carried over passively. He tried to look courage into her. She took a gulping breath, he thought to steady herself, but the tremble grew bigger, grew to a positive shake, so that she rattled from side to side in his hands; and when she took another, still more convulsive, her eyes still fixed on his, her face began to heave and twitch, and to pull out of true. Something was coming loose in her, boiling up from beneath, struggling to the surface. —He nodded. —Her eyes swam, and he expected tears, but the drowning look in them wavered, held; helpless, unable to help herself, but strangely, very strangely, *content*, almost smiling, as if she had decided not to help herself, but to surrender to some oncoming pleasure. And her mouth kinked, stretched, worked, widened, into a desperate grin; and then stretched on and out and into a vibrating black square from which burst a scream so loud and painful at close quarters it felt as if a knife had been stuck in Smith's ear.

He reeled back with his hands clapped to his head, and without ceasing to scream she whirled about and began to sweep objects off the mantel, seizing them in spasms and twitches and flinging them down to shatter on the boards. A china shepherdess—smash—the matching shepherd boy—smash—the clock and the Meissen candle-sticks—smash, smash, smash.

Smith tried to reach into the whirlwind, and she snapped at him with her teeth. Feet came pounding up the stair; Zephyra burst into the room, still holding the cloth with which she had been polishing silver.

"What you said to her? She not like this for months!"

"I—" said Smith, "I—just—"

"Step back from her. Mistress," said Zephyra, who rather than entering the zone of Tabitha's fury was carefully drawing pieces of furniture away from her, "you settle down, now; it be all alright; you be a good girl, and take some breath; you hush yourself, now. *You,*" she said to Smith, with a furious jerk of the chin, "go!"

"But—"

"Don't you see you make it worse?"

"But—I am responsible—"

"Go!"

Seeing that Smith still gaped, and that Tabitha seemed now to be locking into place, a stationary banshee with fists rigid at her side, eyes closed, lost in an ecstasy of protest, Zephyra, sighing, grabbed his sleeve and towed him from the room, and down the stairs.

"You go before the Mister comes," she hissed.

It was too late for that, however. Lovell, issuing falteringly out of the passage-way from the counting-house, moving as if against a hurricanoe-headwind of his own reluctance, met them at the foot of the stair with his hands clutching at his wig.

"*You!*" he cried. "What has—what have you—?" He made a grab at Smith's lapel, but the shrieks from above, the rising howls, distracted him, and instead he pushed past. "Oh God, not again," he could be heard to mumble.

"Now, out!" said Zephyra, and she thrust Smith ahead of her along the passage; to the street-door, and out into the cold.

And stopped dead, on the threshold, seeing what was waiting for Smith there in the snow: what he had accomplished at last, in New-York, with his thousand pounds.

Mr. Smith had been shopping in the slave-market. There, in two of the largest possible sizes of sleigh, hitched up to driving horses, twenty or so silent Africans were packed. He had dressed them all in winter furs, but he must have selected his purchases according to some peculiar principle, for they were an unlikely crowd to choose for labour: old women, children, sullen-looking wenches, a girl with a wall-eye, another whose visage had the far-off serenity of deafness, and a crew of men most owners would have found intolerably villainous, for they were blue-black of skin, with the nakedly belligerent expressions of those not yet resigned to the country. Two had tribal scars.

Smith bolted across the snow-crust of the street in two bounds, like a cat escaped from a scalding. But then surprised her by turning back, when he had reached his strange cavalcade. He was weeping, but he smiled, and held out his hand to Zephyra.

"Aane, me ara ni nnipa a wo twen no," he said.

What a difference a frame makes. The aching winter light that glared up into the glassy humour of her eye from the street, where the blue shadows were beginning to lengthen, was just the same; the sight before her was unaltered; but in her unmoving dark face, armoured to stillness by long sorrow, the pupil through which the light flowed in flared wide of its own accord, in minuscule astonishment, for the meaning of the scene was suddenly reversed. There was Smith, still shaking with the early shock of what he had just lost, and with much more to feel of it ahead of him, and yet with a tension falling from his face—no, more than that, with a whole role falling from it, in flakes and pieces and cascading blocks, like a collapsing wall—that had been maintained in place without a pause since he landed. And there was Achilles from the Fort, who, the word had been, was sold now down to a tobacco farm in the Carolinas, here instead in gloves and furs, holding the reins of the front sleigh to drive it; and there was Smith, jumping up beside him, and the others around him all budging up, shuffling up, to give him his place among them. Smith looked at her again; again held out his hand. The messenger of her new fortune had indeed arrived; if she was willing to hear him.

Which she was. Zephyra dropped the rag she was still holding, and without looking back, without even closing the door, clasped her hand across her belly and walked out of the house on Golden Hill forever: a step, and another step, and one more step through the crunching snow, to the dark hands reaching to lift her up. Ten seconds later, the street was empty.

9

A LETTER

to Gregory Lovell, Esqr., Golden Hill Street,
City of New-York: by the ship
Crown of Heligoland

Banyard & Hythe, Partners: Mincing Lane, London,
10th December 1746

My dear Sir,

I received yours of the 2nd November, and confess Myself
surprised at its indignant Tone. For though it is true, that
the Balances owing between your Office and ours, are usually
settled by means of the Jamaica Trade, yet, a Debt is a Debt,
and while it rests upon our Books, it is our Right to issue any
Bills whatever upon it that We see fit. The mulatto Smith having
presented Himself here with a thousand Pound (Sterling) in
right Currency, it was a Matter of straightforward Advantage
to Us, to sell Him immediately what He desired to buy
immediately.

The Bill is a true Bill and may therefore be paid with
Confidence. Nevertheless, it is understandable that You may have
been taken aback by his sudden Appearance with it, and for your

greater Surety of Mind, We have made the Enquiries concerning Him that You have requested.

The Tale is certainly a striking One. Richard Smith is, it seems, the Descendant of a Slave of the late Lord —— (the present Lord ——'s Father) by Way of two Generations of Marriage to Englishwomen. His Grandfather Hannibal was a favourite Page of this elder Lord's Wife, who being brought to England in the Seventies of the last Century, was enfranchised at his Majority and became a Servant, taking the Sur-Name of Smith. Or, truer to say, became as it were a favoured Ward of the Family, to the Extent that his Son (your Smith's Father) was upon showing Proof of promising Parts, actually sent to Oxford as a Servitor or Scholar-Servant to Lord ——'s Son, and later rewarded by the Living of one of the Churches in Lord ——'s Gift, and consequently settled there in Dorset as a country Parson, where He presently remains. The same Strategy of Benevolence was purposed to be followed for the Parson's Son, but the Boy ran off, pertly objecting to the Fate planned for Him. Rather, He endeavoured to make his own Way, here in the City of London, tricking Himself out first as a Dancing-Master, where He had but little Success, and then as an Actor in small Parts: where He shone more, being as You will have observed handsome of Face and pleasing of Manner, yet not so much as to secure Himself a Competency. This He found instead as Secretary or Factotum to the Mimick Club of Drury Lane, a dining Society not unlike the Beefsteak, where He has mingled for the last two Years with a Scattering of Persons prominent in Drama, the News-Sheets, and the Exchange.

But the Errand on which He came to You proceeds, it seems, from his Sunday Affiliation rather than his Week-day one. He is a Worshipper, in a small Congregation where the Fringes of Aristocratic Zeal meet London's Population of emancipated

Africans: the Countess of Malmesbury's Abyssinian Connection. This Group receiving a Bequest of a thousand Pounds from one of its Patrons, it was decided that it should be laid out for the Purchase, the Freeing, and the Establishing in Independency of their Country-Men and -Women. New-York was chosen as a Market far enough from the West Indies Hub of the Trade for the Transaction to be unobtrusive, and Richard Smith volunteered to accomplish It, as the Person among Them most fitted to pass without Difficulty in different Companies. He had a written Commission for the Business in his Pocket-Book, which He shewed Me.

The Bill, then, to repeat the essential Point, is good, and You may pay It without Demur. Indeed, if the Seas be as usual, You will have paid It long before this Assurance can reach You. But I trust this Information will set your Mind at Rest, and that, after the initial Surprise, the Transaction proceeded on your Side without any further Difficulty or Perturbation.

With a warm Protestation of the Value we place upon our long Association with the House of Lovell, and my best Regards to Mr. Van Loon, I have the Honour to remain,

Your Servant,
Barnaby Banyard

10

August 1814

Well, I still hate novels. They still seem to me to be tissues of exaggeration, simplification, a sweetness that falsifies; and now I know this truth from, as it were, the inside, having written one myself, and marked all the sleights and tricks required to tease out a very partial understanding, a perished cloth more holes than thread, into what seems a smooth continuous fabric. I, who did not know what Mr. Smith was thinking, lend my own spirit to set in motion a puppet of him who does not know what I was thinking. Nonsense, absurdity upon absurdity! I, who have never fought a duel, or played piquet, or shared in various other of Mr. Smith's experiences, find I can concoct the necessary passages by a winking charm, by talking faster, by a conjurer's distracting busywork. How can such farragos be trusted? And yet what else is there, to catch in any shape at all the fragile pattern of particular acts and hours long ago, before oblivion blows them to the winds? They are the best, worst chance to coax into anything like a durable existence the *feeling* of those weeks when Smith was with us, sixty-seven years ago: even if the cost is lies at every turn. Lies are better than nothing.

Besides, they never bothered me very much when I was doing the lying. In fact, there has been a strange kind of satisfaction, like a ghost of my old pleasures, in withholding or denying in these pages most direct views into my past self, as if I was contriving all over again thereby to withhold myself from *him.*

And now I do not want to stop. I sit at my window in the farm-house here, and listen to the hoot-owls drifting across the Fishkill like ghosts in the last of the short summer night, with the lamp lit that I may burn till all hours if I wish to, for we are rich and lamp-oil is a cheap indulgence to keep a nasty old lady happy: and I wish the story not to be over, though it is, and has been these many years. Once again, I have made Smith depart in the snow, with stolen Zephyra and Achilles, and since we never heard any more of those in the sledges ever again, that is that. I have no more to tell. No more I want to, anyway.

The reader must imagine, if they desire it, the scene of chaos and confusion Smith left behind him. The outbreak at first of derisive laughter directed at my father, when the news spread that he had entertained a n—— unawares, and let him carry off a good share of his fortune, and pressed upon him the society of his daughters; and then the rapid smothering of that laughter in embarrassment, and effortful silence, when it was realised, all across the snowy city, what else had been done unawares, and by how many, in relation to Smith. That judge, lawyer and jury together had excused a black man for the death of a white one. That the whole audience of *Cato* had adored him. That the Assembly had thought him worth woo-ing, and threatening. That for sixty whole days he had been treated as a person of consequence. That Terpie had— Well; enough of that. The Tomlinsons obtained a posting shortly afterward to the Philadelphia garrison, and soon, without any discussion, the city's embarrassment over Smith thickened into the pretence that there had never been a Smith at all. He became unmentionable. No-one would talk about him; no-one but me. I have written this to conjure him. To *insist* upon him. My tale begins suddenly, as he arrives, and ends, just as suddenly, as he departs.

But if my pen stops moving, if there are no more fresh words in glistening black flowing out of it, to somehow keep all the preceding ones irrigated and live, if my ink all dries to autumnal brown—then the past too crackles and fades. The people go away, and so does the city.

It is a striking thought that the New-York of my story *only* exists in my story, now. I remember it, unchanged, because I left it in 1750, after writing some letters at which the neighbours took offence, and have not been back. (Indeed, I have not been anywhere but here my whole life since, except once in the year '60 to Princeton, to see the scholars play *The Tempest*, and that did not work out happily, confirming the family in their sense that I had best be stowed safe away.) In my pages, and in my head, the Dutch houses stand, and the mansions of Broad Street, and the spire of Trinity, and the cows grazing on the Common, and our house on Golden Hill: but in Manhattan, apparently, all this is gone without a trace, ruined in the Revolution and burned in the great fires. Scarcely a brick stands. Septimus' grave must still be there, unchanged until the trumpet sounds and all sleepers wake, but with a new New-York billowed up around it. Trinity is a different Trinity, City Hall is demolished, and the streets march north up the island carrying the homes of the wealthy with them, and leaving a scurf of slums behind. There is a De Lancey Street now, they say: but no De Lanceys, for they came out for the King at the Revolution, and so are all scattered to Nova Scotia and beyond. The judge himself was long dead by then, but very probably he would have concurred: for after all, he was Governor himself, after poor hopeless Clinton, and in that role a great supporter of the Crown prerogative.

I do not think I could explain to the younger ones I see, when the family comes up-valley to join me here for the summer months, how such a man as the judge could have been a royalist: how we all were. For they recite the litany of the King's evil deeds every July Fourth as if they were sacred history, and I perceive that for them all kings called George are hobgoblins, who prowl at night through the cities of *their* imagination kicking puppies and eating kittens. "The British" are a species of especially venomous foreigners, tyrannical by nature, enemies to all liberty, and of course the White House–burning villains of the recent war. I perceive I have lived out of one epoch into another one, quite mutually unintelligible, so that if I cried, like the solitary servant surviving the wreck of Job's house, "I only am alone escaped to tell thee," I would be looked at as if I were making animal noises. I am looked at like that quite often anyway.

My father died in the year '64. Flora is dead too. She had four children, of whom one did not survive, perhaps luckily, for he looked much more like her estate manager than boring old Joris. I grew no nicer with age. However, around about the point I passed from aunt-hood to great-aunt-hood, the passion of my contrariness (as they all decided to call it) seemed to leave me, or at least to diminish into a more easily domesticated form. So that now, when I regard those earlier times, and especially the days on Golden Hill, I find I possess two incompatible reactions to them, two feelings that run along beside one another but without mixing, like the snaking currents of dye you now see running along under the transparent skin of the Hudson. I both wish that I felt again that burning pleasure of opposition: and at the very same time I regret with all my heart that I sacrificed so much else to it. With all my heart? No, with only half of it; and half a heart, I suppose, is not enough to make you bold for the business of loving. It is a vote cancelled by the suffrage of the other half.

My great-great-niece says I am the oldest thirteen-year-old girl in the United States. She is thirteen herself, and so, she says, she should know. Heloise Van Loon, born with the century: as sharp as me, but I hope better fitted for happiness. Being clever never did me much good, for you can know perfectly well why you do something, and still not be able to desist from it.

I do not know what became of Smith. I do not think he can have perished directly in the snows of '46: he was hopelessly incompetent to travel through a continental winter, but Achilles will not have been, and I imagine they will have arrived wherever they were going. But after that, all is conjecture, and I can only wonder. Whether he found the learning at Harvard, for example, that he had refused at Oxford; or whether he was reconciled to his father and returned to England; whether he adopted the destiny of his un-apparent colour, or whether, going back to London, he went where it became again a mere personal peculiarity. Whether he yet lives. Can he, possibly? He would have to be even older than me, and women live longer than men, and I suspect I have been pickled into durability somehow by wickedness, like a preserve in vinegar. But I can imagine him, several ways, somewhere sharing this ember of a world with me. An ancient roué of a Smith, who totters at ninety to the gaming-tables, rouged; a Smith who lives in retired pomp in the English countryside after a long success on the stage; a Smith simply enthroned in honour beside a hearth, surrounded by children of whatever colour; or a Smith snoozing venerable in the study of a manse with a thousand brown books of divinity about him, for he had that possibility in him too, from his father.

Does he think of me, if he lives? I think of him, often. Heloise brings me my hot milk, and while the house sleeps and I do not, I return again and again to the moment when Mr. Smith asked me to go with him, and I did not. I wish that I could hover at the shoulder of that stubborn girl (that frightened girl) and nudge her, push her, shove her out of her solitary fear, and into the sleigh, like Zephyra; into a wider life. But I also wish that I could feel again the rejecting fire that was in me then. And I remember how good it was to scream.

Author's Note

After five books of nonfiction, or fiction blended with nonfiction, it feels very strange to me not to say anything about the way this book uses history, but with a mighty effort I will only point out that Mr. Smith is not being unfair about the relative sizes of London and New York as he knows them. New York in 1746 had a population of about seven thousand, while London, then the largest city in Europe, had one of seven hundred thousand: genuinely a hundred-fold difference.

I owe thanks to a lot of people. My brother-in-law Jonathan Martin made a vital suggestion about the mechanism of the plot. My father, Peter Spufford, inducted me into early-modern finance. My younger daughter, Theodora, helped with the conversation at the Lovells' dinner party. My wife, Jessica Martin, put up with Mr. Smith and Tabitha as perpetual guests at *our* dinner table. The gentleman who led me round Iran in 2000 always punctiliously referred to those who ruled his country as "*Mister* Khatami" and "*Mister* Khamenei," alerting me for the first time, member that I am of an anti-formal generation, to the comedies of formal naming. Long-ago conversations with Jenny Uglow about Fielding and Hogarth turned out to have been secretly at work in my imagination. Regine Dugardyn briefed me on Sinterklaasavond. Marina Benjamin saved the middle of the story from sagging. Zoe Adjonyoh, Professor

Author's Note

Graham Furniss and Dr. Kwadwo Osei-Nyame guided me to two accurate sentences in Ashanti Twi, which I then had to alter to fit pre-twentieth-century typography. Jacob and Melina Smith lent me and my family their Episcopalian rectory to stay in for a week, up in the open fields and wild pasturelands of 23rd Street, but with easy access to the eighteenth-century city on the 6 train. Shawn Maurer showed me eighteenth-century Boston, and behaved at an early stage of the book's gestation as if a colonial counterpart to *Joseph Andrews* or *David Simple* was not too crazy an idea. At the other end of its composition, my agent, Clare Alexander, and my editor, Julian Loose, backed me uncomplainingly in various acts of stubbornness. In between I wrote most of Mr. Smith's story in CB1, the oldest cybercafé in the English Cambridge. Gabi gave me my billionth cup of Americano free.

The book was kindly read and commented on in draft by Felix Gilman, Claerwen James, Sarah Leipciger, Henry Farrell, Patrick Nielsen-Hayden, Elizabeth Knox, Tim Parnell, Oliver Morton and Anne Malcolm.

Thank you all.

Feast of St. Michael & All Angels
64 Eliz. II

About the Author

Francis Spufford is the author of five highly praised books of nonfiction. His first book, *I May Be Some Time*, won the Writers Guild Award for Best Non-Fiction Book of 1996, the Banff Mountain Book Prize, and a Somerset Maugham Award. It was followed by *The Child That Books Built, Backroom Boys, Red Plenty* (which was translated into nine languages), and most recently, *Unapologetic*. In 2007 he was elected a Fellow of the Royal Society of Literature. He teaches writing at Goldsmiths College and lives near Cambridge, England.